Praise for

DEFY THE STARS

★ "**Nuanced** philosophical discussions of religion, terrorism, and morality advise and direct the **high-stakes** action, informing the **beautiful**, realistic ending. Intelligent and thoughtful, a highly relevant far-off speculative adventure." —*Kirkus Reviews* (starred review)

★ "**Poignant and profound**...A tale that examines the ethics of war and tackles questions of consciousness, love, and free will. Gray's characters are nuanced, her worldbuilding is intelligent, and the book's conclusion **thrills and satisfies while defying expectations.**"
—*Publishers Weekly* (starred review)

"Replete with rebels, bots, and battles, this **top-notch space adventure** features a well-developed plot and an unexpected, satisfying ending. This is a complex and well-told tale about loyalty, love, and the meaning of life. **A must-buy for sci-fi readers.**" —*SLJ*

"*Defy the Stars* is a **unique** and masterful sci-fi space opera that will take readers across the galaxy on a fast-paced thrill ride.... **Brilliantly done.**"   —*Romantic Times*

"With a love story that sweeps across the galaxy and a heart-racing high-action plot, *Defy the Stars* brilliantly explores what it means to be human. **This book shines like the stars.**"

—Beth Revis, *New York Times*–bestselling author of the Across the Universe series

"**Startlingly original and achingly romantic**, Abel and Noemi's adventure will linger in my imagination—and my heart—for aeons. *Defy the Stars* is **nothing short of masterful.**"

—Kass Morgan, *New York Times*–bestselling author of The 100 series

DEFY THE WORLDS

DEFY THE WORLDS

CLAUDIA GRAY

(L)(B)

LITTLE, BROWN AND COMPANY

New York Boston

Copyright © 2018 by Amy Vincent

Cover art copyright © 2018 by Sammy Yuen. Cover design by Marcie Lawrence. Cover copyright © 2018 by Hachette Book Group, Inc.

Little, Brown and Company
Hachette Book Group
1290 Avenue of the Americas, New York, NY 10104
Visit us at LBYR.com

First Edition: April 2018

Little, Brown and Company is a division of Hachette Book Group, Inc. The Little, Brown name and logo are trademarks of Hachette Book Group, Inc.

The publisher is not responsible for websites (or their content) that are not owned by the publisher.

Library of Congress Cataloging-in-Publication Data

Names: Gray, Claudia, author.
Title: Defy the worlds / Claudia Gray.
Description: First edition. | New York ; Boston : Little, Brown and Company, 2018. | Series: Defy the stars ; 2 | Summary: "Sophisticated robot Abel must save teenaged soldier Noemi from capture on a hidden planet, while outwitting armies of deranged service robots and securing medical aid for a plague on Noemi's home world"— Provided by publisher.
Identifiers: LCCN 2017034001| ISBN 9780316394109 (hardcover) | ISBN 9780316394086 (ebook library edition)
Subjects: | CYAC: Soldiers—Fiction. | Robots—Fiction. | Plague—Fiction. | Immortality—Fiction. | Interstellar travel—Fiction. | Orphans—Fiction. | Science fiction.
Classification: LCC PZ7.G77625 Dej 2018 | DDC [Fic]—dc23
LC record available at https://lccn.loc.gov/2017034001

ISBNs: 978-0-316-39410-9 (hardcover), 978-0-316-39409-3 (ebook)

Printed in the United States of America

LSC-H

10 9 8 7 6 5 4 3 2 1

DEFY THE WORLDS

1

NOEMI VIDAL WALKS THROUGH THE TWO LONG LINES OF starfighters in the hangar, helmet under one arm, head held high. She doesn't wave to her friends like she always used to—until six months ago.

Now no one would wave back.

Chin up, shoulders straight, she tells herself, taking what comfort she can in the familiar smells of grease and ozone, the hiss of repair torches, and the thump of boots on tarmac. *If you want them to see you as a fellow soldier again, you act like one. You don't back down from mech fire, so you won't back down from this.*

But Earth's warrior mechs only aim at the body. Noemi has shields for that. The point between her and her fellow squadron members aims at the heart, for which no protection has ever been invented.

"Vidal!" That's Captain Baz, striding across the hangar with a dataread in her hand. She's wearing her uniform, a dark-patterned head scarf, and the first smile Noemi's seen all day. "We're putting you on close-range patrol today."

"Yes, ma'am. Captain, if I could—"

Baz stops and comes nearer. "Yes, Lieutenant?"

"I wanted to ask—" Noemi takes a deep breath. "You haven't put me on Gate patrol in months. I'd really like to take on a shift sometime soon."

"Gate patrol's the most dangerous gig there is." Baz says it matter-of-factly as she scans through her dataread. Everyone on Genesis knows that the Gate ties them to Earth and the other colony worlds on the Loop, holding one point of a wormhole in place and making instantaneous cross-galactic travel possible. It also makes possible the war that's devastating their world. "Most pilots would be glad to stick a little closer to home."

"I'm willing to share the danger." More than willing— by now, Noemi's very nearly desperate. Protecting Genesis is what gives her life meaning. She hasn't been allowed to truly defend her world for months, not since her return.

It takes Baz a few long seconds to answer. "Listen. That day's going to come, okay? We just have to give it time."

The captain is on Noemi's side, which helps a little. That doesn't mean Captain Baz has it right. In a lower voice, Noemi says, "They won't trust me again until I'm pulling a full load."

Baz weighs that. "Maybe so." After another second's contemplation, she nods. "We'll try it." Her voice rises to a shout. "Ganaraj, O'Farrell, Vidal's with you today! Let's get up there, people—gamma shift's ready to come home."

The other two pilots stare at her from across the room. Noemi simply heads straight for her starfighter.

She's going to earn their acceptance the only way she can: one flight at a time.

Wait and see, she tells herself. *Soon they'll like you just as much as they did before.*

She figures it shouldn't be hard. They never liked her that much to begin with.

* * *

Ten percent of the time, Gate patrols are the worst, most frightening duty assignment of all. At irregular, unguessable intervals, Earth sends Damocles ships full of warrior mechs—Queen and Charlie models, designed only to kill. They've more than decimated Genesis's antiquated defense fleet in the past five years; every battle they win brings them closer to the day warrior mechs will land on the surface of Genesis, unleash a ground war, and begin reclaiming Noemi's planet for Earth's use. Every battle alarm has to be sounded as soon as possible. The starfighters on patrol are expected to engage Damocles ships immediately, without waiting for backup. Most don't survive.

However, the other 90 percent of the time, Gate patrols are boring as hell.

In the pilot's seat of her starfighter, Noemi circles the Gate at the outer perimeter; Arun Ganaraj and Deirdre O'Farrell stick closer. She's still close enough to watch the monstrous thing in the sky, a massive silver ring illuminated along its various panels so that it shines in the darkness of space. It's orbited by various bits of debris from the war, from metal shards no bigger than splinters to chunks larger than her starfighter.

An entire ship remained hidden in that debris for thirty years, until Noemi discovered it, and inside she found—

"You seeing that?" Ganaraj's voice comes over the speaker just as her screen brings up the Gate in greater detail. The faint shimmer in the middle of the ring has taken on a familiar, ominous look—a cloudiness like a pond about to frost over.

"Yeah, I see it," Noemi says.

"It might be nothing." Ganaraj sounds like he's trying to convince himself. *"Doesn't always mean something's about to come through."*

"Usually doesn't," Noemi agrees as she zooms in tighter on the image and sets her weapons to ready. Segments of old wreckage and shrapnel from past battles often create the illusion of incoming traffic. Even a faint hint of intrusion is danger enough to set her on edge.

"Or it could be a bunch of mechs coming through to dice us all." O'Farrell makes herself sound happy about it, so

happy the sarcasm is unmistakable. *"But you'll just want to give them milk and cookies and send them home again, won't you, Vidal?"*

"Pack it, O'Farrell," Noemi snaps back.

"Well, that's what you do, isn't it? You love mechs sooooo much that you'd rather leave Genesis exposed to war and death than destroy a freakin' hunk of metal—"

Ganaraj cuts in. *"Could we pay attention to the Gate, everybody?"*

"Never stopped," Noemi says. But her cheeks feel like they're burning, and her pulse throbs angrily in her temples. She can handle it when they pick on her, but not when they turn on Abel.

When she found that ship six months ago, she also found the mech inside it: Mansfield Cybernetics Model 1A, the pet project of the one and only Burton Mansfield, and the single most advanced mech ever created.

Model 1A prefers to be known as Abel.

At first, Noemi saw him the same way everyone else on Genesis does: a machine fashioned in the shape of a human but with no soul inside. An enemy, one she could use before destroying. He was the tool that could blow up the Genesis Gate—sealing Genesis safely away from Earth forever, winning the war in one split-second blast.

However, blowing up the Gate would've meant blowing up Abel with it, and by the end of their journey through the colony worlds of the Loop, Noemi knew that Abel was far more than a machine. She could no more have killed him to destroy the Gate than she could've sacrificed a child on an altar.

God asked for that once, whisper her old catechism lessons. She's getting better at ignoring those. Maybe too much better—

Red lights flash on her starfighter console. Noemi's hands tighten on the controls as she spots the signal. "We've got something coming through."

By now, though, their sensors are telling them the same thing. "*Confirmed,*" says Ganaraj, fear threading through his voice. "*But it's not a Damocles.*"

"*A scout ship,*" O'Farrell suggests. "*Getting advance intel before the Queens and Charlies come through.*"

"Since when do mechs use scout ships?" Noemi zooms in tighter on the intruding ship.

No. Not a ship. Something else.

The metal object is shaped into meter-long delicate points that extend in every direction from the small spherical center. To herself she whispers, "It's like a star"—the way she pictured them as a child, pretty and shining, not monstrous and powerful. The prettiness makes it more ominous.

"*Is it a bomb?*" Ganaraj asks.

Noemi knows it's not. She can't say why she knows it, but she does. Call it intuition.

O'Farrell provides more concrete confirmation: *"Scans negative for explosives."*

The Gate shimmers once more, and another star bursts through. Then another. As Noemi stares, the stars keep multiplying until her sensors give her a final count of a hundred and twenty. They rush through space, a constellation as brilliant as it is terrifying, streaking toward Genesis.

"Inform command, and let's stay on them," Ganaraj orders. He's been a lieutenant nine weeks longer than Noemi has. *"The second we get clearance, we're blasting these things to oblivion."*

Noemi would blast them now and trust that clearance would follow later. There's less than no chance that Captain Baz and the other higher-ups are going to allow anything from Earth to get close to home—explosives or not. But Ganaraj is in charge, and Noemi's on thin ice, so she grits her teeth and flies tight on the stars as long as she can—

—which isn't that long, because they're spreading out, widening the distances between them. When the stars first emerged from the Gate, Noemi's three-fighter patrol could have destroyed them in a quick spray of blaster fire. Every second that elapses makes targeting more difficult and time-consuming. The stars zip through the solar system, miniature mag engines making them glow bright in the darkness, traveling fast enough to reach Genesis within fifteen minutes. Noemi scans the "stars" nonstop and knows the others are doing the same. The results on her screen reveal nothing about what these things are or what they could mean.

Maybe they're peace offerings, she thinks. It's a private joke. There's no way Earth would make an offer, not now. The situation in the larger galaxy has grown more dire than ever. Earth won't be habitable much longer, and the other colony of the worlds can only house so many more millions of people; that leaves billions who need a place to live, billions who would destroy her world the same way they destroyed their own. The Liberty War began thirty years ago because her people realized they had a moral, religious duty to protect their planet.

Despite their lower technological reserves, they held out for decades, even enjoying a period of relative quiet. But in the past few years, Earth has resumed the fight with a vengeance. Genesis is the only prize worth claiming— anywhere, for anyone.

"Ganaraj," she says. "They're getting too far apart."

"*Regulations state—*" Ganaraj breaks off. "*We have clearance. Take these things down.*"

Four and a half minutes. It took four and a half minutes for that decision to be made. But that's Genesis's leadership for you, all the way from the top of the Elder Council to midlevel military command—always cautious, always hesitant, always waiting to be acted upon instead of taking the initiative to act—

She catches herself. All her life, she had revered the Council, trusted in their judgment, and followed their guidance even when that meant volunteering for the suicidal Masada Run. Then came her journey through the Loop of colony planets and Earth itself, a trip that opened her eyes to other perspectives on the Liberty War…and made her acutely aware of the Council's fatalism. Even after her report made it clear that Earth had new vulnerabilities due to the changing political situation throughout the worlds, the Council hadn't canceled the Masada Run. Only "postponed" it until some unknown future date. And all these months later, the Elders have yet to take one concrete action to capitalize on the intel Noemi has given them.

At least she can take action now. Noemi targets the first star and tightens her fingers on the triggers. It dies in a cloud of bluish dust and a brief flash of light quickly snuffed by the cold of space—as satisfying to her as any explosion could ever be.

If only she could blow them up faster! They're casting a wide net now, clearly preparing to encircle Genesis itself, which wells larger through her cockpit window, its green-and-blue surface placid beneath this strange assault. The stars have individual targets, she realizes, and those targets are all over her world. Her hair prickles as it stands on end. "Ganaraj, we need backup ASAP."

Another star flares bright with energy as her blaster hits it, then disintegrates—that one was hit by O'Farrell, who yells, *"We can take these things out on our own!"*

Noemi shakes her head, as though O'Farrell could see her. "Maybe, but we can't take that chance."

"I've asked ground to weigh in," Ganaraj says. *"Hang on!"*

Hang on? These stars are about to enter atmosphere and he still wants to get approval? Noemi bites back her frustration and resumes firing, targeting every star she can scan.

But she can't scan them all any longer. Their three ships fly farther apart as each tries to take out the stars aimed at the three major continents of Genesis. One after another, Noemi blows them to bits—but they're too spaced out. Too far. In the same moment that she destroys her twentieth star, she sees one glow bright with the heat of atmospheric entry. Then another glows as it enters the far horizon. And another, and another—

Don't focus on what you can't do, she reminds herself. *Focus on what you can.*

In the end, according to scans, forty-seven stars make impact with the surface of Genesis. Every single star hits a populated landmass, most of them in or near major cities and transit hubs; not one lands in the ocean, despite her planet being 60 percent covered with water. This suggests targeting. Yet the stars don't explode on impact, or smash into government buildings, or do anything else obviously destructive. One of them lands on a monorail track, damaging it slightly, and another gouges out a thick gash in a public park. But that's as serious as the property damage gets, and the reported injuries are not life-threatening— small cuts from debris, a minor transit accident when a driver was so startled he failed to watch signals, and one person who fainted in fear and bruised her head in the fall.

No one is seriously hurt—only Noemi's reputation is.

* * *

"Ganaraj reports that you repeatedly argued against getting approvals from command," says Captain Baz as she sits in her office. Noemi stands in front of her desk at attention. "In other words, you wanted him to ignore standard protocols."

"Captain, we're allowed to use discretion on our patrols. Shooting down projectiles sent from the Earth system is well within that discretion."

"Arguably." Baz's voice is dry. "Almost certainly, in fact. But not explicitly. The problem isn't that you wanted to shoot them down, Vidal. It's that you advocated against your commanding officer contacting *his* commanding officer, which can sound an awful lot like urging him to rogue action."

"Rogue action?" Noemi manages to hang on to her temper, but it's close. "Forgive me, Captain—I meant to say, shooting down those stars hardly constitutes 'rogue action.'"

Baz nods tiredly. "Those are Ganaraj's words, not mine. And if you feel that's an unfair interpretation of your actions, I agree." She leans back in her desk chair, loosing her head scarf like she sometimes does when it's only women around. "You've had to deal with that a lot the past few months. The others are hard on you. It's tough, and you're holding up despite the pressure. That takes guts. Don't think I don't notice."

Noemi swallows down the lump in her throat. "That means a lot, ma'am."

Baz sighs again. "Ganaraj won't be happy we didn't put you on report. It might be a good idea to…take a break from flying for a while. We'll find something for you to do on the ground. Preferably a duty you can fulfill all alone, without anybody else to piss off."

"Yes, Captain." This solution strikes Noemi as one that will compound the problem. "But I need to find a way to be a part of the squadron again. More than I was before, if possible. I think that would be better."

Always, she's stood at the fringes. Sometimes she feels like she's been lonely her entire life since her parents died. Esther was the only friend who ever understood her, and

Esther's grave is in the heart of a star all the way across the galaxy.

Baz doesn't seem to see it that way. "You've always been independent, Lieutenant Vidal. That's not a bad thing. Learn to embrace it. Not everyone has to be a 'people person.'"

It's all Noemi can do not to laugh. That's not something she's likely to be mistaken for.

Since Esther's death, she's only been special to one person. One who saw her more deeply than even Esther ever did.

One nobody else on Genesis would admit is a *person* at all.

The captain's tone turns gentler, more thoughtful. "Some Second Catholics meditate, I know. Do you?"

"I've tried. I'm not very good at it."

"That's the secret about meditation—nobody's good at it." A quick smile flashes across Baz's face. "You need to find center, Vidal. You need to refocus. If you do that, I think the people around you will sense it."

"Maybe so," Noemi replies politely. She gives this about a zero percent chance of success.

Either Baz doesn't pick up on Noemi's skepticism or she doesn't care. "The next time you meditate, I want you to ask yourself two questions. What are you fighting, Noemi Vidal? And what are you fighting for?"

The questions resonate more deeply for Noemi than she would've thought. Disconcerted, she stares at the floor as she nods.

"You're free to go," Captain Baz says. At least she won't push the meditation thing any further. "Try not to step on any toes on your way out?"

"Yes, Captain. But—I wanted to ask about the stars. Have the scientists figured out what they are yet? What they were supposed to do?"

Baz shrugs. "So far nobody has a clue. Nothing obvious has shown up. Nothing not so obvious either. Maybe it wasn't official, or serious. Maybe some Earther with more money than sense decided to make harassing us his new hobby."

"Maybe," Noemi says. But she can't bring herself to believe it. Those projectiles from Earth could only have been intended to do them harm.

If they failed, that means others will be coming. This time, she won't have a chance to shoot them down.

2

HALF A GALAXY AWAY, ON A LUSH RESORT ISLAND OFF the coast of China, Abel is crashing a party.

"Thank you," he says to the George model who hands back his identibadge, the one Abel personally programmed with false data. George mechs are only equipped with enough intelligence for uninteresting bureaucratic tasks, and this one performed only routine checks, all of which Abel had taken into account. It would take a far deeper inquiry to discover any issues. Even a human would've been unlikely to determine that the man walking into the party is not actually named Kevin Lambert, is not a lifelong resident of Great Britain, and is not a potential investor in Mansfield Cybernetics.

The party fills a large, oval, translucent bubble suspended not far above the ocean, surrounded by a few smoky side rooms and corridors that wind around it like the precious-metal setting around a jewel. So far, attendees number approximately two hundred and seventeen; he'll finalize this count once he's certain he's accounted for people who might be in bathrooms or hallways. There's at least one service mech for every three partygoers, a mixture of Dogs and Yokes handing around food on trays, a couple of scantily clad Fox and Peter models no doubt provided for after-party entertainment, and three Oboes in the corner, playing music just loud enough to ensure people can still converse.

Abel's information about popular music aged badly during the thirty years of his confinement. He's still catching up. After nearly a century of slower, gentler, neoclassical music, up-tempo tunes have returned to popularity. This song, with a hundred and forty beats per minute, is clearly meant to echo a human heartbeat in a state of excitement, thus stimulating listeners on both conscious and subconscious levels....

Then he stops analyzing the music and simply asks himself, *Do you like it?*

Yes. He does.

A slight smile on his face, Abel walks into the heart of the gathering. He's surrounded on all sides by the rich and beautiful—slim bodies garbed in richly patterned kimonos, jackets and trousers cut to emphasize attractiveness, and silk dresses that do little to conceal every curve and plane of the bodies within.

Only 3.16 meters beneath the transparent flooring, the dark water ripples past, waves forming under their feet to break on the distant shore. Soft bands of light sweep downward repeatedly as if the illumination were flowing along the walls into the sea.

The dataread tucked into Abel's black silk jacket pulses once. Rather than pull it out, he simply taps his chest pocket and localizes the range of his hearing. The crowd's murmuring instantly becomes muted.

"How's it going down there?" asks Harriet Dixon, who works as the pilot of Abel's ship, the *Persephone*. She's generally full of bubbly optimism, but she gets nervous when she can tell Abel isn't telling her the full story. *"Finished trading the 'big and sparkly' yet?"*

He snags a glass of champagne from a nearby Yoke's tray to complete his image as a partygoer. "Not yet."

This is untrue. He sold the diamond they mined from a meteor near Saturn as soon as they made landfall on Earth. His other tasks do not concern Harriet and her partner, Zayan Thakur. Involving them would only put them at risk. Abel has begun calculating the morality of lying in more complex ways, of late.

"As long as you're not losing it at a casino," Harriet says. *"That stone's going to fetch us enough to live on for months! If you manage it right."*

"I will," Abel says. In fact the price he got could probably pay for a full year's operating costs. He will cut Harriet and Zayan in for equal shares of the haul, but he has chosen to distribute larger windfalls in smaller, scheduled installments. When he met his crew members six months ago, they were very near the point of starvation. The natural psychological result of such privation is the impulse to spend any funds as quickly as they come in, sometimes on pure extravagance. This isn't unique to Harriet and Zayan; most Vagabonds are so used to living on scarce resources that they're often unsure how to handle prosperity. Such luxuries don't tempt Abel.

His one temptation lurks at the far edge of the Earth system, monitored by security satellites—the Genesis Gate.

The pathway that would lead back to Noemi, and probably to his own death.

Sometimes that journey seems worth the price.

"I promise I won't gamble it away," Abel adds. "I should be back on the *Persephone* within two hours."

"You'd better be." That's Zayan, clearly shouting over from his ops station. *"Or we'll turn Earth upside down looking for you."*

"Security stations, too." Harriet's picked up on the fact that Abel uses false identification and tries hard to avoid interacting with Queen and Charlie models. She is highly intelligent, but understandably has not figured out precisely why he avoids them. No doubt she's assumed he's in

trouble with the law on some system or another. *"You're the luckiest Vagabond I ever saw. But everyone's luck runs out someday, Abel."*

Abel doesn't have "luck." He simply has a better understanding of probabilities than any biological life-form. The effect is much the same. "You won't have to search any security stations. I promise." As a George model steps to the acoustic center of the room, he adds, "I'll be in touch once I'm done here. Captain out."

No sooner does he silence the dataread than the music stops midbeat. The human partygoers fall silent just as quickly as the mech band.

A spotlight falls over the George, who calls, "If we may have your attention, the program is about to begin. Our Mansfield Cybernetics presents your host for tonight, renowned scientist and philosopher Dr. Gillian Mansfield Shearer."

Applause breaks out across the room as a woman in her early forties walks to the heart of the light. In the distance Abel overhears someone whispering, "I can't believe she's here tonight. I thought she would've sent a representative—"

"This is important," says that person's companion. Abel doesn't bother looking to see exactly who it is. Gillian Shearer is his lone point of focus. The brilliance makes her red hair gleam. At 154.12 centimeters in height, she stands shorter than the average human female, but her posture and intensity suggest greater power. The plain black dress she wears looks out of place in this room of glamorous gowns and silk suits—as if a funeral attendee had suddenly walked into the party. It hangs slightly loose on her, as though she had lost a great deal of weight in a hurry, or she is one of those humans who considers fashion a waste of time.

Dr. Shearer has a strong nose, and her hair has a widow's peak. These are features she and Abel share, because they inherited them from the same DNA.

Abel is Burton Mansfield's creation; Gillian Shearer is his daughter.

Abel steps halfway behind a taller partygoer. Probably Gillian's human eyes can't make out anyone's features past the glare of that spotlight, but Abel's taking no chances. She might notice his strong resemblance to a younger Mansfield, or she might simply remember him.

Abel remembers her.

"I wish I could talk with Mommy again. Mommy always knew how to make it better." Gillian looks up at him, tears welling in her blue eyes as he carefully applies the synthskin to her bloody knuckles; she says he's better at it than the household Tare. In this moment she is eight years, one month, and four days old. "Daddy says someday I'll get to talk to Mommy, but why isn't it now?"

Robin Mansfield died some months before Abel achieved consciousness. He has assumed Burton Mansfield believed in no supreme being, but perhaps the concept of heaven would comfort a child. "That would be very far in the future."

"It could be now! Daddy got it all wrong." Gillian's scowl is too fierce for her tiny face. "Instead he made you to take care of me."

"And for other purposes," he said, smoothing the synthskin with his fingertips, proud to have been chosen ahead of the Tare. "But I'll take care of you."

Perhaps he should remember her fondly. But everything that reminds him of Burton Mansfield has been poisoned for Abel, possibly forever—and that includes his daughter.

"Assembled guests," Gillian says. The greater depth and resonance of her voice is to be expected post-adolescence, but it nonetheless startles Abel. "For two generations, Mansfield Cybernetics has stood alone in its capacity to create, update, and perfect the artificial intelligences that support our society. It's now hard to imagine how we would manage without Bakers and Items to handle complex but mundane tasks, Dogs and Yokes to perform manual labor, Mikes and Tares to care for us when we're sick, Nans and Uncles to tend our children and our elderly, and the Queens and Charlies that keep us safe throughout the galaxy."

Polite applause briefly fills the room. A meter from Abel,

a Yoke stands still, tray of champagne glasses in her hands, a useful object in human form. He cannot reject Gillian's assessment of a Yoke as no more than that; the sense of self within him—his soul, Noemi called it—is shared by no other mech. But he still looks into the Yoke's eyes and wishes he could see another soul looking back.

Gillian gestures at a nearby screen, which lights up as the spotlight falls dark. Different models of mech appear in rotation—leonine Queens, designed to fight; humble Dogs for manual labor; silvery, inhuman X-Rays that project the faces of others. "We're constantly updating and perfecting each of the twenty-five models of mech in current production. However, those models have remained fundamentally unchanged for decades—primarily because the service they provide is capable and consistent. But my father and I had another reason for maintaining the models as they are: We didn't want to dramatically alter the market until we had an innovation worth altering our entire galaxy." On the screen, the mech tanks growing shapes in rough human form shift into red bubbles—Force fields? A polymer? Abel can't tell from visual input alone—with shadowy fetal shapes inside. Gillian doesn't smile, but she lifts her chin so that her face is bathed in the crimson light of this vision of the future. "Now, at last, we believe we've made that breakthrough."

Applause bursts out again, more enthusiastic than

before, as the screen image shifts into the forms of two embryos with brightly glowing mech components in the area of the head. The embryos rapidly shift into fetuses, into infants, and then into two fully grown mechs—not a Charlie and a Queen, but with faces like the children those two models would have, if they could reproduce.

Now, it seems, they can.

"Organic engineering," Gillian says. "Superstrong structures within made up not of metal but of organic compounds, manipulated to create material far more resilient than bone. Mental capacity that will allow for greater individuality of programming while maintaining the essential separation between human and machine. Self-repairing capacities that go beyond healing minor injuries, rendering the next generation of mechs nearly immortal. We're calling them Inheritors: mechs that can carry on the best of what came before, while helping us realize our ambitions for the future. That's what we believe we'll be able to offer this galaxy—not decades from now, but within the next two to three years."

Excited murmuring rises as the lights go up. Abel understands why. These people are anticipating not only better, more useful mechs, but also investment opportunities that will make them even wealthier than they already are. (He's observed that human avarice almost always outstrips human need.)

His principal thought is different from theirs: *Soon I'll be obsolete.*

In some ways. Not all. The new mechs will be limited mentally; they will not develop souls. Yet knowing any mechs, anywhere, will be more advanced than him in any way—it's a new sensation, one Abel decides he doesn't like.

He'd gleaned rumors of this, mostly through various bits of research chatter coming from Cray, in particular from Virginia Redbird. It was his curiosity about a potential new cybernetic line that brought him here. But he'd hoped the new mechs might be more like him. That they might be people rather than machines.

That he might no longer be alone.

Gillian says, "Organic mechs will be able to reproduce, thus reducing manufacturing costs." Raising one eyebrow, she dryly adds, "Reproduction will be on command only, so no one need worry about any unwelcome surprises. And we're pretty sure we can improve on nine months' gestation time—something human mothers might be jealous of."

As the crowd chuckles, Abel imagines the possibilities. The thought of a pregnant mech, carrying something that is more device than child—something intended only for servitude—revolts him profoundly. A human might call the reaction "primal." All Abel knows is that he cannot abide the thought of it.

Gillian seems disquieted as well, her eyes downcast, but her tone is even as she continues describing her creations. "They'll be cheaper to create and therefore to own. They'll retain all the advantages of mech labor while removing the disadvantages. Tonight, I hope to speak with each of you personally about our research, and about the potential that lies ahead for our company, for your participation in our next great endeavor, and for the betterment of our entire society—all through the creation of the most sophisticated mech ever."

Abel feels like this title belongs to him still, but mentioning him would undoubtedly upset the flow of her sales pitch.

"My father's vision has transformed this galaxy once." Gillian's blue eyes have taken on the intensity of a gas flame. "His legacy has the potential to be greater still. Mansfield Cybernetics intends to lead the way not only in mech engineering, but also through a revolutionary vision of the future that promises to expand the capacities of humanity itself. With your help, we can transform the galaxy again...together."

The loudest applause of the night breaks out as she steps off the dais and nods at the Oboes, who all resume their song on the very note where they left off. None of the Oboe mechs show the slightest reaction to this revelation. They're not programmed with enough intelligence to care.

Abel, however, will be thinking about Gillian's speech for a long time. It did not fulfill his hopes of finding another mech like him, but it is nonetheless significant—

His visual field of focus shifts upon identifying a threat: Gillian Shearer, who is staring straight at him.

Her look lasts only 0.338 seconds, not long enough to immediately betray him but more than long enough to create an unacceptable level of risk. Abel doesn't even glance backward as he turns to go.

He weaves through the crowd, moving against the tide of those pressing forward to get nearer to Gillian so they can hear more about this vision of the future she's offered. Walking speed must be calculated to balance the value of haste versus the cost of drawing attention.

His calculations must have been incorrect, however, because through the din he catches Gillian's voice. "That man—the blond one—he looks familiar, can you get—"

Abel ducks into one of the cloudy side passages that lead to bathrooms and food-preparation areas, finds a bathroom that's empty, and locks the door behind him. Then he kneels down and punches through the transparent floor.

The sound and spray of the waves roar into the room as he rips out a segment approximately forty by forty centimeters and jumps into the ocean.

Water closes around him, shockingly cold. He strokes

and kicks through blue-black seaweed and tiny silvery eels, fighting the current, grateful for his unerring sense of direction and the ability to hold his breath longer than any human could.

They will find the damage to the floor in no less than three minutes, no more than ten. If Gillian fully recognized me, she will already have sent a signal to the security mechs on land. If she only suspects my identity or is unsure due to inferior human memory, she won't send the signal until the damage is discovered. In the latter case, he has a chance to make it to the *Persephone*'s hangar. If the former—

He resolves to handle this negative outcome only upon its occurrence.

As soon as Abel's foot makes first contact with the shifting sand near the coast, he digs in, stops swimming, and starts running. Dashing straight out of the waves, he sees guests at a nighttime beach party skittering backward, laughing as a wild man bursts out of the waves to run past them. Sand sticks to his shoes and sopping-wet clothes, but it doesn't slow him down.

No point in restricting himself to human speed once he's off the beach. He accelerates past that within 1.3 seconds and aims directly for the hangar. With one hand he taps the dataread as he runs. "Harriet, Zayan, do you read me?"

"*Abel!*" Zayan's voice comes through instantly. "*Another couple minutes and we'd have been worried.*"

"Worry now," Abel says. "Also start the engines now. Get ready for takeoff as fast as you can."

Harriet yells, *"We told you not to—"*

"Scold me after preparing the ship to fly." He makes a quick time estimate of his possible capture as he runs beneath an elevated rail into a small, scrubby park. Every moment the sky grows darker as night becomes real. "If I'm not on the ship in ten minutes, leave without me, and the *Persephone* is yours."

"Oh, God, Abel, what did you do?" She's become more terrified than angry.

"Nothing, actually, but the authorities won't believe that. *Go.*"

By the time he reaches the hangar 6.1 minutes later, his hair and clothes are almost dry from the sheer speed of his run. Abel doesn't slow down as he heads toward the doorway to their docking bay, except for once when he sees a crowbar lying unattended near an old Vagabond junker. Stooping to grab it only costs him 1.3 seconds, and besides, if he's going to run into resistance—

Approaching the door, Abel grabs the jamb and swings around the entrance, slamming the crowbar straight into the head of the waiting Queen, who was of course concealed in the spot on the other side of the wall her programming would've targeted as most strategically likely. She falls like the inert machinery she has become, and Abel tosses the crowbar back before covering the final distance to the *Persephone*. Its silver teardrop shape seems to shine in the dark bay. When the door spirals open for him, he's finally back home.

"Immediate departure is advisable," he calls, trusting the comm system to be on. Sure enough, the mag engines instantly fire and his ship takes flight. Whatever signal Gillian sent didn't trigger a planet-wide alarm, or at least she didn't know to target the *Persephone* specifically, because he feels the ship escape planetary gravity without resistance.

When he walks onto the bridge, Harriet calls over her shoulder, "Have you gone completely mad?"

"I'm no more mad than I ever was," Abel replies.

This wins him a scowl from Harriet. "That's not as encouraging as you think it is."

Noemi's voice echoes in Abel's mind. *You're really bad at comforting people—*

"Doesn't look like we've got company coming," Zayan announces. "Our path to the Earth Gate to Stronghold checks out as clear." Gillian must not have fully recognized Abel after all—only saw him as an intruder, someone to check out at the nearest spaceport, not someone to chase down and entrap no matter what.

But she easily could have. In another fraction of a second, she *would* have. Abel had let his curiosity override his good judgment; in so doing, he endangered not only himself but also his crew. This is unacceptable. He must be more cautious in the future.

"What, are you *wet*? Did someone try to drown you?" Harriet demands.

"I'm much too good a swimmer to drown." Abel doesn't expect this correction to improve her mood; sure enough, her scowl only deepens. "I'm back, Harriet. Isn't that enough?"

"Of course it is." She glances back at him, her long braids falling past her shoulder as she does so. Both she and Zayan wear traditional Vagabond garb, loose flowing shirts and pants in vibrant patchwork colors. On the stark black-and-silver bridge of the *Persephone*, the young couple seem as brilliant as butterflies. "We worry. That's all."

Zayan laughs. "Yeah, we'd never find another boss who pays as well as you do."

A possibility occurs to Abel that had not presented itself before—an inexplicable flaw in his logic. "You could've taken off without me. The audio record of my last transmission would've allowed you to make a legal claim to the *Persephone*."

"We'd never do that to you," Zayan protests. "C'mon, Abel. Don't you know that?"

Harriet looks at him again, but this time her eyes are less angry, more troubled. "Have you really never had a friend before, that you could think something like that? Besides Noemi, I mean."

"No. I haven't." Abel isn't sure he wants this conversation to continue. "I should change my clothes."

Although he's aware of his crew members staring at him while he heads off the bridge, neither tries to stop him.

Neither Harriet nor Zayan knows why their captain doesn't fear drowning. Why he uses a constant series of fake IDs and stays out of range of security mechs as much as possible. They're loyal enough not to ask. They are, as Harriet just said, not merely employees but friends.

Would they do things differently if they realized Abel wasn't human? That he was not only a mech but the special project of the revered Burton Mansfield himself?

If they knew that Mansfield wanted Abel back because Abel's cybernetic body is the only one designed to contain a human mind—*Mansfield*'s mind, which can save the old man from his impending death—would they trade Abel's life for Mansfield's?

Those questions disturb Abel sometimes, but he prefers never to know the answers.

As far as he knows, only one human has ever valued a mech's life as equal to that of any other person. She's on the other side of the Genesis Gate—far away from him, forever.

What would Noemi Vidal say about the organic mechs? Abel feels certain her fascination would match his own.

His mood darkens as he imagines the future of this technology: mechs becoming more and more humanlike. Someday, surely, a soul will awaken within one of them— but Mansfield learns from his mistakes. The next mech with a soul will be bound by programming so strong it will make Directive One seem like a mere suggestion.

We will no longer be individuals, Abel thinks, counting himself among these unmade brothers and sisters already. *We will no longer be free.*

We will be slaves.

3

WHEN NOEMI RETURNED TO GENESIS WITH LITTLE evidence to support her story about traveling through the galaxy, she could've wound up in the brig, if not cashiered out of the service. Every young person on the planet capable of serving in the military does so; her status as a dishonored former soldier would've made her an outcast— even more than she already was. One person alone saved her from this fate: Darius Akide, Elder of the Council, and once the prized student of Burton Mansfield himself.

Now they meet every few weeks. She's conspicuous climbing the stairs of the Hall of Elders, a teenage girl in her emerald-green uniform among gray-haired, august people wearing serene white robes. That's by Akide's design, since he knows how alone she is otherwise. By summoning her here, he sends a public signal of the Council's trust in her version of events. He is her primary defender. Noemi's grateful, or knows she should be.

But knowing a member of the Elder Council has only made her more sharply aware of the Council's flaws—and how those flaws endanger Genesis itself.

"I suppose it's not surprising that you've never seen any technology like those mysterious star probes." He sits at his hewn-stone desk, salt-and-pepper hair pulled back in a knot. Like most rooms in the great hall, it is illuminated during daytime only by the sunlight flooding through the oval windows carved into the wall. "But can you remember anything from news sources, or perhaps picked up in conversation? We've still no idea what the stars were intended to do. Any hint could help our investigation."

"I wish I could help." Noemi keeps her tone even. Akide is the closest thing she has to a friend these days, but sometimes she thinks he expects her to have learned everything about the other worlds of the Loop during her whirlwind journey. "But I don't remember anything like that at all."

Akide sighs. His next words seem to be spoken as much to himself as to her. "Were they probes? Weapons that malfunctioned? Meant only to scare us? As if we don't know the threat Earth presents. As if we don't know how little chance we have."

"Don't talk like that." It hits Noemi that she just said that to an *Elder*, and her cheeks flush red. "Excuse me. I meant—we have reasons to hope. Potential allies out there on the Loop, for one."

He pats her arm, a touch meant to be fatherly, but to Noemi it feels patronizing. Maybe she'd respond to it better if she could remember more about her late father, but he's just a dim memory of smiles and hugs, an even fainter idea of what it felt like to be cherished, valued, *seen*.

"Lieutenant Vidal," Akide says. "You've grown up on a planet at war. You've known from an early age that victory was unlikely, and that your life would very likely be forfeit to the fight. You've never shied away from your duty, even from the ultimate sacrifice, but I don't think you've ever come to terms with defeat as the most probable outcome of the Liberty War. I know it's hard to come to peace with that—but for your own sake, you must try. Otherwise the pain..." He bows his head. "It would be too much to bear."

Always sacrifice. Always duty. Always resignation. For a planet at war, Noemi sometimes thinks, Genesis seems to have forgotten how to fight.

●　●　●

That evening, she decides to visit the Temple of All Faiths. It's one of the largest buildings on Genesis, certainly the most revered—a great dome of gray granite mottled with blue, held aloft by enormous columns as thick around as century-old trees. Smaller chambers set off from the central dome are reserved for different services of different religions, whether those involve chanting, dancing, prayer, or the handling of snakes. But Noemi is here for the one practice most faiths of Genesis share: meditation.

She settles herself on one of the large cushions. It's old, patched here and there, the cloth soft with age. The light filtering through the high arched windows casts beams through the vast space of the temple. Breathing in deeply, Noemi smells incense.

In this place, even her noisy mind might quiet down.

Closing her eyes, Noemi calls to mind Captain Baz's two questions:

What are you fighting, Noemi Vidal? And what are you fighting for?

She doesn't expect to get much out of that, really. It's a starting place, no more. Because of course she knows the answers. She's fighting Earth, fighting its mechs. And she's fighting for Genesis.

But suddenly she realizes that's not the answer—or at least, not the complete answer. She's also fighting her fellow soldiers, because they don't trust her any longer. She's fighting for Akide to listen to her, to see her planet taking more aggressive action to defend itself.

And I'm fighting to carry on without Esther. Without Abel.
I'm fighting to continue on alone.

She's always known most other people don't like her much, and she's never expected them to. Her one real friendship was with Esther Gatson, the foster sister who had no choice about whether or not to let Noemi into her home and her heart—and Esther's death has become one of the crimes the others blame her for.

Before, at least, Noemi had hoped her solitude might be temporary. That someday, somehow, she'd figure out how to get closer to people, or stop scaring them off—that she'd figure out just what her problem was so that she could solve it. And when she was out in the galaxy, meeting Harriet and Zayan on Kismet, Virginia on Cray, or Ephraim on Stronghold, she seemed to have figured it out. Making friends was easier when she could make a fresh start.

No fresh starts here. Whatever lessons in friendship she learned out there don't seem to apply here. Her isolation has become even more complete, and she's trying to accept that it's probably permanent.

Relax, Esther used to say. *Let people get to know you! Don't be so nervous and defensive all the time. If you're not afraid of being rejected, then people are less likely to reject you.*

Esther was telling the truth. Noemi knows how people avoid the loneliest among them. But if the trick to making friends is to stop being lonely, the paradox is inescapable. Bitterly she thinks it's like telling someone starving to death that they can have all the food they want if they'll just stop being hungry.

Only a few times in her life has she felt that maybe the famine might be over. Really, though, there was only one

time she wasn't utterly alone—one time a person understood her and cared for her—loved her, he said—

Noemi pulls herself out of the memory. Thinking of
Abel hurts, for a thousand reasons but mostly because she
knows she'll never see him again.

Sparing Abel's life was the one moment of religious
grace Noemi has ever been granted, the one time faith
became a living force inside her. She'd thought that if she
ever had such an instant of profound connection, her questions about God would be answered. Everything was supposed to come clear. But it turns out not to work that way.
She is still small in a vast cosmos, unsure what is right and
good.

Try again, she tells herself, closing her eyes. *Use the man-
tra Baz gave you.*

It doesn't help. Meditation brings her no peace, only
reminds her how alone she is—and how afraid she is that
the loneliness will endure forever.

•   •   •

"Will you want toast this morning?" Mrs. Gatson says it
the way a server in a restaurant might speak to a customer.
A new customer, not one of the regulars. Noemi has lived
in the Gatsons' home for nine years.

After Esther's death, the Gatsons commissioned a portrait of her from an artistic neighbor. The drawing hangs

on one of the walls, a soft sketch in pastels that captures her golden hair and blue eyes. But the silence she's left behind expands to fill the house every morning, until it feels as though Noemi doesn't have room to draw a single breath. This place will never completely feel like home.

Their house is a typical one on Genesis—bedrooms underground, general living space above, with large "windows" of translucent solar panels. Vegetables sprout from window boxes that line the perimeter of the one large common room, and herbs grow in long, skinny beams that stretch from floor to ceiling and divide the space into areas for cooking and eating, for socializing, and for work. Entertainment is found outside the home, unless a family is fond of music: Vids, books, and the like are kept in libraries, and pools and fitness equipment are at public gymnasiums. Noemi thought nothing of this until she went on her journey through the galaxy, along the worlds of the Loop, where she saw Virginia Redbird's lab/hideout/opium den on Cray, Kismet's luxurious resorts with their lavender seas and lilac skies, and the overwhelming, vibrant blizzard of activities and entertainment that dying Earth revels in to distract itself from its approaching end.

Once, hiding on an asteroid in the middle of a nebula's rainbow cloud, she and Abel watched an old twentieth-century "movie" together, one with former lovers reunited unexpectedly in Casablanca.

If only I could see Abel one more time, she thinks. *Without the weight of two worlds pressing down on us. When we could just . . . be.*

"Noemi?" Mrs. Gatson's smile is stiff at the corners, like a napkin starched into precise folds. Dark circles under her eyes hint at a sleepless night, and her voice is hoarse. Is she getting sick? Maybe she was crying for Esther; for the Gatsons, grief is private. They don't share theirs with Noemi, and have shown no interest in helping with hers. "Do you want toast?"

"Yes, ma'am. I'm sorry. I'm distracted this morning."

Mrs. Gatson's more at ease once she has something to do and no longer has to look at Noemi directly. "No problems on base, I hope?"

Her foster parents know perfectly well that Noemi's dealt with nothing but problems since her return. This is not a nice subject to discuss. The Gatsons only like to talk about *nice* things. When Esther was alive—so naturally, easily, genuinely good inside and out—conversations centered on her, and the sense of strain was less. Now every single chat feels like a test Noemi has to pass.

"Everything's fine," Noemi says.

Mr. Gatson walks in, and she startles. He looks terrible. He's pale, visibly sweaty, and shambling along, his legs shaking. "Mary, I'm not—not shaking off that cold."

Mrs. Gatson doesn't go to him, but instead gestures to a chair. "I'll get you some juice," she replies, voice wavering.

"No, no, let me get it." Noemi quickly pours a couple of glasses while Mrs. Gatson settles herself beside her husband. "You're both coming down with something, looks like."

"You might be next," Mr. Gatson warns her. "Keep your distance and wash your hands, you hear?"

"Yes, sir." Noemi gives him the glass and a smile. They do care for her, in their own remote way. They'd never want to see her come to harm.

But it will always be Mr. and Mrs. Gatson, never *uncle* and *aunt*, never any nicknames that would acknowledge they've spent as much time raising Noemi as her late parents did. They will never light up at the sight of her returning home. They'll never hug her good-bye.

Mr. Gatson rubs his forehead. "Do we have any ginger tea?"

"I think we're out, but I could go to the store for some," Noemi offers. Until she receives her new assignment from Captain Baz, it's not like she has anyplace more important to be.

"That would be good," Mrs. Gatson says. That's about as close as she gets to *thank you*. There is an unspoken sense from the Gatsons that their foster daughter owes them courtesy and help—it's the way she earns her keep.

Halfway to the neighborhood market, Noemi begins to realize fewer people than usual are walking along the paths, and only one or two cyclists zip by. Not as many children are playing outdoors. None of this is remarkable, but the quiet that surrounds her makes her feel cut off from the world.

In the market, she finds her way to the tea stall only to learn they're out of ginger, as well as chamomile and peppermint—all the ones she'd turn to first for someone sick. As she takes up a packet of elderflower tea, a shopper nearby staggers to one side, then sits on the wooden floor heavily, the way people do when they're sitting so they won't faint.

"I'm sorry," the man says, holding up a hand as if to wave off the woman behind the counter who's hurrying to his side. "Running a fever this morning. Oughtn't to have chanced it. If I rest for just a couple of minutes—"

Noemi doesn't hear the rest. She can't hear anything over the sudden rush of blood in her ears. Her breath catches as she stares at the man's outstretched hand—and at the telltale white lines snaking across his skin.

"Impossible," she whispers, but then she remembers the stars that hit Genesis, the ones meant to harm them in a way they couldn't understand. She understands now.

Immediately she runs through the market, weaving between stalls and carts until she finds the area comm station. Her fingers shake as she inputs the code for Darius Akide's offices. "Yes, hello, this is Lieutenant Noemi Vidal calling for Elder Akide."

An image takes shape on the screen—not Akide's usual assistant, but someone else filling in. He frowns at the young woman who somehow has the code for this inner chamber. "Elder Akide has many demands on his time—"

"Tell him it's me, and tell him it's an absolute emergency." Noemi takes a deep breath. "Earth's using biological weapons. They've infected Genesis with Cobweb."

• • •

The Elder Council doesn't question her, instead immediately going into action. Noemi might have been gratified by their trust if it had done a damn bit of good.

Reports of infection come in from all corners of Genesis. The areas with the most cases of Cobweb are those closest to where the stars made impact, but already people have fallen sick in more remote places. Public advisories go out, encouraging people to wear masks and gloves, to take care of themselves, to recognize the symptoms such as the white lines on the skin. But nobody can tell the citizens of Genesis what they need to know most: how to treat it.

"You described Cobweb as an infectious disease," says

one of the senior government doctors, speaking to Noemi the next day through the Gatsons' comm unit. "But this level of virulence wasn't indicated in your report."

"I didn't think it could've been this bad. When we were on Stronghold, they had quarantine protections in place, but still—it wasn't like everyone on Stronghold got sick at once." She rakes her hand through her chin-length black hair. "But maybe—maybe it was the amount of whatever they put in the stars?"

Her own ignorance makes her wince. It's absurd to be advising senior government officials as a teenager with no medical training at all. They've called because Noemi's the only person on Genesis with any firsthand knowledge of Cobweb. She's seen it. She's survived it. That doesn't mean she has the answers.

"Earth may have manipulated the virus," says the doctor. "Made it even more virulent."

"It was man-made in the first place, so maybe so." Not that anyone knows why Earth bioengineered the Cobweb virus, only that they did. If she'd been able to learn the reason—if Ephraim Dunaway had known it—maybe she could give them some clue about the virus that would actually help. But she's powerless.

Looking across the room, she sees Mrs. Gatson huddled under a blanket, shivering. This is the only time she's been out of bed today. The spiderweb rash across her skin barely shows against her pallor. Mr. Gatson hasn't even tried to rise. Noemi can't leave the house while they're this sick, even though she doesn't know what to do for them.

"When should someone go to the hospital?" she quietly asks the doctor. "How high a fever, or—"

"I'm not sure hospitals will be able to help," the doctor replies. "They're already overcrowded, and the situation's going to worsen when the advisory goes out."

"What advisory?"

The screen answers her as a brilliant orange border appears, the one the government usually uses when making significant announcements via personal comms. Noemi could read the full text at the bottom, but a single word jumps out, one that blots out everything else:

PANDEMIC.

That one word tells Noemi that Earth has done what it meant to do. It's weakened their planet and made them vulnerable to attack.

Genesis has withstood thirty years of war, yet one virus may bring down this entire world.

4

ABEL HAD THOUGHT TO PUT IN FOR RESUPPLY ON Stronghold itself, but as soon as they enter the system, that plan collapses.

"Oh, bloody hell," Zayan breathes as the operations console lights up with warning signals. "The entire system's on lockdown. Is it another Remedy attack?"

"Unknown." Abel's sharp eyes are already looking for either Remedy fighters or security mechs in pursuit of them, but he sees nothing. No space traffic at all, actually. Maybe people have fled the scene of yet another terrorist incident.

Eight space stations and four transit vessels have been destroyed by Remedy since their first, most public strike against the Orchid Festival on Kismet. The death count from these attacks has risen to nearly ten thousand—and that's if Earth is accurately reporting all the deaths, which Abel doubts. The radical wing of Remedy claims violence

46

is justified to overcome the greater violence Earth visits on its colony worlds, but when he looks at this, all he sees is bloodshed.

He can't condemn them entirely, because not every member of Remedy is a terrorist. Ephraim Dunaway, the doctor who helped Noemi and Abel escape Stronghold six months earlier—he is a decent man, one who's trying to reveal Earth's wrongdoing in order to help people. But they met another Remedy member, too. Riko Watanabe claimed to want justice but sought only revenge.

If Noemi were here, they could discuss whether violence can ever be justified in the pursuit of freedom. She might have a different point of view.

"Abel?" Harriet has an odd look on her face. Abel realizes he's smiling softly. Remembering Noemi has this effect on him.

Amending his expression, he decides to test his ability to make jokes. He's been working on that lately. "I'm just relieved we're running into more trouble. When things go too smoothly, I worry."

He must've done it right, because that makes her laugh. "Come on. Even we catch a break sometimes."

"Not today," Zayan says with a grimace. "Receiving signal now—it's a planetwide quarantine warning. Cobweb."

Harriet swears in French. Abel says nothing, because for

a fraction of a second he's not in the here and now. He's remembering six months ago, when Noemi's skin was covered in the telltale white lines of Cobweb and her fever had spiked so sharply he thought he might lose her.

All Abel's knowledge, all his many talents, did no good. It was the quick treatment she got on Stronghold, and the assistance of Ephraim Dunaway, that saved Noemi's life. He doesn't like remembering his own powerlessness.

Zayan's console blinks, informing them they have clearance to land on one of the outer peninsulas, where the disease has apparently been contained, and Harriet's hands are already on the controls. "Go in for landing?" Zayan asks.

Abel weighs the potential risks, then shakes his head. "I'm not willing to risk your health."

"Or your own," Zayan says. "You're not immortal, you know."

"True." Abel's life span is most likely somewhere around two hundred and fifty years. He still has more than two centuries to go.

"Let's get out of here." Harriet begins turning the ship away from Stronghold. "Back through the Earth Gate, then? Even if we shouldn't land there for a while due to— well, whatever it is you're not telling us—we could pick up some more mining work in the asteroid belt."

"Not right now," Abel says. After Gillian's demonstration, he badly needs to talk about what he's seen, and there's only one person he can discuss this with. "Take us to the Stronghold Gate to Cray, top speed."

"Cray?" Zayan frowns. "Nobody gets landing clearance on Cray unless they're preapproved by the scientists. To do that, you have to be a researcher or a merchant or—"

"Or a family member." Abel decides upon the best stratagem. "Let's go."

· · ·

"Cousin Abel!" Virginia Redbird throws her arms open wide. Her long, red-streaked brown hair hangs free almost to her waist, and her orange coverall is decorated with badges and pins from dozens of different sources. While they've been in occasional contact via holos and data transmissions, this is the first time he's seen her since their escape from Earth nearly six months prior. "My beloved, long-lost cousin! I've missed you *so much*!"

Abel submits to the hug, which gives him the chance to whisper in her ear: "I think the human phrase for this is 'laying it on too thick.'"

Virginia laughs. "Remember who you're talking to. I lay *everything* on too thick."

This is true. The others standing around the geometric

perfection of Cray's Station 47 landing dock pay absolutely no attention to Virginia's over-the-top welcome. Only Zayan and Harriet are staring. They'll get used to her in time.

"Did you come all this way just to visit me?" Virginia slings her arm around Abel's shoulders, leading him into one of Cray's underground corridors. The planet's surface may be a seething red desert, but down here everything is cool and crisp, mostly in various shades of white, orange, and gray. Every shop offers games, snacks, or holos to pamper the brilliant scientists who live here, working with the massive supercomputer powered by the planetary core. "I'm touched by the depth of your family feeling, Abel. Deeply touched."

He tries to get into the spirit. "Anything for you, Cousin Virginia."

She laughs out loud in glee. "Who are these friends of yours?"

"Harriet Dixon, Zayan Thakur, this is Virginia Redbird, one of the top science students on Cray." Abel gestures toward his...friends. Yes, that's the right word. "Virginia, my friends Harriet and Zayan work as crew on my ship."

"What's that ship named these days?" Virginia had seen a few of the fake IDs he had to use during Noemi's whirlwind trip through the Loop.

"The *Persephone*," Zayan offers. When Virginia looks

over at Abel, her expression becomes softer. She knows he renamed the ship in Noemi's honor without his even having to explain the connection. Abel finds himself touched at being understood.

Meanwhile, the George mech that checked the *Persephone* into dock shows no sign of recognition of either Abel or the ship, though it may well be the exact same George that dealt with them six months before—when a security alert went out for him and Noemi. He has no worries about any human recognizing him from that; their brains discard far more information than they retain. Probably the Georges undergo periodic memory purges, a factor Abel took into account when deciding to return to Cray.

Yet he cannot forget that Burton Mansfield is still looking for his creation. Still eager to destroy Abel's consciousness—his soul—and replace it with his own. Surely he's programmed certain mechs to recognize Abel, and then work toward his recapture. That's a threat Abel lives with every day.

Either he's been very lucky not to be spotted, or Mansfield knows his location. Tracks him. Waits.

Abel catches himself. *Paranoia can lead to a spiral of recursive thoughts.* He must remain focused on the moment.

"Harriet, Z, you guys seem great." Virginia thumps Zayan on the shoulder. "Abel and I need to talk family business for a while. But how about you meet us at Mont-golfier at 1900 hours? It's this restaurant where all the dishes and tables and chairs are made out of energy fields, so it's like your food is just hovering in space in front of you!...Okay, it's kind of disgusting, but it's flash at the same time. You should try it just once."

Harriet laughs. "Okay, you're on. Pretty sure we can find plenty to amuse ourselves with around here." Already Zayan has his sights on one of the games shops. Abel thinks they might have wandered off even without Virginia's suggestion.

Now he can discuss the advent of the next generation of mechs—without having to hide the fact that he's a mech.

The Razers' new secret hideout looks very much like the old one, with the same hodgepodge of computing equipment, inflatable furniture, multicolored string lights, and makeshift ashtrays that smell strongly of controlled substances. "This location, though?" Virginia scoops some abandoned clothing from a chair and motions for Abel to take a seat. "They'll *never* find us here, unless Mansfield sends more crazy mechs after you."

Abel sits in the inflatable chair with as much dignity as he can muster. "I don't think we have to worry about that right now. My creator seems to have turned to new concerns. I followed up on the research you sent to the

Persephone. Mansfield is creating a new kind of mech—one almost entirely organic."

Virginia's eyes light up. Other humans react this way when offered sexual intercourse or perhaps that endangered rarity, chocolate. "Jupiter Optimus Maximus! That's gigantic, Abel! How come it's not on every news feed in the galaxy?"

"The information is being kept secret, except from a select few wealthy individuals I suspect to be investors."

"This is amazing. We need specs. We need their data! So we're going to have to break into Mansfield Cybernetics." Virginia ticks that off on her finger as if it were any ordinary errand.

"No." Then he considers the question. "Not yet. Most of the work is only theoretical at this point."

"Theoretical work is *data*. Data is *our friend*. C'mon, man."

"I understand this, of course," Abel says. "What I mean is that I think the specifics of Mansfield's plans are less important at this point. I'm as curious as you are about organic mechs, but another aspect of this is harder to understand. We also need to investigate what he's finding investors for."

"For the project with the new organic mechs…which will make him a kajillion dollars, and he already has ten kajillion dollars, so yeah, why does he need investors?" She taps her desk. "You suspect shenanigans."

"...For lack of a better term, yes."

"This is *ultimate*." Virginia spins her office chair around, then rolls it halfway across the room, her red-streaked hair streaming behind her. She catches herself at the chosen desk and presses a panel that brings up the preliminary data she "skimmed" from Mansfield Cybernetics a few months ago. The holographic blueprint of a mech skeleton hovers in the air, Abel's own version of the Vitruvian Man. "They've probably begun construction—or growth, whatever they're going to call it with the organics—at least on a limited number. Where do you think they're doing this?"

"I'm uncertain," Abel admits as he rises from the inflatable chair, gratefully, to join her across the room. "Not at one of the main laboratories or factories. Otherwise word would already have spread, despite Mansfield Cybernetics' best efforts to keep it quiet."

Virginia's grin widens. A Razer likes nothing better than a puzzle, and he's presented her with an excellent one. "So we need to find a secret lab. And we're working *in* a secret lab. How great is that?"

He judges this question to be theoretical and says only, "They revealed no specific locations to the investors."

"Where was this fancy clambake you went to?"

Clambake appears to be the current slang for *party*, for

reasons Abel has not attempted to fathom. "Earth, off the coast of China."

"That's pretty far from Mansfield Cybernetics' main HQ. Pretty far from Mansfield himself, and from the sound of it, he's in no shape to go traveling these days."

"True." And odd—Virginia's right to point this out. It's unlike Mansfield to place himself so far from the central action. "But his daughter, Gillian, was in control. He would have perfect faith in her if in no one else."

"And speaking of Dr. Gillian Shearer..." Virginia brings up yet more data. "Since you told me she's the boss's daughter, I've been following up on her. Mansfield Cybernetics' corporate dealings remain as hidden as data gets— like, *no one* will ever trace their money—but Shearer's not as careful. Got some bank account info, plus a few personal shipping records. Divorce decree about three years old. The only thing I couldn't track down was any school record for her son, Simon, age seven, but maybe she's having a Nan or an Uncle teach him?"

"No doubt." A memory flickers in Abel's mind: a holo of Simon as a baby, displayed for him by Mansfield the last time they were together. Mansfield wanted to show him off to Abel only moments before wiping Abel's memory forever. Mansfield demonstrates his pride in strange ways. Pulling himself back into the moment, Abel adds, "The amount of data you've collected—it's impressive."

"Yeah, I'm awesome." She kicks back, folding her lanky arms behind her head. "I'm bad at false modesty, so I figure, why bother?"

"Entirely rational." Abel's never seen the point of modesty either.

"Here's the kicker," Virginia says, pointing to a glowing column of data. "Shearer's part of a small group of neo-transhumanists."

Abel frowns. Transhumanism—the belief that humans can adapt chemical and/or biomechanical additions to their bodies to become superhuman—was largely abandoned in the mid-twenty-first century. While the philosophy is an understandable development from the human ego, the reality fell far short due to tissue rejection, spiking cancer rates, and unpredictable results. By the time the technology had caught up, cybernetics had taken hold, and humans no longer wished to manipulate their bodies to do what a mech could simply do for them. "Perhaps Mansfield Cybernetics intends to create such technologies."

"Then why get into organic mechs?" Virginia shrugs as she brings up a holo of Gillian speaking before a group. It must be some months ago, to judge by her different weight—or perhaps years, even. Gillian's energy there makes her seem far younger. "Here, watch this."

"*We can overcome human weakness*," Gillian says so fervently it startles him—like something out of a theatrical production rather than real life. Yet her sincerity is unmistakable. *"Indeed, we must overcome it. Consciousness may have arisen from physical existence, but why should it be bound by it? We're caged in prisons of blood and bone. Humanity must be freed!"*

Virginia snaps off the holo. "There's a lot more in that vein—no pun intended. Nothing concrete, though, at least that I can tell."

Abel isn't sure what to make of Gillian's stranger philosophies, but he feels certain they're linked to the organic-mech project. "I should investigate more thoroughly. You've already been very helpful, and I hesitate to ask for more assistance—"

"Come on. You know I love this stuff. Besides, we've had a lull in our workload lately, which at first was awesome, but has kind of turned boring. So I need a new project." She brings up another holoscreen to reveal an image of the noted celebrity Han Zhi, whose physical beauty stupefies humans of all genders and sexual preferences. Even Abel, who experiences desire only after being touched, finds himself staring at the perfect symmetry of Han Zhi's face. Virginia sighs. "I've been reworking his latest holo to give it a better ending. Why do they even make the sad ones where the lovers don't end up together? Nobody wants that!"

This should be Abel's cue to defend *Casablanca*, by far

his favorite fictional narrative. If Ilsa didn't leave Rick at the end, the film would lose much of its power. But another memory comes upon Abel too strongly to deny.

For an instant it's as if he's back on his ship, saying good-bye to Noemi forever. Her fighter slid out into space as Abel's vision blurred with the first tears he ever shed—

"Abel?" Virginia stands up. She's a few centimeters taller than him, and her expression is worried as she looks down at him. "Are you okay?"

"My condition is unchanged." By this Abel means that it is operationally satisfactory. There's nothing "okay" about remembering he'll never see Noemi again.

"One thing I've been asking myself," Virginia says easily, as though he hadn't drifted away from their first conversation, "is why you're so gung-ho about all of this. I mean, I get you being curious, but going super-spy commando at Mansfield Cybernetics parties? That's pretty risky for plain old robotics research."

Abel blinks. He's never questioned his reasons for vigorously investigating Mansfield's work. Its necessity seemed self-evident, but he finds he cannot define it. What controls his behavior outside his conscious thoughts is his programming—the programming Mansfield himself installed.

He will never be completely free of his creator.

"Directive One," Abel says. He envisions the multi-colored string lights all around them as the guts of a computer, as if they were conversing in the center of his own mechanical brain. "My core command demands my devotion to Burton Mansfield. Even though I can defy him, I remain interested in him. I have a strong need to understand his actions and motivations. I am even...invested in his welfare, and want him to be safe and well."

Virginia leans onto her desk, her expression wary. "That doesn't mean—Abel, you're not thinking about turning yourself over to him, are you?"

"Don't worry, Virginia. I'm in no hurry to die," Abel says. "As Burton Mansfield knows."

With a grin, she holds up her hand for the archaic, obscure human gesture known as a "high five." Apparently this is a fad on Cray. Abel returns the gesture, but as their palms slap together he gives silent thanks that Harriet and Zayan aren't here to see it. They'd never stop teasing him.

Yet it is pleasant even to have people who might tease him.

Which makes him miss Noemi again. Why is the pain always fresh, as if they had just said good-bye? How long will it take him to heal? Humans talk about "moving on" in ways that suggest the process should begin in weeks, if not days. Five months after Noemi's departure, Abel still has to consciously steer his thoughts to other topics, daily.

Maybe human love is different. Maybe it's weak, as variable as the weather and so as ephemeral as a breeze.

Abel's love is not.

5

WITHIN FORTY-FOUR HOURS—TWO GENESIS DAYS—THE
entire planet is in chaos.

Not every single person is sick. No disease is that contagious, not even Cobweb. However, more than one in five
individuals have come down with the illness, and surely
the virus is incubating within others. Noemi, having survived the illness, is immune. That makes her literally the
only safe person on her world.

Everyone else is terrified, and that terror is ripping them
apart.

On the first day, everything goes very still. The markets—
and all other public places on Genesis—are closed by
decree. It's a desperate attempt to cut down on infections,
but probably it was too late as soon as the first star hit the
ground. Noemi spends the whole day looking after Mr. and
Mrs. Gatson, who grow more feverish and weak with every
passing hour; she feels as if she can do nothing but watch

the white spiderweb rash spread across their bodies. That night's a hungry one, because the emergency ration drop-offs won't be ready until tomorrow. Noemi eats a solitary dinner of leftover vegetable stew and two cups of coffee, willing herself to stay awake.

The Gatsons need her. They've never welcomed her as a daughter, but they took care of her when she was sick, and she pays her debts. And deep on a level she doesn't like to admit, she's glad they finally have to rely on her for a change.

But on the second day, she's past any feeling that petty. Nothing is left but sheer terror.

"Please!" Noemi pleads as she tries to walk Mrs. Gatson through a gathering crowd outside the hospital. "Please, let us through, she needs help—"

"Why do you think the rest of us are here?" snaps an old man. "Wait your turn!"

But there's no such thing as turns, or a line, or any kind of order. The crowd's panic is so thick in the air Noemi imagines she can feel it, like a vibration in her very nerves. Mrs. Gatson is heavy against her shoulder, barely upright, shivering despite the blanket Noemi wrapped around her shoulders. People bump into them, pushing them roughly from side to side. The hospital's white walls seem to gleam against the storm-cloud-dark sky, promising hope, but there's no reaching it through the desperate scrum. Sick people who can't stand throng the sidewalk, laid out on blankets or just on the grass. The pale rectangles of cloth in their long rows remind her uncomfortably of tombstones in a graveyard. Some of the patients groan or cry; most of them lie quietly. A few are so still that Noemi suspects they're already dead.

She remembers how Cobweb feels. Remembers the bone-wrenching ache of it, the chills that swept through her, the hot scratchy dryness behind her eyes. She'd tried to get to sick bay from her cabin and had instead collapsed in the ship's corridor, unable to walk another step.

It was Abel who found her, lifted her up, took such gentle care of her—

Don't think about him, she tells herself. *Abel can't help you. You're on your own.*

"Hang on," she whispers to Mrs. Gatson, but she doesn't think the woman can hear her any longer. Eventually, as the first drops of rain start to fall, vehicles pull up to collect the sick. They're less like ambulances, more like…cargo trucks. The nurses inside look harried and worn; they're doing their best, but their best isn't good enough. Noemi has no choice but to let them take Mrs. Gatson away.

Returning home means hurrying along streets empty of people or vehicles. People have begun hanging red scarves at windows to signal that someone in the house is infected; nearly every home has one. She's not the only one who keeps looking up at the stormy sky, searching not for signs of thunder or lightning but for Earth's Damocles ships penetrating Genesis's atmosphere at last—for fighting mechs descending like fallen angels to claim their world.

When she gets back to the house, she's able to bring in some emergency rations. She checks and sees that her messages to Captain Baz have gone unanswered. Official information is all about the plague, with no word on who—if anyone—is patrolling the Genesis Gate. Noemi doesn't know if the government is refusing to tell them anything, or whether it doesn't have enough resources left over to even gather the information. None of the possible answers are good.

In the great room, the faint light from the cloudy sky illuminates the surroundings—almost unchanged from yesterday morning, when Mr. Gatson took ill. The teacups still sit on the edge of the sink. Noemi hasn't washed them because she badly wants some reminder of normality. Some evidence of regular life.

Although Mr. Gatson got sick first, he's not as bad off as his wife. He sits on the low couch near the largest window, staring at the dark sky, a knitted blanket around his shoulders even though fever flushes his face. Either he doesn't hear Noemi come in or he doesn't care.

She has to assume it's the first one, just in case. "Mr.

Gatson?" One long step brings Noemi into his field of vision. "Is there anything you need?"

"Yes." His voice quavers. "Tell me about the star."

Noemi knows he means Esther's star. After her death, her body couldn't be kept aboard Abel's ship; if they'd been boarded and searched, they no doubt would've been arrested for murder. When Noemi rejected the horrifying idea of ejecting Esther's body into the cold of space, it was Abel who came up with the idea of burying her within the heart of a star—the star of the Kismet system, one that gives heat and light to an entire living world. She still thinks it's the most beautiful tribute to Esther that could possibly exist.

Yet the Gatsons never asked about the star before. Noemi doesn't know whether that's their rejection of the mode of Esther's burial, or their reluctance to talk about Esther's death any more than necessary.

She goes to the couch and sits beside Mr. Gatson, though she leaves half a meter of distance between them. Habit. "You know the constellation Atar?" That formation of stars is one of the most famous in Genesis's southern hemisphere. "The brightest star in the base of the cauldron? That's Kismet's star. That's where Esther is."

Mr. Gatson leans his head back on the edge of the sofa, gazing up at a sky too cloudy to show them any stars. The faint spiderweb rash on his face is almost invisible in the dimness. "That's—'Atar' is holy fire for the Zoroastrians, isn't it?"

"Yes." Noemi isn't particularly familiar with that faith, more common on the northern continents. But she looked up a few things after Esther was buried there. "It purifies. It knows guilt or innocence. It's the divine glory of God."

After a long silence, Mr. Gatson says, "Then it's a good place for her."

That's as close to forgiveness as Noemi's ever likely to get. She knows better than to respond out loud.

A rap at the door startles her. Mr. Gatson doesn't even seem to hear. Noemi hurries to answer it; when she sees a nurse standing there, medkit in hand, the sight is so welcome she almost wonders if she's imagining it. "Thank God you're here. But Mrs. Gatson—I shouldn't have taken her away, I wouldn't have if I'd known—"

"I'm sent to help out here while you answer the summons." The nurse hands her a small dataread—a confidential summons to meet with the Elder Council, immediately.

●　　●　　●

Noemi doesn't travel to the Hall of Elders. Instead, she's been called to meet with them in an emergency ward.

"Everything we know about Cobweb," rasps Darius Akide, from his place in a hospital bed, "we know from you. To whatever extent we've been able to respond to this crisis, it's because your intel prepared us."

"That's not much," Noemi says. Though she knows in her mind that there's nothing more she could've done, she still feels as though she failed somehow. "Ephraim Dunaway told me the Stronghold doctors figured out I was from Genesis because I was too healthy. Because I responded to Cobweb treatment so quickly. But this disease—it's destroying us."

"You responded to antiviral drugs we don't have," Akide says. "Ours are older and, it seems, much less effective against Cobweb."

Another elder says, "Earth appears to have made Cobweb more contagious before they sent it to Genesis—and perhaps they've made it deadlier, too. Something our drugs can't treat."

"Then we need to—" Noemi stops mid-sentence. The idea is so tantalizing, so liberating, that she can't give it voice. If she admits it's even possible, she'll be admitting how much she wants it. Admitting she wants something means she won't actually get it. She pushes her mind down another route. "Is it—does my body carry Cobweb antibodies, or something like that? Could they use my blood to synthesize a cure?"

The silver-haired elder shakes her head. "Our doctors doubt it, and the research would take time Genesis doesn't have. Earth sent this disease to paralyze us. They could send Damocles ships through at any moment, and we could put up little resistance. Within another few days, we'll have no ability to resist at all."

"We need the better antivirals," Noemi says. It's really happening. "You'll have to send me through the Gate. That's why you called me here, isn't it? I'm immune and I've got contacts in Remedy who could help us. I'm ready."

One thought overwhelms her beyond any others: *I'm free!*

Then Noemi wonders what the hell is wrong with her. Genesis is in terrible danger, maybe the worst it has ever faced. The mission she's going on will be dangerous; surely Earth will be guarding the Genesis Gate closely, which means her chance of capture is high. If she fails, it's the death of her world, and she'll actually deserve the hate she's received.

She knows all that. She believes it. She's going to get the antivirals back to Genesis or die trying.

But then Darius Akide slowly shakes his head. "That would take time we almost certainly don't have. We must face the inevitable."

Nausea twists Noemi's gut. *No.*

"You're not my first choice of diplomat," he says with as much humor as he can muster, which isn't much. The gravity of his words is unmistakable. "But you're the only individual we know will remain healthy and uninfected."

Please, no.

Akide concludes: "That's why you must be the one to offer Earth our surrender."

The war is over. Noemi's world is lost.

•   •   •

The next few hours pass in a blur: Fueling and provisioning her starfighter, and charting her course to the Genesis Gate while scanning all sectors at maximum intensity for any potential mech patrols. Tears periodically blur her eyes, but she keeps going, driving herself on because the first time she stops to think about this, it's going to kill her.

On the journey to the Gate, though, there's nothing to do but think.

How could they do it? How could they just give up? Yes, Genesis is stricken, but Earth hasn't invaded yet. The delay can only be because they want the virus to wreak maximum havoc before the invasion, to make their takeover as easy as possible. That cruel arrogance could be turned to Genesis's advantage if they'd only try to get the antivirals. *I could've done it if they had let me. It would've been easy!*

Well, maybe not easy. But it would've been possible. I'd

have reached out to Ephraim, if I could find him—or maybe
Riko, if I could figure out where she is—

—Kismet would be a place to start, if I could—

I could do it.

Noemi has been reprimanded for reacting instead of acting. She knows her temper and her impulses don't always point in the right direction. And what she's thinking of doing is even more serious than disobeying a military command. She would be making a judgment that will determine the destiny of her entire planet, overruling the Elder Council itself.

But if Remedy could help her get the antiviral drugs in time... she could save Genesis.

The Gate beckons. Noemi hasn't made her decision yet—or at least she tells herself she hasn't—but she feels like she'll know what to do the minute she's on the other side. Time to fly.

She urges her starfighter forward into the shimmer at the very center of the Gate. The ship hits the event horizon, and reality cracks.

In an instant straight lines seem to bend, and light varies its brightness from millimeter to millimeter. It's as if the serene image of her cockpit a moment ago had been turned into a jigsaw puzzle and someone just dumped the pieces on the table all out of order. Noemi's stomach drops, but she keeps her hands on the controls, full speed ahead.

For one moment she closes her eyes, just to steady herself. In that moment she recalls going through a Gate for the first time, Abel at her side, his hands sure on the controls. He'd been so arrogant about his skills, so pleased with her fear. And she'd hardly even wanted to look at the thing she would later destroy—

Reality restores itself instantaneously as the starfield before her shifts, showing an entirely new set of constellations. The planets shine brighter, and quickly she figures out which one is Earth. She stares at it and knows what she has to do.

I have to find Remedy. I have to at least try.

The decision feels like another moment of grace, one so beautiful she has to blink back tears.

Then her sensors begin to shriek, and Noemi swears.

Eight—no, ten fighter mechs, all lying in wait for her. They must've been here the whole time.

She has been betrayed by what she thought was grace, and her folly scalds her like boiling oil.

The Queens and Charlies swoop in, encased in the metal-framed suits that turn them into warrior and warship simultaneously. It's as though she's surrounded by birds of prey, their talons reaching for her from every side. Noemi fires immediately, picking off two of them before her sensors begin to go haywire. She jabs at the controls until she realizes she's caught in a kind of electromagnetic net, one made up of mini–tractor beams emanating from mechs.

That's not standard fighter mech procedure. Not their standard weaponry. Have they evolved a new way of fighting, one Genesis will be powerless against?

But that can't be right, she thinks. *If this was an Earth patrol, there would be even more mechs. A Damocles ship would be nearby. If they're guarding the Gate this closely, where's the Damocles? And why bother with just a few mechs when they're going to invade any day now?*

Her comms speak in the voice of a Queen, scratchy through the speaker: "You have been reclaimed and will be returned."

"Returned?" Noemi talks to it more on instinct, out of pure bewilderment. "You mean to Genesis?"

"To your owner," it says. "You are the property of Burton Mansfield."

"Property? I'm no one's *property*!"

But the mechs don't listen to her. They are Mansfield's property and incapable of knowing why humans should be any different. Instead, one of the Queens swoops close, her metal exosuit carving a stark, angular silhouette against the surrounding stars. Clamps lock on to Noemi's starfighter, jolting her so hard she bites her tongue. To her horror, a thin tube extends from the exosuit, spinning like a drill, to pierce her cockpit.

"No—no no *no*—" She can't imagine why mechs would want to kill her by robbing her of air instead of shooting her down, but *why* doesn't matter, not with that thing coming closer by the second. Heart pounding, she scans her controls for something, anything that might help her, even though she knows there's no way.

The tube pierces the cockpit. Shards of transparent aluminum sparkle like snowflakes as they float freely around her. But the drilling doesn't stop. Instead the tube spins closer and closer, and her horror intensifies as she realizes it's going to go right through her helmet. Maybe through her skull.

Noemi turns her head, even though it's useless. She won't save herself, but at least this way she won't have to watch the thing drill right between her eyes.

Her helmet shudders with the first impact. Now she can hear the high-pitched sound of it, getting closer millimeter by millimeter. Closing her eyes, Noemi begins to pray. *Hail Mary, full of grace, the Lord is with thee—*

The tube breaks through the helmet, just shy of her left temple, then stops. She has no time to be relieved before greenish gas fills her helmet, her lungs, and dizziness sweeps everything away into the dark.

6

AT 1842 HOURS, ABEL ALLOWS HIMSELF TO BE PULLED away from the data to meet Harriet and Zayan at Montgolfier. He had understood Virginia when she said the furnishings and place settings at this restaurant were only energy fields, but this factual knowledge did not adequately prepare him for the oddness of the sight.

"There you are!" Harriet waves cheerfully at Abel and Virginia from the corner where she and Zayan are, seemingly, hovering. "Come on, you've got to see this."

"No, they don't. I wish I hadn't." Zayan's nose wrinkles as he regards his meal, a generous bowl of pho—but since the "bowl" is an invisible energy field, the soup hangs in midair, where its brownish broth looks decidedly less appetizing. (At least, if Abel properly understands the usual causes of the human emotion disgust.) "Floating food is interesting for the first thirty seconds. Then it's just gross."

"It's not anybody else's fault that you ordered badly." Harriet sounds almost prim as she gestures at her "plate," where an ample sandwich levitates. "I say, if you're bored with a flying sandwich, you're bored with life."

Virginia chortles as she takes her invisible seat next to Zayan. "Oh, you think the pho is bad? Just wait until I order the *spaghetti*." Zayan's eyes widen in dismay.

Apparently to take mercy on Zayan's stomach, Harriet changes the subject once Abel's seated next to her. "So, did you sell the 'big and sparkly' yet?"

"What's big and sparkly?" Virginia catches Abel's look and shrugs. "What? I'm easily distracted by shiny objects. It's a failing."

Perhaps it would be better to be straightforward about the diamond. Abel gives Virginia a look that hopefully communicates the message *We shouldn't discuss it in depth at this time.* To his crew members he simply says, "I sold it before we left Earth."

Zayan and Harriet share a look of dismay. "Why'd you lie about it?" Zayan says. The word *lie* sounds wrong to Abel's ears, but he must acknowledge its justice. "If you don't want to cut us in equally on the price . . . you know we never really expected that, right?"

"You're already the best Vagabond boss there is," Harriet says. "We don't take it for granted."

"You'll receive equal thirds of the price," Abel says. "But

I wanted to pace out your payments to prevent another submersible incident."

Zayan hangs his head, sheepish, as Virginia says, "What submersible incident? If you guys got up to hijinks in a submarine, I want to hear every detail."

"It's not that," Harriet says. "The first time we received a big payout after we joined Abel's crew, Mr. Thakur here got it into his head that he needed to rent a personal submersible to cruise the ghost reefs of the Indian Ocean. Which would've been expensive enough, even if he hadn't promptly driven it straight into a reef and needed a tow to get out."

"The tow cost more than the sub." Zayan sighs. "Okay, I got carried away. We'd just been so broke for so long! I wanted to do something special, really memorable—and I did. Just not the way I wanted to. Trust me, I'm never doing that again."

Trust me. That's what Abel hasn't done. He nods. "All right, Zayan. We'll settle it on board. Please forgive the delay."

At this moment, the Montgolfier waiter—a Zebra model, designed for customer service—walks up to the table. Virginia tries to wave him off, saying, "Abel here hasn't even glanced at the menu."

The Zebra ignores her and turns to Abel. "Professor Mansfield has a message for you."

As startled as Abel is, it takes him only three-tenths of a second to react. "If you've coded in your payment for the meals," he says to Zayan and Harriet, "let's go. Now." Virginia has already hopped off her energy-field stool, wild-eyed with sudden fear. But Abel's always known Mansfield could be tracking him. He's had time to steel himself.

Yet beneath his calm exterior, he cannot deny that he is afraid.

The Zebra pays no attention to his attempt to leave. "The message is urgent."

"Walk away," Abel commands the others. Probably he should ask them, be more polite, but Harriet and Zayan have figured out that this is a crisis, even if they can't possibly understand it. Meanwhile, Virginia knows exactly how wrong this is. They fall in line as he walks away from the table, out the door of Montgolfier, and into the corridor of the vast underground shopping complex.

In the corridor is a Yoke model, fit only for manual labor, mopping the floor. She doesn't pause in her work as she looks up at Abel. "Because of your reluctance to cooperate with Burton Mansfield's plans, he has been forced to find another form of motivation."

"What, this one, too?" Virginia says.

Abel quickens his pace. Another Yoke steps in front of them, and Abel doesn't wait for her to speak, just pushes her to one side. He'd always hoped that when Mansfield made his move, Harriet and Zayan would be far away, safe from any harm. While he is willing to take risks with his own life, he cannot allow Mansfield to endanger his friends.

The hangar. They have to get to the hangar, immediately. Such linked communication among several mechs is highly unusual, if not unprecedented. Whatever Mansfield has planned, he's compromised any number of mechs on Cray and could have reprogrammed them to do absolutely anything. They could slaughter his crew and Virginia at a stroke. He is willing to defend them to the death—and since Mansfield has left him alive, that gives him a chance of saving them.

He doesn't think past "a chance." He senses that he doesn't want to calculate exact probabilities.

As they hurry into the hangar, a Charlie mech standing sentry smiles as if he's been expecting them. Abel tenses, preparing himself to fight, but the Charlie doesn't make a move. Instead he says, "Noemi Vidal is in Burton Mansfield's custody."

"Impossible," Abel says. He believes it. Mansfield has great power, but not even he could send a kidnapping force to Genesis. This can only be a lie, flimsy and crude—

—but Mansfield is a good liar, when he wishes to be. So why this?

The Charlie continues, "Proof of life and captivity will

be provided to you as soon as you contact Mansfield from any Earth communication station. You have forty-eight hours from now to present yourself at his home in London, where you will surrender without resistance. Once you are adequately secured, Miss Vidal will be released to safely return home."

"Why is Burton Mansfield after Abel?" Harriet whispers, but Virginia shushes her.

The Charlie's dark eyes are empty—soulless, Noemi would say—as he concludes, "Should you fail to surrender before the deadline, Noemi Vidal will die. The choice is yours."

Then the Charlie model straightens, a motion that indicates realigning subroutines. Within another second, he stands at attention as usual, unaware of the words he has just uttered.

Abel takes one step backward; Zayan's hand closes around his upper arm. Virginia's the first to find her voice. "Hey, we don't even know if that's for real."

"It is," Abel says. "He promised proof, and in such matters, Mansfield never bluffs."

Noemi is "in custody." What does that mean? His imagination pictures her in a cell, a highly melodramatic and improbable circumstance, but he fixates on the idea anyway. Is she hungry? Is she scared, or cold?

(She hates the idea of being alone in the cold. That's

what happened to her when her family was killed, when she lay in the snow for hours.)

He can't know the physical constraints of her captivity. But Noemi must know herself to be a prisoner.

That means she's scared.

"Let's go," Abel says. "Virginia, I apologize for walking away from the project. I trust you'll continue investigations on your own."

"Wait, he wants you to come to him and you're just going to do it?" Virginia protests.

"I have to act." That's the only answer Abel knows for certain.

Once they're walking toward the *Persephone*, Zayan mutters, "What the hell does this guy want with you, Abel?"

To erase everything I've ever done or been. To erase my soul and claim my body as his own. Abel says only, "That remains between me and Burton Mansfield. I can only promise you that you won't be put in any danger."

"Why would he go after Noemi?" Harriet plays with the ends of her braids, like she often does when she gets nervous. "Is he angry with you for some reason? Did you guys do something to him?"

"Knowing the truth can only involve you in it," Abel says, "and, as you can see, being involved in this is dangerous."

Only Virginia understands the whole story. Her face

looks different when she's not smiling—longer, thinner. "What exactly are you going to do?"

Abel had finalized his plan before the Charlie finished talking. "We'll take the *Persephone* back to Earth and dock in an unlicensed port." The planet holds thousands of these, not all of them vectors of illegal behavior, but many are staffed by those willing to overlook certain protocols for a small bribe. "Zayan, Harriet, you'll get payouts equivalent to six months' pay. You should consider yourselves on leave until you hear from me, which may be some time in the future."

"Wait. You're doing what Mansfield wants?" Zayan shakes his head. "No way. You can't let that guy win." Like most Vagabonds, Zayan and Harriet loathe Mansfield, creator of the mechs that perform most of the jobs that would otherwise employ, house, and feed countless millions of desperate, homeless humans.

Harriet turns on Zayan. "He wouldn't do that! You're going to fight this, aren't you, Abel? You don't have to do it alone. Noemi's our friend, too, and besides, we're not going to let some antiquated egomaniac steal away the only decent boss we've ever had."

Abel puts one hand on each of their shoulders. The buzz of activity in the hangar seems to flow around them, oblivious to the drama taking place. "I appreciate your loyalty, and your friendship." It's still strange to him to have real friends, to have a life that Mansfield's plans play no role in. To Mansfield it must be unfathomable. "But this is something I should do alone."

Zayan protests, "Stop being noble!"

"I'm not being noble. I'm being practical. Putting you two at risk serves no purpose, except perhaps giving Mansfield other targets with which to threaten me." Abel resumes walking, eyes straight ahead. Purpose steadies him; perhaps seeing that will steady Harriet and Zayan as well.

But it's Virginia who gets in Abel's face. "Listen to me for a minute, all right? You say Mansfield definitely has Noemi; okay, I believe you. But we also know what kind of person Noemi is. The sacrifices she's willing to make, and the ones she won't. She wouldn't want you to do this for her. You understand that, don't you?"

"Yes," Abel says. "I do."

Virginia continues, "I know you care about her, Abel. But that doesn't mean you have to die for her."

"I don't intend to."

That stops her, and she and the others exchange glances. The slowness of human brains must be agonizing at times.

Taking pity, Abel explains, "Obviously I have to help Noemi if I can. If ultimately there's no way to save her except by sacrificing my own life, I will." He offered to do that for her once, volunteering to destroy the Genesis Gate.

But he's never stopped looking for another way.

"Mansfield believes he can control my actions," he adds. "So he presents me with a binary choice, never understanding that I would look for a third option."

The smile returns to Virginia's face. "You're not turning yourself in. You're going to break Noemi out." When he nods, she laughs out loud. "Now that's the Abel I know."

"We'll help," Harriet promises, but he shakes his head.

"If this can be done at all," he tells her, "I can do it alone. If it can't, you won't be able to help me. You'll only be other people I have to worry about."

She and Zayan share a troubled look. They don't like Abel's orders, but they'll follow them. It would never occur to Mansfield that Abel might try to outwit his creator. Even less would the man imagine that Abel would have friends who'd help him. Abel feels as if he's beaten Mansfield already. In one sense, he has.

But he can take no comfort in that, not when Noemi's forty-eight hours are already running out.

7

NOEMI AWAKENS IN THE WOMB.

Or so it seems to her at first—she's floating, surrounded by a blurriness that's faintly tinted pink. In her daze, she wonders if reincarnation is true after all.

As the drugs begin to fade, however, she becomes aware of bars around her, almost like a cage. The faint prickling on her skin starts feeling like a force field. Beyond the rosy haze, she can discern movement more clearly. Shadowy figures take on human forms. One steps closer, getting near enough that she's able to make out a face.

Recognition jolts her awake. "Mansfield."

"Welcome, Miss Vidal," Mansfield wheezes. "It's very good to meet you at last."

Burton Mansfield's face looks pale even through the pinkish glow of the force field. He's more frail than he was when she saw him on-screen six months ago, and she would've sworn that was impossible. A Tare model supports him on one side, her face revealing no acknowl-edgment that Noemi's in the room. Mansfield wears a plush robe swaddled thickly around him. His gray hair is so wispy as to be almost nonexistent.

But Noemi's blurry mind can't help but see, beneath all the wrinkles in his skin, the outlines of Abel's features. This is what Abel might look like as an old man, if he could get old.

How could someone so wicked create someone so good?

"Forgive the limitations of my hospitality," he says, ges-turing vaguely about her. Noemi hangs suspended in a force field projected from a metal framework that forms the illusion of a cell—one she could step through easily, if she could only get to the ground, but she can't. "You're a strong young lady, and a trained soldier at that. Can't treat you like the average houseguest...though you are very, very welcome."

She tries to remember how this happened. Her mind offers images of the drill piercing her helmet—then goes back to her journey through the Gate—and finally mem-ory returns. The first terror she feels isn't for herself, but for Genesis. "Did you—you infected us with Cobweb?"

"What? Good lord, no. What's the point in that?" Appar-ently Mansfield doesn't think of poisoning a world as evil, only as impractical. "I have certain political connections, you know. Word reached me of Earth's biological-warfare plans—mostly because a few government ministers felt smug about cutting back their orders for more Charlies and Queens. But I didn't see a shortfall. I saw an opportunity. I knew once the plague took hold, Genesis would send either someone to get help or an envoy to surrender, and you were by far their likeliest candidate. Assuming you hadn't already blown yourself up, that is. You do have a temper on you. Now, I suppose you're wondering why I've brought you here."

She hadn't gotten that far through her haze yet, but as soon as the question is suggested, she knows the answer. Her horror deepens. "You're setting a trap for Abel." Her voice is hardly more than a whisper. "And I'm the bait."

"A simple bargain: his surrender for your release. He says he loves you; I suppose we'll see, hmm?"

It's too much. Noemi's never shut down in a crisis; she rises to the moment. But there's no rising to this. Genesis is dying from Cobweb. Abel's life is in danger. She can't even set her own feet upon the ground. If it weren't for Mansfield standing in front of her, weak of body and poisoned in his heart, she might faint.

Instead, she gets mad as hell.

"Coward," she growls. "You've had your life, but you're taking Abel's away from him. You can't accept that you're mortal. You think you should be some kind of a god."

Mansfield hadn't expected that. "You think it's cowardly, the need to survive? Then every living thing's a coward, every living thing in the galaxy."

Which is total crap. Noemi has been afraid to die, but she never let that fear stop her from doing what she needed to do—or force her into doing something so profoundly wrong.

She would tell him that, but he keeps talking. "Hasn't it ever occurred to you how useless flesh is? How pointless? Consciousness is an accident of evolution, and I intend to liberate it from its visceral beginnings." Mansfield's voice has become dreamy. "Some people deserve to live forever. Some of us have shown that spark of the divine. But most people are automatons, as surely as any mech is. Being human is no guarantee of being fully conscious. The vast majority think what they're told to think. Do what they're told to do. Live their whole lives within the dull, safe borders of conformity and complacency. Maybe they should die on schedule, just like they've done everything else. Those of us who want more, who can offer more—we shouldn't be shackled to mortality."

"You think you should get to decide who lives and who dies." Millions will die on Genesis. Abel will die. "You're sick."

Mansfield shakes his head as if fondly exasperated with her. Nothing she says can touch him. "You, with your knee-jerk temper and your Genesis prejudices—you're as much a mech as anything I ever created in here."

She realizes she's in some sort of a basement, one with brick walls and slender windows at the very top. Laid out all around her are tanks—long, coffin-shaped, translucent containers filled with goo. From Akide's lessons, she knows tanks like this are for growing mechs. "Where are we?"

"My house. In fact, the most important part of the house, my personal workshop and laboratory," says Mansfield. "This is where I did all my finest work. The entire history of the galaxy would be different without this room."

This must have been where Abel was born. Where Mansfield attempted to make so many other versions of Abel, and failed every time. "How many of your creations did you kill here?"

" 'Kill' isn't the right word, my dear."

"Isn't it? They live. They breathe. They bleed. Abel wants and thinks and hopes and—" The word *loves* won't come out of her mouth. "How is destroying one of them less a murder than it would be if you destroyed your own child, or grandchild?"

"Stop." Mansfield's tone could turn this room to ice.

Noemi realizes she's hit a sensitive subject. She's not sure what it is, but it's a vulnerable spot, so she keeps pressing. "Abel deserves better from you."

"I gave him his life. I'm trusting him with my soul. And you're not the one in charge of deciding who deserves what."

Noemi tries to move within her force field, and with difficulty she reaches her hand to the metal frame—and encounters sharpness. It's covered with long metal points, ensuring no prisoners will be able to tamper with their newfound jail.

Taking no notice of her futile movements, Mansfield continues, "Now, Miss Vidal, there's nothing much left for us to do but wait. I can find Abel wherever in the Loop he may be, but it could take a little time, so I've given him a generous deadline. We've already dosed you with a few things that will keep you from needing the facilities any-time soon, which means we need just one more—damn it, left it in the tank. My memory's going."

He falters on the last words. The image of invulnerabil-ity he has tried to project shatters. Noemi sees a little old man, scared of his body's breakdown, more fragile than ever before.

Mansfield carefully goes to a tank filled with some kind of coolant and removes something from a canister inside. Only when he totters back to the Tare does Noemi see that he's holding a tiny golden pellet. The Tare loads it into a syringe, then pushes her hand through the force field—sparks flying off her skin—to capture Noemi's wrist in her vise-like grip. Before Noemi can even try to pull back, the Tare presses the device to Noemi's inner arm and a jolt of pain spears through her flesh.

"That little ampule won't do you any harm," Mansfield says. She can feel the knot inside, uncomfortably wedged in next to a nerve. "Unless I trigger it to release, that is. Which I won't do, assuming Abel arrives on time. So no need to worry, right?"

Will she finally see Abel again, only to watch him die for her?

8

ABEL'S INTERNAL CLOCK IS AS FINELY CALIBRATED AS any atomic clock. He knows down to the fraction of a second how much time he has left to save Noemi.

Forty-seven hours, three minutes, twenty seconds.

"So he wants you to go to his house in London," Virginia says as she and Abel huddle together in the Razer hideout to plan. "But you think he'll be holding Noemi there, too? Not at, you know, a second, undisclosed location?"

"I approximate the probability of Noemi's imprisonment in Mansfield's home at 88.82 percent."

Virginia's nose wrinkles in confusion. "That can't be the most secure place."

"Mansfield can control virtually every mech in existence," Abel replies. "He can secure any location he wishes. His health wouldn't permit him to move around very much."

He remembers the last time they were together, how fragile Mansfield was, how Abel had felt so protective of his elderly creator. All that time, Mansfield had planned to kill him that very night.

Virginia leans close. "Cray to Abel. Cray calling Abel. Come in."

As though he hadn't stopped speaking, he continues, "The house is the most logical base of operations. What we must determine is the exact nature of the threat to Noemi, so that I can arrive prepared to counteract it."

Forty-five hours, two minutes, twenty-eight seconds.

"If you screw up my ride," Virginia says, one finger in Abel's face, "and fail to bring it back to Cray in one piece, there won't be anywhere in this entire galaxy far enough away for you to hide from my vengeance."

He nods, glancing across the docking bay to see Zayan securing Virginia's flashy red corsair in the *Persephone*'s bay; his movements on Earth can only remain undetected if he's traveling in a ship that wasn't previously owned by Burton Mansfield, one Mansfield would know how to track. Virginia's generosity means he can dock the *Persephone* elsewhere but remain mobile. "Understood. If I damage the corsair, I'll need to find a wormhole to another galaxy."

"That's *not* what I meant!"

Twenty-three hours, thirty-seven seconds.

A landing dock in Namibia provides as good a hiding place for the *Persephone* as any. Long-term storage fees are reasonable, and security is tight. Abel pays Harriet and Zayan their advances and tells them farewell.

"It may be some time before I can return," Abel says. "If the two of you find other work that interests you, I'll understand if you choose to take it. But I hope you'll decide to stay."

They look at each other in mutual, almost comic disbelief before Zayan says, "Abel, do you really not get it? We'd never make this much doing anything but radium mining." The radium mines on Stronghold's largest moon are notorious for paying well but providing inadequate radiation shielding. Miners regularly die within five years of taking the job. Some people take it anyway. "Besides, we *like* you."

More subdued, Harriet says, "Noemi's a survivor. If anyone can make it through, she can. And you'd better come back to us safe and sound, too. Got it?"

"Got it." Abel finds her words illogical. No one can know the future. But he is unexpectedly pleased to realize how concerned Harriet and Zayan are about his welfare. These people he met only months ago care for him more truly than his "father" ever did.

They depart on a noontime shuttle to Rangpur to visit Zayan's family. For no reason he can name, Abel watches their shuttle take off and fly away until the distant dot in the sky disappears from even the farthest range of his vision.

Twenty-two hours, thirty-six seconds.

One hour provides sufficient time between Harriet and Zayan's departure and his own that no random security check should find any link between the two. The instant he can, Abel slides the corsair's cockpit closed and prepares to fly.

Virginia's corsair is a top-of-the-line personal cruiser. It can seat three at most, and sleeps perhaps two, assuming those individuals are sexually involved or extremely good friends. The lone mag engine may not compare to the massive ones on the *Persephone*, but it's powerful enough to take this ship from one side of a system to another in good time. While the interior is luxurious, the exterior is even more flamboyant to Abel's eyes. Shiny red paint, exaggerated curves, chrome trim and fins that serve no aerodynamic purpose: The aesthetic reminds him of ancient automobiles of the mid-twentieth century.

It's also a ship that tends to attract attention, but Abel isn't worried about that. Mansfield believes he has the situation under control. He'll expect nothing from Abel but compliance.

The vision clarifies in Abel's mind so swiftly, so vividly, that it feels almost real: *Walking into Burton Mansfield's home again, hearing the soft chimes of the grandfather clock, seeing Mansfield sitting in an easy chair with his hands outstretched. Mansfield saying, "You came back. You came to save me after all."*

"Yes, Father. I could never abandon you."

If this were actually to happen, Abel would swiftly be shown into the basement laboratory, invited to lie down on a metal table, and, he suspects, be strapped down. Mansfield wouldn't trust him not to change his mind.

But when Abel imagines the scene, he envisions a different ending:

Mansfield saying, "I could never hurt you, my boy." Holding out his arms. "Your girl is safe. I'm so sorry. Everything's all right again."

Abel being folded in his creator's embrace. "I love you, Father."

"I love you, too."

Directive One should be such a simple piece of programming to obey, but it turns against him sometimes, providing dreams like that one. Delusions. Falsehoods. Directive One lies. He must remember that.

The ready lights glow green on the corsair's console.

Abel hits ignition, and the corsair streaks upward, aiming beyond the sky.

Twenty-one hours, twenty-six minutes, two seconds.

London looks even more worn-down to Abel than it did when he was last here not quite six months prior. Upon reviewing his memory files, he cannot justify this impression; the state of disrepair is actually very similar. But apparently something deep within him insists upon comparing this to the London he remembers from thirty years ago, the one that still possessed more of its vitality and hope. For him, that past vision is more real than reality.

A curious paradox. He'll have to discuss that with— someone, someday.

After stowing Virginia's corsair in a public dock, using a false name, he hurries to a public-access info station. This takes him through Trafalgar Square, past the remnant of Nelson's Column that still stands after a lightning strike a century before. The bustle of a large Earth city is like nothing anywhere else in the galaxy: the crush of humans, the numerous mechs of every model hurrying about their labors, storefront lights, banners in front of museums advertising the few great works of art not yet in private hands. Abel has read that most people support the sale of classic paintings and statues because only individual collectors will take them offworld. Humanity wants these works to survive Earth. It's a beautiful impulse in its way—though Abel would admire it more if humankind could've spared some of that concern for Earth itself.

The info station provides private booths for an extra fee. Abel settles himself into one—a tall, narrow room with walls, ceiling, and floor as black as obsidian. Its metallic darkness is broken only by the slender control bar, a single line of silver.

His first action is to input codes that should make it difficult to trace his location. Mansfield will know he's being contacted from someplace on planet Earth, but no more than that. Only then does he send a signal to Mansfield's home. (The contact information for his creator's domicile was programmed into him before his awakening as a conscious being. Burton Mansfield never wanted Abel to stray far.)

A hologram shimmers into existence, revealing a standard Charlie model. It speaks first. *"Model One A. You will be linked momentarily."* Then it shimmers out.

There's a seat in the booth, as black as its surroundings, but Abel remains standing. He will not bow before Mansfield. Reminding himself of the minutiae of human body language and arranging himself to project confidence, he braces himself for the sight of his creator.

The hologram shimmers back into brightness, taking on human form. But it's not Mansfield before him.

Noemi seems to be suspended in air. She wears the black tank and leggings that go beneath a Genesis flight suit. Her arm bears a red mark along its inner curve, and her chin-length hair is unkempt. Her head is tilted to the side, buoyed by what must be a force field, and her eyes are shut. Noemi's muscles are slack. Abel's first thought is that she's dead. *Mansfield broke his word. Or the mechs got the deadline wrong. They've killed her—*

Before that terrible pain can fully pierce his shock, however, Abel realizes her chest is rising and falling with slow, even breaths. She's alive, but unconscious. A Tare steps closer and presses a syringe against Noemi's arm, and then she twitches. She struggles against the force field that holds her as she becomes fully conscious. Her eyes focus on him at last, and her horror matches his own. *"Abel!"*

"Noemi," he breathes. He seems to know no word but her name. How many times he's longed to see her just one more time—but never would he have wanted to see her like this, his fierce, strong Noemi held captive and afraid.

But she wastes no time on her own fate. *"Don't turn yourself into Mansfield, no matter what. Do you hear me?"*

Abel still doesn't intend to surrender, but he can't say that during a conversation he assumes is being listened to. "I have to make sure you're safe—"

"Forget me! You have to save Genesis." At first he thinks she's still delirious from the sedatives she must've been

given, but she's in earnest. *"Earth sent Cobweb to Genesis—biological weapons, and they've engineered it to be so much worse—the whole planet's sick—"*

He understands Earth's strategy instantly. Biological warfare has never played a large role in human conflict, largely because such viruses and bacteria tend to backfire. They spread beyond borders on a map. They ignore the color of uniforms. They infect target and shooter alike. But to use them against a completely different planet? How safe. How simple. Earth will wait until the pandemic has fully run its course—ensuring the virus dies out for a lack of hosts, and will be unable to infect any invaders—then strike with full force. This could end the war within weeks. Their plan is as effective as it is morally reprehensible.

Abel extrapolates all of this within 1.41 seconds, without ever losing focus on Noemi's stricken face.

She pleads, *"You have to find Ephraim. Do you understand what I mean? Get out of here and* find Ephraim. *Save Genesis."*

"I can't leave you to Mansfield—"

"Yes, you can." Her stubbornness has returned to her. Even as a captive, Noemi still has the same fire burning within her. *"I volunteered for the Masada Run, Abel. I was ready to give my life for my world. That's exactly what I'm doing now."*

Abel completely comprehends her plan; his mental

circuits swiftly trace the path from Ephraim Dunaway to the moderate wing of Remedy, with its medical connections, and then to improved antiviral drugs that might give Genesis a chance to recover. He feels sure he can activate that plan without surrendering either her life or his.

Still, he can't say so in the hologram. "Hold on. I'll find a way out of this."

She shakes her head. Her dark brown eyes well with tears. *"On Genesis, sometimes, I'd wonder what I would say to you if I ever saw you again, and I decided—it's just, thank you. Thank you for loving me. At least I know someone did, just for once in my life."*

"Noemi—"

But the hologram fades out, only to be replaced by an image of Mansfield. His creator could well look mocking and superior—he has the power, and they both know it—or he could try to be fatherly and warm, in the manner that always deceived Abel before. Instead Mansfield looks... shaken. Even stricken. He says, *"The terms of our deal have changed."*

"What do you mean?" Abel can't imagine what higher ransom he's supposed to pay than his own life.

"You'll come home no sooner than two hours from now," Mansfield says, in the oddly detached way that means he's thinking as he talks. This plan is as new as the words he speaks. *"You'll find information, coded for you alone, on*

where and how to proceed next. Then you'll meet us at that location within—what is it? Dear God. Within twenty hours, you come to me at the new location, or else you'll force my hand." He's trying to shift the blame for Noemi's ultimate fate onto Abel, a noxious psychological tactic, but there's no time to call him on it. Mansfield continues, *"Twenty hours, my boy. Something in you wants to come. Listen to that inner voice. Save Noemi. Save me."*

The hologram blinks out, leaving Abel standing alone in the dark. For the first time, he understands how humans can be shocked into immobility, an animal instinct from deep within the limbic system, an instinct Abel had thought he didn't have until now.

With Noemi's life on the line, Mansfield is changing the terms. He's not happy about it. His creator is afraid—afraid of something besides his own death—and this unknown variable destroys all of Abel's plans and calculations. He has no way of knowing how to rescue Noemi—

—besides accepting Burton Mansfield's bargain.

9

WHEN ABEL'S HOLOGRAM GOES DARK, NOEMI CHOKES back a sob. That's the last time she'll talk to him, or to anyone she's ever cared about. It feels like her farewell to life itself.

Noemi expects to die here, in Mansfield's laboratory. She hopes to. That will mean Abel's not only safe but doing everything he can to help Genesis. Her death is a small price to pay for that.

But it's one thing to know that. Another to hang in the prickly heat of a force field, to smell the ozone, with no action to take and no one to talk to and nothing to think about except the horror that's coming.

The basement door opens, and multiple feet thump on the stairs. Instantly Noemi can imagine the rescue—but the people coming downstairs aren't police or soldiers or even Abel. It's Mansfield, a couple of his mechs, and a red-haired woman whose face is thin and drawn.

"You couldn't convince them to wait?" Mansfield's demanding of her as he leans on her arm. "Couldn't get them to give us a couple more hours?"

"I tried." She bows her head, as though she can't bear to disappoint him. "It was impossible. We have to go, now."

"Gillian—I'm so close—"

"Abel will find us. We'll make sure of it."

"What's happening?" Noemi doesn't expect an answer, but she's not going to hang here like a painting on the wall. "Go where?"

"Does it matter?" Gillian says, then nods toward the Tare mech. "Get Miss Vidal ready for transport."

Transport?

As the Tare mech moves toward another syringe, Noemi sees Mansfield sit down in front of a holo-recording device. "We'll have to encode this, you know," he says to Gillian. "So nobody but Abel can get it. If we're so close to being discovered that they're pushing up our launch, the authorities could get here at any time."

Gillian nods and kneels by Mansfield's side. Gently she says, "I'll start the encryption now, Papa."

His daughter—Noemi thinks, but then the Tare's hand seizes her arm, another needle pierces her flesh, and the world swirls away into darkness.

• • •

Noemi's asleep, but not asleep. Aware, but unaware. Everything shifts and gyrates around her as though she were tumbling over and over in a bubble in a waterfall.

Abel appears before her again as he did in the hologram—shadowy, half-transparent, yet more real to her in this moment than anything else. Whenever she'd imagined seeing him again, she'd imagined it being so sweet. So *joyful*. Instead it's only anguish and fear so intense they strip her nerves raw.

She tries to think about the more distant past, about her journey with Abel through the stars. The haze from the drugs makes memory feel as real as experience, and soon she's caught up in the exhilarating rush of it all—racing together through a lunar spaceport, staying up at night on Cray and talking about faith while they sat under twinkling string lights, pretending to be husband and wife on Stronghold, watching *Casablanca*, their one kiss in zero-G, and the moment they met, when Abel stopped firing at her and handed her his weapon instead.

When they met, they tried to kill each other. Now they want to die for each other.

I'm going to win, Noemi thinks blurrily. *I'm going to be the one who dies. It has to be me.*

It has to.

• • •

She awakens lying down, on what feels like a comfortable couch. The pinkness of her eyelids reveals that whatever space she's in now is extremely bright. Only a few soft murmurs and the low hum of electronics are audible. Noemi lies very still, keeping her eyes shut, to maintain the illusion of unconsciousness as long as possible.

Mansfield's voice is reedy and ragged, his breathing labored. "You remembered to bring your mother's box, didn't you?"

Gillian has a rich voice, deep for a woman, one that would sound more natural giving commands than deferring to her father. "Of course. I'd never forget that. You're only nervous."

Mansfield: "Why wouldn't I be? This is damned irregular business."

Gillian: "We always knew this could happen. We're no more than a few holo messages from total chaos."

None of this makes any sense to Noemi yet, but she listens intently to every word. Soon, hopefully, she'll have enough pieces to put the puzzle together.

As the soporific fog of the drugs wears off, she notices more details of her new surroundings. The few footsteps she hears fall on soft carpet. Faint vibration suggests they're in a vehicle, and since Gillian and Mansfield were talking about a "launch," it's probably a spaceship. Someone seems to have slipped clothing on over what she already wore;

whatever it is feels soft against her skin. Yet the thought of lying there limply while somebody put clothes on her—it feels like almost as big a violation as if they'd taken them off her.

It occurs to her that a mech was probably the one to clothe her, a mech that couldn't have cared whether it was dressing a human or a turkey. That helps a little. But her heart can't stop pounding in her chest. She's always been able to stand strong against her fear, but it's coming at her from so many directions at once.

Genesis has a chance now, she reminds herself. Abel can find Ephraim if anyone can. Surely Remedy will help if it's at all possible. She's done as much as she could do to save her world. Will it be enough?

At least it's better than surrendering.

Now if only she could be certain that Abel will save himself along with Genesis—

"The captive has awakened," says the Tare, who must be standing very close. "Eye movements suggest consciousness."

"Why are you pretending to sleep?" Mansfield calls. "Get up, girl. We need to have a talk with you."

Noemi opens her eyes and pushes herself up on her elbows. As she'd suspected, they're aboard a spaceship, a luxurious personal cruiser. Everything—the gleaming polymer walls, long, low couches, and thick carpet—is white and plush, so spotless she doubts the ship's ever been used before. The cruiser seems to have only one main chamber, set up as a kind of great room. A few mechs stand about in their plain gray coveralls, either serving humans or waiting to serve. On the far edge of the chamber, Mansfield reclines on a chaise the same snowy color as everything else, Gillian fussing at his side. They've changed into...evening wear? Which seems absurd. But Noemi sees Mansfield in a tuxedo and Gillian in a glittery black dress, and either the drugs have warped her brain or they're going to a party.

Then she realizes she's wearing a silky, silvery jumpsuit. Apparently they're *all* going to this party—whatever it is.

"We should talk," says Gillian. "The terms of your captivity have changed."

"You decided to make my kidnapping...more festive?"

Mansfield chuckles, still acting like they're all good friends deep down, but Gillian's face remains starkly unmoved. "When we arrive at our destination, you'll be introduced as one of our guests. You will behave like a guest and be treated like a guest, unless and until you attempt to inform anyone of your real reason for being present. It's unlikely you'd be believed—but we can't take the chance."

Gillian lifts her hand as though to show off her cuff bracelet. Most people would think it was only a bracelet and look no further. But Noemi sees that the thin metal lines and tubes on its surface aren't only a pretty pattern; they're a hint that this is working machinery.

"I can activate the poison ampule within your body at any time," Gillian says. "It would take less than a heartbeat. Even if you tried, you couldn't kill me fast enough to save yourself."

Give me a chance, Noemi thinks but doesn't say. Instead she sits up straighter, lifts her chin. "So what's more important than your father's next chance to murder Abel?"

Mansfield scoffs when she says the word *murder*, but it makes no impact on Gillian's almost eerie stillness. "My father's work, and my own, represents the single greatest leap forward humankind has ever made. There's no sacrifice too great for this. No price too high to pay."

"That's easy to say when Abel and I are the ones paying," Noemi shoots back, but the truth is that Gillian's fixed stare unnerves her almost as badly as being trapped in the force field did. "I hate to tell you this, but your dad stealing someone else's body isn't that big a leap forward for anyone but him."

"This is about more than one man's survival, even as great a man as my father." Gillian turns toward him with a look of utter devotion—but not the kind usually shown by children to parents. It reminds Noemi more of worshippers before the Cross.

She doesn't miss the faint flash of exasperation on Mansfield's face. He may have plenty of high-minded things to say about his work, but he doesn't care that much about "humanity" or "the greater good." Mansfield's saving himself.

But Gillian is after something bigger. Something she sees as almost holy, something she's willing to do evil for. This woman is a zealot following the false god of her father's ego.

"Approaching Neptune," reports the pilot, a King model hard at work at a small central console.

Neptune? Noemi frowns. Humans neither live nor work anywhere near Neptune. If she remembers her exoastronomy correctly, it's hardly a place where anyone would take a tropical vacation, with average temperatures around negative two hundred degrees Celsius and winds that can reach twenty-four hundred kilometers per hour.

The King adds, "Bringing us into Proteus orbit." Mansfield simply waves him off.

Proteus. That's the largest of Neptune's moons, and as far as Noemi knows, no better a destination than the planet itself.

The only thing Proteus would be good for is as . . . a hiding place.

Noemi gets to her feet and is grateful to feel steady again. Nobody stops her as she walks closer to the small viewscreen that hangs on one wall, more as a decoration than a guide for anyone. Neptune's silver-blue surface now takes up nearly half the screen as they fly past it on their way to the moon looming larger every second.

Narrowing her eyes, she picks out one strange detail on-screen—a kind of shadow that takes on greater detail.

Then the magnification zooms in on that shadow, and she sees the ship.

Its size astonishes her—larger than any other vessel she's ever seen, even the resettlement carriers, even the most fearsome Damocles ships. The shape reminds her of an egg, if the sides were more sharply angled, the tip closer to a point. Purposeless running lights trace every decorative swoop along the surface, and there are dozens of those. Deep black lines grace every edge, along with tiles in terra-cotta red and lapis blue. The patterns suggest ancient Egyptian motifs. The ship is cradled within a spiny construction dock, like a jewel nestled in a metal setting.

This ship would be difficult to land. It's too enormous to dock at most ports; it expects, demands special accommodation. There's no retrofitting it for future uses. *How many millions of credits—no, billions, maybe even trillions—were spent just on decorating this thing? How can Earth's leaders claim we're the ones responsible for people starving and dying while their people are wasting resources on* this?

While Earth was plotting her world's death, it was also building this extravagant, useless ship. Making itself a new *toy*.

Oblivious to her wrath, Mansfield struggles to his feet and holds out one hand toward the image of the grand, golden ship. "Welcome to the *Osiris*."

Gillian murmurs, "Where we will be reborn."

By definition, a spacecraft can't be a final destination. "Where is this thing taking us?"

"Someplace almost no one else has ever been," Mansfield says.

Noemi wonders how sinful it would be to slap an old man if he was very, very evil and also incredibly irritating. "Thanks for that helpful answer. How's Abel supposed to find you somewhere nobody's ever gone?"

Her taunt hits its mark. Mansfield pales as he sits back down on the low couch. The thought of missing his chance at immortality obviously shakes him. It's Gillian who answers, and she's talking to her father, not to Noemi. "Abel's going to come to the ship. It won't be long, you'll see. He won't let us leave without him. Even without the girl, Directive One will bring him to us in the end."

Mansfield's eyes meet Noemi's. They're blue like Abel's, cold like Abel's could never be. "You'd better hope so, anyway. Because your fate is my fate, Miss Vidal."

"Then I hope I die," Noemi says.

"That can be arranged," Gillian says. She touches Noemi for the first time, laying a hand on her arm. Her flesh is cool, and she grips the sore, tight spot where the ampule lies beneath the skin, waiting to kill Noemi on command.

10

ABEL'S NEXT MOVE MUST BE HIS MOST DANGEROUS one yet: returning home.

His DNA mirrors Mansfield's in many regards. This means he's able to get through the security fence via a simple scan. No mechs or human sentries are in sight. As the ornate metal gate swings open to admit him, Abel looks up the hill toward the house silhouetted by the periwinkle of early dawn, its shape comforting and familiar. Each panel of the geodesic dome seems to glitter from the city lights all around.

The house is currently uninhabited. He can tell that from the lack of energy use within, the lack of light, the lack of guard mechs rushing out to seize him. Abel had calculated that Mansfield's instructions were genuine; his words were too peculiar, too rushed, for him to have been laying a trap. Mansfield's traps would be more careful. Still, Abel's relieved to have his calculations verified.

As he walks closer, he sees signs of disrepair. Mansfield's garden has become a brown, withered shadow of its former self, even though mechs had been taking care of it until recently. Enough time has passed for vines to begin reclaiming the carefully shaped hedges. Dust dulls the sheen of the lower panels. Weeds poke up between pathway stones; even on this dying planet, life fights for every inch.

Mansfield left within the past few hours, in the physical sense. The disrepair tells Abel that Mansfield stopped thinking of this house as home some weeks back. Why?

A few twigs have been blown onto the steps that lead down to Mansfield's basement laboratory. Abel had planned to enter through this door, but he halts a meter short of it, unable to go farther. He keeps replaying the last time he was on those steps, running up and out and away, escaping with his life. The memory shakes him, and so he walks toward the front instead.

Anyway, why shouldn't he enter through the front door? He has the right.

Mansfield always wanted me to call him Father, Abel thinks. *If he were truly my father, I'd inherit a share of his estate. I hereby declare this house my share.*

But walking through the front door is even worse, because the wreckage is almost complete.

All those books are gone. The holographic fire has gone out, and nothing remains but an eerily blank wall.

Even the grandfather clock has been whisked away, leaving a bright square on the carpet where the light never had a chance to fade the colors. Swiftly he checks Mansfield's bedroom; this, too, is empty. Patterns of dust suggest the home's contents were emptied out within the previous day or two, possibly within the past few hours. Nobody is present, either human or mech, and the silence is total. The house has been hollowed out, as if all the days Abel spent here were nothing but an illusion. He feels as if he cannot trust his own memory banks.

Why bring me here for instructions and then hide the instructions? Abel thinks with what he's learned to recognize as the human emotion of irritation. He welcomes the feeling; it's an effective distraction from his fear for Noemi's life.

He frowns as he walks back into the living room and sees something left behind, a relatively small, brightly colored oil painting by Frida Kahlo, *Tree of Hope, Keep Firm.* Mansfield had acquired it when he bought the entire collection of a closing museum, and he displayed it prominently as a masterwork by the greatest surrealist of the twentieth century. However, Mansfield had little personal feeling for the painting. If anything, he disapproved of it: *Some people throw everything they think and feel up on the wall for everyone to see, my boy. They don't understand subtlety.*

But Abel doesn't understand subtlety either. The direct

emotions of the Kahlo appeal to him. In this picture, Kahlo had painted two self-portraits stranded on a parched and barren landscape, one self in day and one in night. One lies on a hospital gurney, face hidden, bandages askew to reveal the still-bleeding cuts in her side; the other sits upright, brilliant in a red dress with flowers in her hair, holding the brace Kahlo was forced to wear after her spinal injury. This one stares at the viewers, challenging them to understand.

What's most interesting about the painting, in Abel's opinion, is that the self who is prone and bloody is the one in the daytime. The prouder Kahlo, the stronger one, sits in the night. Even then, she clutches her brace to her, so part of her can be seen only through its lattices.

Most humans choose to hide their pain and weakness. Kahlo acknowledged that everyone saw hers. It was her power that was hidden by darkness, and the proof of her injury is part of that power.

(This is his interpretation alone. Although scholarly writing about the painting is stored deep within his memory, he's never consciously accessed it. He wants his opinions to remain his own.)

Abel likes the brace especially. Primarily made of metal, it was nonetheless a part of Kahlo, a part she acknowledged to the whole world. He doesn't have to call on Freudian texts to know why that element would speak to him. Sometimes, during his earliest days, when Mansfield was busy with other things, Abel would sit in this room for hours, studying every facet of the painting, trying to connect with the spirit of a centuries-dead human who nonetheless understood what it meant to be part living, part machine.

Mansfield has packed up most of his other valuables, but he left this here to rot. Abel's beginning to wonder whether his creator ever really appreciated any of his treasures. He takes the painting from the wall, tucks it under one arm, and braces himself to search the place he least wants to go to: the basement.

This was Abel's *birthplace*, for lack of a better word. Originally it was the basement of a Victorian-era house that stood here centuries ago. Mansfield refitted it as a modern laboratory for his most advanced experiments. So while old brick lines the walls and a few stained-glass windows edge the small area just above ground level, the room is filled with tanks for growing mechs—

—and a force field generator standing starkly in the center of the room, an empty cage with sharp points. This was where Noemi was kept, in the dark of the basement, unable to touch anyone or anything without pain.

The feeling Abel's having now is one he hasn't experienced often. It's one he finds difficult to reach, because it's so utterly forbidden to mechs, so alien to the core programming of his nature. But he knows it instantly, from the way it twists and burns in his mind.

This is anger. This is *fury.*

His emotions don't change what Abel has to do. He shifts his vision to infrared so he won't have to turn on any lights. (Probably no one is watching the house, but no point in running the risk when he has other ways of seeing.) The long rectangular tanks are empty of mechs, though a few are still filled with the milky-pink fluid that helps nascent mechs grow. A few smaller tanks had been added since Abel was here last; Mansfield had explained that people longed for child-size mechs to take the place of the offspring they couldn't afford to have. Organic mechs might make that unnecessary, giving birth to babies for humans to cuddle—until they get old enough to be discarded, sent off to be other people's machines.

On one table, abandoned, sits a cybernetic brain stem with its receptor cord, the seed of any mech. If Mansfield had ever coated it with the right amino acids and synthetic DNA, and then lowered it all into one of these tanks, it would have grown into a mech. It would have had the power to walk, talk, and even think, to a degree. Instead it sits here forgotten.

Abel picks it up and stares at the metal box. What is it that makes this some*thing* and him some*one*? There *is* a difference—Abel has seen that for himself—but no one understands exactly what it is, not even Mansfield.

Then he sees the extra memory device clipped onto the

brain stem, its metal newer and shinier than that around it. Of course this is where Mansfield hid the message. He realized exactly where Abel would look.

It's disturbing to be known so well by someone who means you harm.

He goes to the chair where his creator used to sit, with its small workstation, and activates it. As the room is illuminated by the faint blue glow of the screen and its workings, he plugs in the memory device. When he sees the extraordinarily high encryption level, he wonders whether Mansfield really meant for him to decode this at all.

Frowning, Abel gets to work. This could take him hours to crack, and deciphering this message is his only hope of saving Noemi.

After thirty-two minutes and four seconds, his intense concentration is broken by the chiming of the disposable comm unit he purchased at the public-access info station. Mansfield had demanded Abel wait two hours before coming here, no doubt because he felt his party would be more vulnerable to attack in transit. Abel had put those two hours to good use, searching through various Earth archives of medical personnel. Most people don't hide their secrets as well as Burton Mansfield hides his.

He pulls out the disposable comm with its old-fashioned flat screen and activates it to see the face of Ephraim Dunaway.

"Abel." Ephraim's unease is obvious. "How the hell did you find me?"

"I cross-referenced people in medical fields who had taken new jobs on Earth approximately five months ago against names that had never appeared in previous records before that same time. Your new identity was then fairly easy to determine from demographic information." Abel realizes that's not exactly what Ephraim was asking. "I strongly doubt any human would be able to find you as easily, if at all."

Ephraim relaxes slightly. "I never expected to hear from you again. Glad to know you're all right." In the background of the viewscreen, Abel sees a window, which in turn reveals palm trees swaying in a strong wind beneath the weak gray sunlight of a stormy sky. Ephraim must be on the other side of Earth completely. "But this isn't just a call to catch up on old times, is it?"

"No. I need Remedy's help—or, rather, Genesis does."

When Abel explains what's happened on Genesis, Ephraim's expression shifts from confusion to horror. "Dear God," he whispers. "This is mass genocide."

"Not if we can get them better antiviral drugs." Abel has been calculating the probabilities. Earth virologists would have assumed that Genesis could receive no medical supplies from the worlds of the Loop, and thus would not have bothered reengineering Cobweb to be more drug resistant. "It would mean sending medical supplies to Genesis en masse, and if any entity is capable of doing that, it's Remedy."

"That's a big if, my friend." Ephraim shakes his head. "We have the people. We can get the drugs. What we don't have is the *network*. Remedy is made up of individual cells that don't know that much about one another; it's safer that way, for everyone involved. Of course, that means we aren't all on the same page about what we should be doing, and why, and how. Communication between cells is strictly limited."

Ephraim breathes out in understandable frustration. The radical wing of Remedy sees the moderates as weaklings; the moderate wing sees the radicals as terrorists. Abel agrees with the latter philosophy but knows better than to take sides in a fight not his own.

"We've never acted in concert before," Ephraim continues. "Never stood up as—as an army, mostly because your brother and sister mechs would kick our butts. Earth outguns us by a factor of ten."

"More like a factor of one hundred and seventy." Perhaps that correction was unnecessary. Abel quickly adds, "Forgive my interruption."

"The thing is, what's happening on Genesis—that's what Remedy's been waiting for! It's a *war crime*, something so heinous Earth had to do it in secret. Plus, the bioengineering makes it clear that Earth was behind Cobweb all along. Even the bloodthirsty bastards who might be okay with biological warfare against Genesis would be furious to know Earth messed with its own people first. If the citizens of the colony worlds learn the whole truth about this, they might finally rise up. Earth's own population might join us!" Pounding his fist into his open hand, Ephraim adds, "But we need *proof*. We need Remedy to band together to *get* that proof. And I don't know how to make that happen."

"There must be some form of communication," Abel reasons. "Riko Watanabe had wider connections—"

"Yeah, but Riko and I parted ways more than four months ago. She got me set up with a new name, new identification—and I'm thankful for that—but we were never going to truly agree." The narrowing of Ephraim's eyes suggests regret, even hurt. Even as Abel registers this, Ephraim's emotion is wiped away by new focus. "Higher-level operatives have relay codes for use only in major emergencies. Plug those codes into your communication, and you could get information to the large majority of Remedy pretty damn quick."

The rest is obvious. "But you don't have any of the relay codes, nor any idea how to obtain them."

"Bingo," Ephraim says. "Riko might have access to those, but again, she's God knows where by now."

"I found you within two hours," Abel points out. "It seems rational to conclude that I can also find her."

Ephraim turns out to have a booming laugh. "You're the best detective I've ever known. How long do you think it's going to take you, searching multiple planets? A whole day? A day and a half?"

"Noemi's in trouble. I have to help her first." Abel's peripheral vision has been tracking the decryption this entire time.

"Wait. What's happened to Noemi?"

Abel shakes his head. "You shouldn't get involved. The situation is—complicated."

Although Ephraim clearly doesn't like the vague explanation, he accepts it. "Then what I'm going to do is reach out as broadly as I can. Right now it's tough—we're in a hurricane zone, about to see some people through a superstorm that's making landfall within the day."

Such superstorms have become more and more frequent during the past three hundred years—mega-hurricanes capable of lashing half a continent with their fury. Abel's memory banks make it clear that during such times, chaos reigns. "You won't be able to fully reach out until communications are unblocked after the storm."

"Doesn't mean I can't make some progress," Ephraim insists. "I might not be able to contact many Remedy cells, but I might be able to find one that does have the relay codes. Regardless, I *know* I can get us connected to plenty of hospitals and medical ships. As soon as this storm's passed, we'll start gathering together as many antiviral drugs as we can. That way, once we get the info we need, we'll be ready to act."

The decryption glows brighter and clicks: Mansfield's message has been unlocked.

"I have to go," Abel says. "Proceed as quickly as you can, and don't wait to hear from me again. According to Noemi's account, Genesis has very little time."

"Got it." Ephraim's facial expression indicates concern. "How much trouble are you and Noemi in?"

"You would find it more psychologically reassuring not to know." Abel shuts off the communication without another word. He can't waste even the few seconds it would take to reassure Ephraim Dunaway, not with Noemi's life on the line.

He inserts the memory device into the holography unit and inputs the full decryption code. The hologram flickers into action and a blue-tinted image of Burton Mansfield takes shape—wearing a bathrobe, sitting in the same chair Abel occupies right now. His creator looks terrible, more dead than alive, and the creak in his voice pierces Abel through. But his words are even worse.

"So, you found the device right where I knew you'd look. You thought I didn't understand what you've become, didn't you? I do understand, Abel. That's why you're so precious to me." This means *That's why I intend to take over your body.* But Abel remains focused as Mansfield adds, "I'm giving you another chance to save your girl. *One chance.* I'd like to posture and pose and tell you it's because I'm running out of patience, but the truth is, I'm running out of time. So is Noemi Vidal."

Abel pays no attention to the taunts. Instead he analyzes the uncertainty in Mansfield's body language. The strange, rushed quality of these instructions. Even the way Mansfield's eyes dart from side to side, as if he's watching some action play out around him. Something fundamental has changed about Mansfield's short-term plans—suggesting a large, important element at work that Mansfield has no control over. This element could help Abel, or it could doom Noemi. Until he discovers what it is, he can't determine which probability is greater.

Mansfield continues, "Come to Neptune, Abel. To Proteus. Find the *Osiris.* I'll even extend your deadline, but not far. Meet me there within one Earth day, no more. That's the last chance for all three of us to get what we want. Once you've done your duty, I promise you, Noemi can go safely home. I'll even allow you two the chance to say good-bye."

The memory of their first good-bye floods Abel's mind—the feel of Noemi in his arms, the softness of her mouth against his. It sharpens his longing for her so much he's glad Mansfield didn't mention a chance at good-bye in his first kidnapping demand. If he had, Abel might've surrendered.

"Find the *Osiris*," Mansfield repeats. "Until then." With a wave, he vanishes. The hologram is over.

●   ●   ●

In Namibia, Abel docks Virginia's corsair, puts in a flight clearance request, and walks upward through the *Persephone*'s one long spiral corridor until he reaches the equipment pod bay. He was marooned in this pod bay for nearly thirty years, completely alone. For most of that time, he'd wondered whether he would ever be freed from that prison. However, he's found that when he's especially confused or upset, this is the place he most wants to go. It makes no rational sense, but he's trying to dismiss the expectation that his emotions should be rational. To judge by the humans he's observed, no one ever accomplishes this.

Here on Earth, he can't turn off the gravity to float in zero-G like he did before. The darkness and the closed door are enough. He lies on the floor, gazing up at the marks carved into the ceiling. When he was first stranded, he scratched one for each day; his plan was to keep track of them all until he was rescued. He gave up after only 5.7 years. The habit became too depressing. If he'd kept going, nearly every centimeter of this pod bay would be scarred.

This was his prison. This was his home. This was where he learned to endure the terrible burden of not knowing. Now, when he must go on without any sure knowledge of how Noemi is, and without any concrete plan of saving her, he has to call on that endurance again.

A light begins blinking on a nearby interface; take-off clearance has been granted. Immediate departure is necessary.

But he hesitates at the door for almost 2.3 seconds, looking up not at the marks on the ceiling but at the spot in midair where he held Noemi in his arms. Where they kissed.

He always knew it would only be once.

11

As Mansfield's cruiser pulls closer to the behemoth ship *Osiris*, Noemi starts planning her escape.

I can't overpower the mechs on board Mansfield's craft in order to steal it, and even if I could, I wouldn't be able to get away in this ship. They're close enough now for her to see that dozens, maybe hundreds of mechs swarm around the *Osiris* and the surrounding area, swooping around the docking framework like vultures over prey. *Once I'm on the Osiris,* she decides, *I can look for other chances.*

The sore flesh around the poison ampule in her arm throbs with every heartbeat, reminding her that her captors have the power to kill her at any moment. But she knows they're unlikely to try anything before Abel shows up, which she hopes will be never.

Abel's helping Genesis, Noemi tells herself. The second she escapes from this ship, she intends to join him. Her world has so little time.

The cruiser's comms buzz. *"The Columbian Corporation welcomes you to the launch of the* Osiris, *the first stage of the most incredible journey in the history of humankind."* It's obviously an automated signal, and Burton Mansfield scowls.

"We're the largest investors," he grumbles as Gillian helps him to his feet. "You'd think we'd merit a personal greeting."

"We still don't have a majority." Gillian's tone suggests she's said this many times before. "Besides, does it matter?"

The question seems to irritate him. "Status always matters, my dear." People from Earth have strange priorities.

But Gillian doesn't think like her father. Her eyes take on the distant, fiery glow of holy purpose. "Soon they'll know what we've really accomplished." Noemi has no idea what the woman is talking about, but she's certain it means nothing good.

"Docking instructions have been autocoded into your personal cruiser," the message continues. *"Upon your arrival, our team of mechs will take care of your every need. So sit back, relax, and enjoy the miracle that is about to unfold."*

"What the—" Noemi feels a slight tug as the *Osiris* begins towing them in. "Did they say 'miracle'?"

"Hyperbole. I advised the other board members against that kind of language, but they outvoted me. But haven't I performed miracles before, Miss Vidal?" Mansfield asks as he settles back onto his chaise.

Abel surely counts as miraculous, but that's not only Mansfield's genius at work. Something else happened within him to make him so much more than his creator.

To Mansfield she says only, "You're no god."

The *Osiris* looms larger before them, its ornate golden hull blotting out the stars. One of the mechs steps closer and fluffs Noemi's hair, then spritzes her with something that smells of pear blossoms; it startles Noemi until she remembers that she's being passed off as Mansfield's invitee. As the golden well of the docking bay swallows their vessel, Noemi takes a few deep breaths and straightens. She'll walk onto this ship not as a prisoner nor as a party guest, but as a soldier of Genesis.

It doesn't matter if nobody else knows what she really is. She knows it. That's enough.

The cruiser passes through the silver sparkle of a force field and settles onto the deck. When the cockpit pops open, scented air rushes in, thick and seductive as perfume.

A Zebra model comes up to them, holding out his hand. "Professor Mansfield, Dr. Shearer, welcome to the first stage of the great journey. Your suites are fully prepared."

"I'll want to see the labs," Mansfield says. "Not right away, of course, but soon. Sometime before we get going. How long is that again?"

"We plan to set off as soon as Minister Cheng arrives in approximately ten hours."

Mansfield and Gillian exchange a look of horror. Ten hours isn't much time for Abel to catch up to them. Noemi ducks her head to hide her smile. *He'll never make it. Mansfield will never get his claws into Abel again.*

Now if only I can get out of his claws myself—

The Zebra turns its attention to Noemi, though he speaks to Mansfield and Gillian. "May I inquire as to your guest?"

"Her name is Noemi Vidal," Gillian says, taking Noemi's arm as though they were on some kind of date, "and she's to be kept away from any sensitive ship areas. Put together sensor checks that will alert us if she goes anywhere near a weapon or an air lock. And put her into one of the empty cabins, preferably the one closest to mine."

Any human would immediately understand that those are nothing like the normal instructions for a "guest." The Zebra nods politely, his smile unchanging. "Let us know if we can do anything for you before our departure, Miss Vidal."

Noemi sees the chance and pounces on it. "Our departure to where, exactly?"

But Mansfield waggles one finger as his Tare model helps him into a low-hovering chair. "Don't tell her a thing. I want it to be a surprise."

If the Zebra's programming allows him to recognize how weird this is, he gives no sign. "The prelaunch cocktail party is already in progress. I can escort you there now if you'd like."

Inclining her head, Gillian says, "Please." As they all set out, Noemi walks behind them, trying to figure out this charade. But each event is more surreal than the last. Her heart remains on Genesis, imagining all the pain there. Her body still trembles from the adrenaline of being taken hostage and of fearing for both her life and Abel's. But her mind has to somehow gather the self-control for a...cocktail party.

Maybe the gas they pumped into my starfighter didn't just knock me out, Noemi thinks. *Maybe this is all one big hallucination.*

The Zebra leads them from the docking bay. A Yoke hastens by with a tray of glasses filled with something fizzy; Mansfield shakes his head, but Gillian takes one, and Noemi figures she might as well, too. When she gains a swallow, she's startled to realize it's strongly alcoholic, but manages to get that mouthful down without coughing.

They walk through a corridor with carpets so thick they seem to caress her feet with every step. A faint gold shimmer lines the curving walls, and cobalt-blue sconces are shaped like scarab beetles. This doesn't look like a spacecraft to her. It's more like the way she always envisioned a palace. The air not only smells but *feels* pleasant; it takes Noemi a few seconds to realize that's because there's some humidity—not much, but more than the usual arid conditions aboard a spaceship.

Humidity wears out a ship. Damages the pipes. Noemi was trained to vent her starfighter and her suit after every flight, because too much water in the works will break it down faster than anything but an explosion. Whoever built a spaceship this extravagant and advanced has to know that.

Are the passengers too rich to care about using up this entire ship?

Finally the Zebra leads them to a tall set of arched doors, inlaid with enameled tiles. The Zebra steps back to allow their party through as the doors slide open to reveal a gold-plated room filled with a swirl of beautiful people—young and glamorous, dressed in sumptuous clothes—carrying their own glasses of bubbling wine. Honey-colored light filters through panels of what looks like real amber. As the partygoers laugh and chatter, they seem more than cheerful. The mood is closer to exuberance, delight, even elation. Mechs are everywhere, catering to each human whim: Two Oboes and a William play string instruments on the dais while Yokes offer fine wines and finger food that smells richer than any meal Noemi's ever had.

When Mansfield and Gillian come through the doors,

all the guests turn as one. Everyone smiles, and a few people even clap softly. A crowd begins to form around them, eager to personally greet the great cyberneticist and his famous scientist daughter. Seeing them so fawned over is more than Noemi can stand, so she edges away through the throng—still in the party, still obeying Gillian's dictates. But now she's able to take stock of her surroundings, plus do some quality eavesdropping.

Noemi pretends to be very interested in picking out a petit four from a Yoke's tray while she focuses her attention on Gillian and the black-haired man talking with her.

"—feel sure you entirely agree that pushing up the launch schedule was unnecessary." The man smiles, but it's the fierce, teeth-bared smile of someone who expects to get his own way and hasn't this time. "I hardly had time to pack my baggage, much less get it here!"

"Of course, Vinh," Gillian says. She can sound pleasant when she tries. "Yes, if they've picked up ionization trails, maybe we have a few small ships scouting this location, but that's no reason for panic. My father and I have our own vital reasons for wanting to delay the launch. This greatly interferes with his . . . medical treatment. But we don't have veto power over this."

Vinh's anger is clear even without its target being in the room. "How dare they inconvenience you, two of the most illustrious passengers on this ship? Especially when your family has been through so much lately." The side of Gillian's face twitches; Noemi glimpses it and wonders what it means, but Vinh doesn't even notice. "We should lodge a protest with the captain immediately. Your names on a petition would carry real weight."

Hearing Abel's murder described as Mansfield's "medical treatment" is too much to take. Noemi takes another few steps back and begins weaving her way through the crowd, trying to get a sense of the room's dimensions. She notices one tray in a Yoke's hands: It's filled with cheeses and breads, and also on the tray is a knife for trimming the cheeses to the guests' demands.

It's not much of a knife, but it has a pointed tip. Noemi could pierce skin and flesh with that. Later on this trip, she may need to. She can't really steal it while dozens of people are looking on, but she makes a note for later: *They're careless. The only weapons they think about are blasters. They won't be watching the cheese knives.*

She keeps working her way around the room. As she goes, she jostles a girl a few years younger than she is— no, someone a few years older, an adult, although this woman's not quite five feet tall and so thin that she looks more like a little kid. The woman's champagne spills on Noemi's jumpsuit. "Oops! So sorry! Let me get that," she says, gesturing at a Dog to dab at Noemi's clothes. "I'm Delphine Ondimba. I don't think we ever met at one of the prelim retreats, did we?"

"No, I don't think so."

"What a beautiful outfit!" Delphine beams. "It sets off your figure wonderfully. I wish I could wear things like that—but when I do, I look even tinier than I am, and people start acting like I should still be playing with dolls."

"You look great," Noemi ventures, and she genuinely likes the look of Delphine's flowing white silk caftan and heavily jeweled earrings. But she feels like she's playing an elaborate game of dress up. More to the point, she's not learning anything about this ship's layout, which means she's no closer to figuring out her escape. Time to keep moving. To Delphine she says, "I'm sure we'll run into each other later."

It's a mundane brush-off, which is why Noemi's so surprised when Delphine breaks into peals of laughter. "'Run into each other'! Yes, I bet we will, at some point in the next fifty years or so."

Fifty years?

Noemi opens her mouth to ask—then goes silent as the ship shudders beneath her feet. The entire party changes mood in an instant as smiles melt to frowns. All the musician mechs stop on precisely the same beat. "Well, what in the worlds is that?" Delphine says. "Are we taking off already?"

"My last shipment hasn't arrived!" Furiously Vinh stomps toward a side door, which slides open to reveal a large plasma window that shows the starfield around them. "If they've moved the launch even closer, I'm going to demand a full—"

Brilliant green light flares through the window, blinding everyone in the room, and the entire ship rocks so violently that most of the passengers fall to the floor. Noemi manages to stay on her feet, barely. Staggering to the window, she peers into the darkness beyond. Only her military training allows her to pick out the faint glints of metal and slashes of movement that hint at what's going on outside— a pitched battle between the *Osiris*'s mechs and a swarm of unknown fighter craft.

The ship shudders again—another blast must've landed somewhere else—and then the soft gold illumination in the room switches to blinking red alarm lights. Over the speaker, someone shouts, *"All hands to emergency stations! We're under attack!"*

A few people begin screaming. Noemi turns back to the window, realizing that the fight outside involves at least hundreds of combatants—maybe more than a thousand. Whoever came after this ship came in force.

Delphine holds one hand to her chest, as if that's all that's keeping her racing heart inside. "Attack? Who would be attacking us?"

It's Gillian Shearer who answers, her oval face gone an even starker white. "Remedy."

12

THE JOURNEY TO NEPTUNE COULD BE COMPLETED MUCH more quickly if Abel put the *Persephone*'s mag engines into overdrive mode. However, that would tax them to the limit, holding him to slower speeds for some days to come. Abel projects that he'll probably require the ship's highest level of velocity to escape with Noemi after freeing her.

This means he won't reach Neptune for hours. He has no solid data nor even any theories as to what he will find there. Therefore he can't construct any meaningful plans, much less calculate their relative probabilities of success. Abel will spend the hours of the journey with little to do besides worry about Noemi.

He'd always understood himself to have greater capacities for patience and calm than humans. This self-assessment will have to be reconsidered.

As the *Persephone* clears Saturn's orbit, he stands in his cabin, which used to be Mansfield's, and attempts to fix his full focus on the wall. He doesn't dislike the once-famous painting already hanging there, one of Monet's Water Lilies. But impressionist techniques aren't as effective on mechs. Humans look at the swirls of paint and see the translucency of water. Abel sees swirls of paint. Understanding the illusion is not the same as experiencing it.

The Kahlo is propped in one corner. He'd thought to hang that one instead, so the room would reflect his preferences instead of his creator's, but it's so small—and it's not the kind of painting to be peacefully stared at while falling asleep. It demands attention and analysis. It disquiets.

Right now, when Abel feels as though his every circuit is overloading with the need to reach Noemi, he doesn't need any more disquiet. The water lilies can stay where they are.

What could pull Mansfield so far from home when his condition is so frail—and when he believed Abel to be within hours of his possession? A move so dangerous suggests other involved parties with power even greater than Burton Mansfield's, and urgent priorities still unguessed. Still, whatever cards Mansfield has left to play will be played in pursuit of one primary goal: immortality. Noemi's kidnapping proves that Abel is still Mansfield's only sure route to avoiding death—

Your thoughts are becoming highly repetitive, Abel reminds himself. *This is counterproductive. Find other points of focus.*

He takes another step back, trying yet again to see the

Monet as a human would. He ought to have asked Noemi about it. Maybe that night after he nearly froze doing work on the outer hull, and she lay in here beside him as he thawed—he could've asked her then—

A chime sounds, indicating an incoming communications transmission, a response to his earlier signal. Abel instantly dashes to the nearest console because he finally has something useful to do.

The screen lights up to reveal Harriet and Zayan, crowded together into what looks like a public, open-air comm booth. In the distance behind them he sees green hills shrouded in clouds, serene and beautiful; they appear to be visiting some of the last surviving tea gardens on Earth.

"You're all right!" Harriet says, a huge grin on her face. *"Noemi's safe and we're getting back to work."*

Zayan laughs. *"That wasn't much of a vacation! Still, if Noemi's okay, that's all that matters."*

"Nocmi is not yet safe, but your vacation has ended—if you choose to take on this work, which I hope you will." Abel cannot require them to do this, only ask.

"What's going on?" Harriet asks. *"How do we help Noemi?"*

"I don't need your help to rescue Noemi," he replies. "I need you to assist a friend of mine who is a member of Remedy."

Both Harriet and Zayan sit back, with near identical expressions of shock. It's Zayan who finds his voice first. *"You swore to us you were never in Remedy."*

"Nor have I been. But I have contacts within the group, and one of those contacts needs help."

Harriet's shaking her head so vehemently that her braids shake. *"No. No way. Abel, we love working with you, but signing up with terrorists? Never."*

"Ephraim Dunaway is a member of the moderate wing of Remedy," Abel says. He uses Ephraim's name deliberately. Harriet and Zayan will see it as a show of trust, which it is. Even if they won't help, they won't turn Ephraim in. Abel needs them to understand that he knows this. "He's one of the people who're working to get control from the more violent wing. More to the point, he's a doctor, and he's trying to save Genesis."

"Genesis?" Zayan shakes his head, as if to clear it. *"Wait, how did Genesis come into this?"*

Abel's explanation plays a symphony of reactions over their faces—horror, then hope, then uncertainty. He has no idea how they'll answer, but he must ask: "I can send the contact information for Ephraim. If you can reach out to him and help him find a few ships to hire—Vagabonds you personally know and trust—"

"Can't do it." Harriet folds her arms across her chest. *"You were at the Orchid Festival bombing the same as us.*

You saw what they did. You tell me this Dunaway wasn't a part of that, all right, I believe you. But I don't trust Remedy, and I'm not putting my neck on the line for them. Right, Zayan?"

But Zayan doesn't answer. Only when she's turned to him, eyes wide, does he say, *"I think we have to do something."*

"Are you batcrap crazy?" Harriet explodes. *"This is* Remedy. *You seriously want us to join Remedy?"*

Zayan turns toward her, and Abel is no longer a participant in the conversation, only an observer. *"Of course not. But that's not what this is. We wouldn't be attacking anyone, just helping run medicine to Genesis. That's different."*

"You really think Earth's going to let medical ships or anything else go through the Genesis Gate?" Harriet demands.

Abel doesn't get a chance to answer, because Zayan immediately says, *"That's where Remedy comes in. They'd be—you know—the muscle. But we'd be doing good. Helping people."*

Harriet's ire has faded, but her eyes remain wary. *"We could get caught."*

"Yeah, well, nobody said doing the right thing was easy. And I know you. You'd never be able to live with yourself if you walked away from this." Zayan turns from Harriet back to Abel. *"So, what, we'd help this Ephraim Dunaway guy find some good Vagabond ships to hire—"*

"*No*," Harriet cuts in. Her tone of voice has changed, become electric. "*We reach out to lots of Vagabonds. Tons of them. If you're going to get a shipment through the Genesis Gate, you're going to need as big a fleet as possible. You're going to need…hundreds of ships, probably. If we put the word out that we're standing up to Earth, putting together a rescue convoy, strength in numbers and all that—I bet we'll find lots of volunteers.*" To Zayan, who's staring at her open-mouthed, she says, "*Well, if we're doing this thing, let's not half-ass it.*"

Zayan grins at her. "*This is why I love you.*"

"*Is that the only reason?*" She arches an eyebrow.

Abel knows from experience that Zayan and Harriet are fully capable of flirting and taking care of key tasks at the same time, but this practice will leave them with no attention left over for him. "I'll be out of contact for a while," he says. "Work with Ephraim, trust your own judgment, and don't wait to hear from me."

That brings them back to him, concern clear on both their faces. "*All right,*" Harriet says slowly, "*but if you need help, you call us. Anywhere, anytime. Got it?*"

"Understood."

It occurs to Abel to wonder whether Burton Mansfield has ever had friends who would pledge their loyalty to him, despite danger, without any hope of personal reward. Maybe not. Maybe that was one reason why he made Abel and wove Directive One so thoroughly throughout his brain. Mansfield chose to program love rather than earn it.

• • •

Abel knows down to the second the moment he'll be within sensor range of Neptune's moon Proteus. Yet he waits on the bridge for almost an hour beforehand, unable to focus on anything else, staring at the viewscreen and willing the alert to sound.

Without Zayan and Harriet, Abel doesn't bother with his captain's chair. Instead he sits at ops, checking and double-checking every system on the ship, waiting, waiting—

The proximity alert sounds. Instantly he brings up the long-range images of the moon Proteus. His viewscreen fills with unexpected details; he frowns as he identifies a docking framework and a passenger ship—an enormous passenger ship, one that could carry perhaps ten thousand individuals on shorter journeys, or thoroughly provision and entertain a small number in great style. Given the appearance of the ship, Abel suspects the latter. This vessel—surely the *Osiris* Mansfield spoke of—is as intricate and golden as any piece of jewelry found in an Egyptian pharaoh's tomb, with designs in styles no doubt meant to evoke that comparison.

Abel frowns at its gaudiness. The extravagance is of course wasteful, so it must serve some purpose.

Its use can't be tactical, he thinks. *Therefore it is emotional. The passengers of this ship are no doubt rich, and they may wish for the ship to reflect their wealth and status. So the elaborate decoration is . . . symbolic.*

He wonders whether Burton Mansfield helped choose the ship's name. As Abel knows from experience, Mansfield likes symbols and allusions. In the ancient Egyptian myth, the great god Osiris is murdered by his brother Set, who dismembers the body and scatters the pieces far and wide. Osiris's wife, Isis, and the other goddesses bring the pieces back together, though there's one part they never find: the penis. So Isis creates a phallus out of gold for Osiris, then copulates with her reequipped husband, causing him to be resurrected as king of the world of the dead.

Mansfield would of course be drawn to the idea of rebirth. Surely, Abel thinks, it can't be about the replacement phallus, though Freudian theory might find a link between that and the enormous size of the *Osiris*.

Movement at the edges of the ship's framework proves to be a large squadron of fighter mechs, swooping through the area and skimming the surface, protecting every millimeter of the hull. It may be impossible to sneak aboard. Abel considers turning himself over to Mansfield—or appearing to, feigning his defeat just long enough to get on board—but that would require him to fight his way out—

The border of the viewscreen flashes yellow: new ships in proximity. Abel's sharp vision picks up motion around Proteus and Triton as well. Immediately he focuses multiple lenses on each motion, bringing up several dozen vessels of various sizes, all of which seem to be moving in on the *Osiris*'s location, faster than normal passenger ships or freighters.

"Remedy," Abel says aloud.

Not the Remedy faction he sought either—not the moderates and medical professionals who founded the resistance movement. Those people wouldn't be attacking a passenger ship. These can only be the radicals. The dangerous ones. The terrorists.

The *Persephone* is still several minutes away, and his ship can't turn back a force of that size on its own. Abel, used to easily overpowering and outthinking humans, is unprepared for the knowledge that he's outmatched. Even if the *Persephone* had weapons, he'd be hard-pressed to take out more than a handful of the attackers.

But Mansfield and Noemi have to be aboard that ship.

Directive One pulses within Abel, demanding that he do something to protect his creator. *Anything.* He takes hold of his control panel and braces himself as though for impact: The urge to protect Mansfield is that strong. Something far more powerful urges him to save Noemi, to get her out of there even if it costs his own life.

He hits the controls and sends the mag engines into overdrive.

The *Persephone* flashes into the battle in mere seconds. Abel kills overdrive right away; the engines buck in protest but his ship remains ready. Unfortunately the *Persephone* has no weapons, only mining lasers that can do damage when needed. So Abel can offer little more than escape.

Reach the docking bay. Use the damage Remedy has done to get on board. Then find Noemi and free her from custody. Directive One repeats within his mind, but Abel ignores it, or tries to. *We'll notify Remedy of our neutrality as soon as we leave the* Osiris. *Perhaps there will even be a chance to discuss the mission to help Genesis, to get relay codes from someone on one of these ships—*

Laser cannon fire slices so close to the *Persephone* that every alert goes off at once; every console lights up almost solid red. Another meter closer and his ship would now be wounded almost past repair. Abel decides informing Remedy of his neutrality should be an earlier step in the process.

He slaps comms on for wide-frequency transmission. "To any Remedy vessels within communications range, this is the *Persephone*, a noncombatant vessel. Please respond."

No reply. No other ships fire but Abel can't determine whether that's due to his message or because they're focusing their attack on the *Osiris* with even greater frenzy.

The Remedy ships blast the spacedock surrounding the ship over and over, until the skeletal framework shatters into metal beams that rotate out through space. As Abel watches, unable to intervene, Remedy ships circle the *Osiris*, darting toward and away like stinging insects, until a few manage to penetrate the landing bays.

Once on board, the Remedy members will no doubt assume control of the vessel. Then Noemi will be at the mercy not only of Burton Mansfield but also of the most dangerous wing of a terrorist organization.

Notify Earth security. Abel usually tries to avoid interacting with the authorities any more than necessary; he doesn't know who might be under Mansfield's pay, or even whether someone might finally penetrate his fake identification. He doesn't care. Not if Earth ships could save the *Osiris*, and Noemi along with it.

"Free vessel *Persephone* calling any Earth ships in range," he says, adjusting his signal to ensure it more swiftly reaches the comm relays between planets. "Suspected Remedy action against a civilian vessel near Proteus. Repeat, suspected Remedy action—"

Four Remedy ships swoop in sharp arcs to zoom straight toward his ship. The problem with open comms is that anyone can hear you, and now Remedy knows he's endangering their mission. That makes him the enemy.

Abel had calculated this, so he's prepared. He shifts the

Persephone's course, diving toward Neptune. The last thing he sees before switching his view is the *Osiris* beginning to move. As still more Remedy ships dart inside, it lumbers from the debris of its frame and begins to fly toward open space.

They can't get far, Abel reminds himself as he focuses primary instrumentation on Neptune, fast approaching on his viewscreen. From here, even in overdrive mode, no ship can reach either the Genesis or Earth Gate in less than four hours. What he has planned will take far less time.

He wheels around toward the moon Naiad, the innermost of Neptune's satellites. As he'd anticipated, the Remedy fighters follow him. Naiad is small and irregularly shaped, and its orbit is erratic. Abel brings them around in a curve that is in fact a collision course. Their computers will inform them of that in 3.8 seconds.

Changing course in time to avoid a crash must occur within 3.1 seconds.

In the last moment, Abel banks sharply to stern. He doesn't shift the viewscreen to show him the scene of the crashes behind him. Watching the smaller, abstract symbols on his console blink out of existence is sufficient.

Killing humans to save his life and his ship is within Abel's parameters. Given that he was acting to save Noemi from a crisis these pilots helped bring into being, he feels morally justified. Yet the knowledge that he's taken human life haunts him. He will have to consider this from many religious and philosophical viewpoints—but later, after rescuing Noemi.

The *Osiris* has already traveled a great distance, and at a higher speed than the *Persephone* can reach. He's not that far behind, however, and Abel feels sure that the ship will soon come to a stop. Whether Remedy gains control of the ship or is defeated, the captain will need to cease flight and take stock of the damage.

Yet the *Osiris* keeps flying, getting farther and farther ahead by the minute. As its path becomes clearer, Abel begins to frown. It appears to be headed to the Kuiper Belt of asteroids and detritus that circles the far end of the solar system.

In other words, it's headed toward nothing.

Perhaps this is a random course, set by Remedy to escape Earth authorities, if they've taken control of the ship. That's the only rationale Abel can devise. That attempt is doomed to failure—the ship's ionization trails will be traceable for days yet—but it is possible the Remedy members don't know that. He magnifies the image of the ship so that it nearly fills the domed screen, giving him the best possible view—

—and the *Osiris* disappears.

Abel at first assumes a sensor malfunction. He runs through the ship's systems looking for a fault and finds none, then examines his own internal workings. Everything reports normal.

He pushes the engines faster, and even considers putting them into overdrive again, dangerous as this would be. But within 2.31 minutes, he's close enough to get better readings on the area. He turns up various far-flung asteroids, one distant gravity anomaly, but absolutely nothing that could be a ship. Even if the *Osiris* had been destroyed, there would be wreckage, radiation, or other evidence.

Instead the ship has simply vanished from existence— taking Noemi with it.

13

THE MAIN LIGHTS FLICKER, LEAVING ONLY THE STACCATO red alert for illumination. Panic crackles through the passengers like near-fatal voltage, galvanizing them all.

"What do we do?" Delphine clutches Noemi's arm, probably because Noemi's one of the few not shaking with fear. "If Remedy captures this ship, they'll kill us all!"

"How did Remedy learn about our voyage?" demands the older, more hostile man named Vinh. "We were assured of total secrecy!"

"I'd like to know that myself." Mansfield has gone ghostly pale. "They said we'd had proximity alerts, but they never said—"

Another blast near the window floods the room with a flash of intense green light. The ship rocks again, and Mansfield nearly topples from his chair; Gillian manages to catch him. She says, "Someone betrayed us. Someone inside the Columbian Corporation—no one else could've known."

Vinh says, "I demand an inquest!"

Noemi thinks, *This guy has no idea that we might all be dead in an hour.* As scared as the other passengers are, they're not taking any actions to save themselves. They stare upward, almost motionless, like rabbits in a vehicle's light.

Heavy clanking through the walls suggests a major system shutdown. Everyone tenses, and Noemi's palm itches for the holt of a blaster. Standing here in a ship she doesn't know, with people she doesn't understand, unnerves her more than straightforward combat ever has. She prefers it when she can see what's trying to kill her.

Over the comms comes the captain's voice, now hoarse with panic. "We're being boarded! All hands to emergency escape pods! All hands, abandon ship!"

It's like throwing bread to pigeons. People scatter in every direction at once, screaming with terror, knocking over trays and one another. A flume of champagne splatters across Noemi's face; she spits it out and yells over the din: "Everyone *listen!*"

Everyone does. They halt in place, staring at her. At first Noemi's surprised—she thought she'd get the attention of just a few people—but then she realizes she's the only one trying to act for the group. That turns her into an authority on a ship she'd never heard of, with capacities she knows nothing about.

"You," she says to Gillian, who must know more about the vessel than most. "Where are the nearest emergency escape pods?"

"Near the cabins. In other words, up several decks." Gillian remains crouched by her father's side; Mansfield is trembling with terror, which would be satisfying at any other time. "We'd have to move through the main public areas of the ship to reach them."

Realization sparks Noemi's temper. "In other words, you had escape pods for the passengers but not for the crew."

"The crew's ninety percent mechs!" Mansfield snaps.

Noemi wonders whether they care about the lives of the other 10 percent.

Gillian adds, "If Remedy's boarding the ship, then they'll be in those same public areas. We can't go there without turning the corridors into a shooting gallery, with us as the targets."

"Okay, then," Noemi says, thinking fast, "what's the nearest area of the ship we could secure?"

"What do you mean, 'secure'?" Delphine's small hands cling to Noemi's arm; her silky white caftan has glittering trim tinted pink by the alert lights.

The subtle vibration of the engines shifts under Noemi's feet. They're breaking free of the docking framework already. The *Osiris* is on the move, and regardless of who's driving, Noemi doesn't want to go where they're headed. "I mean, we get weapons and barricade ourselves within an area of the ship that we can keep Remedy from taking."

"There's no point in this," Vinh snaps. "We have mechs on board for this."

"Exactly right." Mansfield nods, as if he's encouraging himself rather than the others. "The mechs will defeat the Remedy members."

Maybe being rich and pampered turns you into an optimist. Noemi's never had that luxury. "If the mechs win, great. If not, we need to be prepared."

"Who put you in charge?" Vinh says.

Gillian rises to her feet and puts one hand on her bracelet—the one containing the trigger for the poison in Noemi's arm. "That's a very good question."

Noemi's gaze scans the partygoers around her, half of whom are still holding their glasses of fizzy wine instead of running for the escape pods as they were just told to do. They wear velvet capes, thigh-high boots, jewels the size of bumblebees on their fingers and in their ears. The terror on their faces makes them pathetic; otherwise they'd just be laughable. "I'm not in charge," she says, "but I'm betting I'm the only person here with any military experience. Yes?"

A few of them glance around. Delphine timidly offers, "Probably."

"All right, then," Noemi says. "Since this ship is already on the move—"

"You don't know that," retorts Vinh.

Does this man not even know how to gauge when a large ship is in motion? "Yes, I *do* know that, and so does anybody else who's paying attention to the vibrations under their feet. If your crew still has control of the engine room, where are they taking us?"

"You don't need that information," Gillian says sharply. The passengers look confused; it's sinking in to them that Noemi isn't just another partygoer.

"Fine, then. Doesn't matter," Noemi says. Her heart's beating fast in her chest, because it's not like she's had tons of experience with this either. Taking on an entire Remedy army sounds like a good way to end up dead. She's out of her depth—but less so than anyone else on board. That means she has to do what she can. "We still need to secure an area before Remedy's forces fill every part of the ship."

"How do you know that they haven't already?" Apparently Vinh hopes to show her up, but he's doing a really bad job of it.

"I know that because *none of them are in here yet.*" After giving that a second to sink in, which hopefully will keep him quiet for a while, she goes on. "All right. What weapons do we have on board?"

Mansfield draws himself up in his chair. "No weapon for you."

But Gillian bends down to him. Her intense blue eyes focus on Noemi as she says, "It doesn't matter, Father. She's of use, for the moment, and we don't want this ship to go far." She puts one of his hands on her arm; to those around, it must look like a comforting gesture, but Noemi sees that Mansfield is now touching the bracelet that could kill her. More loudly, Gillian calls, "There are a handful of blasters in emergency lockers throughout the ship. They were intended for use if the ship was infiltrated during final construction—but nobody's removed them."

Noemi tries to take heart from that. "Okay, so, we'll pick up a few weapons on our way to our base."

"We have a base?" Delphine asks in a wavering tone.

"We're about to. You guys know the layout of this ship better than I do," Noemi says, thinking fast. What kind of place would they need? "What we need to do is—is seize control of one critical area as fast as we can. The main engine room, the food supply, something like that."

"Won't those areas be the first Remedy goes after?" says Vinh, who has a point for once.

She nods. "Yeah, they will. But we should still try to claim one, just in case Remedy does get control of the ship. We can negotiate on equal terms if we can hold just one room on the *Osiris*, as long as it's the right room."

Gillian stands up, and instantly the attention of the room shifts to her. That's the authority they already know—a leading shareholder in whatever the hell the Columbian Corporation is—and are more comfortable with. "Follow me," Gillian says to the passengers and Noemi both, as she opens the nearest door.

Normally Noemi would be relieved not to have to carry the burden of leadership alone in a situation like this. Now, not so much. But at least they have a guide.

She jogs through the corridor, alongside Shearer, ahead of the passengers huffing and puffing behind them. Mansfield's chair hovers slightly above the floor and, to Noemi's disappointment, is able to keep up. The ship rocks once more—but from fire within the decks, not outside the ship. If the fight has shifted inside, then Remedy must be close to gaining control.

The emergency lockers are hard to spot at first: Normally they'd be painted a bright yellow or orange, but here they're a sedate gold that matches the pseudo-Egyptian decor. Noemi stoops by the first locker, cracks it open, and pulls out three blasters. She tosses the other two to people nearby—Delphine and Vinh. Dr. Shearer just keeps running, leaving the rest of them to catch up.

"I've never fired a real blaster!" Delphine says between gulped-in breaths. Obviously she's not used to running this fast. She *is* fast, though; her white caftan flutters around as if she were caught in a strong breeze. "Is it like in games? Because I'm pretty good at games."

"Of course it's like games!" huffs Vinh. "What's the point of firing simulators if they don't simulate firing?"

On Genesis, war games are only for the literal practice of warfare. What must it be like, to shoot at human figures and think of it only as play?

The comms crackle, and a different voice comes over the speaker. "This is Captain Fouda," he says, "of Remedy. The *Osiris* is ours. Surrender yourselves at the main docking bay, or consider your lives forfeit."

People begin to shriek and cry, but Gillian yells, "This doesn't change anything! Keep going!"

Noemi expects half the group to ignore her and turn themselves in, but instead they keep running after Gillian. Either they have more gumption than she thought, or they're too scared to do anything but follow their leader.

It's harder to tell while she's running, but it seems to Noemi that Gillian's taking them farther from the engine room, not closer. That would've been her call: Take down primary engines and wait for Remedy to come begging for help. But there are other valid targets, like food storage or water systems. She just keeps looking out for lockers—which are few—and distributing the handful of weapons they're able to muster.

The vibration of the engines suggests that the *Osiris* is

definitely on the move, at what feels like full speed. Where is Remedy taking them?

Gillian leads them all into an enormous room lit only by the alert sirens. Noemi lets her blaster drop to her side as she squints to make out the various shapes. They're surrounded by walls of tanks. At first she thinks this must be the water supply—a solid target—but then she realizes most of the tanks are filled with opaque pink goop. Within them she can see vague dark forms, bobbing slightly, waiting to be born.

"You led us to the mech chambers?" Noemi says. "How does that help?"

"The mechs can fight," Delphine offers.

Noemi shakes her head. "Not until they're finished, which could be hours or days from now. How does this help us?"

"This is the most important area on the ship," Gillian says evenly. "This is the area we need to hold."

The passengers seem unwilling to argue that point—except for Vinh, who remains prepared to argue about anything. "We were told there would be top-level security! But our departure date is moved up because of the 'threat of discovery,' and we still get attacked by *terrorists*? I demand at least a fifty percent refund."

The other passengers launch into similar complaints. Maybe they're distracting themselves from their fear;

maybe they really think they're safe now. Either way, Noemi can't take any more of it.

The far wall of this chamber is next to the outer hull. A few plasma windows reveal the stars outside, so she at least has a view. The sight of the stars might give her some peace.

Instead she sees a smaller scout vessel gliding alongside—a Remedy ship, no doubt—and in the far distance...

"What the *hell*?" she whispers.

The silvery ring ahead of them, only a few moments away—that's a Gate.

This Gate isn't as polished as the others. Not as perfect. Long sections reveal its inner workings, as jumbled and ugly as the entrails of a living thing. Still, there's no mistaking it for anything else.

But the *Osiris* is nowhere near the Earth Gate to Stronghold. Nor has this ship had time to travel all the way back to the Genesis Gate, even if they'd accelerated to overdrive, which Noemi doesn't think they did.

This is another Gate. A secret Gate. A shortcut across the galaxy to...where?

The *Osiris* hits the Gate's horizon, and light fractures around Noemi as they pass through to a destination unknown.

14

"WELL, IF IT ISN'T MY BELOVED COUSIN ABEL BACK ONCE more! It's so wonderful to see you again so—oh, crap. What's wrong?"

He stands in the geometrical white-and-orange dock on Cray, staring at Virginia Redbird, unable to find any words.

It would seem that having more emotions within would lead to having more to say, since there is naturally more to discuss. But now Abel knows it doesn't work that way. Emotions don't take turns; they crowd in together. His different feelings blot each other out, like writing words atop other words in ink, until nothing's legible any longer. What remains is a darkness that says nothing and contains everything.

Virginia comes closer and puts her hands on Abel's shoulders. "Abel?" she whispers. "What happened with Noemi?"

"I don't know," he manages to say. "Let's go back to your lab. We have some data to analyze."

. . .

In the Razers' hideout, they find Ludwig and Fon sitting on the floor, immersed in a game of Go, until it becomes clear that Abel's brought them a new puzzle to solve.

(That's how they think of problems—as puzzles or games. Abel knows some humans would find this insensitive or at least immature, but he doesn't want sympathy or sensitivity. He wants answers. Answers are data for him to work with, and if he has enough data, then he won't have to think about the black-ink jumble of feelings inside.)

"This is beyond bizarre," Virginia says as they replay the disappearance of the *Osiris* on one of the 2-D screens. The flicker of light and shadow carves her distinctive features more sharply, setting off her strong cheekbones and square chin. "If it had been destroyed, we'd either see some cataclysmic event or at least some debris floating around afterward. Instead it's like the whole ship gets—*swallowed* by the void."

"That's not a realistic hypothesis," Abel says.

Virginia shoots him a look over her shoulder. "I *know*, Abel, don't trip a breaker. It's just an expression. This is weird, is all I'm saying."

Abel nods to show her he understands—he always did,

of course—but it appears that even the deepest grief can manifest as irritability. He must take this into account when dealing with unhappy humans in the future. "We have to determine whether or not the ship still exists. Burton Mansfield and Noemi were almost certainly on board."

"How can you know for sure?" Fon asks from her place on a nearby floor cushion, hugging her knees to her chest.

"Burton urged me to find him there. Logically he would've taken Noemi with him to the ship immediately after leaving Earth."

Ludwig points out, "He might have gone somewhere else, planning to join the *Osiris* later."

"Burton Mansfield is in very poor health. His body is frail, and he requires mech assistance for almost all daily activities." *Mansfield's papery skin, the veins showing through in soft blue.* "He could send mechs or trusted associates to take care of any other business." *Abel, my boy.* "Therefore Mansfield would minimize travel, going directly to the *Osiris*, which may well have been destroyed."

All his concern, fear, and grief ought to belong to Noemi. She's the only one who should matter, the only one he wants to save. But Directive One remains insistent within him, demanding that he care about Mansfield, too. Even now. Always.

"Destroyed by nothing, leaving behind nothing?" Virginia says. "No way. Think this over, Abel. Your emotions are clouding your judgment, which is kind of exciting in terms of the evolution of your psyche, but it's not helping us analyze the situation. So maybe dial down your human side for a minute."

My emotions are clouding my judgment, Abel thinks. At any other time, this revelation might be wonderful to him. For the moment he can only refocus himself.

"Do we know where the *Osiris* was headed?" asks tiny Fon.

"Irrelevant," Abel replies. "We can only speculate whether Remedy flew the *Osiris* along its original course or diverted it to another destination. So we have to analyze the data to determine its course and extrapolate from that."

Pointing at one corner of the screen, Ludwig zooms in on it. "Do you see the blur here? That doesn't look like a problem with the *Persephone*'s sensors. It looks like a distortion field at work."

"Mansfield has used distortion fields in the past," Abel says. "Mostly to camouflage deep-space mech facilities, particularly those near the Genesis Gate in the earlier days of the Liberty War, when Genesis troops sometimes came through to fight in the Earth system."

Virginia lights up. When she gets a new idea, it's like setting fire to a fuse. "Speaking of Gates, these energy readings—don't they kind of look like a ship passing through a Gate?"

Fon makes a scoffing sound. "Come on. There's no Gate out there."

"The size and intensity of a distortion field that could eclipse a Gate completely, beyond any detection—that's far beyond anything Mansfield has done in the past," Abel says. A Gate requires more than a visual screen. "Massive energy readings also have to be concealed. Such concealment is difficult to begin with and grows exponentially greater with the size of the object to be concealed."

"The distortion field didn't conceal all the energy readings," Virginia insists. "Yeah, this is like the mini-pocket-baby version of Gate-transport readings, but maybe that's all that bleeds through."

Abel sticks to mathematical realities and probabilities for the time being. Math is comforting. It is rational and unchanging. His emotions cannot cloud his math. When he runs the numbers, it becomes increasingly clear that she has a point.

"Could Mansfield build a field that size?" Virginia presses. "You know him better than just about anyone, Abel. We all know he's got the money and the power. And he's definitely got the brain. Does he have the—drive, I guess you'd call it?"

Drive. Will. Purpose. Mansfield broke every law of cybernetics to build himself another home for his soul. He joined in the building of that enormous ship for some grand purpose still unknown, at a cost that must total in the billions of credits. When Abel filters this through his knowledge of his creator, the probabilities shift. "He does. He could."

"Earth built another Gate without telling anyone?" Ludwig scowls at the screen as if demanding answers from it. "That would mean they've found another habitable world."

Fon chimes in, "Not necessarily. They could be exploring something else, like a system with materials we need, even if humans can't live there."

"Or they built an artificial planet somewhere," Virginia says. She's playing with a lock of her red-streaked hair, eager and alight. "It could be a massive space station, maybe. Even a Dyson sphere! Something really flash, you know?"

"Any such structures may well have defenses," Abel says.

How would those defenses react to the *Osiris* arriving under Remedy control? Would they negotiate or shoot to kill? Not to mention, such security would mean Noemi is in a prison—no, a fortress. Rescuing her would be extremely difficult.

But not impossible.

Ludwig hesitantly says, "You mentioned—you said that Genesis was under attack? Earth used biological weapons?"

"Cobweb was disseminated planetwide," Abel confirms. "Possibly the virus was modified to be both more contagious and more deadly."

The Razers all stare at one another, stricken to a degree

that surprises Abel. He doesn't doubt their horror at the use of biological weapons, but their reaction seems more... personal.

Fon speaks up first. "That's going to be level 110."

"I think Ricardo works down there sometimes," Virginia murmurs. "Mei, too."

Only then does it occur to Abel that the reengineering of the Cobweb virus might've been done at Earth's request, but it wouldn't have been done on Earth. That would've been performed by the greatest virologists in the galaxy—who, like the top specialists in every science, live and work on Cray.

"Are there any Razers who work on that level?" Abel asks. "Could they get information about how it was done?"

Ludwig lets out a low whistle. "That's going to be under tight security. Really tight."

"Doesn't mean someone couldn't get past it," says Fon, and the others take on that look of excitement that means they've found a code or rule they plan to raze.

Swiftly Abel inputs contact codes for Harriet and Zayan. "Don't endanger yourself for that intel, Virginia—but if you get it, please inform these people immediately. Tell them I asked you to. They may be able to hand the information on to doctors who could work on a cure."

"You've got it," Virginia promises. "Oh, we are forever captains for *this*."

"Thank you for your help." He shuts off his screen; Virginia and the other Razers stare up at him in surprise. "Your insights have been extremely helpful, but ultimately I must investigate in person. I should leave immediately." Abel gives them another nod instead of saying good-bye.

As he strides through one of the rough-hewn stone tunnels leading back to the dock for Station 47, he hears footsteps coming up fast behind him. "Abel!" Virginia calls. "Wait up!"

He slows his steps, but not by much. "Did you discover something new within the data?"

"No, but you're running out of here like somebody set your ship on fire."

"What I observed demands direct investigation, immediately. Looking for alternate viewpoints and theories is— an interesting intellectual exercise, and you've provided valuable insights about the distortion fields and a potential Gate—but this is all irrelevant without further data. I don't know why I didn't see this from the beginning."

"You didn't come here just for intellectual exercise," Virginia says. "You also came here because you were hurting and you needed a friend."

Abel starts to say that this isn't true. He's functioned without friends for the large majority of his existence. Even if he did need emotional support, he would be consciously aware of it. Wouldn't he? But humans are often oblivious to the psychological reasons for their behavior. Abel's mind operates at a human level of complexity. He's already determined that he has a subconscious—yet this is the first time he's realized his subconscious affects his behavior. "Maybe I did. Thank you for listening to me, and going over this data. You helped me assess the situation more clearly. But the fact remains that I have to return to the site immediately."

Virginia shakes her head. "Give it one hour."

"Why one hour?"

"That's how long it's going to take me to put in for emergency leave. Well, I guess I should pack, too, but that's not going to take long. Basically I only wear about six variations of this." Virginia wears her usual deliberately oversize jumpsuit, baggy except for the broad belt tight at her waist, with various pins and badges proclaiming her fidelity to every piece of entertainment she's ever loved. "I can have that done before the request's even turned around."

"You don't have to come with me. I'm more than capable of handling the *Persephone* on my own." Sometimes it's a stretch even for him, but Abel manages.

"For the most advanced artificial intelligence ever created, you can be kind of stupid sometimes." Virginia sighs. "Backup is *good*. Backup is *your friend*."

"No, you're my friend, and I'd rather not put any more of my friends in danger." Even knowing what Harriet and

Zayan are attempting makes him feel uneasy. The risk to Virginia would be far more immediate.

She is unconvinced. "If you go out to investigate something, you're just going to leave the *Persephone* abandoned? You might as well put up a huge glowing holosign that says 'Free ship to good home.'"

Abel considers that, but only briefly. "You've raised a valid tactical point, but it's still not worth endangering you."

"Worth it to who?" Virginia demands. "I'm interested in this, too, you know. Scientific mysteries are my lifeblood. If I stay here, I'm just going to be running more data for Professor Fernandez, who can deal with a couple weeks' delay. And Fon and Ludwig can handle the Cobweb project here."

"None of this changes the risk to you. I'm sorry, but—"

"Listen to me, dammit!" Her smile has vanished; she's not joking any longer. "The people aboard that ship, the *Osiris*—they may have traveled through a hidden Gate. That means Earth is possibly hiding an entire habitable world. They're doing that while people around the galaxy starve. More than five months ago, right after I left you and Noemi, I went home to see my parents. We've always talked via comms every few weeks, but—you never know who's listening to those, right? The signals are programmed to catch words that sound disloyal to Earth. Maybe I could get away with some of it because they've invested so much in educating me, but my parents? I hadn't really been able to talk to them, to hear everything they had to say, since I was six years old."

Abel remembers what it felt like to be separated from Mansfield for a long time, back when he still thought of him as "Father." The ache is both indescribable and undeniable.

She continues, the words spilling out of her in a rush. "I've always felt like being chosen for Cray made me special. I love it here, but I never asked myself how it felt for my mom and dad. Not really. The teachers tell you here what an honor it is, that your parents brag about you—and they do—but to Mom and Dad, Abel, it's like I was *stolen*." Virginia stops, hand to her lips like she can't believe she dared to speak the words. But she doesn't hold herself back for long. "Historically, this is not a new issue for my people. Same crap, different package. I couldn't see it for myself before, but now I do, and it makes me mad as hell. Why couldn't they have taught these classes on Earth instead of here on Cray? Why is it so 'impossible' for my parents to ever visit, when game traders can get landing clearance any time they want?"

These are rhetorical questions, but when humans ask them, it's often because they want to hear the answer repeated by another. "They bring top students here to weaken the bonds between family members and to ensure that your strongest loyalty is to Earth rather than to any individual."

Virginia blinks. "Okay, wow. I knew that, but—I hadn't put it in those words. But that's it. That's it exactly."

"Your anger at Earth is understandable, but that doesn't require you to come with me," Abel points out. "Unless you mean to join Remedy? I should warn you, they're unlikely to accept a new recruit in the middle of an operation on this scale." Given the number of ships he saw attacking the *Osiris*, Abel considers it likely that this is Remedy's most ambitious strike yet.

"Join Remedy? Are you having some kind of system meltdown?" Virginia mock-punches him on the shoulder, then winces and shakes her hand. "Ow. You're way more solid than a human."

"My skeleton contains—"

"Yeah, okay, I know about your skeleton, that was stupid of me, skip it. My whole point is, no, I'm not joining a bunch of terrorists. But that doesn't mean I want to go back to the way I was before either. Growing up here, you're always taught to look for new solutions, new ways of doing things. To search for new truth, you know? Instead they've been lying to us the whole time. After what I've learned, and what I've realized about how I grew up, I'm done being lied to. Whatever's going on out there behind that distortion field—it's real. It's true. And it's something the people in power don't want us to know about. That means I *need* to know all about it, right now." She pauses and catches her breath. "Did that make sense?"

"Yes, it did." Abel could point out that her reasons for wanting to join him are almost entirely emotional, no matter how understandable those emotions might be. But so are his own reasons. Besides, she's correct on one strategic point: Having a second person along will improve his odds of a successful resolution. "If you're sure it won't raise suspicion—"

"It won't." Virginia lights up. "I'm an *amazing* liar."

"Don't admit this to too many people."

She laughs out loud as she jogs off to prepare, and calls over one shoulder, "You're developing a sense of humor, you know that?"

It wasn't a joke; it was a sound tactical suggestion. Nonetheless, Abel smiles.

15

NO SOONER HAS THE *OSIRIS* APPEARED IN THIS NEW system—whatever and wherever it is—than the comms crackle. *"As your new commander, I should introduce myself."* He has an accent Noemi recognizes from Stronghold. *"You may address me as Captain Fouda. The final actions of the bridge crew were to inform us that many main shareholders of the Columbian Corporation are on board. Is one of them perhaps brave enough to speak to me?"*

Mansfield steers his hoverchair to a small console with a screen, only a few steps from where Noemi stands. He pokes the controls with a bony finger. "This is Burton Mansfield, creator of every mech in existence—many of which are headed up to destroy you even now. What's happened to our captain?"

"Something you'd better hope doesn't happen to you." The screen coalesces into an image: a man in his late fifties, with coloring much like Captain Baz's, sitting in a

high-backed command chair. Thin white scar lines etch one side of his face and run down and around his neck, maybe evidence of a long-ago battle. He and the ragged crew around him all wear simple, functional clothes in shades of beige; Noemi remembers that from some of the Remedy bombers she and Abel saw on Kismet. *"The great Mansfield,"* Fouda says slowly. *"More interested in mechs than in humans, it seems."*

"What's your business here? Remedy's always had an argument with Earth," Mansfield says. "Not with private citizens."

"It is private citizens who make the choices that render Earth a tyrant instead of a motherland." Fouda steeples his hands in front of him. *"Private citizens who hoard the precious resources that could make life easier for billions throughout the galaxy. But this—this goes beyond any hoarding, any theft, in the history of humankind. You've hidden a Gate. You've hidden a world."*

Noemi hadn't had time to think this through, but instantly she sees that no other explanation would've made sense. Somewhere in this system, there's another habitable planet, capable of supporting thousands or millions or even billions of people.

But nobody else knows about this world. Earth's government shared the information exclusively with its wealthiest, most privileged citizens, allowing nobody else even the possibility of traveling to this system. The desperate Vagabonds and hardworking miners will never be told this place exists. This new chance at life isn't for everyone. It's being hoarded selfishly—or it was before Remedy got here. Noemi experiences one moment of solidarity with Remedy, when she feels like they're on the side of right.

That vanishes when Fouda says, *"We'll keep the members of your crew who can still be of use. Otherwise we have no need to maintain a supply of leeches."*

She sees Delphine trembling with fear, and gets even angrier for her than Noemi is for herself. These people have done something impossibly selfish, but nobody deserves to be murdered in cold blood.

"Our sensors show you in one of the mech chambers," Fouda says. *"Easy enough to vent the oxygen from those rooms, I think."* Wails of terror go up from the passengers, but Noemi just gets furious.

She moves to the console, shouldering Mansfield's chair to the side so roughly it rocks. "Listen to me. If you think the passengers on this ship are passive prisoners, think again. We're here in numbers. We're armed. You may control the bridge, but trust me, we still have ways to make this a *very* unpleasant trip for you. So you'd better stop threatening us and start negotiating."

"Or else your mechs will get us? We turned every mech we found to scrap metal. Remedy is made up of human fighters.

Real *fighters. We don't send toys to do the work of warriors."*
Fouda laughs. *"Don't worry. It shouldn't take more than ten minutes to die. A reasonably merciful end, and more than you deserve."*

More screams, and weeping. Delphine sways on her feet as though she is about to faint. Noemi banks her fear down deep. If only the passengers had taken the water supply or the engine room, something worth bargaining with.

She still has a card to play—the worst one ever, but it's all she's got.

Noemi says, "Ten minutes should be plenty of time for our blasters to punch a hole in the hull. Since you'll have shut off the airflow to this area, you won't be able to adjust the ship's internal pressure in time. You'll lose hull integrity and destroy the entire ship. I forget—when people are exposed to outer space, do they implode or explode? One or the other. Either way, I'm sure you'll enjoy it."

His smile fades. *"You'd kill yourselves, too."*

With a shrug, Noemi says, "Once you've cut off our air, we're dead already. Might as well take you with us."

The pause that follows stretches out for several seconds. Actually Noemi has no idea whether they could punch a hole in the hull; blasters might not be that strong, even if set to overload. As long as Fouda isn't sure either, though, she's able to negotiate.

At last he says, *"We'll address the issue of your survival after our arrival on the world you call Haven."*

Haven. A small thrill goes through Noemi at the sound of it. Whatever else is going on here, another home for humanity's been found, and that has to be good news.

"If you only planned to kill us, you would've done so without contacting us," says Gillian, who's come to her father's side. "You want something, obviously something you thought we'd be motivated to give you for our own sakes. I'm guessing those are our landing coordinates. Correct?"

Fouda looks impressed. Noemi probably does, too. She'd known Shearer and her father were intelligent, but that's the kind of leap Abel himself might've made....

"Yes," Fouda says. *"We wanted the coordinates."*

Gillian nods, keying them in. "No point in having you land us far away from the supplies. We're going to need those."

"We'll see." With that, the Remedy captain shuts down the link.

A second of silence follows, broken by Delphine saying, "Noemi, are you a security expert? You seem very useful."

Gillian answers for her. "Let's say that Miss Vidal's a last-minute addition to the party."

"Why didn't we have a security expert?" demands Vinh, who can't be blamed for feeling angry but seems determined to aim that anger in all the wrong directions. "Humans in charge of protecting us instead of just those damned mechs?"

"The mechs can do the job," Mansfield says. His face is pale, his voice tremulous. "But Remedy brought more ships than we thought they had."

"And you shouldn't trust our new friend too much," Gillian says, turning to face Noemi. The gas-flame blue of her eyes seems as if it could burn through Noemi's skin. "She's a soldier of Genesis. The enemy."

A flush heats Noemi's cheeks. From the huddled passengers, she hears someone whisper, "Since when do Genesis soldiers show up on our side of the Gate?"

"Tends to happen when we get kidnapped," Noemi says. Gillian's hand moves to her bracelet, and Noemi feels a cold flash of fear, but she lifts her chin and keeps her voice even. "You need someone military right now. I may not be the person you would've chosen—but I'm all you've got."

After a long moment, Gillian exhales. "Fine. Make yourself useful."

How is she supposed to do that? Noemi thinks fast. "Well, first we need to take control of more of the ship than this." She gestures around at the mech tanks, hoping at least one other person in this room realizes how absurd this is as a home base. "What's both useful to us and close to this location?"

Gillian thoughtfully taps one long fingernail against the screen. "Passenger luggage hadn't all been distributed to cabins yet. So there should be clothing and such in the cargo bay seventy meters farther along this corridor. Next to that would be more of the supplies for our celebrations— champagne, chocolate, petits fours, so on and so forth."

Seriously? Noemi wants to shout. *You're counting party supplies as one of our big advantages?* But she bites back her tantrum. At this point, even champagne and petits fours count as food reserves. "Okay. We secure this corridor."

"How do we do that?" Delphine says, her eyes wide.

"We get out there with blasters and blow away anyone or anything between us and what we want." Noemi checks the charge on hers. Nearly total.

"You mean shooting people. We have to actually *shoot people* who will be *shooting at us.*" Vinh's fury hasn't abated; it's still ricocheting in every direction. He sounds more upset that he has to do real work with real risk than he is at the thought of taking human life.

"The Remedy members won't be shy about killing us," Gillian says to Vinh. "I suggest you adopt their attitude."

"We know what we have to do." Noemi gestures toward the door. "Are you guys going to do it or not?"

The passengers continue staring glassily at Gillian, who finally gives them a short nod. "Go. Hold the ship." She turns her head toward the tank in front of her, filled with its pink milky liquid. "I have work to do."

"Okay, everyone," Noemi says to the passengers, readying her blaster. "Let's go."

• • •

At first Noemi doesn't see so much as a single Remedy fighter; maybe not all the Remedy people involved in the Proteus battle boarded the *Osiris*. Still, they obviously have enough of a crew to bring the ship firmly under their power. The lifts have been locked down, plus most computer interfaces provide only minimal information and no controls beyond the nearly automatic: lights on, lights off.

"Don't suppose Mansfield or his daughter could get into the computer system and help us," Noemi grumbles.

"Well, they can't do everything," Delphine says, as though reasoning with a small child.

"They've done enough," Noemi agrees.

"I feel so sorry for them," Delphine confides as they hurry down the hallway to the next bend. "This must be even worse for them than it is for us."

"Why? Because being rich and powerful is such a burden?"

Delphine gives Noemi a look. "Because of Dr. Shearer's son, Mansfield's grandson. I think his name was Simon?

Anyway, he died about four months ago, from Cobweb complications. Only seven years old."

After a pause, Noemi says, "That's terrible," and she means it. She remembers Cobweb's blistering fevers, the sickly sweet delirium that dizzied her, the utter exhaustion that made it impossible to even walk. She thinks of the suffering she witnessed on Genesis—Mrs. Gatson's feeble coughing, the groaning patients lying helpless on the ground. Noemi would never wish such misery on an innocent child.

But grief should be, among other things, a call to compassion—a chance to recognize the pain in others' hearts mirrored in your own. It doesn't seem to have had that effect on either Mansfield or Gillian Shearer.

The *Osiris* has few corners; most corridors bend in gradual arcs. As their group takes the curve leading to the baggage stores, Noemi stops short in horror. Her first thought is massacre, but then she sees the wires poking from the severed limbs and torsos.

Dozens of mechs lie jumbled on the ground, all of them sliced down by blaster fire. A few of them aren't totally inactive; a Yoke keeps trying to brush away the detritus near where she lies, even though her hand has only two fingers left. A Baker stares up at the ceiling, blinking, his face passive. They're all broken beyond repair.

Noemi's destroyed plenty of mechs in battle. They aren't

like Abel—aren't people. Yet the sight of so many mangled limbs unsettles her.

If Remedy's fighters can do this to things that look human, does it make it easier for them to kill actual humans?

● ● ●

After securing the baggage area with a few makeshift trip wires, and grabbing as many edibles as they can carry, Noemi and her group make their way back to the mech tanks. The presence of Shearer and Mansfield makes this room their de facto headquarters, so this is where they'll need to take stock.

As the others begin bickering over whose box of chocolates is whose, distributing luxury clothing around, Noemi walks away to catch her breath. Mansfield sits in his chair, giving no orders, saying nothing, not even to Gillian, who's hard at work at a nearby terminal. He appears profoundly shaken, and Noemi knows why.

"Abel will never find us," she says.

Mansfield looks up at her, his face gone even paler. "You don't know that." His voice is hardly more than a whisper. "He has the intelligence to—to extrapolate from existing evidence—"

"What evidence? There's no ship for him to find. Remedy even blew away the station where the ship had been.

Then we flew through a Gate nobody in the galaxy knows about, one you must've hidden with some kind of distortion field, and now we're headed to a planet that's been kept so secret Abel would never, ever hear a word of it." She leans closer, every word as sharp as a knife's point. "You failed. Abel lives."

"That means you die." But Mansfield's threat has no venom to it. He's nearly broken, facing mortality as he must never have done before. Death will demand its due of him after all—and before too long.

"If I die, then I die to save both Genesis and Abel. That's fine with me."

Noemi walks away from him, between tall columns of mech tanks, half-expecting to feel the hot spur of pain in her arm at any moment. When the ampule blows, the poison will enter her body, and that's it. But Gillian Shearer keeps working hard at her terminal, not distracted by the strangeness around them. Apparently Noemi's death will have to wait until later.

One of the items grabbed from the baggage area was a ship entertainment device, portable within the hull. Delphine has set it in her lap and is eagerly tapping away at the screen. Her priorities could use some work. But she's the one passenger who's still friendly to Noemi, so maybe that lack of perspective is worth something. Noemi comes up and looks at the screen, which shows a list of available

holos, at least half of which seem to star Han Zhi. "You're…
searching for something to watch," she says slowly. "Now.
With all this going on."

"No, not yet. See, I had this idea." Delphine points at
the top of the screen, at a label reading OTHER ENTERTAIN-
MENT OPTIONS. "Remedy locked down all the essential systems, right? Entertainment isn't essential, so that's still
open to us. These portables are still hooked into the computer. And one of the options on the entertainment chan-
nels is FLIGHT PROGRESS. So if we go in here—" Jabbing at the
screen a couple more times, she brings up a diagram of the
star system that shows the *Osiris* clearly just shy of Haven.
A small square over to one side shows the view from the
principal bridge screen, in which a white-and-blue world
surrounded by many moons grows larger by the second.

"That's brilliant, Delphine," Noemi says sincerely. Just
because nobody's ever asked this woman to use her brain
before doesn't mean she doesn't have one. Her admiration
shifts into dismay as she begins realizing what's on this
screen. "How many moons does Haven have?"

"Fifteen! All of them in fairly close orbit, a couple of
them nearly as big as Earth's." Delphine claps her hands
together. "Won't the night sky look amazing?"

"Yeah," Noemi says absently. Her pilot's training has
kicked in, and she's estimating gravity, imagining vectors.

The thing about a planet with multiple satellites,

particularly when they're this large and orbiting this tightly, is that a pilot can't land without accounting for gravity wells. It's doable, but it's tricky, and the larger the ship, the more difficult it gets. Noemi would have to work to land her starfighter on this planet. Something the size of the *Osiris*—

"Shearer!" Noemi calls across the room. "Who was going to land this ship?" *Please let it be the original crew. Remedy's probably left them alive; they can handle it—*

Over her shoulder, Gillian replies, "They'd specially programmed an Item for the task. What difference does it make?" Apparently piloting isn't one of Gillian Shearer's many concerns.

The *Osiris* shudders, and Noemi sucks in a breath. "It's about to make a big difference."

"What's happening?" Delphine looks from Noemi to the viewscreen and back again. Haven's white surface grows ever larger until it completely blots out the stars.

People cry out as the ship lurches beneath them. Noemi yells, "Do we have access to any stabilizers? Any force fields?"

The shaking finally gets Mansfield's attention. "The tanks are braced with emergency force fields, of course—"

"How do we use them to brace ourselves?"

Gillian has caught on. She dashes to her father, pulling his hoverchair back toward the walls. "Just get to the tanks. Everyone brace themselves on one of the tank platforms!"

Noemi obeys this woman for what she hopes is the last time ever. On her heels, Delphine says, "It's going to be a rough landing?"

"You could say that."

It would be more accurate to say they're almost certainly going to crash.

People are already clustered near the bottom of this column of tanks, so Noemi quickly climbs the frame. An antigrav force field flickers on in response to the turbulence, trapping them all in a red bubble. That's okay; the force field makes her distance from the floor irrelevant. Delphine follows on the climb, even though her caftan nearly trips her up. Once they're close to the top, Noemi settles herself in the framework like a kid balancing on the monkey bars. All around her, the force field tickles with the faintest hum against her skin. When they hit a jolt, the field's going to get a lot stronger, but she'll deal with that later.

Not much later. From here she can still see the console Delphine was working at lying on the floor. There's nothing on the viewscreen now but whiteness.

The *Osiris* lurches violently. Noemi grabs the framework harder, by instinct, but she can feel the force field tightening around her in an almost painful grip. They've gotten close enough to the surface for artificial gravity to shut off. That's a standard ship function, normally an energy saver,

189

but here it's going to be deadly. Without internal gravity, everyone on board could be battered to death by the ship's ragged descent.

"Are we spinning?" Delphine cries. "It feels like we're spinning!"

It's hard to tell from the way it feels—the dizziness could just be panic, but the force field's hold mutes that. The evidence is all visual: boxes of chocolate and silk negligees, stylish shoes and monogrammed suitcases, tumbling around like bits of glass in a kaleidoscope.

We're going down, Noemi thinks. *We're going down hard—*

The first impact is the worst. Noemi's flung forward so violently her neck pops, her forearms slam into the framework, and the force field around her feels like it might snap her in two. Debris smashes tanks, strikes passengers, thuds against metal and bone. As screams fill the air, Gillian yells, too late, "Brace yourselves!"

A second impact slams into them, knocking out main lights and leaving only the orange emergency glow. Then there's a third impact. A fourth. They're skipping across the surface like a stone against water, Noemi realizes. Even the best skipping stone sinks in the end.

The *Osiris* strikes something—a rock, a ridge, no telling—and slides sideways until it begins to roll. Noemi closes her eyes and hangs on as they tumble over and over, debris flying in every direction. Something heavy within her force field strikes a glancing blow to the side of her head, and she feels the heat and wetness of blood at her temple. There's no up or down any longer, just a terrible dizzying rush that seems as if it will never end.

Finally, though, the ship makes one last flip and skids to a halt—upside down.

Noemi gasps as she looks down at what had been the ceiling of the tank room but is now the floor. She's clinging to the framework, only partly held up by the force field, which is no longer working at full strength; some of the fields appear to have shorted out completely. The console Gillian had been working at hangs uselessly from above. Below is a bloody, smoldering pile of dazed humans, broken machinery, and wrecked luggage. Main power flickers on again, then goes off, probably for good. In the dim orange emergency lights, the huddle below looks even more surreal and monstrous.

This ship will never fly again, Noemi thinks. *We're stranded here.*

Forever.

16

ABEL HAD ANTICIPATED THAT EARTH FORCES WOULD soon investigate what had happened near Proteus. However, he'd failed to anticipate the scale of the investigation.

"Did they send every ship on Earth ever?" Virginia grumbles from her place at the helm. She keeps the *Persephone* close to Halimede, one of Neptune's outermost moons. Her bright orange jumpsuit is the one flare of color in the otherwise darkened bridge.

"You're exaggerating for humorous intent," Abel says, "but this is a far larger search party than I would've anticipated, even considering the scale of the Remedy attack."

To his surprise, Virginia laughs. "You still don't get it, Abel. If Remedy had hit a Vagabond convoy, we'd see about one and a half scout ships out here taking readings. A luxury ship with Burton Mansfield aboard? Earth won't stop until they get to the bottom of *that*, I promise you."

"Your point is well taken. But this investigation is still limited."

That earns him a puzzled frown from Virginia. "What do you mean?"

Abel expands the relevant area on the viewscreen and lights up the vectors he's calculated as green shimmering lines against the starfield. "It's very easy to tell which direction the *Osiris* flew in. Once they're scanning that area, these ships should be able to pick up on the anomaly in the Kuiper Belt. If they were genuinely searching for the passengers, they'd be pursuing the *Osiris*, not merely gathering data on the Remedy assault."

"Oh, man. You're right. Why aren't they doing that?" Virginia scowls as if the search parties were personally offending her.

"My guess is that they've received orders not to. Why they got those orders, and from whom, I can only guess."

As a rule, Abel tries not to guess without good cause. Assumptions can be useful mental shortcuts, but they can also mask dangerous gaps in logic. Yet he finds it hard to dismiss his set of conclusions:

1. The anomaly they've detected must in fact be a Gate.
2. This Gate was built as a passageway to another habitable world, space station, or other place where large numbers of humans could live.

3. Whatever is hidden on the other side of that Gate is something only the powerful know about. Some of those powerful individuals were on the *Osiris* at the time of its disappearance—Mansfield's presence alone proves that—but others were not. Some of those left behind must intend to follow the *Osiris*'s path.

Given the limited investigation, Abel must conclude that whatever fear these shadowy others have for the friends and family who went ahead isn't as strong as their need to keep the secret.

Humans frequently (and inaccurately) speak of mechs as "cold-blooded," unable to care. It seems to Abel that humans deserve the term far more. Mechs don't have the ability to care; humans do, yet often choose not to care at all.

The *Persephone* remains where it is until the rotation of the planetary system gives the ship an obscured path to approach the hidden Gate. Once they're within range of the distortion field, Virginia gasps. At first Abel is confused, because he sees nothing but dark, starry sky.

Then he remembers, *Distortion fields are made to deceive electronic sensors. Not human eyesight.*

Swiftly Abel limits his vision to wholly human frequencies to see what Virginia sees—and there it is.

"We have ourselves a Gate," she says, "don't we?"

"Yes." But this is unlike any other Gate Abel has seen.

Most Gates are massive, built to be nearly indestructible, and they shine like the beacons of power they are. This Gate has been constructed to the same dimensions as any other, but were it not for the telltale shimmer across the center, it would be easy to believe it wasn't completed. No outer plating is bolted to the inner mechanisms of the Gate for long-term protection. Instead, the panels and circuitry are exposed.

"They haven't finished it yet," Virginia suggests.

"Possibly. Or possibly this Gate isn't meant to last for very long." When she gives him an alarmed look, he adds, "In relative terms. It would remain operable for fifty to seventy-five years, but that's still far less time than the other Gates will endure."

"Why did they waste time building some half-assed Gate? They're gonna wind up cut off from the rest of the Loop within a couple of generations."

Abel nods. "I suspect that's the idea."

Virginia goes very still as she sees the truth Abel's understood from his first look at this Gate: Whatever's on the other side isn't going to be a permanent addition to the Loop, one of the many possible homes for humanity in the future. Whatever world or station awaits them—it will be open for a select few, for a short time. Then it will be sealed off.

Something very precious lies on the other side of this Gate.

Several minutes pass before either of them speaks again. Once they're within a few minutes' travel of this ramshackle Gate, its messy workings beginning to fill the domed viewscreen, Abel says, "I have to make this trip, but you don't." Virginia's argument on Cray was vigorous and heartfelt, but he wouldn't blame her if she had reconsidered her decision after seeing the scale of the nearby investigation. "If you'd rather I dropped you off near one of the Saturn stations—"

"Forget it." She shakes her head as if waking herself up and leans over her console with refreshed concentration. "Maybe some people could walk away not knowing what's on the other side, but me? Virginia loves a mystery. I accept this about myself."

Abel has learned not to be deceived by her jokes. "You're a very loyal friend."

"If you get mushy on me one more time, I swear to you, I'll reprogram you in your sleep. You'll be singing 'God Save the Queen' every hour on the hour."

"You're joking." He waits for the response, then ventures, "... Aren't you?"

"Push me and you'll find out, Robot Boy."

•   •   •

The hours of their trip are uneventful. Despite this Gate's strange appearance, their voyage feels exactly the same as it would through any of the other Gates of the Loop. Neither Abel nor Virginia says a word until they finally spot the world on their sensors, and Virginia brings it up on the viewscreen.

"It's beautiful," she says as they take in the snowy surface of this unknown planet. Her tone is gentler than usual, softer. "It reminds me a lot of—when I was little, before Cray, sometimes we'd go up north and visit my grandparents way at the top of the Rockies. The snow would be a meter deep all around, as far as you could see."

Abel has already worked out the planet's orbit, its likely climate, how the sky would look from its surface. Its fifteen moons will make landing tricky, but the night should be illuminated by reflected light. "This is their summertime."

"Really? How deep does the snow get in winter? Don't answer that."

"Its orbit and rotation suggest minimal variations in the seasons," Abel adds. "I'd guess the average temperature fluctuates less than two degrees Celsius through the year."

This is the chilliest of the habitable worlds yet discovered. Stronghold is cold, but still warmer than this—just as lower Scandinavia is warmer than northern Alaska on Earth. Stronghold's arid surface makes snow extremely rare. Here, the atmosphere has enough humidity for blizzards and frosts. While the oceans he sees are smaller than those on Earth, they're still vast enough to provide ample moisture for this world. Fish likely dwell within those oceans, and trees adapted to the chill will produce fruit even in a snowy springtime.

This splendor they see matters little, compared to what they're not seeing. Abel says, "Can you detect the *Osiris*? I'm not picking it up on my sensors."

"Mine neither—though we know it's been here." She hits a panel on her console that makes hazy lines of orange appear on the starfield in front of them, crossing the new planet's white surface. The ionized trails mark the *Osiris*'s path. "Looks to me like they landed, terrorists and all."

"Do you think we should scan the surface?" Abel is careful not to give Virginia orders. Unlike Harriet or Zayan, she is not his employee, and her ego is sturdy enough to sometimes outweigh her good heart. As the possessor of a healthy ego himself, Abel understands how inconvenient it can be.

Virginia responds to the suggestion as swiftly as she would've rejected a command. Within moments, the screen fills with the image of the *Osiris*... or what was once the *Osiris*, and is now only a wreck.

"Oh, crap," Virginia says, even as she zooms in tighter on the image. "But—that looks survivable to me. Right?"

"I think so."

Abel feels oddly bifurcated. Half of his brain performs the necessary calculations, projects a scenario in which the pilot of the *Osiris* failed to account for the gravitational pulls of so many different moons at once, and is content to have solved the logical puzzle. The other half feels as though he has been plunged underwater for an hour or two, as long as his cybernetic lungs can hold out, and his body is now screaming for air as desperately as any human's.

Stay alive, Noemi, he thinks. *Stay alive.*

He doesn't send the same message to Mansfield, but Directive One ensures he has to look for his creator, too.

"I'll go down and search the surface. Look for Noemi, see if there are any survivors." He doesn't mention Mansfield by name.

"Whoa, whoa, hang on." Virginia spins her chair around to face him. "What's this talk about 'I'? We're a team, remember?"

"Any surviving members of Remedy or ship passengers will be desperate for an intact spacecraft. The *Persephone* should remain in orbit at all times, with a pilot aboard, to ensure it isn't stolen."

She crosses her arms in front of her chest. "Then why don't you stay while I go?"

"Because I am physically stronger, better able to operate in conditions of extreme cold, more powerfully motivated, and have greater mental capacity than you."

After a long, flat stare, Virginia says, "You really have zero concept of tact."

"I understand it. But I prefer honesty." He'd felt Virginia, who is well informed about cybernetics, would be able to accept these simple truths. Instead perhaps some nuance is called for. "You are of course extremely intelligent, given the limitations of a human brain."

"Stick with the ego, buddy. You *suck* at tact." Her mood has improved, but her position hasn't. "What if you get yourself blown up? Going alone is dangerous, Abel!"

"This entire mission is dangerous. The relative increase in risk upon leaving the ship is irrelevant."

At last Virginia sighs. "Fine." As Abel gets to his feet, she adds, "But I'm monitoring you the whole way!"

"I'd expect nothing less."

A few minutes later, the launching bay doors open and Abel flies Virginia's corsair down toward the surface, spiraling in a long arc. The moons' gravity wells tug at him like spiders crawling along their webs toward trapped prey, but he keeps the ship steady. Quickly the snowy planet becomes Abel's entire sky.

The *Osiris* stands out even from a great distance, its gold-and-terra-cotta surface vivid against the pristine snow. Although it crashed into the surface, leaving a kilometer-long gash of broken trees and upturned soil, the ship's structure appears largely intact. Abel readjusts his assessment of the crash. Assuming internal shock absorption and artificial gravity functions remained operational, most of the passengers are likely to have survived.

Noemi is alive. Probably she's alive. And she's strong enough, enterprising enough, to endure the aftermath of something like this—

He pushes away the thought. Even hope can't be allowed to ruin his focus. For now, he has to determine how best to infiltrate the wreck of the *Osiris*.

Abel brings the corsair in closer, swooping low to the ground until he's skimming just above the treetops and rolling hills. The conifers here grow dark blue needles instead of green, but otherwise they're not so different from pine trees on Earth. In the near distance, a spectacular mountain range scrapes the pale sky. Soon, the sunset will filter between the peaks. A waterfall flows down one of the nearer mountains, its crest framed by a shell of ice the color of beach glass. The path of that river can be traced to a large lake that borders a broad plain, which seems likely to be the planned site of the first human settlement; a large structure shows up on his sensors, but absent any life signs, so it's not important to investigate it at this time. While animal life is abundant in this planet's oceans, relatively few species live on land, and the air is occupied primarily by pale gray clouds of what seems to be some kind of marsupial bat. Everything about this planet appears both beautiful and benign. Abel understands why people would hope to settle here, why they would consider living with the omnipresent cold a small price to pay.

What he doesn't understand is how they overlooked every other danger sign. Because now that he's in the atmosphere, able to take his own readings—

This cannot be accurate across the planet, he surmises. The toxicity rates must be specific to this locality, through a mechanism as yet undetermined. Otherwise humans would never have attempted to settle this world. No doubt he just flew over one rare, uninhabitable area, one that begs for further study.

Abel intends to study it, later. His focus must remain on the *Osiris*, and on what and who he may find within.

He lands the corsair roughly two kilometers from the crash, behind the crest of a hill. Although he'd like Noemi to know he's coming for her, very few on board will welcome his presence. Remedy attackers won't be pleased to see him; Burton Mansfield would be—only because he could then attempt to capture his prize creation. Abel must remain undetected as long as possible. He puts on his white hyperwarm parka, holsters his blaster at the belt, and sets out just as sunset begins to darken the sky.

The terrain's rougher going in this area, with multiple boulders and dangerous scree hidden by the snow. The *Osiris* lies on the edge of a large plateau, near a sharp drop-off—and now that Abel can study the surface up close, he realizes deep crevasses may lurk underneath, hidden by the snow. So he slows his movements, examining every element of the path ahead.

The site crash is very near this planet's equator, which means twilight falls swiftly. The sky above becomes luminous with five visible moons, casting enough reflected light to glitter on the snow. He extrapolates orbits from his observations in the *Persephone* and realizes no fewer than three moons will be visible at all times, every night of the year. Nighttime is rarely very dark here.

Convenient, perhaps, for future settlers—but for Abel, it only increases his chances of being detected.

He stays low, following the terrain. When he reaches the ship itself, he reassesses its condition. Equipment will have been badly damaged, or may be unusable simply because it's affixed to what was once the floor and is now the ceiling. That will include hospital equipment, biobeds, anywhere an elderly man might be expected to rest.

Abel finds one air lock just above the line of the snow. He tries the automatic entry, but that's broken. So he presses in with all his strength until he's bent the seal itself, which allows him to painstakingly pull back the door. The effort is enough to tire even him. Once he's cleared enough room for him to squeeze through, he does so, adjusting his vision to the darkness within. The floor beneath his feet slopes sharply to the right, and is curved like the ceiling it used to be. Fortunately his sense of balance is not so easily undermined.

No intruder alarms go off. As he heads for the inner door, he reasons that any alarms may no longer be operational. This area of the ship would've been near main engineering, which is now completely nonfunctional and therefore unlikely to be a priority for Remedy. He may yet get in undetected. The panel to open the door out of the air lock, inverted, is high enough that he has to jump for it, but at least it works. Once it's open, stale air flows in and he eases out—

—to see a small huddle of people at the end of the corridor, each one armed and pointing straight at him.

Abel pulls back 0.17 seconds before the blaster bolts would've hit him. His weapon in his hand, he gauges whether to run out of the air lock and try a different entrance—but no, they'll be on the lookout for him now. Instead he fires, not intending to kill anyone, but he aims close enough for them to know he could.

Someone shouts, "You heard Captain Fouda! All passengers are to surrender immediately!"

So these are Remedy members. "I'm not a passenger," he calls back.

Another person yells, "You're not one of us!"

"I never said I was. But I'm not a passenger either."

A pause follows. Their confusion is rational enough, Abel decides. But how should he best present his case to them? If they're warring against the passengers, as seems likely, they won't think well of his coming here to save one.

A third voice calls, "Identify yourself!"

And somehow, this voice is one he knows.

17

NOEMI WINCES AS SHE TURNS HER NECK FROM SIDE TO side, but it doesn't feel like it's been injured. Only sore. The cut on her temple's not too deep either. She drops to the floor (once the ceiling), her silvery boots crunching against metal shavings and bits of debris. "Is everyone okay?"

For the most part it seems that they are. Delphine, like several other passengers, is crying and sporting a few cuts and bruises to rival Noemi's. Most of them cling to the tank frameworks like raindrops on a spider's web, shaken but not seriously hurt. Mansfield lies in his chair, which is tilted against one wall; he looks like a marionette with cut strings, his limbs slightly akimbo and no strength in his form, but he's breathing. The fields around the tanks kept them all alive.

The bridge probably had emergency field protection, too. Most of the rest of the ship won't have, though. Noemi says, "Some Remedy members probably died in that crash.

Maybe lots of them. So they're weakened. If we can pull ourselves together and get back out there—"

"Pull ourselves together?" Vinh sounds almost hysterical. "After what just happened? Are you heartless?"

"I just mean—this is probably our best chance." Noemi double-checks her blaster. Her hands are still trembling, but she suspects she can shoot straight. "Remedy has to be as messed up as we are. Maybe we can catch them off their guard."

A low, mournful cry startles her, as well as the others. The sound is coming from the once-unshakable Gillian Shearer, whose cheeks shine with tears. She's trying to climb up to one of the tanks she was working on earlier, one that has cracked and is draining pink goo down the sides. In the controls is set a diamond-shaped octahedron roughly the size of a large human fist, which is blinking in a strange pattern.

"Simon," Gillian sobs. "Oh, God, Simon, no."

That was the name of her dead child. Gillian must've been hit on the head so hard she doesn't know where she is, or maybe temporary amnesia just wore off and reminded her of her loss. Embarrassed for the woman, Noemi looks away—until she hears glass cracking.

She looks up. In the murky cargo bay with its dim orange emergency light, it first seems as though the leaking tank is splintering of its own accord. Then, through the gloom, she makes out a shape within the tank.

The shape of a tiny human hand pressed against the surface—

With a great crash, the side of the tank gives away. Fluid gushes down in a waterfall, soaking Gillian and splashing on everything nearby. In the rush, the shape of a human boy falls, too, hitting the floor with a heavy thud. Noemi stares as he tries to get to his hands and knees; he fails, maybe because everything's slippery but also maybe because he doesn't know how to move yet.

This isn't a little boy, Noemi realizes. *This is a mech....*

The mech raises his head. He has long red hair that stretches past his shoulders; he's sopping wet and completely naked. His features aren't totally formed yet; there's something soft about his face, something fetal, even though his height is that of a six- or seven-year-old child.

But it's still plain that he's terrified.

Gillian, pushing her damp hair back from her face, approaches the crawling mech. "It's all right," she says, trying to smile. "I'm sorry we had to rush—it's going to be all right—"

The mech says, in a shaky child's voice, "Mummy?"

Oh, my God. That's her son.

Her dead son.

Mansfield's always planned to put his soul within Abel's body and so be immortal. That means he must have some procedure or ability to record or store his soul—in effect, an entire human consciousness. Yet Noemi had never considered that he might use this power to preserve someone else, much less his own grandchild.

She looks up at the octahedron, now gone dark.

"Yes, that's right, Simon. It's Mummy." Gillian's smile pierces Noemi's anger with the woman. Nobody could be invulnerable to such naked pain. "We weren't supposed to wake you up for a while yet. I'm so sorry. Something's gone wrong, but don't worry. I'm here, Grandfather is here, and we'll take care of you. We'll put everything right later."

"My thoughts are noisy." Simon paws at his head. His fingers are slightly webbed. "Make them stop."

"That's because you're different now, but we can help you learn to handle all those thoughts." Gillian moves tentatively toward him. The wet, shivering child in front of her must bear almost no resemblance to the son she lost, but she holds her hand out to him just as she would've before. "Come here and let Mummy help y—"

"No no no!" Simon wails. "I don't want to!" Gillian stops where she is.

Mansfield pushes himself up with one arm. Noemi expects him to call to Simon, too, but he speaks instead to his daughter. "This one's botched."

Shaking her head fast, Gillian says, "No. It worked. It's *Simon*. Can't you see that?"

Simon presses his tiny webbed hands to either side of

his head. "There's all this talking in my head but it's not words."

Noemi's knowledge of Abel helps her understand what must be happening in Simon's head. "It's your programming," she says gently, crouching low as she approaches so she won't be any taller than the child. "You've got lots and lots of information in there that you can use."

"I can handle this, thank you." Gillian's tone could carve ice.

Probably Noemi is out-of-bounds. But what are the boundaries in a situation like this? All she knows is that she sees something—someone not very different from how Abel must've been when he was new. The thought tears at her heart and makes her want to do anything she can for him.

Maybe there's nothing to be done, because Mansfield croaks, "Gilly, you need to let this go."

His daughter ignores him, crawling half a meter closer to the shivering mech that is also her child. "Darling, come here to Mummy. I'll set things straight, you'll see."

Simon gets to his feet, unbalanced and shaking. Gillian freezes. No one else in the room says a word. He takes one step toward his mother, then another, and then he runs at her as fast as he can—

—at mech speed, which is too fast. He slams into Gillian so hard she goes flying backward, hits one of the broken tanks, and slumps to the floor.

At the sight of his mother's collapse, Simon screams—a raw, anguished sound—and rushes away crying. The door is now suspended overhead, flush with the ceiling rather than the floor, half open. Simon leaps to it, squeezes through, and vanishes, a wild thing lost in the wreck.

After a long pause during which no one so much as moves, Vinh says, "What the *hell*?"

Noemi agrees completely.

She hurries to where Gillian lies amid puddles of pinkish mech fluid. Although the force of that collision could've broken bones or at least knocked her out, Gillian's awake, only dazed. Noemi kneels by her side. She means to be helpful, if possible, but Gillian turns her head away. "Why don't you tell the others, Miss Vidal? Tell them all what we've done." Her voice sounds strange, difficult to read. Does Gillian feel guilty and want Noemi to condemn her? Or is she proud of their resurrectionist powers, no matter how imperfect the execution might be?

Noemi keeps her voice low and sticks to the most immediate facts of the situation. "What you were going to do to your father—save his soul until you could put it into Abel's body—you did that with your son when he died. You were creating a new body for him, one just like Abel's."

Gillian laughs, a hoarse, unhinged sound. "Model One A is already obsolete. My father needs him just to tide him over until we can make the next generation of mechs."

"The next generation?" Noemi asks.

"Organic. But they're so much more than merely organic. They're Inheritors." Slowly Gillian sits up, wincing as she touches the side of her head. "That's the brand name our marketers came up with."

"Inheritors?" Delphine comes closer; her tear-streaked face is clouded with confusion.

"This doesn't concern you," Mansfield snaps. He's managed to push his hoverchair level again, though it must have taken some of the last strength he has. "The rest of you, get away from here."

The other passengers scurry to the far corners to take stock of their cuts and bruises. Noemi doesn't budge. Apparently neither Mansfield nor Gillian expects her to; she already knows too much.

"We need more time to perfect the technology." Gillian puts out a hand in the universal gesture for *slow down*. "So much more time. I wasn't going to transfer Simon until we'd triple-checked everything—made sure we had backup storage—but the tank cracked in the crash, and I wasn't going to have a chance to draw a full genetic backup from his bone marrow. I had to do something." Her lower lip trembles. "Now he's out there. He must be terrified, and Remedy could go after him at any moment."

They put a soul into a mech's body. They've actually made it happen. Noemi doesn't feel outraged the way she does whenever they threaten to do this to Abel. The mech Gillian made for Simon hadn't finished growing; it had no soul of its own to be displaced. But just knowing that it's possible—that they really could've done this to Abel, if this hijacking hadn't separated them forever—sends a shiver down her spine. "So it wasn't just about Mansfield," Noemi says. "You planned to make the whole family immortal."

"We could've shared this with the entire galaxy eventually." Gillian pulls herself together. "We intended to do our final experiments here, on Haven. My father would've been able to get used to his new body without others asking difficult questions. We wouldn't have had the same... let's call them, regulatory concerns. We could've emerged through the Haven Gate with news of Inheritors for all the greatest minds of the galaxy—with the promise of immortality for the best and brightest. Now it's all in ruins, like this damned ship."

Noemi's head reels from the possibilities. "If you can make other, uh, Inheritors, why did you bother going after Abel?"

It's Mansfield who answers. "For the consciousness to transfer, you need a genetic link," he rasps. "We've yet to prove precisely why—one body ought to be as good as another—but we've demonstrated it in the lab twenty times over."

Twenty consciousnesses, lost to experimentation. Lost to Burton Mansfield's fear of death.

He continues, "And it turns out, you need young genetic material to build an Inheritor. Abel is one—the most primitive Inheritor, but still, he counts. I built him when I was forty-nine years old, and he came out perfect on the first try. So I didn't bother trying to create another until Abel was lost. By then, I'd aged too much. My genetic structures weren't as strong. Honestly, it's a miracle I was even able to make him at forty-nine—the cutoff would be closer to forty, for most. So he's my only chance." His voice cracks. "Was my only chance. Lost now."

Noemi feels exactly zero pity.

He pulls himself together and speaks to his daughter. "You jumped the gun, Gillian. You have to have nerve for this business. You can't panic the first time things go wrong."

Gillian bows her head, ashamed to have been found wanting. Noemi can't believe he's talking like that about his daughter's fear for his grandson's soul.

Mansfield takes a deep breath, then coughs. "Get Simon back. Recopy the data and sample the marrow. Then do what you can with the version we've got."

"Yes, Father." Restored to a sense of purpose, Gillian lifts her head and squares her shoulders. Mansfield has given her permission to think of this replica of her son as something less than human. Is that all there is to it, for her?

Noemi turns to Gillian and pitches her voice for her alone to hear. "I realize this is a weird time, but we have to reestablish our base on this ship. There might be some localized emergency force fields we could use to seal our area off. And if we set up force fields, that would keep Simon close to us instead of exposing him to Remedy."

Hope animates Gillian's face. Regardless of what her father said, she still holds on to some belief that Simon might be saved. "Yes, we have to do that. We should get started."

Some of the passengers have already brushed themselves off, getting ready for action; these few are hardier than their privileged lifestyles would suggest. They're ready to follow as soon as they have a leader—and somehow, that leader is Noemi.

"Abel might still make it," Mansfield murmurs. "He's smart enough. Curious enough."

Noemi shakes her head.

"That's what you want to believe, I'm sure. But Abel has a fate," Mansfield says, maddeningly calm again. "I know that. I designed his fate for him, wove it into his very DNA. His fate is in every strand of his hair and every cell of his skin. His fate is fixed. In the end, he'll always return to me."

"Like he always obeys your orders?" The last direct order Mansfield gave Abel was a command to shoot Noemi in the chest. She's still alive and well.

"If he won't come for me," Mansfield says, "he'll come for you."

"He's not coming." Not even Abel could follow a trail this obscure.

"Miss Vidal," Mansfield rasps. "You're giving up hope. I haven't."

"You'd better." She says it savagely, to herself as much as to him.

Gillian puts one hand on Mansfield's forehead. "Father, don't strain yourself."

"I'm all right." His eyes, frosted by old age, fix on the broken tank. "Can't we find my things? I'd like to have them about me, if—I'd like to have them."

Things, Noemi thinks. *Not people. I wonder if you've ever really loved anyone.* He doesn't even look up at his daughter.

Oblivious to Noemi's reaction, he continues, "Really, I should've brought the Kahlo. Abel would've enjoyed seeing it again. He always liked that painting so."

He can look at Abel, see that Abel loved a piece of art— behold an impulse that intelligent and human and *alive*— and still want to use Abel up and throw him away like a piece of trash.

Noemi's unsure of Second Catholic Church doctrine,

sometimes; she's still discovering her individual faith. As she stares down at Mansfield, though, she realizes at least one thing the Church taught her is utterly true: There are worse fates than death. One of them is to live without the capacity for love.

Abel could never have saved you, she thinks. *If you'd ever seen him for what he is, you might've saved yourself.*

• • •

Noemi fans out with the other passengers, doing what they can to secure the area once more. Force fields still work and can be activated to cut off various corridors; Noemi's able to plant a few homemade incendiary devices in some key locations, including an auxiliary fuel gauge. She notices that the passengers never leave her completely alone. Maybe they think she'll abandon them the first chance she gets.

But where's she supposed to go? To Remedy? They know her as the maniac who threatened to kill them all earlier today—

—no, yesterday. Isn't it? Everything's blurring together. Her body ran on pure adrenaline for hours and hours, but has now run out.

Just get back to the mech area, she tells herself. Simon has to be captured, but she's in no shape to do it. Remedy has to be negotiated with, but first they'll have to reestablish contact; with comms damaged if not destroyed, that next contact seems likely to be a while away. If the force fields hold long enough for them to regroup, they might be able to devise a strategy to take the ship back from Remedy, and then—

Better to ask that question later, assuming she ever gets the chance.

Noemi stumbles over something on the floor-ceiling, glances down, and sees that it's a chandelier. Or it was a chandelier. Now it's just an etched-crystal hazard underfoot. *Who puts chandeliers in a spaceship?*

Irritated, she turns the corner that leads back to the cargo bay. In the distance, she can just make out a small huddle of passengers under one of the emergency lights. They can't see her at all. One of them whispers, "How much longer is this going to take?"

"Two days, maximum," says Vinh. "That's what I was told, pre-treatment."

Treatment? And how much longer is *what* supposed to take?

"So we wait, then," says the first speaker. "How do we stop that Genesis girl from going after Remedy in the meantime? It's a risk we don't have to take."

Vinh shakes his head. "I doubt we'll have to worry about her much longer."

Noemi knew the passengers didn't much like her. She hadn't guessed they were counting on seeing her dead.

18

ABEL CANNOT EVALUATE ENOUGH VARIABLES TO DETER-
mine how probable, or improbable, this circumstance
might be. However, it is not impossible.

"Identify yourself!" shouts the same voice he's heard
before.

From the place where he huddles behind a chunk of
wreckage, he checks the timbre and inflections against his
memory banks, rechecks them, and nods. "My name is
Abel," he calls. "And yours is Riko Watanabe."

Footsteps come closer—just one person, small of build.
A few people mutter, *"What are you doing?"* and *"Come
back!"* but she doesn't stop until she sticks her head
through the door. Despite the tan fatigues and goggles
she wears, he identifies her easily. It is indeed Riko.

She has the same short haircut she did before, the same
wary expression. This is hardly a joyous reunion. But she

lowers her blaster rifle, which in the current situation counts as a good sign.

"This is Abel," she calls to her fellow Remedy fighters. "The mech I told you about, who broke me out of prison." After another moment's hesitation she adds, "He's a friend."

Abel is not sure he would've described her as a friend; he is even less sure whether he's willing to apply that term to anyone who freely takes part in terrorist activities.

Under the circumstances, however, he must take what allies he can find.

"What are you doing here?" she asks. "How in the worlds did you find us?"

"I was following Burton Mansfield, who is holding Noemi captive," Abel replies. "I believe they are both on board." Impossible to tell whether they survived the crash—but he refuses to speculate further. Not until he has more data. He won't give up on Noemi one moment before he has to.

Riko nods slowly. "Mansfield's on the manifest, yeah, but Noemi? How did he manage to take her hostage? Hadn't she gone back to Genesis?"

"It's what humans would refer to as 'a long story.'" Abel risks getting to his feet. The Remedy members closest to them tense and clutch their weapons tighter, but nobody aims at him. They appear to have trust in Riko's judgment. So he adds, "All I ask is for a chance to look for her."

"Fair enough," Riko says. "In return, we could use a little help."

"Whatever I can do."

Whether Abel likes it or not, for now, he's on Remedy's side.

· · ·

The extravagance of this ship struck Abel as wasteful, even cruel, as soon as he saw its golden exterior. However, he had failed to account for the danger presented by that gaudiness until he encountered the interior, and had to follow Riko and her party across endless rooms and hallways littered with the remnants of chandeliers, champagne flutes, and stained glass.

"Think of how many people could've been fed for the cost of that thing," says Riko as she nudges one of the larger crystal prisms aside with her booted foot. "Four dozen? A hundred? And how many chandeliers are there on this ship?"

"I haven't seen enough of the layout to come up with an informed estimate." Abel remains within half a meter of Riko, partly because she is his guide, but also because the other members of Remedy are far less sure of him than she is. They've hung back approximately three and a half meters, following at a careful distance, muttering among themselves. He doesn't object. On a crashed ship, on an isolated world, it would be tactically unwise to needlessly antagonize terrorists.

Riko Watanabe is such a terrorist. He has known that since her connection to the Orchid Festival bombing. Yet this information refuses to fully process when she gives him a small, uncertain smile; the expression makes it clear how young she really is, no more than twenty-one or -two.

"We've got to introduce you to Captain Fouda," she says. "Explain to him exactly what you can do. With your abilities, you might be able to help us get some of this ship back in operating order. I mean, I know it's never going to fly again, but at least we could get it running as some kind of shelter."

Given the extremity of the crash, Abel doubts this. "While landing, I observed a large structure some kilometers distant. The most rational conclusion is that this was the shelter built to house the first settlers here. Your group should send a team there to investigate. It would undoubtedly provide better long-term shelter than the wreckage of this ship."

"Of *course* they had homes waiting for them already. These bastards would never come here to settle the land through hard work like any other colonists." Riko clutches the blaster rifle she holds a little closer. Abel's very glad not to be standing in its crosshairs. "The Columbian Corporation's fancy-pants passengers are too good to dig ditches, or winter in ready-huts. No, they have to be surrounded by luxury at all times, taking a luxury ship to keep them comfortable until everything's set up to their satisfaction. It's ridiculous!" She nods toward an ornate mural on one wall, an upside-down portrait of the falcon god Horus.

Her irascible mood seems likely to cause complications. Abel keeps his tone even. "You're entirely correct that the use of resources for this ship was wasteful. But the *Osiris* has been destroyed. We should move on."

Riko stops midstep. The orange emergency lighting catches the spikes in her short black hair and the thoughtful expression on her face. "I know you're right, but it's hard," she finally says. "I've been fighting this kind of evil since I turned ten. Moving on—that's never been an option before now. It's always been about tearing something down. Never about building something up."

"New worlds offer new possibilities." Abel continues making his way through the *Osiris* corridors, and as he'd anticipated, Riko stays with him.

By this point on his visit to a new vessel, he's usually mentally constructed a rudimentary layout of his surroundings. Form follows function, and the fundamental structures within any station or ship usually conform to basic templates. The *Osiris*, however, is different. Its corridors wind and bend in illogical ways, more like the tangled streets of an ancient city than anything designed. Even though maps of the ship are posted at every stairwell and lift, they won't illuminate without main power, which means they're as useless as the nonfunctioning lifts and the stairs that seem to dangle from the ceilings. They walk through a spa with saunas and hot tubs hanging down uselessly, a ballroom with ridged acoustic tile that would've caught sound from beneath efficiently but is tricky to walk on, and finally a banquet hall with long opalescent tables dangling from the ceiling.

This extravagance seems likely to set Riko off on another tirade against waste. Abel decides the best means of distracting her would be to obtain more information for his own purposes. "Since you were ten?"

Riko, still gazing at the shimmering tables above, doesn't quite catch it. "What?"

"You said you'd been fighting since you were ten. I wouldn't have thought Remedy accepted recruits that young."

"Oh. They don't. That was a—turn of phrase, I guess."

Abel considers what he knows of the human subconscious. "Even turns of phrase mean something."

Taking another couple of steps, her boots crunching against broken glass from the tables, Riko shakes her head. "I was ten the first time I saw a food riot on Kismet. You wouldn't think people would be starving a couple miles from a beach party, would you? But we were. You could hear people laughing while you lay in your bed hungry."

"Kismet hides that fact very well." Even Abel, who is hardly naïve about humanity's unkindness to its own, hadn't realized hunger would be one of that planet's problems.

"There's plenty of fish in the ocean, and humans can eat most of them, but you have to serve the resort guests first." She stares into an unseen distance, focused only on the past. "Tons of edible fruit grows, both on Kismet-native trees and the ones we imported—the palms with their coconuts, or the bananas, or the pineapples—but the resort guests love those. They eat it all. Every alcohol distiller in the galaxy ships to Kismet, plus we were able to ferment the local bellfruit into a wine so sweet you could hardly believe it. And the guests drank all the wine. Every glass. Nearly every drop. You could spend every day harvesting food, every night serving it to the guests, and then at the end of it go to bed ravenous."

"That sounds difficult." Hunger is one human experience Abel can't share. He doesn't think he's missed much.

"We have it pretty good on Kismet, at least better than the Vagabonds or laborers on Stronghold. But compared to the people who visited our world to eat and drink the best we had, and who lay around on our beaches all day while we slaved to make them comfortable? We were desperate, and we knew it." Riko leans against the wall, and suddenly the blaster rifle looks too large for her slim arms and tiny frame. She could be a little girl playing soldier, if Abel didn't remember the sight of dead bodies after the Orchid Festival bombings. "Sometimes the anger boiled over. We'd have riots. Strikes. Lootings. Then the mechs would sweep in and arrest or kill however many people it took to restore order. I saw friends of mine die. Can you imagine what that feels like?"

Abel thinks of Noemi lying on her biobed, nearly delirious with fever, Cobweb tracing white lines on her skin. "Yes," he says to Riko. "I can. Let's move on."

She furrows her brow, clearly aware she's troubled him in some way. However, she says nothing, for which he's grateful. Maybe tact has more utility than he'd realized.

Once they've secured this door, Riko pushes open another in a corner to reveal something far less dramatic: a bathroom, or what was once a bathroom before it turned upside down. As he looks at the ceiling, he says, "Relieving wastes may prove to be ... a challenge."

Coming up behind him to take a peek, Riko groans. "*Shit.*"

"I wouldn't."

A faint creaking farther down the corridor compels

Abel to focus his hearing on that area. Two more creaks and he's certain. He straightens and gestures at Riko, who takes another moment to realize what he's already determined: Someone is walking toward them.

The other Remedy members are far behind. This person is approaching from ahead.

It could be another Remedy patrol, Abel surmises from Riko's reaction, which is wary but not panicked. He follows her lead, keeping hold of his weapon but not yet aiming it.

The footsteps enter human aural range, and Riko's dark eyes widen. However, the proximity of this unknown intruder is less disquieting to Abel than the arrhythmic steps; this person isn't walking through the corridor as much as stumbling through it. A sound-wave analysis indicates that this individual is barefoot and extremely small, possibly even a child.

Not an attacker, then. More likely a passenger injured and dazed from the crash. But even a small adult, if injured, dazed, and afraid, might fire if startled. Abel remains on alert.

A figure appears in the doorway, silhouetted by the dull orange emergency light. The individual is male-presenting, approximately one hundred fifteen centimeters in height, with childish body proportions, pale skin, and long hair, unclothed. Abel's analysis stops short when he recognizes the scent in the air. The smell is one he remembers vividly from the first moments of his life—the oddly sweet odor of mech generation fluid.

When the figure takes another step forward, emerging from shadow, Abel sees a small boy holding what appears to be a severed mech hand, as if it were a plaything. Mansfield has indeed begun making child mechs. The boy mech's features are ill-formed, incomplete. This one wasn't finished yet. How can he be awake?

"I'm lost," the mech says. In his voice Abel hears emotions he's never heard from another mech, even himself—terror, misery, and confusion. "I don't know where we are."

"We're on a ship called the *Osiris*." Abel keeps his tone even and calm. He's aware of Riko gaping at the two of them, but she says nothing. "Can you tell me your model designation?"

"I don't know what that is." The mech curls into one corner and flops down, just like the exhausted child he appears to be. He hugs the severed hand to his chest.

"Your name," Abel says gently. "What is your name?"

"I'm Simon Michael Shearer," the mech announces automatically, as though called upon in school. His fear and disorientation remain strong. "Why are there things in my head? There are thoughts in there I didn't think."

Shearer. Gillian's surname is now Shearer. She lost a child some months ago. The information filters through Abel's mind, combines with his knowledge of Mansfield's obsession with immortality and his and Gillian's hopes for organic mechs, and delivers a conclusion that radically changes the situation: This can only be Gillian's son, Mansfield's grandson. Simon, not Burton Mansfield, is the first individual to have his consciousness resurrected in a mech body.

Abel is looking at the only other mech in the entire galaxy who possesses a soul. Every other day of his existence, Abel has been totally unique—and he knows better than most that to be unique is, in some sense, to be alone.

He's not alone any longer.

Empathy floods his emotional capacities, and he holds out one hand. "It's all right," he says gently. "You've changed, Simon. It takes a while to get used to changes. But I can help you."

Simon trembles, afraid even to hope. "Can you get all the weird thoughts out of my head?"

That must be how his childish mind interprets data input. How different is a human brain from a mech one? What feelings are the same, and which have changed? Abel longs to know the answer to these questions, but Simon is not yet in any condition to answer. "I can't remove them," Abel says, "but I can help you understand them. Focus them."

"But I want them gone!" Simon shoves himself up to his feet. He's on the verge of tears. Abel takes another step toward him, only for Simon to skitter backward, stumbling on his chubby, childish legs. "Make them stop!"

"I would if I could." Abel can do nothing for this child but exist alongside him. At least Simon will never endure what Abel endured; he will never be alone.

"You said you could help!" Simon shouts, and he lifts the hand up, as if to throw it at Abel. It wouldn't be much of a projectile, but it's the only weapon the little boy has.

"Watch it!" Riko gets between Simon and Abel, even though protection seems unnecessary. "Just calm down, and—"

Simon shoves Riko, hard. Harder than any human child could. She flies across the room, hitting the wall solidly before slumping down semiconscious.

At the sight of what he's done, Simon makes an anguished cry that seems to pierce Abel through. The child doesn't understand his own body or his own mind. He is in a world literally and figuratively upside down.

Before Abel can stop him, Simon runs out again, escaping deep into the wilds of this crashed ship.

To pursue or not to pursue? Abel must remain here. Riko's the only member of Remedy who is loyal to him at this point; if he goes running through the *Osiris* without her, other members are likely to fire on him. He badly wants to help Simon, but he can't do that by being destroyed or disabled.

Abel will set things right with Simon, but that has to wait.

Instead he goes to Riko's side, where a brief examination reveals she isn't injured beyond being winded and stunned. But as he checks her over, part of his brain plays another thought on infinite loop: *I am not alone. I am no longer alone.*

• • •

Captain Rushdi Fouda of the Remedy fighters has only an honorary title. Within 3.2 minutes of meeting the man, Abel has determined that Fouda's never been in military service. He enjoys the idea of command more than the reality—and surely whatever preconceived idea Fouda had of leadership looked nothing like this: control over only isolated pockets of a crashed ship on an unfamiliar world. The *Osiris* might as well be a city under siege, with certain streets and neighborhoods barely held, others destroyed, others hostile.

Nor is Fouda eager to welcome a mech into his ranks.

"It's like I told you, Abel's no ordinary mech," Riko insists. She puts one hand to her forehead for a moment, wincing.

Although Abel determined she suffered no traumatic brain injury from Simon's attack, she's nonetheless had a headache for roughly the past eight minutes. It occurs to him to wonder about the toxicity zone he flew through on the way to the *Osiris*; exposure to such elements would certainly harm humans in short order, and a headache could be the first symptom. However, given that everyone else seems fine, Abel surmises that the dangerous zone is far enough away, and that the air filtration aboard the *Osiris* must still be functioning as adequate protection against any effects at distant proximity.

Riko continues, "Abel rescued me and Ephraim Dunaway from prison."

"Dunaway," Fouda sneers. He is a wiry man, sinews showing through leathery skin. Faint lines tracing a pale pattern along his face and neck. "One of the *moderates*. Your good friend."

"We tried to find common ground, yeah." Riko's cheeks flush with anger. "The point is, Abel got us both out."

"He's a mech." Fouda gestures at Abel the way he might indicate some mess that needs cleaning up. "In the end, that means Burton Mansfield controls him."

"He does not," Abel says. This point is one he must make himself. "Mansfield has tried very hard to recapture me, and has failed. I came here to investigate him, and to search for my friend Noemi Vidal, who may have been brought here as his prisoner."

Riko interjects, "Noemi's the Genesis fighter I told you

all about! We can't pass up the chance to have an ally from Genesis."

Would Noemi be so quick to join up with Remedy, especially after this? Fortunately this is not a question Abel has to answer. To Fouda he says, "All I ask is a chance to look for her, perhaps also to search for whatever data Burton Mansfield may have cached on board." *And to check on Mansfield*—though that's something he prefers not to admit even to himself.

Fouda huffs. "You came here with demands, then! Well, we have demands of our own first."

"That's reasonable." Abel stands in military at-ease position, calculating that this will influence Fouda to believe him obedient. He *will* obey if it doesn't conflict with his core programming; he can readily assist in restoring power, for instance. Getting the information he needs—finding Noemi—is worth some labor. However, it is not worth slaughtering innocents.

But Fouda says, "We'll start small. See if we can trust you." When Abel inclines his head—again, like a subordinate—Fouda calms even more. "The passengers are pretending to be soldiers. They've set up force fields, blocking us from some areas of the ship. That's how they hide from us. We don't intend to let them hide any longer. A mech like you—you'd be effective against them, wouldn't you?"

"Yes." Given sufficient firepower, Abel could outfight large numbers of humans, but elects not to mention this. Fouda should not have that information before he decides whether to give Abel a weapon.

"Fine." Fouda nods at him. "Let me show you what we're up against."

He leads Abel down a side corridor, toward what must have been a separate operations room. Their entire path is lined with mech bodies.

Dozens of them. Possibly hundreds. Some have literally been smashed to pieces—an arm here, a torso there—making an exact count difficult. Abel prefers not to try. Mechs bleed as humans do, and the scent of the air has that metallic tang to it. Some blood spatters the walls and has puddled on the concave ceilings-turned-floors. Internal coolant fluid pools there, too, milky-white streaks amid the red; it doesn't mix with blood.

"We couldn't leave them for Mansfield to turn against us," Fouda says. He's not apologizing for this; he's proud of it. "The Charlies and Queens went down hard. The rest? Easy."

"I should imagine so. They weren't combat models." A Nan lies at Abel's feet, her scorched face staring up blankly at him. Nans nurse children and the elderly.

"What, do you feel bad for your fellow machines?" Fouda mocks him.

"No." He doesn't. Abel knows better than any human the vast gap between regular mech minds and his own capacity. They don't have *selves*; the bodies on the floor weren't alive in the way he is. "But I find it interesting to evaluate how humans treat those who present no threat to them."

Fouda isn't pleased enough with this answer to continue the conversation.

Only one display in the ops room still functions, but it reveals the layout of the *Osiris* in thin green glowing lines. Abel realizes they haven't inverted the layout to reflect the ship's upside-down state and quickly punches in the commands to do so.

Fouda seems irritated he didn't think to handle that himself. But he only points to a few areas glowing orange. "Here, near their mech chambers and the baggage hold—that's where they're holed up. Closed-off areas with force fields."

"Standard force fields?" Every ship has them amply distributed throughout, in case of hull breaches. When Fouda nods, Abel says, "Those are easy to activate, but just as easy to deactivate. It can't be accomplished remotely, but a small, targeted strike team would be able to handle it—provided you have someone with sufficient knowledge of field mechanics."

"We do now," Fouda says. "We have you."

Abel's in no position to argue.

One of the consoles overhead blinks, and the Remedy fighter monitoring it (from a repair ladder) says, "We've got another mech patrol incoming."

Fouda scowls. "More? How many of them can there be?"

"Quite possibly thousands, extrapolating from the size of the vessel," Abel says. Nobody thanks him for this information.

The Remedy crew member continues, "I can't tell for sure, but it looks like—like the mech patrol is working to clear a major corridor that would connect the passenger territory to the bridge—Corridor Theta Seven. That would give them a clear path to attack us."

"Except that it goes straight through the theater," Riko says, and a few people laugh. Abel's unsure why, but at this point asking seems more risky than useful.

Fouda's begun to grin. "Then let's put on a show, shall we? We'll take out their mechs, and any passengers foolish enough to be with them. And this time, we're going to fight fire with fire." He turns to Abel and says, "To kill a mech, we send a mech."

Again Abel considers protesting and decides against it. He doesn't *want* to protest.

Even though he disagrees with Remedy, he's ready to take up arms against the passengers—because the passengers are the ones holding Noemi captive. Mansfield has her even now. If he believes Abel will be unable to find Haven, which would be a rational assumption, Burton Mansfield has no more need to keep Noemi alive. She's in mortal danger, and the only things standing between her and Abel are a set of force fields and a mech patrol.

Neither will remain standing long.

Fouda says, "Do we have your oath that you'll help us, mech?"

Abel looks up evenly at him. "Yes. You have me."

19

NOEMI RUNS THROUGH THE FIELDS NEAR THE HOSPITAL, *surrounded by the dead on every side. She has to be careful not to step on their swollen bellies or trip on their outstretched arms. Their Cobweb-streaked faces stare blankly up at the sky, searching for the God who didn't come. Despair fills her—utter futility—and yet she has to keep running, because there's something she could do, something vitally important that would put it all right. But she can't think what that something is.*

She stumbles and falls to the ground, between the corpses. Her revulsion turns to shock as she realizes the body lying next to her is Esther's. Why isn't Esther in her star? They left her in a star so she would always be warm, so she would always burn bright.

Esther turns her head to face Noemi. She is alive and dead at once, which somehow makes sense. The expression on her face is so completely, utterly Esther's—compassionate and yet knowing, almost as if she were about to say I told you so.

Instead she whispers, "It's your turn."

Noemi startles awake, disoriented for the few seconds it takes her to remember where she is: lying on a pallet of evening wear and luxury pillows, in a cargo area of a shipwreck where half the people on board are trying to kill her, and the other half seem to be plotting the same. The scant few people in the entire galaxy who care about her are literally billions of miles away, while she's stranded on a planet almost nobody else in all the worlds even knows about.

Being disoriented was better.

She breathes in through her nose, out through her mouth. This is the first quiet moment she's had in days, her first chance to center herself. Probably it's the last she'll get for a while to come. Possibly ever. Noemi closes her eyes and tries to meditate.

What are you fighting, Noemi Vidal?

Remedy, even though I partially agree with them. The passengers, even though I'm allied with them. Gillian Shearer and Burton Mansfield. My situation on this planet—

Noemi catches herself. She's naming trees and ignoring the forest.

I'm fighting my own powerlessness.

And what are you fighting for?

My life.

That's not it either. Noemi accepted long ago that she might have to sacrifice herself for what was right. Saving Genesis—protecting Abel from Mansfield's plot—those things together are worth dying for. So why is she still living?

I'm fighting for my free *life. For the chance to decide how I'll live and how I'll die.*

She's not sure she's ever had that power. Here, in this wreckage on Haven, she finally has it—and nothing else.

Noemi sits up and glances around. The cracked tanks hover against the walls and hang from the ceiling, tinted semi-opaque by the remnants of pink goo, strangely and unsettlingly biological. In a few intact tanks, mechs float in stasis, their silhouettes suspended above; Noemi has no idea when they'll awake, if ever. Other passengers slumber nearby, all of them seemingly dead to the world. The hard work they've done the past day or two—Noemi can't tell how long it's been—that's got to be the most effort they've put into anything, ever. They're too exhausted to be kept awake by their unfamiliar surroundings, or by the occasional dull thud or vibration through the ship that marks Remedy's efforts to keep their territory.

The chill in the air has deepened. Although the hull

of the *Osiris* in this section of the ship has kept out the worst of Haven's deep winter, the cold has begun to sink in. Probably the ship's climate controls were destroyed in the crash, and Noemi wonders whether other areas of the hull were more severely damaged, letting the weather in. Rubbing her hands together briskly, she examines the pile of clothes serving as her bed. Maybe something better got tucked in between the layers. A white jacket looks promising; it hangs too big on her shoulders, but it's warm, so it will do.

"Noemi?" whispers a tiny voice. It's Delphine, who's curled on the far edge of the pallet under what looks like a fur coat. "How are you?"

"Scared and angry." Hungry, too, but Noemi doesn't mention it. They have nothing to eat but petits fours, and at the moment she thinks if she ever eats another of those things again, she'll puke it back up. "Trying to figure out where we go from here."

"We wait for the mechs to come and save us," Delphine says. "From the Winter Castle. They must be on their way."

"The 'Winter Castle'?"

Delphine's face lights up. "Our settlement. Mechs built it for us ahead of time, so it would be ready when we arrived. Beautiful suites of rooms with windows overlooking the mountains—hot springs and steam baths—fully stocked and equipped kitchens—entertainment libraries—oh, just everything. All we'd have to do is move in our clothes and our decorations, and we'd be right at home." Her voice turns wistful on the last words.

Noemi says, "And there were other mechs there, too?"

Delphine frowns. "Of course. Bakers for the kitchens, Tares for the medcenter, Williams and Oboes for music, Foxes and Peters for—well, you know, and—"

"How many mechs?"

After a moment, Delphine shrugs. "Hundreds, I'd guess. Maybe even thousands. Enough to overpower Remedy, for sure. They'll be along to get us soon."

Noemi nods, keeping her doubts to herself. There's no way to know if those mechs saw the crash. No way to be sure they'd mount a rescue mission even if they did see it. Independently assessing a situation like that, coming up with a plan, electing to follow it—that's higher-level initiative than mechs generally manage on their own. Unless Mansfield programmed them very, very specifically, those mechs are still sitting in that Winter Castle, smiling vacantly, waiting with eternal patience for guests who will never come. They might wait there for the next three hundred years.

Yet the passengers seem content to bide their time.

"Are you feeling okay?" Delphine props up on her elbows. Her frizzy hair has been freed from its earlier topknot and has become a soft dark cloud around her face. "You're not feverish, are you?"

"I don't think so. It's hard to know. We're all so tired and sore and dirty—" Noemi makes a face. She'd just about kill for a shower.

"As long as you're feeling all right." Delphine's expression is difficult to read. Her concern seems sincere, but why should she be so worried about Noemi's health? It's not like they don't have other problems.

Noemi's distracted by the sight of Gillian Shearer walking toward the center of the room, away from the small pallet that now serves as Burton Mansfield's sickbed. The woman looks years older than she did when the voyage of the *Osiris* began; fear has already carved new hollows in her cheeks. Her dark-circled eyes search the room for something she isn't finding, but Noemi notices her taking a few seconds longer to gaze at the octahedron data solid left over from Simon's tank. That diamond-shaped thing stores information, and once held her son's soul—maybe still holds a copy of it.

Mansfield told his daughter to write Simon off and make another one. Looks like she can't accept that idea.

Honestly, Mansfield's attitude is the less surprising one. Noemi can imagine Darius Akide claiming that Abel could be easily replicated, like any other machine. That's the way people think before they've seen a soul inside a mech—or, in Mansfield's case, before they understand what a soul truly is. Maybe Gillian Shearer understands.

Noemi rises from her pallet and runs a hand through her black hair, pulling herself together as much as possible. Delphine's eyes get big—the universal sign for *What are you doing?*—but Noemi ignores this and crosses the room for a talk.

It takes Gillian several seconds to notice her. Those gas-flame blue eyes have never seemed more intense, more eerie. "You're still here, I see."

Where would I go? Noemi manages not to say. "The Columbian Corporation didn't plan for anything going wrong, did they?"

Irritation flickers over Gillian's face. "If they had turned things over to me—or at least to my father—we could've taken appropriate steps. We would've had proper security around Neptune. Would've had mech patrols ready and waiting to handle any intruders on board. We'd even have been able to program fail-safes in case of a crash. But no. The others resented my father's power and political influence. They relished being able to outvote him just for the sake of doing so. My father's foresight—his genius—he would've saved us all."

Noemi keeps her opinion on that to herself. "When you say 'the others'—who are you talking about, exactly?"

"Other great leaders in technology, politics, commerce," Gillian says dreamily. "The best of the best. The finest Earth's population has to offer."

Crossing her arms, Noemi says, "I'm not sure the actual best humans alive would hide this planet from millions in need."

It doesn't faze Gillian. "You can't imagine the future we'll build. I wouldn't expect you to."

As badly as Noemi would like to tell this woman exactly what she thinks, something else is more important. "Have you found Simon?"

Gillian freezes the way people do when they step on glass—seizing tight with pain. "No."

"Have you been able to figure out what part of the ship he's in?"

"We think he crossed into Remedy territory a while back." When Gillian presses her lips together so tightly they turn white, her agony is so palpable that Noemi feels an echo of it deep within her ribs. It's not Gillian she hurts for as much as it is Simon.

"I could go after him," Noemi says quietly.

"I'm perfectly capable of putting together my own team." Gillian's words are clipped, and she won't look directly at Noemi any longer. "You don't have a role to play here."

"Yes, I do. I'm the only one besides you who understands that this Simon is really your son."

When Gillian turns back to Noemi this time, her face is stricken. "I can—I can do it over again—"

"Maybe you can," Noemi admits. She doesn't know how a soul can be copied over and over—whether it's still really a soul at that point or not—but for now she sticks to what she knows to be true. "It doesn't change the fact that Simon's soul is in *that* body, though, right? He's just a little boy, and he's alone and afraid. Even if you can make another, what happens to this Simon matters. It matters to him, and it matters to you."

"It doesn't matter to you," Gillian says. "Is this meant to, what, drive a wedge between me and my father?"

It is, at least in part, but that doesn't change the truth of what Noemi's saying. "It does matter to me. Because when I look at Simon, I see Abel."

"Abel's different. Abel is for my father."

Temper sparking, Noemi says, "How is that different?"

"Because my father is different!" A few sleeping people nearby twitch and stir; Gillian puts one hand over her mouth, like that will keep her feelings inside where no one can hear. "The Columbian Corporation—this expedition—it offered us the chance to explore the Inheritor project and bring it to its fullest potential. Have you asked yourself how the galaxy would change if the best of us could lead longer lives? Could, in effect, be immortal? Scientific discovery could be accelerated. Artistic works could be created on a grander scale than ever before in history. The skill of an elderly master surgeon could be given to a young, steady pair of hands. The strategy of an admiral who's lived through four wars could be put into a body that's never suffered a wound. But war itself might end, if the negotiators on either side had lived through enough wars before to know how best to avoid it. Have you considered any of that? Have you asked yourself what society might become if our most powerful were no longer motivated by fear?"

"No," Noemi says. "I can't get that far with it. I get stuck on the part where you talk about 'the best' of us. Who gets to decide who that is?"

With a slashing gesture, Gillian says, "Enough."

She's right. This debate isn't helping Noemi's cause. Time to get back on track. "We agree on one thing. We agree that Simon matters. He shouldn't just be—thrown out so you have to start over."

Although Gillian winces, she haltingly answers, "My father—he's made it clear that I should—"

"You don't have to disobey your dad. Let me be the one to go after Simon, bring him back. Then, maybe you can put him right."

Gillian stares at Noemi so long that the whole conversation seems to have backfired. Noemi wonders if she's going to get tossed out an air lock into the snow. At this point she's almost willing to take her chances.

Then Gillian takes out a small scanner and offers it to Noemi. "The scanner is calibrated for mechs. Several are still functioning, at least partially, and Remedy may be using some Tares or Yokes, but..."

"It helps." Noemi closes her hand around it. "Thanks."

Instead of responding, Gillian simply turns back to work on her datareads. The console that might've been more useful dangles from the ceiling; in the deep shadows of night, it could be a gargoyle or a vulture, a dark hulking shape over them all.

•   •   •

The boundaries between the passengers' part of the ship and Remedy's sometimes shift as force fields blink on and off. Power supplies must be as damaged as everything else on the *Osiris*. Noemi walks slowly, scans every room before she enters it, and puts her hand out to test whether the air feels particularly warm, or charged with static electricity; both are signs of a force field in the area. She has no intention of winding up trapped on the wrong side of a boundary line.

Might not be so bad, she thinks as she crawls through one half-collapsed corridor toward what upside-down signs tell her was the grand ballroom. *I could walk up to*

Remedy and go, Hey, I'm from Genesis, we're kind of on the same side here? Except for the part where I don't believe in terrorism, and—

Noemi sighs. She's better off not switching sides at this point. Neither group on this ship likes her much, but at least she understands what the passengers want from her and has earned a little goodwill. If she can find Simon, her stock with them might go even higher.

But her main motivation is looking for someone who's scared and alone, someone who's closer to Abel than anyone else she's ever likely to meet. She'll never see Abel again, never get a chance to explore the mystery of what he is. All she can do is help Simon in his name.

She stops crawling, hit by a wave of sadness so intense it makes her breath catch in her throat. Noemi had believed she'd made her peace with the idea of never again seeing Abel. When she left his ship for the last time, she understood then it would be forever. Nothing that happened in the past several days could've changed that. That one glimpse of him through the hologram—even that was more than she should ever have expected to have again. As horrifying as that moment was, she still treasures it, holds it close. All that ugliness was transcended by the sight of Abel's face, just once more.

If he had found her—rescued her, and they'd been together again—

What would I have felt?

What could we have been?

She pushes the thoughts from her head. There's no point in wishing for what can never be, no matter how... how beautiful it might've been. Abel's on the other side of the galaxy, forever safe from Mansfield, and that's reward enough. She needs to concentrate on saving Simon, and on keeping herself alive.

Once she's through the narrow passage, Noemi gets to her feet and brushes dust and grit from her forearms and knees. She grimaces as she realizes some of it got down the absurdly low front of her jumpsuit. *Why would anyone design an outfit this impractical, much less...*

Noemi pauses, one hand still on the cowl-neck of her jumpsuit, when she hears a faint electronic beeping. Grabbing the scanner from her makeshift utility belt, she sees a small red light pulsing on its screen.

Military training brings her hand to the holt of her blaster before she stops herself. If this is Simon, he's unarmed. He needs to be approached as a friend.

If it isn't Simon—well, any other intact mechs probably aren't a threat.

"Simon?" she calls softly as she takes a step forward. Crushed iridescent ceiling tiles crunch under her boot. "Simon, we met earlier. Do you remember me?"

Movement farther down the corridor makes her go still. Her eyes discern the shape of a little boy sitting on the floor, as if playing with toys. When she creeps forward, one orange beam of emergency lighting turns on; the glow falls across Simon's face, revealing his unfinished features; it's worse than she remembered, although it's hard to say how. Something about the contrast between the blank, masklike visage and the anguish in his eyes makes it terrible. He sits amid a ghoulish display of destroyed mechs, at the center of severed heads and limbs that look all too human in the dim, eerie light.

But Simon's steadier than before. Somewhere he found a gray mech coverall and put that on, rolling up the sleeves and legs almost comically. That part, at least, really seems like what a little kid would do, and when he speaks, he sounds less panicked. "I remember you."

"My name's Noemi. Your mom sent me here to look for you."

That makes him frown. "Mummy did this to me." He paws once at the side of his head. "She put the voices in here."

"She was only trying to make you better, after you were sick," Noemi says, which is the kindest way she knows to put it. "You had Cobweb. I've had Cobweb, too. I know how terrible it feels."

He doesn't care. Little kids forget about feeling sick after they're well—though maybe *well* isn't the word for what Simon is now. "It helps if I talk back to the voices."

"Okay," Noemi says. She just needs to agree with him, to keep agreeing until he calms down enough to return with her to his mother. "What do you tell them?"

"I tell them I'm mad. That I'm mad at the whole world. They want to help me."

Her skin prickles with fear as she hears motion. Noemi hurls herself toward the nearest corner, grabbing her blaster, prepared for Remedy fighters—

—and instead sees mechs. More than a dozen of them, all standing there vacantly, apparently at Simon's command.

Only one Charlie is fully intact. The others are fragments of their former selves: a Zebra with one arm torn off at the elbow, a Jig with half of her face burned away to a metal skull, a Peter who hobbles along on legs stripped almost entirely free of flesh. Real blood and pale coolant spatter their blank faces and ripped clothing. These are only machines—not like Simon, nothing at all like Abel—but that doesn't help. In some ways it's worse. Noemi would feel compassion for wounded humans but these twisted, grotesque figures only horrify her. Every instinct tells her these things are *wrong*.

The stripped skin, the blood—that's just the damage she can see. How badly broken are they on the inside?

Simon's plastic face twitches, rapid spasms at his half-formed eyebrows and too-narrow mouth, until he manages something like a smile. "They're my friends," he says, and his voice is breaking up, frequencies missing from the sound, making it all too clear he's a machine. "They like to play chase. *Watch.*"

As one, every single mech lunges toward Noemi.

There's nowhere to run. She throws herself back into the collapsed tunnel and wriggles through as fast as she can. Bare metal fingers close around her ankle, dragging her back, and she screams. One kick and that's one off her, she's through the tunnel, but they're ripping through the wreckage after her.

Go go go go go. Noemi races down the corridor, leaping over a crushed chandelier, one hand on her blaster. When she gets to a corner, she turns and fires. Green blaster bolts slice through the air, taking out one of the Bakers, but the other mechs pay no attention. They continue on, single-minded in their pursuit.

Noemi runs even faster, pushing herself to her limit. Ahead she sees an upside-down sign proclaiming that the theater lies ahead. *Okay, a theater, that's a large space, maybe I can put some distance between us there.*

The theater is the closest thing to a safe space she can find.

A glance over her shoulder reveals the mechs still

gaining ground. There ought to be differences in the way each model moves—Noemi knows this from battle—but there aren't. Every single mech is coming after her in precisely the same way: with Simon's off-kilter, shambling, too-fast walk.

They're moving as one, she thinks amid her fright. *They're behaving almost like—like an extension of Simon's mind.*

20

THE PATROL ABEL LEADS TOWARD THE THEATER ISN'T large—only six Remedy fighters, five of whom show signs of discontent at being asked to follow a mech. The sixth fighter, however, is Riko, and he hopes their trust in her will translate into a modicum of trust for him.

He can't stop thinking about the force fields throughout the ship, the ways they may be booby-trapped, and how every single one of them is helping to hold Noemi hostage. She'd attempt to escape if possible—he remembers the cruel way she was suspended in the force field, hating her helplessness nearly as much as she must have—but that would only put her in even greater danger. If she hit the wrong force field—

It's as though Abel can *see* it, this horrible thing that may not even happen: the explosion ripping through Noemi, tearing through her skin and bone.

Continue moving, he tells himself. *Dwelling on negative possibilities won't help Noemi.*

As they edge their way through the semidark corridors, weapons at the ready, Riko quietly asks, "So you talked to Ephraim?"

"Yes. I reasoned he was the person most likely to be of help to Genesis at that time."

Riko drops her eyes. "And he seemed—Ephraim was all right?"

"He indicated nothing to the contrary." Abel reviews his memory files. The expressions on Ephraim's and Riko's faces when speaking of each other do not match anticipated reactions for former colleagues, or even friends. He tests this hypothesis by adding, "Ephraim seemed unhappy when he spoke of your departure."

Riko's cheeks flush, and Abel has his answer. She must see recognition on his face, because she quickly says, "It didn't last long. It couldn't have lasted long. Probably it shouldn't have happened at all."

"The two of you are very nearly polar opposites," Abel says. "When we all parted on Earth, I was under the strong impression you didn't even like each other."

This wins him a sidelong glance from Riko. "Noemi's a soldier from Genesis. You're a mech from Earth. I bet you guys didn't hit it off at first either."

Abel and Noemi met while trying to kill each other. "Your point is well taken."

"I'm just glad he's all right. That's all." Riko winces and rubs her temple. "Thinking about this is giving me a headache."

Loud clattering around the curve of the corridor alerts Abel only a fraction of a second before the humans hear it, too. As he rounds the corner, Abel brings up his blaster—

And stops. The damaged mechs before him aren't combat models. Williams are musical performers; Sugars are cooks. Obviously they aren't part of the passengers' attack team, but then what are they do—

The Sugar's fist connects with Abel's gut before his sensors have fully registered the motion. He slams into the wall, hard, his blaster falling to clatter at his feet; he's thrown off as much by surprise as by the force of the blow.

Stunned, he attempts to collect himself. How is a Sugar in warrior mode? She shouldn't be programmed for that.

But now the William's on him, barreling toward Abel at full speed. This time Abel manages to duck out of the way, but his confusion has intensified. Non-warrior mechs should not fight beyond very basic defense of humans— hardly more than a push or a shove—but the Sugar has picked up a heavy metal bar from the debris and seems intent on beating Abel to bolts.

She swings. Abel catches the bar in his open palm, ignoring the impact that sends pain shooting from his wrist to his shoulder. He closes his fist around the bar and pulls it backward, hard; the Sugar doesn't let go, which means he slams her into the ceiling. Her body drops to the floor, twitching erratically. Only now does he see that the entire back half of her head is missing.

The William charges again, and Abel swings the bar around to strike him in the hip, collapsing the joint; as the William model falls, he bashes its head. It drops beside the Sugar, completely still.

"Is that all they've got?" says one of the Remedy fighters, with so much bravado he seems to believe he was part of this fight. "If those are the only mechs the passengers can send after us, they're down to nothing."

"Perhaps." Abel frowns as he rises from the destroyed Sugar and William and reclaims his blaster. "But the larger group of mechs still lies ahead."

According to Abel's instrumentation, the mech patrol is very close, but still on the other side of the nearby theater, perhaps two levels down. He hurries faster through the corridor, motioning for the others to follow.

One quick jump brings him to the level of the stage door, which he's able to pry open with both hands. Abel slides through the narrow opening into near-total darkness; only a few emergency lights at the very bottom of the theater shine at all. He adjusts his visual frequencies to assess the area. The stage itself hangs above him, a gaping space with its old-fashioned velvet curtains drooping beneath. While theater seats remain in mostly neat rows at his head level, underneath the tiers of balconies curve across each level, an image reminiscent of a nautilus shell. The acoustic curve of the theater's ceiling has become a bowl-like floor many meters down.

As Abel prepares an estimate of the exact distance, he hears the banging of a door, and a thud—like someone dropping from that overhead door onto one of the lowest balconies. More noise follows, footsteps multiplying upon one another: The mech patrol has infiltrated the theater. Soon they'll attempt to punch through to Remedy territory.

Instead, Abel intends to punch through them—and clear his way to Noemi.

Without waiting for the other Remedy members to climb through the door, he pulls his blaster, magnifies his targets, and begins to fire.

A Tare model, head badly damaged, somehow operational as it rounds the curve of the balcony: One shot from his blaster and it goes down in a spray of sparks and blood.

A Charlie, completely intact but unarmed, running with great speed and direction—but not toward a door: Abel fires, takes that one down, too.

"What's going on?" Riko demands from her place below.

"I have no more data than you do."

"Is that robot for 'how would I know'?"

"No, although that question is entirely valid." Abel focuses his main attention on the jumble of mechs in the darkness beneath, whose movements make no sense but are too controlled to be random.

They're not yet trying to get through to Remedy territory. These mechs have some other target.

Keeping his blaster ready, he swings the crosshairs forward to the very front of the group, past the far end of the spiral of mechs, all the way to their target.

The human backlit by the distant emergency beacon glow is approximately five feet six inches in height, female-presenting, with chin-length black hair. Her build—her movements—even the way she runs—

Abel goes through all the measurements, because he must be sure. He can't trust his own sensory input; surely it's only showing him what he wants so badly to see.

But every detail lines up.

Identification confirmed.

Abel leans through the door and shouts, "*Noemi!*"

She pauses for one instant, her expression unreadable. That moment is almost enough for the other mechs to catch her, but she begins running again even as she yells back, "*Abel?*"

Within 0.72 seconds, he's assessed every possible means of rescue and made his decision. He leaps from his vantage point at the stage, plummeting at such an angle that he's able to grab one of the golden curtain ropes on his way down, tugging the end down after him.

His feet land on the curved surface beneath as silently and gracefully as a cat. Immediately Abel vaults up to the next level, his path intersecting with Noemi's. She's running toward him, a shadow and then herself. When she flings herself into his arms, they collide so hard he nearly loses his footing.

She's here. She's with me. It is the simplest, most basic of facts, and yet Abel has to register it over and over. His consciousness can't fully process her presence after so many months of longing; he should run a diagnostic later. For now he can only hold on to her.

Noemi gasps so sharply that he first thinks she's in pain—but she swings up her blaster and fires behind him. When Abel turns he sees a King mech within two meters of them smoldering and stumbling backward. She destroyed it only a second before it would have destroyed them. His reaction to seeing Noemi again has overridden his most basic safety protocols. They must leave the area of immediate risk before his malfunction endangers them further.

"Hold on to me," he says. She does. He jumps back down

to the rope and grabs it; Noemi doesn't have to be told to hang on to his back. They've been here before. As fast as possible, he climbs hand over hand, lifting them both up and away from the strange broken mechs below.

When at last they reach the top, Abel swings them onto a small balcony, only a few feet below the Remedy members. At first Noemi falls to her knees, breathing hard, as if unable to believe her own perceptions either. When he stoops beside her, though, she clutches him close—and finally, finally, he's in Noemi's arms again.

She buries her face in the curve of his neck, a sensation so trusting and tender that he can think of nothing else. He hugs her tighter and revels in the sight and sound and shape of her. This one moment is more joy than he ever thought to have again.

"Abel," Noemi whispers, and she pulls back. Their faces are close in the darkness, and he remembers their one kiss with fresh vividness. "What are you doing here?"

"Retrieving you, of course."

"You shouldn't have come after me. Mansfield—when he realizes you're here—" She pauses. "He's about to die. Any day. Any hour. He's completely desperate."

Directive One throbs like pain within him, commanding him to save his creator, but Abel ignores it. "Whatever risk I faced couldn't compare to the danger you were in. I had to find you."

Noemi laughs once, though tears are filling her eyes. "So you just found a hidden spaceship and a hidden Gate and a hidden planet? No big deal?"

"I had to come," he says. For him, it's that simple.

This time her laugh sounds more like a sob, and she hugs him even more tightly than before.

Abel wonders again if he was damaged in the fight, because his thinking remains disordered. Her embrace overrides his ability to concentrate on anything else.

Or maybe this is simply an effect of extreme happiness. Maybe this is what humans experience as joy.

"What's going on down there?" yells Riko. The bubble of unreality around them pops, reminding him of the many dangers of their situation. Normal function must return.

"I've retrieved Noemi," Abel calls back. "We'll need to take another path back to the bridge, but we'll rejoin you shortly."

"Noemi? Hi!"

"Riko?" Noemi laughs brokenly, in disbelief. "We'll be right there."

Together they get to their feet. She's breathing hard, clearly taxed to human limits of endurance. A wave of protectiveness sweeps over him. "We need to get off this planet," Abel says.

"You think?" Her smile is even more beautiful than he'd remembered.

Together they pick their way from that balcony into another corridor, one significantly more damaged than most of the others Abel's passed through so far. The temperature is 2.2 degrees Celsius colder, which suggests a nearby hull breach. He adjusts his assessment of the wreck again and posits that the most severely affected part of the *Osiris* must be nearby. This information is chiefly important, as it affects Noemi's well-being.

Her concentration focuses on something besides the deepening chill. "Genesis—Cobweb—were you able to—"

"I contacted Ephraim. He's working to get the drugs, to get as many members of Remedy involved as possible." Abel pauses to lift a broken strut and clear their path; Noemi walks under his upstretched arms. More destroyed mechs litter the floor, but he tries not to register them. "Harriet and Zayan are helping him arrange transports from sympathetic Vagabonds. And some of the Razers on Cray are searching their bioengineering labs for the modified Cobweb virus."

Noemi blinks. "That's—oh, my God, that's amazing." Her smile begins to return. "And Remedy's really mobilizing to help?"

"For a mass mobilization, Ephraim would need relay codes he doesn't possess. However, Captain Fouda has them, and is willing to trade them for my help in pacifying the ship."

"Trade? He wants to trade with billions of lives on the—" She catches herself. "Okay. We do this thing, then we get back and tell the whole galaxy about Haven. They tried to hide Haven, but we won't let them get away with it. Vagabonds, people on Stronghold, even the citizens of Earth—they deserve to know this world exists."

A set of calculations he's been running for several hours now requires discussion. "Haven's existence has the potential to affect the Liberty War."

"It could change *everything*." Noemi has apparently done the same calculations, and her human imagination has taken them further. "Yeah, Haven's cold—but it's habitable, and it's beautiful. Millions of people could live here. Millions, maybe even billions! If there's another home for humanity, and the galaxy knows it? They don't have to conquer Genesis. We could even take in people then, freely— whoever chooses our way of life—oh, Abel, this could be the answer to everything."

He wants to caution her that absolutely nothing can be the answer to everything. Earth has to have hidden this planet for a reason, one he has been unable to extrapolate. Also, if there are more pockets of toxicity like the one he flew over on his way here, that means some areas of Haven won't support human life.

But then Noemi hugs him again, and these sensible objections are sorted as irrelevant. He wants to store every sensation, every emotion, every millisecond. Despite all the tragedy and terror around them, he's been reunited with the girl he loves, and nothing can fully diminish the wonder of that.

Abel is of course aware that Noemi doesn't love him, at least not in the same way he loves her. This, too, is irrelevant. As he understands it, love is not transactional; it is a thing freely given. The joy is in the giving.

(Many human forms of entertainment seem to misrepresent this, but their information is of course inferior to actual experience, and so he disregards them.)

His absorption in her is interrupted by the sound of rustling overhead, within the damaged, twisted metal above. Noemi hears it, too, and they take a step back from each other as they look up.

To Abel's immense relief, the small figure peering down through the wreckage is Simon. He remains alive, and has even managed to find clothing. This shows attention to normal human social cues, no doubt a sign that Simon's soul is adapting to its new body. His…*nephew* can still be saved.

"Noemi," he says, "this is—"

"I know who it is." Her entire body has tensed. When their eyes meet, she whispers, "I realize what this means for you, but Simon—I think there's something wrong."

She has reacted too strongly to Simon's unfinished

appearance. Humans are sometimes overly influenced by visual stimuli. Abel takes her hand, intending to comfort her and facilitate a conversation between her and Simon.

But then Simon giggles, a high-pitched, off-kilter sound. "Peekaboo," he says. "Peekaboo!"

This alone should tell Abel nothing. But he has human instinct now, and that instinct is telling him Noemi may not be entirely incorrect.

He doesn't yet know what Simon is, only that Simon is not as he should be.

21

NOEMI'S STOMACH TWISTS WITH FEAR AS SIMON DROPS through the wreckage down to them. Above her she hears more rustling; when she looks up she sees a disembodied mech hand crawling along the ceiling like a spider. Simon's still playing with his toys.

Abel is oblivious. The sheer wonder of finding another mech like himself must've overwhelmed all his rational instincts. He holds one hand out toward Simon. "It sounds like you two have met," Abel says. "We're friends, just like you and I are friends."

"She's not my friend. I don't like her." Simon sounds like the playground bully. She wonders if that's the kind of kid he was, or if it's the kind he remembers hiding from. There's no telling how he behaved or what he experienced during his life as a little boy. What remains is neither human nor mech—and while Abel brought together the best of those worlds, Simon may be bringing together the worst.

You're just freaking out because of his—toys, she tells herself. *Maybe we can set things right. Abel can if anyone can.*

But she keeps her eyes on the hand crawling closer along the wall.

Meanwhile, Abel's *smiling.* "Noemi can be rude and abrasive at first meeting. You just have to get to know her."

"Abel," she says. The word comes out breathy and hushed; it's like the sight of Abel near this thing has stolen her strength. "Obviously you've met Simon, but I don't know if you understand who he is—"

"He's Gillian's son and Mansfield's grandson."

Noemi blinks. "Okay. The thing is, Gillian wants him back, and Mansfield wants him deactivated."

Abel turns back to her, and the expression on his face shocks her to the core. She hadn't known he could feel true rage. "Deactivated?"

Maybe just this once Burton Mansfield has a point? But no. She can't give up on Simon so easily. "He's doing strange things with the broken mechs. It's like he's—controlling them."

"They're my toys," says Simon. He tilts his head the way a curious dog might. The effect is much less endearing. "She doesn't like my toys. Noemi blows them up."

Abel brightens, like this is somehow a positive turn in the conversation. "My friend's temper is highly variable. But I've learned her kindness is the truer part of her character. She understands that mechs like us aren't merely mechs. That we're something more. Not so very different from other people—"

"I'm not like other people." Simon stumbles back. He's still awkward in his new body. "Other people don't have all this yelling in their heads. I want it to stop. Why won't it stop?"

"What you're perceiving as 'yelling' is probably your databanks giving you raw information." Abel's smile could break Noemi's heart. He wants so badly to think that Simon is like him. "I can help you learn how to prioritize memory bank input versus current sensory intake. I mean—I can teach you to change the yelling to whispers. Then you won't mind listening."

"Abel," she says in a low tone. "Simon's the one who sent the mechs after me in the theater."

Finally, that gets through. Abel looks back at her, concern furrowing his brow. "That shouldn't be possible."

"I did it! I did it!" This small child in the dimly lit hallway laughs as a severed hand crawls toward him as its master—and somehow his laughter is the scariest part. "My toys are my friends. *Real* friends. They do whatever I want them to do. They help me."

Noemi clutches at the sleeve of Abel's thick white coat. "Please, let's go."

"It's all right…" Abel's voice trails off as the broken mechs at their feet begin to twitch.

As obliterated as these mechs are, they're trying to respond to Simon. A detached arm crawls toward them, pulling itself forward with its bloodied metal fingers. A Sugar model rolls onto her side, kicking at Noemi's feet. Hopping sideways to avoid that, she pulls more insistently at Abel. "We have to get out of here before he calls more of them."

Of course Abel wants to talk technological breakthroughs. "You're controlling other mechs? Remotely? That's a remarkable advance, Simon. Can you explain the method of your—"

"No!" Simon balls his hands into fists. "They're *mine!*"

The Uncle on the floor grabs at Abel's leg but misses. Its motion distracts Noemi from the Sugar reaching for her blaster.

At the first tug, Noemi manages to pull the blaster back, barely. She fires, destroying the Sugar with a single blaster bolt. As its remains collapse and clatter, the disembodied hand drops down on her, skittering its fingers through her hair. All the battles she's lived through can't stop her from screaming as she slaps it away from her.

"Noemi?" Abel's trying to look after her and beat back half a George at the same time.

She takes Abel's hand and runs away from Simon—trusting, praying, that Abel will follow her instead of pulling back.

He does. They dash from the theater, footsteps thudding so heavily that she can't tell whether any of the mechs are chasing them. It doesn't matter where they go, as long as it's somewhere else.

They find a pair of doors that lead them into what was once a kitchen, and Abel manages to slide them soundly shut before any of the other mechs can follow. For a few seconds, they stand there in silence. Noemi finally catches her breath. "What's wrong with him?"

Abel's blue eyes lock on hers with a gravity she hasn't seen in him since he offered to die for Genesis more than five months before. "Simon's only confused and afraid."

"That's what I thought at first. But what he's doing with the other mechs—the way he's lashing out, denying his human side—he's dangerous."

Abel's expression is hard to recognize. It takes Noemi a few seconds to realize that he just doesn't believe her. "I realize Simon has problems, but he can't be…written off so completely. Not yet. You don't understand."

"…I guess maybe I don't."

"You needed a while to understand me, didn't you?"

"Yeah, I did." Noemi's pretty sure this isn't the same kind of thing at all, but they can talk about it some other time.

It hits her all over again: *I get to talk to Abel. He's* here. *The one person in the galaxy who's ever completely seen me, known me—he's here.* What does that mean for her, for them?

She doesn't know. Can't know, not with all of this going on. Noemi is certain only that she's happier to see Abel than she's ever been to see anybody—and that their chances of getting through this have more than doubled, now that they're together.

"We should return to the bridge," Abel says. "Otherwise Fouda will suspect me of deserting Remedy, and Riko and the others will begin to worry."

"And we have to get those relay codes." She doesn't really understand how the codes work—how Remedy itself works—but if that's what Ephraim told Abel, she's going with it. "Genesis doesn't have much time."

"Your fear for your world goes far beyond concern for your own survival," Abel says as they begin walking along the glass-strewn corridor, taking what must be an indirect way back to the bridge. "You've always been selfless. My programming ranks it as one of the highest virtues—and my consciousness agrees."

Does he balance those two? Interesting. They'll have to talk about that sometime. "Saving my own planet hardly counts as selfless. I mean, that's my home. That's almost everyone I've ever known."

"I've lived among humans for more than five months now, working as a Vagabond. This has given me far more insight into human beings than I had before. While what you say is logical, I have found that, when conditions become difficult, most people are quick to save themselves without thinking of others. You supersede that selfishness."

Noemi shakes her head. She's hardly the best person she knows. She's one of the most mixed up, one of the angriest. "I don't think I'm anything special."

"I disagree." His eyes meet hers with warmth that reminds her—suddenly, vividly—of their one kiss.

Flustered, she says, "Protecting Genesis is what I've trained for my whole life."

Abel seems to consider his words carefully before replying. "I've come to believe that even humans have a Directive One. A call they'll always answer, or a goal they can never stop trying to achieve. Something that will always override everything else. Mine is my need to protect Burton Mansfield. Yours is your loyalty to Genesis. Whether it's a matter of virtue, as I believe, or training, as you believe—it makes no difference. You remain constant."

"You defeated your Directive One to save my life. You didn't even flinch."

He says only, "Maybe I'm programming a new Directive One for myself."

She flushes again, but it doesn't fluster her so much this time. It feels...nice. Noemi hugs him tightly, and for a little while, it doesn't matter that they're on a hidden planet, in a crashed spaceship turned upside down. The terrible crises that they have to resolve both on the *Osiris* and back on Genesis haven't gone away, but in this moment, at least, everything is exactly as it should be.

•   •   •

"Where the hell have you been?" Captain Fouda demands of Abel. His smile reminds Noemi of the versions of sharks native to Genesis. He leans back in the captain's chair, which he's gone to the trouble of setting up on the new floor. "A mech can't work any faster than that?"

"Noemi!" Riko emerges from a side room off the bridge. She looks strained—red-eyed and pale—but no wonder, and at least her smile is genuine. "Where were you guys? I'm glad you're okay."

"That makes two of us," Noemi says, though there's a limit to how safe she can feel with Gillian Shearer's poison ampule still embedded in her arm.

When Riko hugs her, she returns the embrace. It feels like too warm a welcome; Noemi's never made peace with the radical wing of Remedy, and the events of the past couple of days haven't encouraged her to improve her opinion. But when Noemi and Abel first met Riko she showed them compassion—and Harriet and Zayan, too. That's worth at least one hug.

Riko's happiness seems to have drained Fouda's to

oblivion. He sits upright. "Wait. I know you. You're the one who threatened to breach the hull and kill us all!"

"You were threatening to kill me first." Noemi folds her arms across her chest. "I'm not going to apologize for defending myself. That's the only reason I'm still alive."

Angry as Fouda is, he seems to recognize she has a point. "Why were you helping those parasites? They tried to hide an entire world from humanity!"

She could answer that she'd made the only allies she could, that justice is best served by sharing this world rather than punishing its would-be thieves, or several other things. With Captain Fouda, though, the best defense seems to be a good offense. "You didn't bother reporting this to the rest of the galaxy either. Were you going to claim Haven for yourselves? If so, you're no better than the passengers."

Sure enough, Fouda flushes. "We only wanted to establish ourselves here first, to make it hard for Earth to conceal it again."

"And of course to set yourselves up as the planetary leaders," Abel interjects. "The hunger for power is an ordinary human failing. In this case, however, it appears you intended to use that power for the common good...more or less."

We have got to talk more about tact, Noemi thinks. But dealing directly with Fouda is more important. "The relay codes," she says. "We need them to save Genesis."

"And you'll get them." Fouda nods, squaring his shoulders, but Noemi can see the traces of shame in his expression. "As soon as the two of you have helped us fully claim this vessel from the passengers. They've taken the docking bay, which means we have no craft to reach their shelter. Until we have that, we're powerless."

She's surprised the passengers had the sense to secure the docking bay. "You're holding an entire planet hostage?"

"No. The passengers are. Only when we have freed Haven will we help save Genesis—so make sure the passengers comply."

Fouda's trying to be proud of his pronouncement. Yet the murmurs around them suggest not every member of Remedy feels the same way. Many of them frown and cross their arms, unhappy that their virtuous mission is turning into a power play.

So how do I best save Genesis? Noemi wonders. *By defeating the passengers or by arranging a mutiny against Captain Fouda? The mutiny would probably take longer—*

The comm unit next to the captain's chair begins to buzz. Fouda grabs it. "Yes?"

"*Captain Fouda?*" Gillian Shearer's voice cuts through the static, as if defying the signal to muffle her words. "*Shearer here. I need to speak with you.*"

"How did you get this frequency?" Fouda demands.

"*Process of elimination,*" is Gillian's only reply. Tension renders every word taut. *"We've been able to review certain security data as well, and now I have reason to believe you're in possession of a mech named Abel. He may not have told you he was a mech—"*

"They're aware of my nature," Abel says. After a pause, he adds, "Hello, Gilly."

That must've been what he called her when she was a little girl. It's so strange for Noemi to think of him knowing her then—*caring* about her—

"I knew you'd *come."* Gillian's breath catches. *"I knew you couldn't stay away, not when Father needed you. He needs you now more than ever. Oh, Abel—he's dying. Today. This hour. Please, come quickly."*

Even the raw pain in Gillian Shearer's voice wouldn't stop Noemi from telling her to go to hell. But the expression on Abel's face does. He's not angry. Not closed off.

Oh, my God, Noemi thinks. *He wants to go to Mansfield. He's still controlled by Directive One.*

22

ABEL OFTEN EXPERIENCES THE SAME PHYSIOLOGICAL
responses to emotions that humans do, although his design
was intended to make those emotions slightly muted. This
renders him more efficient and effective—that's the rationale Mansfield gave, long ago. *So your body won't be shackled to your mind.*

In this, at least, Mansfield must have been correct.
Because hearing the fear in Gillian's voice, knowing that
his creator is dying not in the abstract future, but at this
very moment—it wrenches him apart. If he were human,
surely this would be unbearable. That, or Mansfield was
wrong, and Abel is feeling every bit as much emotion as a
human would. His airways are partly constricted; sounds
seem to be coming from far away. His hairs stand on end
as though it were his life in danger rather than Mansfield's.
Every physical reaction tells Abel to act immediately or
suffer forever.

He remains still.

"Abel?" The desperation in Gillian's voice echoes within him. *"Are you there? Can't you hear me?"*

"Yes, Gillian." The words come out at a lower volume than he would've expected. It's as if he's initiated a partial shutdown to conserve energy. He turns to Fouda and says, "This conversation requires a private channel. I should be able to transfer this to the captain's antechamber, with your permission of course."

From his place in his crooked, battered, repositioned captain's chair, Fouda tries to look stern—but only for a moment. Something in Abel's face, or in Gillian's voice, has made an impression where all their earlier words did not. "All right, then." Fouda's expression turns unreadable as he motions toward the antechamber. "Go."

Gillian, who must have heard the exchange, says nothing. Yet the sound of her shallow, panicked breathing comes through the comms regardless.

As Abel hastens into the antechamber, Noemi follows him. No doubt she realized he would want her close. He's wanted to be so deeply understood again, but his pleasure in it is distant, something he knows rather than feels. As he patches the comms through to this small, darker room, she stoops down, searching through the various shards of debris. It is a strange way of giving him privacy, he thinks, but is grateful for her intention.

All of this he senses at a remove. Directive One seems far away—grief for his father eclipsing even the programming meant to ensure Abel would never outlive him.

The silence has gone on too long for Gillian. *"Abel? Can you hear me?"*

"I hear you."

"Then please, come to us."

"I'm afraid I can't do that."

"You have to," Gillian insists. *"This is about more than one man's life. This is about the next step in human and mech evolution. This is about immortality itself. Don't you see that?"*

"I do now." Everything's very clear to him, in a way it never was before. Perhaps extreme emotional responses serve a mental purpose after all: They clarify thought and intention. Behind him, he hears Noemi breathe out sharply, perhaps in frustration with Gillian's grandiosity, but she doesn't interrupt.

"Abel?" Mansfield's wheezing voice comes through the speaker, so feeble it shatters something within Abel, something intangible but very real. *"My boy—"*

He cannot bear hearing such pain and not seeing his creator. He will not.

Main communications, like almost every other ship-wide system, has been down since the crash. Most components will have survived with only minimal damage;

however, power has been diverted to emergency light and temperature systems. All Abel has to do to restore visual communications is provide an alternate energy source. He holds up one hand and then runs a finger along one of the hidden seams in his synthetic skin; it breaks and bleeds, exposing raw mechanics. The pain is irrelevant. From within the skeletal structure of his wrist he removes a small auxiliary power module, a backup he's never had to call on.

With his red, slippery fingers, Abel shoves the small power module into the appropriate slot on the comm panel. Instantly the holoscreen begins to fuzz and glow. He leans into its speaker and says the name for Burton Mansfield he's tried so hard to forget, but can't: "Father."

The screen shimmers into the image of a sickroom— not in a hospital with helpful Tares and a biobed, with everything optimized for patient comfort, but a pitiful pile of blankets on the floor. Gillian Shearer kneels beside the bed, surrounded by equipment Abel remembers from his earliest days of wakefulness in the lab. And there, lying down, is what remains of Burton Mansfield. It's not all of him any longer; even though Mansfield breathes and moves, something essential has already broken the ties that held it in place.

Gillian tries to smile, a crooked parody of the genuine thing. *"You see now, don't you? You understand what has to be done?"*

"Better than you do," Abel replies.

"You have to come to him! You have to. Even if you push back on Directive One to save others—you can't do it for yourself alone." Gillian's lower lip trembles, and a memory from more than thirty years ago replaces real-time visual input: Her holding up her tiny hand for him to bandage after a fight at school. She had trusted him completely back then. He had not yet matured enough to question whether he could trust her in return.

Abel says, "It appears that I can."

The fragility of Gillian's expression shifts into something stronger and darker. *"I didn't want to do this. Not ever, really—it's beneath us—but my father's work must continue."* She holds up her forearm. Despite her disheveled clothing and dirty hair, she's still wearing an elaborate jeweled bracelet. This seems ludicrous to Abel until he magnifies his vision and realizes the mechanism it contains. *"I still have the power to kill Noemi Vidal."*

"No," Noemi gasps—not in horror, but in pain. "Not anymore."

He turns to see her standing 1.4 meters behind him, clutching her blood-streaked arm. At her feet lies the ragged bit of metal she used to slice into her own flesh; in her fingers is a pea-sized ampule, ringed in almost microscopic machinery, gleaming wetly. The self-control required to keep from crying out during such pain—it is no less bravery than he'd expect from Noemi but it astonishes him regardless. They're each bleeding from their left arm, each wounded in almost exactly the same place.

These wounds are the price of their freedom from Mansfield, forever.

Gillian's face goes pale, and she lets her arm drop. She acknowledges neither the threat she made nor Noemi's liberating herself from it. "*You* have *to do this,*" Gillian insists. "*If you didn't, why would you even be here? You can't have done it only for the girl. Not this. You crossed an entire galaxy, knowing that your life would be forfeit when you were found! You would never have searched for the* Osiris *and* Haven, *not if you didn't understand your destiny. Only Directive One could make you do that.*"

"I believed so, too," Abel says, "until just now. Yes, I came here for more than Noemi. I had to know what had happened to Father. I couldn't go on without knowing. Naturally I assumed Directive One helped to lead me here. But that was an incorrect assumption."

Abel isn't used to learning new truths without evidence; he can't even say when this truth first became clear to him. He's only aware that he knows it as surely as he knows anything else in his experience or memory banks.

Mansfield's breath catches in his throat. "*Abel?*"

"I'm here, Father," Abel says. "Not because of Directive One. I was led here by the part of me that remembered when you showed me *Casablanca* for the first time, and explained Captain Renault's jokes. When you took me out into the garden to trace the constellations. And how happy you were the first time I told you I could dream. Noemi calls this my soul. Whatever it is, it's the part of me that proved you a genius—the part that proved you could create artificial intelligence that was the equal of any human. Yet it's the part of me you have no use for."

Mansfield opens his mouth to reply, but he can't. His breathing has become shallow and erratic. It takes all of Abel's willpower not to magnify the section of the holoscreen where he might read the small machines that measure pulse and respiration. Such details would confirm nothing Abel doesn't already know.

This is the hour of Burton Mansfield's death. Very nearly the minute.

Gillian has begun to weep. Although Abel expects her to keep pleading for their father's life, she instead starts working with some of the equipment piled near. One unfamiliar element draws his eye—a small, glowing octahedron in the shape of a diamond. With a trembling hand, Gillian inserts it into the machine connected to her father by the diodes stuck to his forehead.

Abel knows what this means, but there's no point in acknowledging it. He has very little time to speak, and must say the most important thing first. "I love you, Father. You don't love me, which seems as though it should change my own feelings, but it doesn't. I love you anyway." His eyes blur. This is only the second time Abel has ever cried. "I can't help it."

Noemi leans her head against his back. It comforts him as much as anything could in this moment. That's not much.

Mansfield coughs. Maybe he's trying to speak; maybe it's a spasm, no more. But even that minor exertion is too much. A deep rattle in his chest fills Abel with dread; he's never heard that sound before but he knows what it means. Gillian takes her father's hand, but Mansfield doesn't look at her. His rheumy eyes stare at the screen. At Abel. He's the one Mansfield wants with him, not the weeping daughter by his side.

This is what greed does to humans, Abel thinks. *It makes them ignore the love they have in favor of what they can never attain.*

The rattle chokes off. Mansfield exhales, and doesn't breathe in again. His wide-open eyes are no longer looking at Abel or at anything. Although there is no rational reason for it, his body appears smaller and more frail.

Burton Mansfield is dead.

With her one uninjured arm, Noemi hugs Abel tightly from behind. He covers her hand with his, taking what comfort he can from her touch. But he can only stare at the father who never loved him, unable to turn to the girl who does.

He'd always thought that Mansfield's death would liberate him from Directive One and so would feel like being set free. It doesn't feel like that at all. What Abel felt—and feels—for his father will always matter. That's a burden he'll carry as long as he exists.

Gillian doesn't break down in tears. Instead she lifts the small diamond-shaped data solid in her palms, cradling it reverently in front of her chest. It emits a soft white glow that lights her face from below, which makes her look almost like another person. *"He's not gone,"* she says thickly. *"I've saved him here. And I will save him completely. Soon."* She casts her blue gaze up at Abel, newly intense in both grief and fury.

"You can't do that without capturing me," Abel says. His voice sounds almost normal, which surprises him. It seems as though he ought to have been changed in some fundamental way, though of course there's no logical reason for this. "And you are in no position to capture me."

"I will be." Gillian doesn't say it in defiance. She's certain. She shouldn't be. There is more to her threat, an element he doesn't understand but must discover. *"I've already brought a soul over once. I can do it again."*

Noemi steps from behind Abel. "Simon's not—I'm sorry, Gillian. I did look for him. I kept our bargain.

But when we found him, he—he's turned angry, and strange—"

"If you want me to work with Simon," Abel interjects, "I will." When Noemi glances over at him in evident dismay, he decides they must discuss this again in the near future. "Whatever difficulties you've faced in your son's transfer, I should be able to put them right."

Gillian shakes her head. *"I don't need your pity, Abel. I need you. And within one more Haven day, I'll have you."*

The holoscreen blinks out, and the antechamber goes dark.

In the wake of his creator's death he should feel safer than he has in a long time. He doesn't. Instead he feels damaged in a way he doesn't know how to repair. Mansfield might've known how to fix it, but Abel can no longer ask him.

• • •

The first repair he conducts is Noemi's arm; she, in turn, helps reseal his synthetic skin. Together they wipe away their blood as they sit in a small passageway off the bridge, one that Remedy is using as a kind of crew quarters. Several of their fighters are resting there, apparently exhausted from the days of this siege. Noemi must be tired, too, but she's more worried about Abel than about herself, which seems wrong to him. She is the priority.

"Are you okay?" she murmurs as they sit on the floor,

side by side, her hand wrapped around his. The white ban-dages around her arm contrast sharply with the relative darkness around them.

"I can continue to function."

"That's not the same as okay."

Abel leans his head against her shoulder. "No. But it will do." He's been sad before, but has never been comforted like this. Simply being cared for has a kind of emotional power he'd never suspected. "We should discuss our long-term strategy."

Her hand gently squeezes his, demonstrating that she knows he needs this as both a plan and a distraction. "First we need a short-term strategy."

"This is an excellent point."

"If Gillian Shearer's coming after you..." Her voice trails off and she shakes her head. "They don't have the firepower or the strategy to take down Remedy, and they act like they're happy to wait for servant mechs to come and find them someday, which would've happened by now if it were happening at all. So you're safe."

"They have an advantage we haven't determined yet. Or Gillian believes that they do. Even if she's in error, soon the passengers will act. They'll try to retake the ship in an attempt to recapture me."

She hesitates. "What you said about Simon—you meant that?"

"Of course. I have to help him if I can."

"Are you sure you can?" Noemi bites her lower lip, then blurts out, "I know what he means to you, Abel. He's closer to being like you than anything or anyone else ever has been. But...you have to have seen he's not right."

"I see that he's new, and the product of an untried process. A child's consciousness was a poor choice for an initial transfer, particularly under such chaotic conditions. But he represents a step forward in mech evolution. He's the first Inheritor." When Noemi frowns, he explains, "So Gillian called them. Mechs with greater organic components—and, it would seem, the capacity to house a soul."

Noemi must have witnessed enough to realize some of the rest for herself. "From their base here, they were going to make all these mechs—mechs they could transfer human souls into—" Anger flickers across her face. "He would've made more mechs with souls. It wasn't enough that he had to imprison you in a mech's body forever. He wanted to do it over and over again—thousands, millions of times—"

"I don't understand," Abel says. "Imprison me?"

"It was wrong of Mansfield to give you a human soul and a mech body, with programming that forced you to obey him."

"You mentioned this once, but I didn't realize you meant it so literally." The strangeness of this strikes him; it's as though she's been speaking another language entirely, one he failed to translate in time. "Noemi—yes, I'm angry at Mansfield for some of his programming. But how can I be angry that he created me? He didn't imprison my soul. He brought it into being."

"But"—she struggles for words, and finds the wrong ones—"it just seems so unfair, that you have to live like this."

"What other way could I live? Mansfield could hardly have given me a choice of whether to be mech or human. My nature combines elements of both. Being a mech is part of my soul, of who I am. I don't want to change it. Do you think I *should* want to?"

"You mean you don't want to be human?"

"What would be the point of wishing for the impossible? Besides, I'm faster than humans. Smarter. More durable. I make use of all my capacities and even enjoy them. Why would I want to reject them?"

"That's not what I meant," she protests. "I only know Mansfield shouldn't have done that to you."

"He shouldn't have made me in the first place?"

"Stop twisting my words around!"

"I'm not." Abel looks at her the way he did the first day

they met, when they were still enemies bound together only by her desperate need and a quirk in his programming. She hated him then. He didn't like her either. "You pity me, simply for being. You saved me and spared me because you recognized the value of my soul, but you still don't believe my life is as valid as yours."

"That's not true." She puts her hands on either side of his face. Her skin is rough and abraded, her nails broken down. Blood from her self-inflicted injury still mars her fingernails. The contrast between the proof of her struggle on this ship and the tenderness in her eyes takes the heat from his anger. He's acutely aware of the presence of at least a dozen Remedy fighters sleeping nearby; surely they should be out behaving like soldiers, not present for a moment this intimate between him and Noemi. "Abel, you've talked about how alone you are. How you don't have anyone else in the galaxy like you. Was it right of Mansfield to do that to you?"

"No. But if Simon can be saved—if the organic mechs can prove sophisticated enough to possess souls—I won't be alone for long."

Noemi winces, as if in pain. "Will you just ask yourself if maybe you want this too much?"

Will you question your own prejudices, Noemi? Can you not try to see him as a little boy in need of help? The words are there, waiting to be spoken, but Abel doesn't say them.

He doesn't want to argue with Noemi—not when they're in such danger, and he can't blame her for being afraid. The pain of Mansfield's death is fresh for him, startlingly powerful, with dimensions Abel knows he's only begun to map. Noemi's presence is his only comfort. He doesn't want to push her away, not ever but especially not now.

But she is so horribly wrong.

Footsteps in the hallway make them both turn toward the sound. Noemi lowers her hands from Abel's face as two Remedy members enter on either side of Riko, supporting her on each arm. She looks even paler than before and is hardly able to walk.

"What's going on?" Noemi goes to Riko's side.

One of the Remedy soldiers says, "Another sick one." He rubs his forehead, telegraphing his own discomfort. "Somebody must've caught the flu before we started on this mission. Just our luck."

Abel turns back to the sleeping Remedy soldiers behind him, reexamining them with his full attention. If he's estimated the size of the Remedy attack force correctly, this is a far higher percentage of fighters than would normally be allowed to take simultaneous rest breaks. When he attunes his hearing to check their breathing, many of them have elevated respiration rates; their bodies are not efficiently processing oxygen.

He remembers the readings he took on his flight in. The

toxicity levels in that one sector weren't compatible with human life. No person exposed to that for more than a brief time would be able to continue functioning. Death would follow within mere days—if not hours.

Swiftly he goes to the nearest console and activates as much of the *Osiris*'s sensor array as still functions. When he does a sweep, he realizes that the area he flew over wasn't an aberration. Those toxicity levels stretch out over an enormous area, possibly even planetwide.

That means every human being on this ship is about to die. The Remedy fighters, the passengers—and Noemi.

23

SEVEN HOURS AGO, NOEMI HAD THOUGHT BEING stranded in a crashed, upside-down spaceship with a group of terrorists, their panicked hostages, and a potentially homicidal kid-turned-mech was one of the most danger-ous situations she'd ever found herself in. Now she only wishes things could be that easy again.

Because—for the second time within ten days—she stands at the center of a plague.

She picks her way across the shimmering tiles on the ceiling/floor of what had been designed as a dining hall but has become a makeshift hospital. The emergency light-ing at ankle level makes the tiles glitter and casts surreal shadows in the murky room. Nearly two dozen Remedy members lie on various cots and pallets, each of them pale, shaking, and feverish. Whatever they're suffering from isn't Cobweb, but it's just as vicious. The sick people's eyes are bloodshot, and they murmur as they weave in and out of consciousness. Sometimes they make perfect sense, and other times they rant about explosions, or mechs, or even dragons.

Is this what it's like on Genesis at this moment? Or maybe Ephraim's already led a Vagabond convoy to her world with lifesaving drugs.

Or maybe Earth's already invaded, killing what few survivors remained, and is even now claiming Genesis as its own.

Riko's steadier than most of the Remedy fighters, at least so far. She curls on the floor in a fetal position, arms wrapped around an engraved silver champagne chiller meant for finer things than serving as a vomit bucket. "I'm okay," she murmurs unconvincingly. "I am. If I can just get some sleep—"

"That's right." Noemi strokes Riko's short, spiky hair and notices how clammy her forehead has become. "You need rest. Close your eyes and try not to worry, all right?"

She's not the most nurturing person, under most circumstances. Nursing the Gatsons had been awkward at best, her clumsy ministrations welcome only because nothing better could be had. Today—or tonight, whenever it is—she's drawing on her memories of how Abel tended her when she got so desperately sick with Cobweb. It's amazing how much more natural it feels, being caring and gentle, when she asks herself what Abel would do.

Maybe all this time she'd only needed someone to give

her permission to be...soft. To not have her shields up all the time.

Abel himself is hard at work on the remnants of the bridge, bringing up what few ship functions can be restored, for what little time they can continue to operate. As more and more Remedy fighters fall ill, Captain Fouda grows more anxious. Maintaining control of the *Osiris* with only a fraction of his force will be difficult—or would be, if the passengers could strike. They must be as desperately ill as the Remedy fighters around Noemi. Fouda wants to automate as many force fields and defense systems as possible, so Abel's devoting his attention to bringing up what little additional power the ship still has.

Both Noemi and Abel need to play by Remedy's rules for a while. When they can work out that long-term strategy Abel mentioned, they'll figure out how to escape from this situation.

As if he's sensed Noemi thinking about him, Captain Fouda strides through the room, ignoring the patients and medicines lying around, his boots crunching on the fragile peacock-blue tiles underneath. He doesn't step on anyone who's sick, though he's so careless that's probably just luck. "No one's up yet?" he demands, apparently to everyone at once. "Not one person has gotten better?" He gets louder with every word. Before long, he'll be shouting, waking up all the patients and ensuring they remain sick even longer.

So Noemi goes to him, gesturing toward where some of the sicker ones lie. "Whatever this is, it's serious. Yelling at them isn't going to help. These people are going to need care for at least a day or two." Privately she thinks it might be much longer; for a few, fevers have spiked high enough to cause convulsions.

Fouda scowls and steps closer to her. "That's time we don't have. We're down too many operatives as it is." Then he turns away to stalk through the ad hoc sick bay, as though he could heal these people through his anger alone. Noemi begins to turn away, then catches sight of something on the back of his neck, just above his collar. Straightening, she squints to make it out.

The pale lines on his skin are too random for a tattoo; they match the marks on the side of his face, so maybe that's more battle scarring. Yet the marks are familiar, too, in a way she didn't spot before....

They look a lot like the pale white lines on her shoulder, the ones that won't go away—her scars from Cobweb. He suffered from it, too; he survived, like her.

Probably their shared experience should make her feel more compassionate toward him. Instead she only wonders how anybody could have been that sick, felt that much pain, and not be able to summon any concern for others.

The same way you rationalize setting off a bomb in the

middle of a music festival, she thinks. *You stop thinking of other people as human.*

● ● ●

It's a couple of hours more before Fouda releases Abel from duty. Noemi could time it to the minute, because she knows Abel has come to her as fast as he could. "You're feeling well?" He reaches for her face, then hesitates; she finds herself wishing he'd come those few inches closer, so they'd have touched.

"I'm fine. I mean, I'm exhausted and I'm hungry and I'd give my left arm to take a shower, but I'm not sick."

He doesn't look as relieved as she thought he would. Instead he glances around the sick bay, assessing each patient in turn. "You should be sick."

"Huh?"

"On landing approach to Haven, I measured high levels of toxicity in the air. They were incompatible with human life—really, with any life we know of. At first I thought it might be unique to that location, but my more recent scans suggest a far broader distribution. It's possible the entire planet is toxic to human life."

"But the trees—and there must be animals—"

"They would've evolved to survive in these conditions," Abel says. "Humans have not."

None of this makes any sense to Noemi. "But they set

up this huge expedition here! The richest and most powerful people in the galaxy—they went to all the trouble of building a Winter Castle here and stocking it with servant mechs. There's no way they would've done that if they knew this planet was sick, and there's no way they didn't scan this world top to bottom before any of this began. The *Osiris* would never have been built in the first place."

Abel takes Noemi's wrist in his hand, his thumb above the blue lines of her veins. "Your pulse is normal. You appear to be breathing easily—"

"I told you, I'm fine."

"You can't be," he says flatly. "Before, I thought the ship's air filtration systems must be operating at enough efficiency to keep the humans on board alive. Obviously that isn't true. Every person on this ship will fall ill and die unless they're removed in time."

"If I were going to be sick, I would know by now. Riko started feeling bad more than a day ago."

He frowns. "The passengers haven't asked for help. Nor did Gillian show any signs of illness when Fa—when we spoke to her last."

Is Delphine Ondimba sick like this right now? She's the one passenger Noemi liked, the only one worth worrying about. "It might only have been setting in. There's no way almost everybody in Remedy would come down with this while every single passenger on the *Osiris* would stay well."

Abel ventures, "Possibly the better health care the passengers would've received explains it. They've always eaten better food, had opportunities for optimized exercise without being subjected to hard labor—much as you grew up in a far healthier environment on Genesis."

Briefly Noemi recalls Ephraim Dunaway explaining that he knew she was "too healthy" to be from anywhere but Genesis. If only they had a doctor like Ephraim here. "It's not just me, though. Did you notice that Captain Fouda's fine, too? So are a handful of the other Remedy fighters."

"It's mysterious," Abel admits. She knows he hates confessing he doesn't know something nearly as much as a cat hates getting wet. It would be funny if the situation weren't so desperate. "Still, I'd like to further analyze the possibility that preexisting health makes a difference. Remember how your physical condition helped you when you had Cobweb."

Cobweb. Noemi feels the white lines on her shoulder prickle, and thinks of the scars along the side of Fouda's face. "Oh, my God."

"What?" Abel takes hold of her shoulders. "Are you dizzy? Nauseated?"

"I'm one hundred percent okay," she says. "And I think maybe I know the reason why."

•　•　•

Reaching the ship's real sick bay takes some effort. It's not that far away, but the doors don't reach all the way to the old ceiling, now the floor, so Abel has to jump for it and help Noemi over. Then the consoles and biobeds are suspended so far overhead that she wonders why they bothered coming here when the equipment is out of reach.

But Abel rigs up an emergency platform and is able to work on the consoles just as efficiently when they're upside down. Noemi remains at the base of the platform to steady it while he works. Her head is at the level of his calf. Greenish light from the screen illuminates his face as he says, "The database has files about Cobweb, but they're all locked. Only Burton Mansfield and Gillian Shearer are cleared to access them."

Good luck getting Gillian to help them out. Noemi groans and leans her head against Abel's leg. "So much for that."

"Actually, I suspect they're locked only to a basic DNA scan. If so, we're in luck." Abel holds his hand up to a soft-scanner that reads tissue. In the dim green glow, Noemi can see dark matter crusted under his nails—his own blood. She'll never forget watching Abel literally tear his own body apart only to see his unworthy creator one more time.

The scanner blinks and whirs, and data begins to rapidly unfurl on the screen. She can't read it at this distance, at least not upside down, but she begins to smile. "You got through, didn't you?"

"As far as this ship knows, I *am* Mansfield." He pulls back in surprise.

"What? What is it?"

Slowly Abel says, "They've all had Cobweb."

"Huh?"

"Every registered passenger aboard this ship was infected with a weakened form of the Cobweb virus before departure. This was done under clinical supervision, with antiviral treatment being administered almost immediately. Under such conditions, Cobweb would virtually never be fatal."

Everything begins clicking together. "We knew Cobweb was man-made," Noemi says. "We knew they made it for some purpose, but we couldn't guess what it was."

"We still lack proof," Abel says, "but I believe we both share the same theory."

Whatever Earth scientists were trying to do, they screwed up. If it's a weapon, it escaped into their own population before they were able to use it against yours, said Ephraim Dunaway months ago on Stronghold, when he explained what little Remedy knew about the Cobweb virus at that time. *If word got out that this disease was created by Earth, we'd have mass rioting on every world of the Loop.*

"Cobweb wasn't designed to hurt people," she says. "It must've been designed to *save* them."

Abel nods. "Haven must have been found several decades ago. Earth's government would've realized it would be the perfect replacement for Genesis, if only for the few environmental factors that kept it from being safe for human beings. So they attempted to bioengineer a virus that would rewrite human DNA, only enough for them to endure the conditions here. In that regard, Cobweb does exactly what its creators hoped. But the virus is more dangerous to human life than they knew."

"A lot of people who catch Cobweb get so sick they die." Noemi shakes her head in wonder. "But the ones who survive...they inherit an entire world."

"I put the probability of this hypothesis being correct at approximately 92.6 percent." Abel hops down from the platform to her side, so lightly and easily that she's reminded again—he's not quite human. "There are medicines for Cobweb in storage on the ship, including weaker forms of the virus that might operate as inoculations—"

"Thank God," Noemi says. She has serious problems with Remedy's radical wing, but she can't bear to watch people needlessly suffer and die. "We can help them."

But Abel shakes his head. "The materials aren't stored in the sick bay. They were considered 'high risk' and are kept in the same area as the tanks for growing mechs. That's territory currently held by the passengers."

That was the first place they'd run to, when Noemi told them they needed to control "valuable resources" on the ship. *I believed Gillian was being so selfish, leading us there,* Noemi thinks. *But she knew* exactly *what she was doing. She was the ruthless soldier at war. I was the one in over my head.*

"If Earth made Cobweb a virus," she says slowly, "one that spread organically, with a high level of contagion, so absolutely everyone would catch it—they didn't originally intend to hide Haven. They meant to share it with the galaxy."

Abel considers this, then nods. "That also seems likely. Earth's government still chose to conceal Haven in the end, but it seems likely they did so primarily to cover up the truth about Cobweb."

"That's not a good enough reason. Not to deny this to humanity—to resume the Liberty War—" Noemi gasps. "That's why they did it, isn't it? Why they came back decades after we thought they'd let us go? They ended the war when Haven was found. They started it again when they realized they could never reveal the truth about this planet."

"I can only put that at a 71.8 percent probability," Abel says gravely.

"You mean—probably. Not certainly, but probably."

He nods.

Noemi feels nauseated, not from illness but from the knowledge that her world could've been saved so easily— but someone, somewhere, decided they had too much to hide.

• • •

She expects returning to the makeshift sick bay to be more difficult, now that she knows these people could so easily have been treated. They'll have to break this news to Fouda, who will of course want to attack the passengers immediately—a conflict Noemi doesn't want any part of any longer. Even less does she want to be surrounded by suffering people she can't save; after Genesis and now this, she feels like some mythological bringer of death.

But the worst part of her return is when she sees how much worse Riko is.

"Riko?" She hurries to Riko's bedside, Abel beside her. Riko looks so ragged, so miserable, that Noemi can hardly connect her to the energetic, sarong-clad woman they met on Kismet's moon. Even when Riko was in prison on Earth, her strength shone through. Now she looks like her own ghost. "Hang on, okay? We might be able to help you."

"Doubt it," Riko rasps.

"Shhh. Save your strength." Noemi looks around for

something, anything that might help, and Abel hands her a cool, damp washrag someone must have prepared. It's not much, but it's better than nothing, so she lays it across Riko's forehead. Riko's skin is so hot it nearly burns.

"Tell me one thing," Riko whispers. Every word costs her. Every movement. Yet she manages to clasp Noemi's wrist. "You people—on Genesis—you believe in gods, don't you?"

"We believe—" Noemi catches herself before launching into a detailed explanation of the many various faiths on Genesis. "Well, we believe."

"Before—I thought I'd see people living free—thought I'd know then it was all worth it." The doubts Riko never hinted at before now haunt her eyes. "But I'm not going to see that. I'll never really know."

Noemi opens her mouth to protest that Riko will be okay, but Abel gives her a look that silences her words. Whatever treatment is out there, they're not going to retrieve it in time.

Riko continues, "What if I was wrong the whole while? What if there's no place for us to go? Was it all for nothing?"

Abel says, "You acted on your beliefs, intending to help others. That has worth." He and Noemi share a glance. She knows he doesn't agree with Remedy's terrorist actions any more than she does. But there's no point in punishing this woman on her deathbed.

Noemi remembers Captain Baz's words to her, more

meaningful than ever before. "I think it matters what we fight for. What we choose to die for."

Riko hears in those words whatever she needed to hear. She very nearly smiles. "Yeah?"

"Yeah." Noemi brushes a few strands of sweaty hair off Riko's forehead, then takes her hand.

Riko's grip tightens around hers at first, but slowly, gradually goes slack. Her breathing slows down. Suddenly the image of Esther's final moments fills Noemi's mind, tightening her throat. This is what death looks like.

The doctors always say hearing is the last sense to go. She leans close to Riko's ear. "It's all right. We're here with you. It's okay." Which is utterly meaningless, but it's all she can come up with.

Somehow she must have said the right thing again, because Riko relaxes, exhales in a long, unmistakable rattle, and—

"She's dead," Noemi whispers as she turns to Abel. "Isn't she?"

"The line between life and death is somewhat arbitrary." Only Abel could say this and sound compassionate. "Riko's heart and lungs have ceased to function, but while her brain no longer supports consciousness, it continues sending signals. In its last moments, her body was flooded with endorphins, with every possible emergency boost of strength or will. Her brain will be processing these as pure euphoria, producing the visions reported by so many brought back from clinical death."

"That's what Earth thinks." She wipes at her eyes. "On Genesis we see it differently."

Apparently Abel knows better than to argue the existence of heaven with her here and now. "It's interesting to conjecture."

Although Noemi believes in the afterlife, she isn't sure exactly what kind of reckoning awaits on the other side. She only knows Riko kneels before it now. A power greater than Noemi will decide whether punishment or mercy is called for. So it's okay to mourn what could've been.

If Earth had opened Haven to everyone, Noemi thinks, there wouldn't be such a thing as Remedy. *Maybe Riko would've been a settler here, working hard to set up the first cities of a brand-new world.*

So many lives could've been so much better if Earth had only taken responsibility.

The comms—recently restored by Abel—crackle with sound. Gillian Shearer's voice comes through: *"If our calculations are correct, by now the members of Remedy have learned exactly why this world belongs to us, and not to them. You can't live in this environment—not without the medical treatment we control."*

Noemi and Abel look at each other. *We were right,* she thinks.

Gillian says, "*We're willing to trade that medical treatment. You'll get as much as you need. You simply have to pay for it first.*"

Noemi instantly realizes what comes next. Dread hollows her out, and her breath catches in her throat.

With satisfaction, Gillian concludes, "*Bring us the mech named Abel, alive.*"

24

ABEL'S BLASTER IS BACK IN HIS HAND BEFORE GILLIAN Shearer has finished saying his name. He reaches for Noemi—but she's already on her feet, her own weapon at the ready. She looks down at the body of Riko Watanabe, and for a moment he thinks Noemi won't be able to abandon her. Humans behave strangely around the dead.

Instead Noemi says only a single word: "Go."

He runs for the far door, which leads into a badly damaged corridor. With one leap he's in the door frame, able to pull Noemi with him. Behind them he hears somebody hoarsely shout, "He's getting away!"

Are Fouda's soldiers already after him? Irrelevant. If they aren't, they will be, and he and Noemi have to run without looking back.

They take off through the long, dark corridor, debris crunching under their feet. Even the emergency lighting took damage here, meaning the small orange beacons are far apart. They dash through an area that must have briefly caught fire; the once-delicate murals on the walls have been charred black. Each breath smells of ash. Through the darkness he can barely make out Noemi, sometimes glimpsing only the glitter of her jumpsuit. With her limited vision, she must be running nearly blind.

"What do we do?" she says. "Literally everyone on this ship is trying to capture us. There's no safe space."

"We have to leave the *Osiris*, and Haven, as soon as possible. The corsair is approximately two kilometers away—"

"Okay, great. We get outside and run for that," Noemi pants. "We have to find an air lock."

Under such stress even an experienced fighter like Noemi can make an error in strategy. "They'll check the air locks first. I believe there's a breach in the hull not far from the theater. We stand a better chance of escaping through that breach than through any of the doors."

Noemi is wise enough not to ask the exact probabilities of their success. "Let's go."

Abel calibrates his running speed to match Noemi's. Once they're on more even footing, he'll simply pick her up and carry her. "If I've calculated Haven's diurnal cycles correctly, it should be nighttime outside. We'll have cover of darkness and should be able to get back to the corsair."

"Without a scratch?" Noemi quips. "Promise?"

"We can take scratches. The corsair must not. I suspect

Virginia would refuse to give us a ride back to the Gate. She'd take the *Persephone* as her bounty." He means to joke, but the possibility is in fact plausible.

"Wait." They pause at a sharper bend in the corridor. Abel thinks Noemi's only catching her breath, but she asks a question. "Virginia Redbird came with you?"

"You know how she loves a mystery."

She laughs in apparent surprise. She leans against the wall, clearly gathering her strength for their next run. Although Abel should be focusing nearly all his conscious attention on plotting their course, he nonetheless registers that her jumpsuit is extremely low-cut, revealing the curves of her breasts, which rise and fall with her rapid breathing. This should be irrelevant but somehow is not.

Swiftly he comes up with a reason for observing her wardrobe. "You'll be inadequately protected against the cold." He gestures at his own white hyperwarm parka. "Once we're outside I'll give you this."

"I found a coat earlier and left it behind, like an idiot. Won't you get cold, too?"

"I can endure it for considerably longer than a human, more than long enough to reach the corsair. The flight back to the *Persephone* will also be cold, but should take no more than twenty-nine minutes depending on Virginia's orbital status.

"I'm calculating our path to the corsair," he says quickly,

turning his head to gaze at a broken light fixture instead of Noemi's chest. "I should have it in another few seconds."

Noemi glances at him sideways. "The *Persephone*? That's what you renamed the ship?"

"Yes. In Greek mythology, she's the wife of Hades, the daughter of Demeter. She spends half her time in one world, half in another. In each world she's a goddess, but there's no one place she will ever belong."

"...*Oh*."

When he turns to her again, Abel can see realization dawning in her eyes. He's betrayed his feelings. When will he learn not to do this? Love has to be buried even deeper than he realized.

In a small voice, Noemi says, "You saw that."

He doesn't know how to reply except to say, "I know you."

Noemi shakes her head—not denying him, but as if in wonder. "Sometimes I feel like I've gone my whole life just waiting for someone to see me. And you do, Abel. You might be the only person who ever has."

"Now you know how I felt the day you told me I had a soul."

Their gazes meet in the darkened room, and Abel realizes he's holding his breath, which is highly counterintuitive. Yet the impulse is undeniable.

"Running," Noemi says abruptly. "We should be running."

"Agreed." With that they resume their haste, Abel bewildered by his own reordering of priorities. Escape must be their first and only goal.

The ambient temperature drops a full degree Celsius, then lowers still further. Their destination must be within proximity. At last he makes out lighting at the end of one long corridor that has a blue tint rather than the orange of emergency lighting. When he magnifies this sector in his vision, he detects a few stray snowflakes.

In 3.6 seconds, Noemi sees it, too. "The hull breach. We're almost there!"

Assent seems pointless. Abel runs faster, pushing ahead of Noemi to scout the area. Every meter brings more brightness and sharper cold, until he finally rounds the final turn—

—and stops just short of tumbling down a hundred meters, which even for Abel would be fatal.

He stretches out one arm, which Noemi runs into just after. She gasps in shock. "Oh, my God."

Even for a soldier of Genesis, that's only an expression. However, the physical devastation of the ship could well have been wrought by a vengeful deity. The entire *Osiris* hull has cracked—opening a sort of canyon almost forty meters wide, one that runs almost the length of the ship. From where they stand on the ragged edge, he and Noemi can see nearly an entire cross-section of the ship—each deck its own layer. Dangling sections of wall, flooring, and wires cover the side as though they were vines. Exposed above them is Haven's night sky, brightened by six of its moons; below, at the floor of this artificial canyon, are drifts of freshly fallen snow.

"How exactly are we supposed to get out from here?" Noemi's question is valid. What is now the top of the ship stands a solid eight meters above their head, and no uninterrupted framework for their climb readily presents itself.

Abel leans out, examines the wreckage, and comes to a conclusion. "First, we'll need to climb down this"—he points to a nearby waterfall of dead cables, most of them as thick around as Noemi's ankle—"to a level approximately fourteen meters below us. From there we can shift sideways and reach that piece of wreckage." His gesture indicates a latticework of metal that leads very nearly to the top.

Even the most courageous humans are not entirely unafraid of extreme heights, especially in uncertain conditions like the ones they currently face. Noemi appears pale, but she nods. "That looks, um, doable."

"It is." At least, he believes so. Testing the weight capacity of that latticework is a task he'll turn to later.

He slips off his white parka, which Noemi quickly dons. By mutual, silent assent, she prepares to go first—until, in the distance behind them, they hear a thump.

Turning his head to focus better on the sound, he makes

out at least two sets of footsteps—still faraway, but heading in their direction.

"They've found us," Noemi whispers.

"Not quite." He gestures toward the cables leading downward. "You should go on alone."

"What?"

"They're only after me, Noemi. I can evade them for a time and escape the *Osiris* later. You and Virginia could retrieve me then."

She shakes her head. "I'm not leaving you."

This is enormously pleasing but poor strategy. "One of us has to go first regardless. It makes more sense for that to be you."

Still Noemi hesitates. "You swear you'll follow me? Right away?"

"I swear." Oaths mean more to humans than to mechs; Abel sees little purpose in promising to do what future conditions may make impossible. But for Noemi's sake, he will try to obey.

She begins shinnying down the cables, hand under hand, bracing her booted feet against fragments of wall. He watches her carefully until she's out of sight and only then glances back.

In the darkness, he sees movement. Specifically, he sees a badly broken Tare, one eye missing so that the yellowish glow of her brain circuitry shows through. Behind her, an

Oboe straightens, ignoring her shredded left arm and leg, and begins to hobble toward them.

"We have company," Abel says, knowing Noemi's still close enough to hear. "Some of Simon's—playmates."

She freezes in place; he is able to determine this from the way the cables stop moving. "Can they tell Simon we're here?"

"They already have." Abel knows this as surely as if he'd programmed the mechs himself.

"Come on," she urges. "Hurry. Follow me."

An altercation with Simon must be very close. Although Noemi wishes to avoid it due to her own fears and prejudices—understandable, if regrettable—Abel welcomes the chance.

He had been absolutely honest with Gillian; he believes he can get through to Simon. Calm him, reassure him, maybe even repair him. As long as that's true, Abel has to try just as hard to save him as he tried to save Noemi.

She's the first person who believed I have a soul, he thinks. *I must be the person who believes in Simon.*

"I'll be right there," he murmurs as he gets to his feet.

"*Dammit*, Abel—"

He ignores Noemi's fury. The Tare staggers closer, her half-destroyed face more terrible in the brighter light. Abel doesn't share the instinctive human revulsion at what looks like a life-threatening injury, but there is nonetheless something uncanny about the tilt of her head, the exposed illumination from the circuits of her mechanical brain. When she speaks, she reveals a damaged larynx, sounding more like an ancient type-to-speech reader than either mech or human: "Simon says stay."

"Are you in contact with him right now?" The mechs seemed linked, before—to one another, and to Simon—which means Simon doesn't have to be in the same room with the Tare to speak for her. Abel takes one step toward her, but the Tare points and stomps her intact foot.

"*No!* Simon says *stay!*"

Finally Abel remembers the game human children play, which for some unaccountable reason is attached to this name in particular. No doubt to a child called Simon, this game was even more appealing. "I'm staying. See? Am I speaking to Simon right now?"

"May-be," singsongs the Oboe, who continues shuffling closer. Bloody wire hangs from some of the gashes in her leg.

From below Noemi calls, "Abel? What are you doing?" He doesn't dare follow; at this point in the "game," he shouldn't be moving.

Simon is only a confused child, trapped in a mind he doesn't understand. Abel may be the only individual who can ever help him make sense of it, the one native speaker of a language Simon must immediately learn.

The Tare and Oboe stand on either side of Abel,

effectively pinning him with his back to the enormous crevasse. They're not operating independently; they're being controlled by Simon with a level of coordination that goes beyond any standard protocols. Queens and Charlies perform military procedures programmed into their circuits, or they can respond to combat cues independently. They can't do both. Tares and Oboes lack any strategic functionality—one practices medicine, while the other provides entertainment, usually in the form of music. For them to behave as they are now, they have to be operating as though they are parts of Simon's own body.

"How are you doing this?" Abel looks through the blank golden space of the Tare's missing eye, hoping Simon is looking back at him. "How do you control the others?"

"Well," the Tare says, in the suddenly serious way of small children, "it's like there's a machine part of me and a *me* part of me. I have to forget all about the me part of me and just be a machine. That part's way more fun."

Abel frowns. Virginia said something like this to him not long ago, that he should embrace his mechanical side more often. He's always tried so hard to reach for his humanity. He's not sure how to reverse that.

A skittering sound, then a thud tells him Noemi has successfully reached the lower level from which she might escape. Although he wishes she'd leave the *Osiris* without him, he understands she never would.

The Tare wobbles forward and puts one hand on Abel's chest. "You're like me, aren't you?"

"In many ways." Abel smiles in a way he hopes will read as reassuring. "We both synthesize the human and the machine."

Frowning, the Tare steps back again. Abel curses his own precision; *synthesize* is too formal a word for a small boy. "You don't look like me. You look right. I don't look right. I look all messed up."

"That can be fixed. Everything that's wrong can be fixed. You just need to—"

To what? Abel realizes he doesn't have an answer. The most logical outcome would be for Simon to return to Gillian, who understands both the body and the soul involved far better than anyone else. But Gillian is cut off from her usual resources; if she weren't, Simon wouldn't have been re-created so hastily and poorly. Abel would like to take Simon on as a project, to offer him guidance and friendship, and to figure out his inner workings over time, with the help of the excellent scientific equipment available there. But cooperation with Gillian is impossible. Taking charge of Simon would in effect mean kidnapping a little boy, promising to make him better without being certain that was even possible.

"Abel?" Noemi whispers. His sharp ears catch the sound, but responding is still inadvisable.

Through the Tare, Simon smiles. "You're like me and you're not like me. We're alike and we're different." The Tare model's hand fists in the folds of Abel's shirt. "I want to see how you're different."

"I'm not sure that you—"

"I know! I'll take you apart. *Then* I can see."

Abel blocks the Tare's forearm, breaking her grip on his clothing. He draws upon the few child-psychology texts in his databases and says, simply and firmly, "No."

Both the Oboe and the Tare seize him, and the Oboe yells, "*Simon says!*"

With one shove, Abel pushes them both back—but not far. They're mechs, even if not for combat, and they're stronger than any human opponent. When they both rush at him, he jumps upward as high as he can, which is just high enough to grab the ridge above them. As he dangles there, the Tare and Oboe leap upward, too. The Oboe doesn't make it—her broken leg keeps her off balance, and she clatters onto the floor and rolls off into the crevasse. A series of distant crashes makes it clear she's being dashed to pieces.

One down, he thinks—the Tare is coming nearer, her blank golden light of an eye boring into him.

"Abel!" Noemi cries. "Will you get your metal butt down here?"

My butt is made of flesh and is designed to be pleasant

both to see and to touch, he'd like to say, but this information can perhaps wait.

He lets himself drop, falling past the Tare to Noemi's side, where he catches himself on the floor of her level. Noemi makes a half-strangled sound of fear before he pulls himself up, but the instant he's next to her, she knows to start running.

They dash across the jagged edge of this broken ship, snow blowing through their hair, the deep fatal drop less than a meter to their left. Abel's sharp vision and quick analysis allows him to identify the areas they're running through—a broken-up Turkish bath, devastated living quarters, an upside-down pool—the other half of each mirrored on the opposite side of the ravine. When they run past a transparent wall separating two rooms, a Tare on the other side throws herself against it with such speed and force a human would be knocked unconscious. Noemi has the fortitude to keep going without even glancing sideways.

Abel does not. The Tare claws at the transparent material; there's no way she could break it, but a Tare model isn't programmed with that information, and Simon neither knows nor cares.

And it is Simon doing this. He cannot deny that.

"Come back!" the Tare shrieks, her voice saying Simon's words. "Come *back*!"

The plea wrenches Abel to the core, but he can't take the risk. He has to keep running.

They reach the framework he'd seen before, the one that provides a way for them to crawl to the top of the ship. Noemi pauses, panting and clutching at her arm. She must still be feeling intense pain from those cuts, but she says only, "Can we climb it before they get to us?"

"Possibly." Abel readies himself. "But I can climb one-handed and shoot at the same time."

"Bet I can shoot and climb, too, if it comes to it." However, her focus remains above. She turns up her face to the moonlight and starts to climb. Abel follows her, dividing his attention between Noemi's progress (will her injured arm continue to support her?) and the area below them (in case more of Simon's "toys" pursue).

Their ascent doesn't move as quickly as Abel would like. Noemi is undoubtedly wise to pace herself, conserving her lesser human strength, but he can't forget that Simon or his mechs could reappear at any minute, wanting to play a very deadly game.

Perhaps I can still communicate effectively with him, Abel thinks. *Once controlling the other mechs has lost its novelty, Simon will wish for other forms of amusement. I could structure the learning he needs as a series of puzzles he might find enjoyable.* He doesn't intend to give up on the boy yet.

But *how* is Simon controlling the other mechs?

A far-off glint of light at the edges of Abel's peripheral vision draws his attention just in time for him to refocus and see the blaster in a broken Charlie's hand, pointed straight at them.

"Noemi!" he shouts. She responds intelligently by hugging the metal framework, hard.

Charlies have intelligence, too. The blaster bolt is aimed not at them, but at the very top of the framework they're climbing, and he hits his target. Abel feels the metal shudder, then tilt backward.

"Abel—" Noemi clutches the frame tighter. "We're falling!"

He can do no more than watch as the framework gives way, toppling into the crevasse in the ship's wreckage, taking him and Noemi down with it.

25

THEY FALL BACKWARD, GAINING SPEED. NOEMI CAN ONLY clutch the metal that's clearly not doing a damn thing to keep her from tumbling down into the open maw of the crashed ship. She winces, preparing herself for the worst—

—and the framework stops hard. The reverberation through the metal carries into her bones, and the jolt of it nearly makes her lose her grip, but she manages to hang on. Her blaster tumbles down, a brief flash of moonlight on metal before it vanishes.

What just happened? She looks around as best she can and realizes the metal framework is still connected to the ship by various cables and one twisted but unbroken beam. It sways precariously, suggesting that connection won't hold much longer. The framework's fallen from being parallel to the sides of the ship to perpendicular—stretched across the deep gash, but not nearly long enough to reach to the other side.

"Noemi!" Abel calls. He must be moving closer to her, because the entire framework trembles; she hugs it tighter and tries to ignore her aching muscles. "Are you all right?"

"I didn't fall, if that's what you mean. But this is *not* all right. Not even close!"

Don't look down, she tells herself. *Just go hand over hand back to that side of the ship. Like the monkey bars!*

She's always hated monkey bars.

Abel reaches her side, which would be reassuring if it weren't for the buck and sway of the metal frame with every move either of them makes. One extra-violent dip makes Noemi break her own rule and look down; immediately she wishes she hadn't. The bottom of this gash in the ship lies too far below; the crevasse in the wreckage looks like a deep canyon through stone, except more ragged, uglier, deadlier. She stares into the jumble of sharp wreckage and snow beneath her, knowing at any second she might become part of it. And if they fall, she wants to be holding on to Abel. Maybe then she could bear the feeling of air rushing around them. Maybe she could endure the cold, and the terror. It will just be hanging on to Abel until the obliterating end.

"I doubt Simon's mechs will pursue us here," Abel says. "His control lacks the finesse necessary for bringing any of them across."

"You're wrong." At any other time, she'd be proud of

finally getting one step ahead of Abel. Now she just wants to throw up. "He won't send any of the big mechs, but the—the severed things, the hands and arms—he could send those."

It would only take one mechanized fist slamming down on her knuckles to send her falling to her death.

"True."

"You could fire on them, though. Give us cover. You're strong enough to hold on with one hand, aren't you? So you could still fire your blaster."

"Of course I'm strong enough to hold on with one hand." He sounds almost offended. "However, my blaster, like yours, was shaken loose during the fall."

"Just great."

Abel finally reaches her side and slings one arm beneath her, helping to hold up her weight. Trying to be encouraging, he adds, "The mechs may simply wait to see if we make it back to that side of the ship, to capture or kill us then."

"Fabulous." Noemi's breathing hard with the effort required to hang on, even with Abel's help. "I don't think this framework's going to hold very long. Especially not if we keep moving."

"Agreed."

For a second they hang there in silence. Noemi turns her face from the crevasse below to the luminous moons overhead in Haven's sky. This might be her final experience of beauty, of wonder. Cold wind whips around them, and ice crystals sprinkle her cheeks and eyelashes. Despite the chill, terror has made her hands start to sweat. *Oh, great, this is exactly when I want to be slippery.*

Abel says, "Attempting to return along the framework may be unduly dangerous, if not impossible."

"Yeah, but what else are we supposed to do?"

"I might be able to jump to the other side of the ship. You could hold on to my back."

Noemi cranes her neck to look at the cavernous gap around them. She can't tell exactly how far away the other side is, but—it's far. "Not even you can make that jump with me weighing you down . . . can you?"

Abel remains silent for a second, then says, "We'll find out."

"*Not* reassuring."

"Unfortunately, that which is reassuring is not always true."

She swallows hard. "You'd just be swinging over, using your arms. Not jumping."

"The verb is imprecise, but I felt it would sound more encouraging."

"It did until you explained it!"

Apologetically, Abel says, "You *did* ask."

"Okay." A stronger gust of wind sends shudders throughout the framework. It won't hold their weight much longer.

She takes a deep breath and pulls herself together the best she can, turning her head to face Abel. They're so close together their noses nearly touch. "All right. I know we have to do this. I just don't like it."

"I don't like it much either," Abel admits, "but in this situation, the best solution isn't necessarily a good solution."

"You are the absolute worst at comforting people *ever*."

One corner of his mouth lifts, half a smile, but his mech focus remains absolute. "Our first difficulty will be adjusting your weight onto my back." The air currents whirl around them, dusting them with ice, as Noemi's brain tries desperately to think of a better way out of this, *any* other way out of this, or maybe how she could've avoided being out here to begin with.

"Hold still," she commands, and he braces himself, becoming even more unyielding than the metal they hang from. Noemi calls on her memories of basic training. They had to climb plastic webbing, nets made of thick rope, even trees. She always scored at the top of her squadron. If she did it then, she can do it now.

Swing your arm over OH GOD OH GOD okay you've got it GOD HELP ME grab on to him HARD—

"Okay!" she yelps as she clutches Abel around the neck with her arms, and around his waist with her legs. She dangles from his back like a sloth from a tree branch. "Okay, okay. Got it."

His voice is slightly strangled as he says, "You're lucky I don't have the same respiratory needs as humans."

"I know you could probably hang here all day, which is great for you and everything, but could you *please* jump already?"

"I need to brace myself." With startling speed, he swings around the edge of the framework so that he's crouching atop it instead of hanging beneath. Having him between her and the deep crevasse below feels irrationally reassuring—until the metal framework groans ominously, and a shudder sends vibrations through both their bodies. They don't have long. Abel senses it, too. "Are you ready?"

Noemi grips Abel even more tightly. "Go."

He jumps with such force that it knocks the breath out of her. For one terrifying, surreal instant it seems as though they're flying—the other side impossibly far away until it's rushing toward them, into them. Noemi goes dizzy when they hit one of the floors, pure metal, and hit it *hard.*

Abel manages to grab the edge of the floor, delaying their fall. She hangs there for a terrible moment, swinging back and forth like a pendulum, until he hurls her over him.

He lets go of her—a terrifying sensation—but Noemi rolls onto the other side of the ship, onto a jagged, raw structure.

She lands rough, tastes blood, but instantly scrambles to the edge to help him. He's not pulling himself up for some reason. Then she realizes one of his wrists is badly bent. It must have been damaged in the jump; he broke it to save her, and now he can't save himself.

Noemi leans forward to grab his undamaged arm. "Come on," she whispers. "I can get you inside."

Abel shakes his head. "I'm too heavy for you."

"I'm strong. Look, I can brace my feet."

"My left ankle is broken." He must have hit that wall even harder than she thought. "I can't push myself up. You'd have to take my whole weight. It's too dangerous."

"So, what, you're just going to fall to your death?"

"…I believe you can escape and contact Virginia on your own." Still, he's only worried about her, not about himself.

"Listen to me." Noemi grabs his arm with all her strength and leans so close that he has no choice but to meet her eyes. "You'd better try to help me. Otherwise, you're going to fall and drag me down with you. Because I won't let go of you, Abel. I will *never let go.*"

Abel hesitates, but only for an instant. "On three."

They count together, silently, nodding on each number— and then Noemi pulls back as hard as she can, towing Abel with her. He gets his broken forearm onto the edge of the wall, which must be agonizing, but it takes enough of his weight to pull him over the edge. Then they flop down side by side, wounded and stranded—but alive.

Distantly she hears the metal framework give way, clattering against the sides of the gash in the ship until it smashes into the wreckage. *Another ninety seconds*, she thinks, *and we'd have been smashed with it.*

Once they can breathe again, she and Abel take stock. "Wait, what is this?" she pants. They're surrounded by solid metal, with no doors to speak of. "Some kind of storage tank?"

"Possibly." He remains on his back a few moments longer than her. "As there is no direct means of leaving this spot, we'll need to devise an escape once—once we're capable of it."

Right now, they aren't. Noemi scraped the side of her face badly in their rough landing, and one jagged bit of metal sliced a small cut at her temple. The self-inflicted wound in her arm is bleeding more now than it was before, too, but she's less worried about herself than she is about Abel. He manages to use a bit of torn upholstery to bind up his bent ankle with his good hand, but he winces every time he tries to move the other wrist.

"That joint has been compromised more seriously than my ankle," he reports so calmly he might as well be talking about someone else. "Self-repair would be easier if I hadn't extracted the auxiliary power module in order to speak to Mansfield. Just because I hadn't called on it in thirty years, I thought I never would. I believe this is close to what humans call 'hubris.' "

Noemi doesn't have any tools that would allow her to repair him, even if she knew how. "This is bad."

"The damaged components are organic. Even without the power module, I can repair myself within a few hours if I go into a regenerative state."

She nods. "By then it's going to be very late at night, but still dark, right? We can get out of here without anybody seeing us."

"We'll make a plan once we can assess our situation more fully," Abel says. He's talking to himself as much as to her, she suspects. "For now, we should rest."

"Is a regenerative state like sleep?" Noemi doesn't much like the idea of spending hours in this icy tank without anybody to talk to, but if that's what Abel needs, she'll deal. Maybe she can fall asleep, too. Dozing off somewhere so cold and uncomfortable would be impossible, normally, but at the moment she's so exhausted it seems possible.

"It will be. But the transition takes several minutes."

Abel tries to get comfortable, though there have to be few places in the galaxy less comfortable than a debris-filled, ice-cold metal tank. Noemi lets him choose a spot where he can lie on his side, then spoons behind his back, wrapping one arm around him while the other serves as her pillow. When she touches him, he goes very still.

"You need to stay warm," she says. "If it weren't for this parka, I'd have frozen down here already."

"Even with the parka, you would die of exposure within forty hours. I would go into a dormant state not long thereafter and would require a full reboot to awaken."

"Well, we're not going to be down here that long."

Either they'll be out of trouble by then, or they'll be dead.

Abel's quiet for several seconds, and she thinks the regenerative cycle must have begun until he breaks the silence. "Aren't you going to tell me how badly I'm comforting you?"

"...You didn't seem to enjoy it, before."

"Humans are better at defusing tension through humor."

"*Whaaat?*" She drags out the word; if Abel wants to be teased, she'll oblige. "The greatest mech of all mechs just admitted humans are better at something?"

"For now. I might figure it out eventually."

"Yeah. You might." Noemi hugs him, rests her forehead against the place between his shoulder blades. He's not as warm as a human would be, but she hopes she has enough body heat for them both.

They might've lost each other. So many things between her and Abel are unsaid—so many she's unsure of.

But Noemi knows at least one thing she wants to say to him, and she doesn't intend to waste any more time. "Listen. About before—what I said when we were discussing Simon, and Inheritors—I'm sorry if I hurt you."

"I don't know if 'hurt' is the right word," Abel says. But after another moment he adds, "It will do."

"You're not 'lesser' than me or any other human. I told you once that you were more human than your creator, remember?"

"That proved not to be a very high bar to clear."

She closes her eyes, concentrating to find the right words. "I don't pity you for being a mech."

"But you *do* pity me."

If they were in any other situation, Noemi would walk away now. She'd give him time to consider; she'd think up smarter, better things to say. This would all be so much easier. Yet this is the hour they have. "I pitied you for being so alone. That's all."

"If other Inheritors come into being, I wouldn't be alone. But you said their creation would be a sin."

"Think about it, Abel. Those Inheritors—they'd be hunted across the galaxy. Mansfield never intended to reserve these just for himself or his family, and Gillian Shearer—she thinks her role in this universe is to destroy death itself. Every human who's afraid of mortality, which means every human ever, would try to capture one. The

Inheritors would spend their whole lives on the run. On your own, you can hide, but a whole race of mechs like you? The word's going to get out. After that, you'd all be hunted down every second of your lives."

"...That's your objection?"

"You don't think it would happen?"

"No. You're right, it would, if safeguards weren't in place. But"—Abel's hand closes around hers—"humans can be killed. They can fall prey to disease, or accident, or even murder. That doesn't mean they stop having children."

Is he thinking of them as children already? That feels completely wrong to Noemi, but she can't say exactly why, and she's not going to speak carelessly again. "That's different. Inheritors' souls have been created only to be destroyed. Their bodies will live on to serve as vessels for the rich and powerful, but the Inheritors themselves—the innermost part of them—that dies. Humans aren't created only to die."

"I think your Bible might say differently."

She blinks, taken aback. The entire shape of this question has just changed for her—like the drawing in which a vase suddenly becomes two faces. Every existence is finite; why should one have less value than another?

A creator's intent matters, she thinks, but this is something she needs to consider in depth.

Gently, Abel continues, "You're still thinking of mechs

as living to serve humans. As... secondary. This is a natural assumption, since as of now I am one of only two mechs who lead an independent existence." He turns his face toward the crevasse of wreckage and she knows he's wondering about Simon within that ship, half-formed, afraid and angry. "But it doesn't always have to be that way. Consider the potential."

"I will," Noemi promises. "But will you do something for me?"

"Of course."

"Please consider the possibility that something's not right with Simon. I know you feel for him. I do, too. When I spoke to him the first time, I imagined it was you if you were brand-new, and nobody had ever explained to you what you were. But Gillian rushed the process, and she used a little kid who didn't understand. It went wrong in a way I'm not sure you can put right. Simon's 'games' nearly killed us. They still could. I'm just afraid that—that you want a brother so badly you'll ignore all the warning signs until it's too late."

In the long pause that follows, Noemi curses herself for every word, until Abel finally says, "You may be right. Not about the Inheritors, but about Simon. He's... unstable." Admitting that cost Abel. She hugs him around his waist, offering what little comfort she can, as he continues, "When I was speaking to him through his mechs, I mentioned his mother. I thought he would naturally want to return to her. But Simon felt nothing. He no longer loved her. I know that if I could no longer feel love, I would be irretrievably broken. Simon may be as well. I can't abandon him until I'm sure—but I intend to investigate. And I'll be more cautious in the future."

"Okay. That's all I ask."

When Abel speaks again, his words come more slowly. "The regeneration cycle is about to begin."

"Do you dream while you're regenerating? Or only while you're asleep?"

"I've never dreamed during a regeneration cycle before," he says groggily. "But there's no reason I couldn't, eventually."

Hugging him again, she says, "Then have good dreams."

Abel shifts, as if he's going to turn and look at her, but then his head droops onto the floor and his body goes slack. Regeneration has begun.

Noemi's wired from their narrow escape, and a debris-strewn tank in below-freezing temperatures isn't exactly the most comfortable place she's ever tried to sleep. But she's so exhausted that she thinks she'll be able to grab an hour or two once the adrenaline wears off. Maybe she can try to have some sweet dreams of her own.

As long as Abel's with her, she feels safe. Which at the moment is a total illusion, but she'll take what she can get.

She rests her forehead against his back again, content to feel the in-and-out of his breath—slower than a human's would be, even in sleep, but still comforting. This small comfort feels precious to her. Beautiful, and rare.

Noemi's never questioned what she felt for Abel. By the time he told her he loved her, they had less than one hour left to be together. In the months since, she's often wondered about the nature of his love, whether it was the same as a human's. But there had been no point in asking what she might feel in return. It had seemed so obvious that they could never meet again.

Holding him now, though—the sense of longing and need even while he's in her arms—well, it makes her think.

In her memory she hears what Abel said to her months ago, as they parted at the Genesis Gate: *It hurts more to lose you than it did to give up my own life. Does that mean what I feel isn't only a copy? That I do love you?*

She answered, *I think maybe it does.*

That seems even truer to her now than it did then.

She closes her eyes and hugs Abel more tightly. Just for now, she's going to pretend there's nothing wrong. That there's nothing else in all the worlds but the two of them, together.

26

THE AWARENESS THAT THE REGENERATION CYCLE HAS ended doesn't feel exactly like waking up, but it's close. Abel opens his eyes to near-complete darkness; only a few of Haven's moons are visible at this time of night, and they must be smaller, more distant ones. He adjusts his vision as best as possible, then rotates his wrist. Although some stiffness remains, its condition is adequate for their immediate needs. The ankle feels almost entirely normal.

Next to him, Noemi sleeps soundly, her breathing deep and even. Her arm remains stretched around his waist, although her hand has gone slack. Abel allows himself a few moments to enjoy her nearness, and covers her hand with his own. Hopefully this is not inappropriate. She stirs gently, snuggling against his back in her sleep, and he discovers that love can be a physical sensation, a kind of melting warmth through his chest.

Even if she doesn't love him in return, this feeling is reward enough on its own.

But he can't afford to let such thoughts distract him from their imminent need to escape. He adjusts input so he can listen to the widest possible range of frequencies. His hearing isn't exponentially better than a human's, but the extra sharpness he possesses could make a difference. The bluster of the wind masks almost anything he could possibly hear outside the tank itself. However, he thinks that if Simon's mechs had pursued them to this side of the crevasse, he'd pick something up. Certainly he would hear any Remedy fighters who had made their way over in hopes of collecting the bounty on his life.

Abel and Noemi are alone. They'll get their chance to escape.

For another twenty-six minutes, he allows Noemi to sleep. She can't have gotten nearly enough rest these past few days, even for a young human in top physical condition. However, when the temperature drops further, he realizes they need to act before the chill becomes hazardous for her despite the protection of the parka. "Noemi?" he whispers. Speaking louder would be more effective, but humans seem to value a more gradual awakening. "Noemi, get up."

"Mmph." She stirs beside him, then groans. "I was hoping the tank part was a nightmare."

"We aren't that fortunate. We need to move."

"Can we? Are you okay?" Noemi sits up and touches his arm. No doubt she's only checking his injury, but the contact rushes through Abel like heat or electricity. It's not yet desire, but it could be. Do humans feel attraction at such inconvenient moments? Surely not. This must be some kind of malfunction. Unlike any other malfunction, though, Abel enjoys it.

He says only, "I should be able to climb down the remainder of this side of the ship until we're at ground level, which will provide our best chance at escape. This is of course assuming the necessary handholds exist. What about you? How would you evaluate your climbing strength?"

"I'm not sure. Usually I'm pretty good, but now—" Noemi rubs her hands together; they're red with cold, no doubt numb.

Immediately Abel says, "You should hold on to my back again while I climb for us both."

"Don't put yourself in more danger for me. That's too much weight for you to carry with your ankle and your wrist—"

"It isn't." It's close, but within acceptable parameters. "They're almost back to normal. In addition, you know you can't grip the handholds, not without gloves. This is the only way."

Her frown tells him she doesn't like it, but she nods. "I was thinking—if we get to Virginia's corsair, and return to your ship, maybe we could contact Fouda from there? We might be able to bargain for the relay codes with something else."

"I don't want to leave Simon here."

Noemi pauses, and he anticipates more of her objections to his work with Simon. Instead she says, "We'd have more resources on the ship. Some of Mansfield's original plans for mechs, stuff like that, right? We could regroup and come back for Simon."

"An excellent plan." Its excellence is largely based on the fact that it's the only remotely workable alternative, but Abel feels the need to be encouraging while agreement is still possible between them. His needs and Noemi's will soon conflict. She'll want to help Genesis as fast as she can—understandable—while he knows leaving Simon alone any longer could lead to disaster. He'll make his arguments when the time comes. "Our hike to the corsair will be difficult—about two kilometers from here, but through difficult terrain and thick snow."

She shrugs. "We'll make it or I won't."

Abel wants to correct her statement, as he has no intention of going on without her. But that's something else to mention only later, after it comes up, which, hopefully, it won't.

In some respects, the broken chasm dividing this ship provides a more promising climb than Abel would've thought. Ragged spars of metal jut out at various angles, offering the hand- and footholds they require. Unfortunately, those same spars are mostly crusted with ice. Abel can compensate only so much for a slippery surface.

Noemi's not the only one who could use a pair of gloves.

Quickly calculating ratios and probabilities, Abel decides the likelihood of his making it safely to the bottom is sufficient for him to try it. But it doesn't seem enough for him to risk Noemi. He prefers a wider margin of safety when it comes to her. "I'm not sure I can do this."

"Uh-oh." Noemi rubs her head with one hand. "If you're admitting you have actual limits, that means it's bad, right?"

"Successfully climbing to the bottom isn't impossible. Only . . . slightly less probable than the alternative." This is definitely a time to keep exact percentages to himself.

She exhales, then says, "Well, there's no other way out. No matter what the odds are, we have to try."

Abel knows this, logically, but still wants to argue. Maybe he could escape on his own and bring help back to her—but what help, and when? Most likely he wouldn't be able to return for at least a solid day, by which time Noemi would probably have died of exposure.

"Abel?" She looks at him steadily. "I trust you. I'm

willing to try this. And sitting around here dreading the climb is only freaking me out."

"All right," he says. "Let's go."

They figure out a way to extend his belt and loop it once through the cord around her waist. It's a pitifully weak kind of harness, but it's the best they can do with what they have. Abel positions himself at the tank's edge and lets Noemi adjust her grip on him and her balance. "Ready?" he asks.

Her hands tighten around his shoulders. "Ready."

He bends, grasps the lip of the tank, and drops so that his body hangs over the side. For 0.4 seconds the icy metal seems to deny his hold, but then Abel gets it. Together he and Noemi dangle from this one ledge, she clinging tightly to his back, the crevasse still very far below.

"Oh God oh God oh God oh God," Noemi whispers. "Tell me that was the hardest part."

"It was, actually." Their probability of death is still far too high, but completing the first step means their odds have improved to nearly sixty/forty.

Abel moves slowly, taking his time to make sure every hold is as secure as it can be. His wrist throbs with every movement, which is unimportant as long as his grip remains strong. There's not much Noemi can do to help at this stage, but she remains utterly still, more so than most humans could manage. Because of this, his balance stays constant. With every meter they descend, the drop becomes less dangerous, and their odds improve.

After eleven minutes and fourteen seconds, they reach the bottom. Together they make contact with the ground, then stumble back a few steps before collapsing in the white wet crunch of snow. Noemi's breathing is fast and shallow, like someone trying not to cry; Abel would reassure her if he thought he could speak.

This must be what humans call "exhaustion." He doesn't like it.

Finally Noemi says, very quietly, "Thank you, Abel."

"You're welcome."

"We have to start walking. Can you do it?"

His ankle and wrist ache from the strain of the climb, but as Noemi said earlier—they'll make it or they won't. So he gets to his feet alongside her, brushes ice crystals off his clothes—

—and spots the figure rising from behind a snow-covered pile of debris.

"Abel!" Noemi cries, pushing him to the side just before a blaster bolt arcs through the air overhead. If her reflexes are faster than his, he's even more tired than he thought. They're half-buried in a drift, the snow their only protection. "Was that Remedy?"

"No—the Tare with one eye. One of Simon's. And we're unarmed."

The situation's even worse than that. Even now, the Tare—functioning as part of Simon's mind—is sharing their location with the rest of his mechs. Within minutes the others will be on them.

Abel brought Noemi safely to the ground only for them to both die.

Noemi looks around frantically, her chin-length hair whipping in the wind, before grabbing a large stone and hurling it at their attacker. The Tare has turned so that her absent eye faces them, so she doesn't see the rock coming—and when it makes contact, she goes down instantly, unconscious or inoperable.

"Unarmed, my ass." Noemi scrambles to her feet and tows Abel up with her. She seems to have realized he's not functioning optimally. Snow slips off her parka but clings to his clothes in thick, cold ridges. "We have to go back inside the *Osiris*," she says.

He must protest. They only barely escaped the ship with their lives, and both the passengers and any surviving Remedy members will attack Abel on sight. Simon has yet to be reasoned with. Noemi will be in danger as long as she's near him. "That can only delay our reaching the *Persephone*."

"You're not yourself, Abel. And if you're not at full strength, there's no way we can get to Virginia's corsair." She counts her points off on her red, chapped fingers. "But if we can't fly up to her, she could fly down to us. There's got to be something in the *Osiris* we could use to contact her—right? Or we could maybe find the docking bay and take a smaller ship, if there's one that's still spaceworthy. Either way, we'll be able to help ourselves better in there than we can out here."

"Agreed." It's risky, but so is every other course of action they could take. He stalks through the snow over to the fallen Tare and takes her blaster in hand. If he has to put Noemi in danger again, at least he'll be able to defend her. Then he spies another blaster among the wreckage and tosses it to Noemi, who's very good at defending herself. She's also skilled at attacking, as their opponents on this ship will soon be aware.

And if he sees Simon again—what?

He'll answer that when he has to, and not before. "Let's go."

⬤　⬤　⬤

Their entry point at ground level turns out not to be far from the air lock through which Abel originally entered the *Osiris*. He feels a strange ache at the memory of Riko greeting him here, smiling and exhilarated, little guessing she had less than three days left to live.

Concentrate on relevant facts, he reminds himself. *At the time, this was Remedy-held territory. But Remedy no longer has the workforce to control so much space. This location should be safe.*

"How far are we from a communications station we could use to contact Virginia?"

"Given the depleted energy reserves within the ship, we would probably have to get very near the bridge to find a working comms console. While possible, this course of action would also bring us into likely contact with Remedy members." Who will, of course, be desperate to capture Abel and turn him over to Gillian in exchange for the medicine that would save their surviving friends.

She nods. "And the docking bay?" As they slowly work their way within, it becomes clear that even the emergency lighting has begun to falter. Abel adjusts his vision to infrared so Noemi will remain a warm glow by his side.

"Nearly half the length of the ship away—but closer than the bridge."

She groans. "Let's just start walking."

One corridor proves to be by far the safest and best lit, so they're able to make good time. They walk instead of run, both to be as quiet as possible and to avoid overtaxing Noemi. Or so Abel thinks, until he realizes that for once Noemi's the one slowing down to his pace. Perhaps she's worried about his ankle. It's strangely pleasant, being worried about.

Yet some of his capacities remain at full strength—including his mech vision. Within fifteen meters of the docking bay, he halts midstep, putting his arm out to block Noemi. When she turns to him, confused, he says in a low voice, "Pressurized explosive device, point four one meters ahead."

"How are you—"

"I'm on infrared frequencies right now. Otherwise I would've missed it. Apparently a wire's been fed through the floor of the corridor."

"Remedy *mined the floor?*" Noemi steps backward, a movement Abel copies. They came far too close to activating this device. If he's accurately measuring its explosive content, the resulting blast would've shredded them both. "It has to be Remedy—there's no way the passengers have the know-how for this, or Simon either."

"Agreed. They must've done this when their people began falling ill. Since Remedy no longer had members available for patrols, they went for mines."

"Well, let's find a corridor they didn't mine."

But such a corridor isn't easy to find. Now that Abel knows how to look for the devices, he's able to adjust his vision to search areas human sight could never reach. Remedy's mines are planted deep in the ship's framework, making it impossible to cross from one part of the ship to another. "There must remain at least one route to the docking bay," he says, as much to himself as to her, when they find the fifth blocked passage. "It's the most tactically significant section of the *Osiris*. They wouldn't cut themselves off from it."

"But we'd have to go through whatever remains of Remedy to reach it, which means they'd target you." Noemi leans against one wall. "You see what this is, don't you?"

"A trap." He should have expected as much.

"No. At least, not for us. Even if every member of Remedy dropped dead, the passengers wouldn't be able to leave the surface of this planet. Not now, not ever. Fouda knows he's lost. So he's making sure the passengers die with them, even if it means they starve."

History contains many examples of humanity's capacity for spite, so this shouldn't shock Abel. But he still can't comprehend how a person comes to such a calculation.

He can, however, perform some calculations of his own. "Fouda may have wired the docking bay, too."

"I wouldn't put it past him," Noemi agrees.

"Perhaps we should try to approach the bridge after all. Remedy's forces are weakened. We stand a chance of reaching a communications console."

"No." Noemi squares her shoulders. "We have to set the passengers free."

"I don't intend to abandon them. We should send for

help once we've reached the Earth system." Some of the patrol ships circling Neptune and its moons no doubt know of the *Osiris* and would be able to mount a rescue mission. "As for Simon, I'll reach out to him once we have comms."

Noemi folds her arms across her chest. "What makes you think he's going to listen?"

"I've been considering what would motivate him. He is, at his core, a little boy. So I thought I would offer him a ride in a new spaceship. One where he can sit in the captain's chair. That would work, wouldn't it?"

Her tone gentles. "Maybe. But if he goes haywire up there—"

"I can install safeguards." Abel's already considered this. "There's no way I'd ever let him endanger you. Or Virginia." He hopes Virginia never hears how he had to add on that last.

"Okay. I trust you." She says it more like she's convincing herself than him.

"We must of course do something for the passengers and Remedy members before we go. Their lives are endangered."

Noemi hesitates. At first, their escape seemed like no more than leaving a dangerous situation; however, Abel's programming is at work within him, urging him to protect human life if he can...absent instructions to the contrary from Burton Mansfield, who is no longer a factor. He suspects Noemi's religious belief operates much the same way within her, reminding her of others who need protection.

She begins, "You know how badly I want to get off this planet and help Genesis, but—no, you're right. We can't leave them to die. They don't have tons of food down there—just champagne and petits fours, and they were almost out of those when I left. Those force fields have to be tapping the last of the energy; soon the ship's climate control will fail. The passengers will freeze to death before we can send help."

The fervor in Noemi's voice stirs something within Abel—a sense of purpose that goes beyond his programming. That purpose is as much a part of her as blood or bone.

Quietly he says, "You will always be a soldier of Genesis. A holy warrior."

Noemi nods. Even in the gloom of this dark corridor, he can discern the glimmer of tears in her eyes. "Do you think there's any hope of getting the codes from Fouda? Or will he let my planet die?"

"I don't know."

There is one thing Abel could do, a final drastic measure that would get them the codes. He could trade himself to Fouda for the codes to help Genesis—allowing Fouda to then trade him to Gillian for medicine.

Gillian Shearer would get her hands on Abel at last. His soul would be forfeit, and his body would finally, completely, belong to Mansfield. He would fulfill Directive One.

The very fact that Noemi hasn't argued for this herself is testament to how much their friendship must mean to her. He offered to die for Genesis once before, but she rejects that idea as strongly now as she did then. Still, if it comes down to one life for billions—

Abel curtails the thought. He believes they'll get out of this on their own, because he believes in Noemi. She is the only faith he needs.

27

Normally Noemi would leave the mechanical work to Abel. It's not that she doesn't know how to do most of it, more that she figures the guy who is actually *part machine* has an advantage.

But now she kneels in front of the nearest comm panel, prying it open and using her small emergency light to peer inside. She'll do the labor so Abel can conserve his strength. Their escape from the other side of the ship nearly killed him; she understands that even if he doesn't. As they traveled through the corridors closer to the bridge, Abel walked slowly, and with an almost imperceptible limp. That sort of behavior, coming from him, is proof of real damage.

Even more proof: He lets her do the work without complaint or comment.

Noemi doesn't know how to fix Abel, but she can at least be careful with him. She can't haul him all the way across the ship. They have to figure out a way to handle this where they are.

The comm panel they've got isn't fully powered, but Noemi's jury-rigged it to do something. She only needs to make a couple of transmissions—starting with a couple of deals.

If she handles this right, both Captain Fouda and Gillian Shearer will have to play by *her* rules for a change.

"Okay, I'm about to call the passengers' headquarters." Noemi glances up at him. "Are you ready?"

Abel nods, and she puts it through.

Her voice crackles and echoes through the corridor as she says, "This is Noemi Vidal of Genesis, for Gillian Shearer." The pause feels longer than it is.

The passengers must've been listening for Fouda to issue commands, because the reply comes almost instantly. *"Where is Abel?"* Gillian demands. Her voice comes through the small speaker against Noemi's hand; the vibrating effect feels like she's holding Gillian in her palm. *"Does he still exist? Or did Remedy destroy him?"* She's scared of what Remedy would do out of spite.

"Abel's fine," Noemi says. "So am I. Thanks for asking."

Gillian ignores this. *"I want to speak directly to Abel."*

Abel kneels beside Noemi and leans close to the console. Its golden light glows between them as he says, "I'm here, Gillian."

"*You're not coming back for Father, are you?*" Gillian's voice breaks. She's caught between laughter and tears, so vividly that Noemi can picture her saying, "*Did the two of you call just to torment me?*"

"No," he says. "I wanted to tell you that Simon remains alive, though exhibiting extreme mental and physical malfunction. He's collecting other mechs, somehow controlling them. Simon's dangerous to anyone on this ship—including you—and to himself. However, I still believe I can help him."

"*So you're using the life of a small child as a bargaining chip,*" Gillian retorts.

Noemi cuts in. "And you're using dozens of lives as bargaining chips, so you don't have a lot of room to talk, Dr. Shearer."

"I'll help Simon no matter what," Abel says quietly. "If I can."

"*If this isn't about Simon—*"

"You're smart enough to have kept checking the main passageways, so I'm guessing you know Remedy's trapped all of you on this ship," Noemi says. "If the mechs from the Winter Castle were coming to save you, they'd have gotten here by now. You're going to starve or freeze to death if we don't help you—but we're willing to help you. *If* you accept a few conditions."

"*Conditions.*" Is that anger in Gillian's voice? Resignation? "*Of course.*"

"They're pretty simple," Noemi says. "One, you never come after Abel again. No mech hunters, no hostage situations, nothing. You set him free. Your father had his time, so let Abel have his."

One of Abel's hands curves around her wrist, a gentle touch that lifts one corner of Noemi's mouth in a smile.

Gillian says brusquely, "*What else?*"

"Two, you spare the surviving members of Remedy. You give them the medical supplies they need. Then you bring them to the Winter Castle, share your provisions, let them help build this world. The ones who've had Cobweb are as adapted to Haven as you are."

"*How did you know—*" Gillian cuts herself off, but too late.

"They need new homes as much as you do," Noemi continues. "Yeah, some of them have done terrible things, but seeing as how you guys basically tried to *steal a planet*, I don't think you have much room to talk. They're used to hard work, and they have some of the skills your passengers lack. They'd make good settlers for a new world."

In the background, beneath the crackle of the speaker, Noemi hears Delphine call, "*We need someone who knows how to make snowshoes!"* and has to bite her lip to keep from laughing.

Gillian finally says, *"All right. We can do that. But Simon—Abel, what are you going to do with Simon? I've called and called for him—"*

"Help him stabilize his mental and emotional processes," Abel replies. "I'm not sure whether you can restore him to a growing tank at this point, or whether his memory patterns have been warped by the transfer—there are many variables in play. He began his existence as a human, which makes his experience radically different from mine, but we're still alike in one fundamental way. We're the only two mechs in the galaxy who are also…individuals. If anyone can understand him, I can."

Gillian's response: *"No one understands a child like his mother does."*

No way is Noemi letting her get away with that. "Or like a father? Well, I'm sorry, but Mansfield told you to trash Simon and start over, like that would be no big deal. To me that sounds like your dad didn't understand you at all."

Another long silence falls. Abel's eyes widen as he thinks about Mansfield's dismissal of Simon, even though Noemi already told him about it. Abel's pain remains palpable. Maybe people never stop trying to believe in those they once loved.

Noemi decides it would be merciful to change the subject. "Okay, we have a deal. Wait where you are until we confirm that we've deactivated the mines."

The dry response: *"I don't think you have to worry about that one. We're in no hurry to test them for ourselves."*

"Then let's save comms power. Vidal out." With a flick of her thumb, the intraship comm goes quiet again, and she nods to Abel to change the signal. She's no longer calling the passengers; this time, she's calling the bridge. "Captain Fouda?"

It takes several long seconds for a reply to come. *"Vidal of Genesis."* Fouda's voice is ragged, his tone like that of a man in shock. *"Still alive."*

"So far. We need to talk."

"We need your mech." The defiance has bled out of him. All Noemi hears now is desperation. *"Human lives are at stake—"*

"We've bargained with the passengers," Noemi explains. "They'll give you the medicine you need if you deactivate as many mines as you can—and give me the relay codes for Remedy."

She expects Fouda to argue or posture, but he's past all that. *"We don't have many people left. The mines—I'm not sure how much we can do."*

"Defuse as many as you can," she repeats, adjusting her

expectations. "Abel and I will take out a few, too. But now I need those relay codes."

"Gamma four eight seven delta mu delta five five one eight zeta six pi phi sigma three—"

The string of letters and numbers catches her off guard; this must be something Fouda memorized by rote, something he's spitting out with the last of his mental strength. *I can't record him! There's no way I can remember this!* Noemi momentarily panics, then realizes Abel's getting every word.

When Fouda finally finishes, he says, *"How long? We need the medicine now."*

"Abel and I need to clear at least one of the mines as a show of good faith," Noemi answers. "As soon as we've done that, we'll send passengers with help. All right?"

"All right." Fouda's weariness makes it clear he sees this as defeat, even though it's going to save the few people he has left. *"Fouda out."*

The tiny light between her and Abel goes dark. Her eyes have adjusted enough to the dim lighting to see his expression, though—thoughtful and uncertain at once. "What is it, Abel?"

"You bargained for everyone except yourself." He shakes his head slowly. "You're remarkable."

"I bargained for you. That counts."

Abel's hand slides up her arm, curves around the back

of her neck. The way he leans closer makes her realize he intends to kiss her. Her heart thumps crazily in her chest—

—but he drops his hand and pulls back. "I apologize."

No denying it: Noemi feels cheated. "For what?"

"For acting on my romantic feelings." Abel explains this as easily as he would the workings of the mag engines. "I don't expect you to share them. But my momentary impulse may have made you feel awkward. I won't make the same mistake again."

Slowly Noemi says, "Oh, Abel—that's all wrong—"

"What do you mean?"

She can't come up with the words. Words aren't important. Nothing matters except a truth she didn't know until this moment.

Noemi puts her arms around Abel and brings her lips to his. When she kisses him, he tenses; at first she thinks she's gotten it wrong somehow. But then he embraces her, brings her closer, kisses her back. She gives in to it, opening his mouth with her own.

The first time they kissed, she was floating in midair. Gravity holds them fast now, but somehow it feels the same, like she's flying inside.

No, better. Last time she was only kissing Abel goodbye. It was an ending. This is a beginning.

When their mouths part, Noemi's breathing hard. Abel's expression looks more dazed and wary than elated.

"We shouldn't get caught up like this. Not in the middle of such a serious crisis."

That's what Captain Baz would tell them. That's good military training. Noemi has never given less of a damn about military training in her life.

Then Abel continues, "But as you humans say—to hell with it." And he kisses her again.

This time the kiss goes on much, much longer. Their tiny corner of the *Osiris*—their patch of this new world—feels like all there is to the entire universe. Noemi combs her fingers through his fair hair, leans against him so that he'll feel her heartbeat through his chest; maybe it will feel like a heartbeat to him, too. He doesn't have a heart or pulse of his own. She'll share hers.

Finally, Abel breaks the kiss and folds her deeper in his embrace. Noemi buries her face in the curve of his shoulder.

Tentatively he asks, "Is it bad form to ask for romantic clarification?"

She laughs in his arms. "I don't know. I don't care. Ask away."

"Would you describe yourself as 'in love' with me, or merely interested in exploring a romantic connection?" He sounds so earnest, so unsure. "Either alternative is extremely acceptable. But I'd like to know."

"Probably? Maybe?" Noemi's more confused than Abel could possibly be. She only knows that she couldn't have gone one more second without kissing him. "When I went back to Genesis, my old life didn't fit me anymore. Some of that was because we lost Esther, and some of it was because I was a pariah—"

"Pariah?"

"Skip it for now. Mostly my life didn't fit because I changed on that trip. The idea I had about who I was going to be, and the kind of person I could care about— that didn't apply anymore. Nobody understood that, but I knew you would. I wished I had you to lean on, and to talk to. I imagined what you would say about everything, and I wanted to hear it. Even if you were going on forever or being arrogant! I didn't care."

Abel says, "It is not arrogance if I am realistically assessing my abilities as superior, which generally they are." Of *course* that's the point he'd have trouble with. But she's begun to smile, and so has he.

"I didn't fall in love with you on the journey," she says. "I don't know if I'm in love with you now. But you're probably the best person I've ever known. I care about you more than anyone else in this entire galaxy. I don't know what comes after this, if anything even can. All I know is you're the only person I can't imagine living my whole life without."

Noemi never feels like she's said the right words, except maybe this time. The way Abel's face lights up, the pure hope that's shining from him—she must've gotten at least some of that right.

He kisses her one more time, but when their mouths break apart, he holds up one finger. "…We should probably do something about the mines."

"Yes. Bombs." She pulls back and shakes her head, trying to clear it. "Good idea."

•   •   •

First they turn to one of the largest intact corridors in the ship, the one that will be most useful to both Remedy and the passengers.

In Genesis military training, cadets extensively study both space and planetary mines. Noemi worked harder than most. The last moment she spent with her family was the moment before they drove over an explosive device not so different from a mine; for her, defusing bombs feels like defeating an enemy. Those diagrams come to mind as clearly as if they were still on her academy screen. "Okay," she says as they stand at the far end of the corridor. "I'm going to crawl into the service tube and check this one out. If I can defuse it, great. If it's too thorny, or requires equipment I don't have, we move to the next corridor."

"I should be the one to take the risk," Abel insists, like she knew he would.

Noemi clasps his hands in hers. "I've worked with mines before. I know what I'm doing. You're exhausted, and you're more damaged than you're letting on."

"I still have full dexterity in my wrist."

"Maybe you do. But let me handle this one, okay?" She struggles for the words. "I don't mind letting you do more, because you *are* stronger than any human could ever be. You *do* have more info in your memory banks than any brain could hold. That doesn't mean you automatically have to be the one who puts yourself in danger every time." Noemi brings his hand to her lips and kisses it. His skin is terribly abraded from their icy climb through the crevasse. "Your life matters as much as any human's, Abel. Remember that."

"Not yours. Not to me." He shakes his head. "You're my priority."

"And you're mine."

She can tell he wants to argue more, but he looks down at his damaged hands. If emotion won't convince him, logic will. Sure enough, after a couple of seconds, he nods. "If you run into any difficulty whatsoever—"

"I'll call for you."

"And if you're even slightly uncertain—"

"Same thing."

Abel kisses her hand this time, then lets her go.

Noemi shimmies into the narrow opening of the service tube, pausing after a meter or two to take stock of the few tools she's collected, and to slide a pair of night-vision goggles down into place. In the corridors, she could manage, but down here it's nearly pitch-black. The damage of the crash is strongly apparent here, with the bent girders and collapsed struts of the *Osiris* naked and exposed. When she saw the useless murals and gilding, stepped over the shattered finery, she saw only the waste. Now that she's in the belly of the thing, looking at its raw strength, Noemi realizes how splendid a ship it really was.

It was meant to be a vehicle of resurrection, she thinks. *If it hadn't been for the passengers' greed and Remedy's anger, this ship could've brought an entire planet's worth of settlers to humanity's next home. It really would have been a rebirth.*

In the green-tinted world presented by the night-vision goggles, Noemi spots the mine almost immediately. Its wires sprawl in multiple directions, like one of the heptapod squids native to Genesis's oceans. Still, with a mine, scale is relatively unimportant. Defuse the central mechanism, and all the arms go dead.

Still in the tunnel, she lowers herself into the broader open space beneath the mine. It's barely high enough for her to stand in; Fouda must've sent someone short down here. Still, she can lean back a little, brace her shoulder against one of the walls, and be steady.

Doffing her goggles, Noemi turns on her small light again to check wire and tab coloration. The pattern clarifies and aligns with one she studied back in training, a pretty basic model that practically shows her how to defuse it.

With a grim smile, Noemi takes up the nearby emergency tool kit and gets to work.

What would Captain Baz think of her now? She'd be proud, probably—assuming she doesn't hate Noemi for taking so damn long to help Genesis. As for Darius Akide—

What's that noise?

She ducks, extracting her tools from the mine as she peers through the darkness of the tunnel. Seeing anything is impossible, but she knows she didn't imagine that scraping sound. Swiftly she tugs her night-vision goggles down over her eyes and looks out—

—at Simon smiling back at her.

He whispers, "Peekaboo."

28

ABEL ACCEPTS NOEMI'S DECISION TO TAKE ON THE
mines herself. Although he considers following several paces
behind her, he abandons this plan almost immediately; if he
distracted her at the wrong moment, it could be dangerous
to her. If she felt he didn't trust her to handle something well
within her capabilities... that could be dangerous to *him*.

Besides, she was right. Now that he's sitting still with
nothing to do but rest, he realizes how much his reaction times have slowed. He's drained the reserves of his
regenerative ability; he won't be able to heal until he's
rested. Noemi recognized that even before he did.

My programming prioritizes handling problems for humans.
Naturally I want to do things for Noemi. But perhaps emo-
tional attachment programs humans to do the same.

Fresh wonder opens within his mind as he remembers
that Noemi is emotionally attached to him—that she can't
imagine leading her life without—

He hears metal creak underneath. Localizing his hearing, he determines that the sound is coming from directly under his position, and that in addition to the metal, he can also make out the sound of shuffling feet.

Noemi shouldn't be down there. That's nowhere near the mine. Her position would be several meters ahead—

—which is where the footsteps are headed.

Instantly Abel's on his feet, dashing to the nearest passageway. He reminds himself, *This is why humans should never make the plans!*

The closest hatch door is only a meter away. Lowering himself down is easy, as is moving quickly and silently through the corridor. His infrared vision allows him to glimpse a small human form—slightly too soft, with uneven footsteps—yes, it's Simon. Confirmation comes one second later in the most chilling form possible: Simon's voice saying, "What makes you go?"

"What do you mean?" Noemi sounds so calm, so steady.

"You're not like me and Abel," says Simon. "You're just a person. I don't understand what makes people go."

"I bet you have that information in your databanks," she answers, keeping her tone even. "I bet Abel would be willing to help you figure out how to access it. In fact, I know he would."

Abel's fear for her is mingled with fierce pride.

"Let's go see him together," she continues. "He wants to make things better for you, I promise."

Noemi doesn't trust Simon. She fears him. But for Abel's sake, she treats him with kindness and tries to give him hope. He doesn't have to defend Simon from her any longer... which is why he can see Simon more clearly than before: The awkward way he shuffles forward, though at this point Simon's mind should've adapted to the basic parameters of his new body. The slope of his shoulders, the angle of which has adjusted remarkably wider since Abel first glimpsed him—as though his inner structure hasn't firmed enough to hold. The rawness of Simon's skin, which had to have been even softer than a newborn's when he emerged from his tank, and is now severely abraded with no sign of healing.

"The voices inside say so many things." Simon's own voice breaks up, dropping various frequencies as he speaks. "One of them says that the way you breathe and that sound I can hear in your tummy means you're tired and hungry. That one wants me to get you to a sick bay. I don't know what a sick bay is, but I'm supposed to take you to it."

Tare programming, Abel realizes. Gillian didn't just try to bring back her son; she tried to equip him with Abel's full array of knowledge and skills. She failed. It was too much for one small child mech.

Simon continues, "This other voice says that you're an

enemy, and weakness gives me a chance to kill an enemy. I wait for you to get distracted, and then I rip your throat out."

Probably that comes from a Charlie.

"I'd rather we went to the sick bay," Noemi says, straight-faced. "Let's listen to that voice."

"No. You *are* an enemy, aren't you? You told Abel not to help me."

"I was scared. I didn't understand. That's when we make mistakes. Don't make a mistake now, Simon." She shifts her weight from foot to foot, and Abel realizes she's trying to determine a way out. There isn't a ready one.

The mine stretches overhead, trip wires splayed at roughly thirty-degree angles across the entire floor. In Abel's infrared vision, the small explosive at its center glows like a red jewel. He estimates its explosive strength based on size and the materials likely to have been available to Remedy members on short notice. Then he looks at Simon again.

I'm sorry, he thinks. *You might've been my brother. But they pushed too hard with you. They were impatient. You deserved better.*

He puts his hand on the holt of his blaster.

Abel means to call a warning to Simon, to give him a chance to run. It might be best, in the end, for Gillian to make the ultimate decision about termination. But as he opens his mouth, Simon takes a staggering step closer to

Noemi and says, "I know. I'll kill you and *then* I'll take you to the sick bay."

With that, Simon holds out his own blaster. He must've grabbed one from a fallen Charlie or Queen, like any little boy who doesn't yet understand the difference between a weapon and a toy. It's too big for his tiny hand, but he knows how to fire it. Charlie programming again.

Rushing forward, Abel knocks Simon down but doesn't pause. He grabs Noemi by the waist as he runs; she exhales sharply from the blow but hangs on to him as he runs at top speed through the service tube.

She gasps, still struggling for breath, "He's up—he's aiming—"

"Fire at the mine on my mark." Abel stops short, dropping Noemi. She reacts as fast as any mech could, landing in firing position, blaster leveling. "Now!"

She fires. Point zero one three seconds later, Abel grabs the seam of the metal panel beneath them and rolls over Noemi, pulling the flooring over and around them, wrapping them both under the makeshift shield.

Light brighter than Earth's sun flashes, forcing him to momentarily cut all visual input; compressed heated air hits their metal shield hard enough to dent it and to sear his breath. Noemi hisses in pain, but remains still for another 1.9 seconds, which is when they both smell the fire.

"Go," she says, pushing Abel out. He glimpses the burn

mark on the back of her hand, but there's no time to do anything but run away from the burning blast area—away from what little remains of Simon Shearer.

Neither of them can run at top speed, even with wiring and walls catching flame all around them. The blaze isn't far behind, spreading through the entire service tube at a speed even greater than he'd estimated. In front of them is only darkness; behind them is flickering firelight.

"Service hatch?" she gasps.

Abel doesn't respond with words, instead shoving her to the side. She collides with the ladder and leaps up. He's just behind her, pushing her although she's going fast—he feels the air heating around his feet, heating all around them—

Noemi pushes herself through and collapses into an ashy, crooked corridor. Here, too, they can see the flame, but this must be one of the few areas of the *Osiris* where the anti-fire protections are intact. The sprinkler system squirts up from the floor, not down from the ceiling, but it's enough to keep the blaze contained. Soon it will sputter out.

Simon Shearer has died a second time. Abel wonders how many times the child will be resurrected, and how many of those resurrections will fail.

The only greater punishment than death is to be asked to die over and over again.

• • •

Abel's meditations on Simon's fate absorb him so deeply that Noemi has led him halfway to the docking bay before he registers her actions. Or maybe it's exhaustion, which can be put aside during a crisis but otherwise appears to be extremely persistent.

"We're almost out of here." She hops onto a broken ledge, swings herself over, and pauses for him to follow. "As soon as we find a ship, we're free."

"We have to tell Gillian what happened." Why does he still feel obligated to that family? Why do their feelings still matter to him? "She needs to know about the cleared path, but above all, I have to tell her about Simon."

He can't let her wait for her son in vain.

"We have to tell her what happened once we're safely off the *Osiris*," Noemi says. "Otherwise, she's going to come after you with everything she's got."

He doubts Gillian has much in the way of an attack force, but at this point it wouldn't take much to subdue him. Although Noemi's held up better—astonishing for a human—she, too, is showing signs of weariness. Immediate escape is by far the best course of action.

The docking bay looks more like a child's jumbled toy box than an organized dock for spacecraft. While force fields held some of the smaller craft in place during the crash, most of the ships broke free. The piles of wreckage stand as much as six meters high in some areas. Abel muses that any human in the docking bay during the crash was surely killed.

"Well." Noemi sighs. "Looks like we're going to have to hitch one last ride from Mansfield."

His gaze follows her gesture to a white semi-spherical ship in one corner that's nearly untouched. "It looks like something he would've liked," Abel says quietly.

She notices his reaction—his grief for his father/creator—but only caresses his hand for a moment before becoming businesslike again. "He owes us this one, I gue—"

"Simon says stay."

Noemi jumps. Abel spins around to see a Queen model, largely stripped of skin and flesh beneath the waist. The illusion of semi-nudity is strangely off-putting, as are the Queen's unfocused eyes. She stands amid one of the junk piles; in her damaged state, she blended in with it perfectly.

"Simon is gone," Noemi says slowly, putting out one hand as if to shield them both. "He's not here anymore."

The Queen repeats, "Simon says stay."

Abel runs through likely commands and possibilities. "His final instructions may well have been to keep us in one place until he could confront us in person."

"And those instructions"—Noemi swallows hard—"nobody can cancel those but Simon, who is now dead and so not available to cancel anything ever again. Right?"

"Precisely."

"Meaning we have a problem."

From high above in the coils of fuel hoses and cells, a King shouts, "Simon says *stay*!"

"Affirmative," Abel says. "We have a problem."

Noemi shakes her head as though to clear it. "On my mark—*run*!"

He dashes toward Mansfield's ship at top speed—his current top speed, which isn't fast enough. Abel runs ahead of Noemi this time, because preparing the ship for take-off is the single most effective way of protecting her. All around them, amid the clusters of scrap metal, mechs and pieces of mechs crawl forth, screeching and scrabbling, each one stripped of any purpose or function other than pursuing Abel and Noemi.

Abel feels a split second of revulsion—at mechs, at the very thing he is himself—but pushes it aside as he leaps into the ship.

Its plush interior certainly seems like the kind of luxury Mansfield would—would *have* insisted upon. While Abel checks fuel and power, Noemi dashes in and runs straight to the piloting controls. She slaps the control for the doors, which slide shut—

—partway, until the top half of a Yoke model wedges itself between them, one bloody arm still clawing uselessly at the air.

"Shake her off!" Noemi shouts to Abel as she fires up the engines. The ship lifts from the floor unevenly, hovering with a distinct wobble. "I'm gonna see if the automatic doors still work!"

"By flying directly at them?"

"Got a better idea?"

"Unfortunately, no."

As the ship wheels around, gaining speed, he kicks at the Yoke to dislodge it. Yokes are built for strength, and this one doesn't budge. The doors continue pressing in, but that only grips the Yoke more firmly. He cannot use his blaster without potentially damaging the ship.

Finally he pulls a chair from its stand and bashes the Yoke repeatedly until it falls away—just as he hears the scraping of the docking bay doors, and he and Noemi emerge from darkness into morning light. Fresh cold air whips through their vessel via the still-open doors, and Abel welcomes the chill. They have at last escaped the *Osiris*.

This would be a greater relief if the ship's doors would shut.

"Come on," Noemi mutters, punching at the controls again. "Come on."

Abel grabs the ship's doors and attempts to pull them shut, but the Yoke's clawing damaged them. If the doors can't be closed, the ship can't leave Haven's atmosphere, and he and Noemi will have to land and find the corsair. "Our escape may be flawed."

"And it just got worse." Noemi gestures at the screen, which shows a handful of battered ships leaving the docking bay, no doubt piloted by mechs still mindlessly doing Simon's bidding. How long will these mechs hunt them? Days? Weeks? There's no way to be sure how strong Simon's commands are until they're tested. Reaching the corsair with this many enemies in pursuit will be dangerous; it may be impossible.

Through the doors he catches a flash of red light. Noemi gasps, and he turns back to the screen. Another vessel has entered the atmosphere and is picking off the pursuing craft...not with weapons, but with mining lasers.

Grinning, he goes to the comm panel, activates the signal, and says, "Your timing is impeccable."

"You'd better believe I'm forever captain for this!" Virginia yells back, and Noemi laughs out loud for joy.

29

Noemi hops from Mansfield's freshly landed ship into thick white snow. The cold can't touch her now. In the sky sparkles a familiar vessel, teardrop-shaped and diving toward their location. A broad smile spreads across her face. "The *Persephone*, huh?"

"The *Persephone*," Abel confirms. He moves stiffly as he leaves Mansfield's ship. Noemi feels his pain almost as if it were her own—a strange sensitivity that courses through her nerves—and resolves to get him into regeneration mode as soon as possible.

Aside from worrying about his well-being, it feels kind of good to be the one taking care of him for a change.

The *Persephone* stops maybe half a kilometer away and hovers in place for a moment.

A distant, screeching metal sound makes them both jump, but then Noemi recognizes the faint shimmer of the tractor beam. A moment later, something red and mostly shiny rises through the air—the corsair, no doubt just where Abel left it. The landing bay opens to take it in, and then the *Persephone* spins toward their location, touching down in a whirlwind of snow as its door pinwheels open. Noemi grabs Abel's hand again as they run on board.

"I'm back!" She spins as she looks around the bay. "I actually made it back. I never thought I would."

The ship lifts off again, landing bay door spiraling shut. Abel flips down a nearby jump seat and sinks onto it. "Welcome back."

It feels more like he said *Welcome home.*

The inner door to the corridor slides open, revealing Virginia Redbird wearing an orange coverall and an enormous smile. She bounds toward them. "Noemi!"

"*Virginia.* You did it. You saved us."

"As usual," Virginia says, bundling Noemi into a warm hug. "I'm going to be one hundred percent honest here— I'm orbiting this planet, getting nervous because Robot Boy here isn't checking in, and I figure, it's time to see how things are going for these two. And they were sucking! What with you guys crashing and all. Which meant you needed me, not that you don't always."

"You were right." Noemi slumps against the wall. Relief feels like the removal of a tremendous weight she's had to carry for too long.

Virginia's enormous smile dims the smallest fraction. "Are you guys all right?"

"We need warmth, rest, and food," Abel says. "More regeneration time. Then we'll be fine."

"Then all's well that—oh, *hell*, no." Virginia's eyes widen as she takes one staggering step toward the corsair. As Noemi takes a good look at it, she winces; its surface has been damaged by multiple blaster bolts. "What happened?"

Abel says, "Most likely, when the mechs searching for us found a possible escape vehicle, they attempted to destroy it."

Noemi murmurs, "Simon says stay."

"Luckily their armaments weren't sufficient to destroy the corsair," Abel adds helpfully. "They were only able to severely damage it."

The worst ever at comforting people, Noemi thinks as she puts a hand on Virginia's shoulder. "Um—we're so sorry—"

"It's all right," Virginia says weakly. "You're my friends, and you're more important than my ride. Always. But I just—I need a few seconds to just, I don't know, flail around and make pterodactyl noises. Let me do that, okay?"

Noemi's not sure what that means until Virginia grabs her long hair and makes a screeching sound that does in fact sound like a large prehistoric thing in distress, at least as Noemi imagines it.

I should probably leave her to it, she decides. Besides, she has someone else to take care of.

"You," Noemi says to Abel, bending to sling his arm over her shoulders and help him up. "Sick bay. Now."

"First we have to contact the *Osiris* one last time."

Her heart sinks as she realizes what he means—but he's right. This is one call they have to make.

• • •

"*Abel?*" The comms on the bridge crackle with Gillian Shearer's voice. "*We registered an explosion on our equipment several minutes ago—were you responsible? What's happening? Please respond!*"

"It was us," says Noemi.

Gillian doesn't even acknowledge her. "*And Simon? Have you found Simon yet?*"

When Noemi's dark eyes meet Abel's, she's silently asking whether he wants to say this himself, or whether it's too painful. He lifts his head, accepting the duty. "Gillian, I'm truly sorry. Simon is gone."

A long pause follows, and is broken by Gillian's rough voice. "*You killed him.*"

"We had no choice. Both his body and his mind were breaking down beyond repair, and he was endangering human life. I can tell you that it was—quick."

Gillian Shearer has no use for such mercies. "*You lied to*

me. You lied*! You killed my son. The bargain's over, Abel. We will find you.*"

"We're off-planet, actually," Noemi says. She'd like to rub that into Gillian's face, but Abel clearly has more to say.

He looks upward—maybe remembering Gillian's face— as he says, "Don't stop working on the Inheritors. The project isn't quite ready for Simon, or for your father, or any other human transfer. Still, you're very close. Someday soon there will be other mechs like me. But we're more than repositories for human thought. We're—a new species. Another kind of person. Someday you'll see that. If Simon taught you nothing else, let him teach you this."

"Don't you preach about my son to me, you—" Gillian's voice chokes off. The comms go dead.

Noemi turns her full attention to Abel. He stands behind his own captain's chair, hands resting on the back of it, more weary and worn than she'd known he could look.

"It cost you," Noemi says. "Sacrificing Simon for me."

"I would've protected you no matter what. But I'm not the one who sacrificed him. Simon became a sacrifice when his mother and grandfather chose to experiment with his soul rather than let him go."

The moral dimensions of everything she's learned— of what it will mean when there are other mechs with souls, whether they should exist, whether they can be protected—this is something she needs to meditate on. As the adrenaline of their flight from the *Osiris* fades, her urgency to return to Genesis flares brighter in her mind. Here and now, however, she has a more immediate priority. "We need to get you to the sick bay. They have things to repair mechs in the sick bay, right? You're partly organic."

"My primary medical needs at this time would be better served by a mechanical repair kit than by anything in the sick bay."

"So get yourself down to repair." Noemi takes him by the shoulders and steers him to the door. "Then get some sleep."

"You need rest as well," he points out.

It will take them hours to reach the Haven Gate. Virginia's still mourning her corsair. And Noemi will need her strength for what's to come. "If I go to bed, you'll go to bed?"

Abel had expected her to argue, she can tell, but he nods.

"Don't you dare wake up for at least seven hours," she says, pointing her finger at him.

"As you command," Abel replies, in a soft tone of voice that makes her wonder when else he might say that. Even as her cheeks flush hot, she gestures toward his bedroom and he obediently goes inside, hopefully straight to sleep.

• • •

Noemi takes the world's most glorious shower, then goes to bed in the same crew cabin she used before. Her exhaustion defeats every worry in her brain and carries her off for hours of the deepest slumber. When she awakens, she feels as if she's returned from some completely different, alien realm of the mind.

Fortunately some abandoned clothes of the long-ago Captain Gee remain in store, so she's able to change into a fresh outfit, a simple black shirt and utility pants. She heads to the bridge to talk with Virginia, who isn't there. But Abel is.

Her eyes narrow. "You said you'd sleep."

"I did. I arrived here only twenty-two minutes and twelve seconds before you."

"Are you being super-precise so it won't sound like you're lying?"

"I'm always precise," Abel says, almost primly. Noemi relaxes as she realizes how much better he looks. New pink skin covers his once-wounded hands, and he moves with his usual energy. Even if he's not one hundred percent again, he's recovering.

Now she has to give Genesis that same chance.

They're within minutes of the Haven Gate before Virginia joins them on the bridge. Her eyes are red-rimmed—*she really loves that corsair*, Noemi thinks—but her good cheer has apparently been restored. "Okay," she says. "I'm pterodactyled out. What's our situation?"

Abel has returned to his captain's chair. "Six minutes and ten seconds to the Gate."

"I'm at navigation, but if you want to take ops—" Noemi gestures toward the other main position on the bridge. "And I'm so sorry about the corsair, Virginia."

"It can be fixed. Yeah, it's going to take a while, but projects are good. Projects are fun." Virginia says it with genuine relish before giving Noemi a side glance. "Of course you guys have to help."

"You name it. I spent years learning how to fix up my own starfighter. Your corsair shouldn't be too different."

Virginia raises an eyebrow. "Here I thought people on Genesis stuck to—germinating seeds, or praying, or eating oat bran, whatever you guys think is flash."

"It's not just oat bran," Noemi protests, but she has to laugh.

The dark, rough exterior of the Haven Gate looks forbidding, but Noemi feels a lot better going out than she did going in. After light bends and twists around them, they're back in Earth's system. Abel immediately brings up Neptune on-screen; a handful of ships patrol Proteus, no doubt still investigating what happened to the *Osiris*, but nothing flies anywhere near them.

"We're clear," she says. "Now we use the relay codes. Call Remedy. See if they'll answer."

Abel moves toward the comm panel, but Virginia holds up a hand. "We do that second. I want to run a search for something first."

Taken aback, Noemi says, "Is this really the time?"

"The time to see if Ludwig managed to steal the new, genetically manipulated form of Cobweb they used to attack your planet, to help Remedy find a cure?" Virginia raises her eyebrows. "Uh, *yeah*."

"What if they haven't found it?"

Abel considers this. Given the Razers' ability to obtain virtually any information or materials they desire, generally without being caught, I predict their efforts have proved successful, or will in the near future. Very few obstacles stand in a Razer's way—as I think Virginia would agree.

Her tongue sticks out of the corner of her mouth as she works. "All right, now what?"

"Now we send out a relay code," Noemi says. "One that should signal all of Remedy to listen to our message, and join forces."

"Oh, we're going to call the terrorists!" Virginia's smile is stiff, deliberately fake. "What jolly good fun."

"Not everyone in Remedy is a terrorist. Even some of the ones who are—" Noemi remembers Riko lying on the floor of the *Osiris*, wondering what she'd been fighting, and what she'd been fighting for. Those aren't questions you want to leave unanswered to the end. "—They've had it hard. And if they save Genesis, I think that makes up for a lot."

Virginia doesn't look convinced, but she turns the console over to Abel, who memorized the relay code. He begins inputting it, saying, "After the relay codes, I'll send a second message to Ephraim. He's the one member of Remedy we'll all agree on trusting."

It jolts Noemi to realize that she'll actually get to see Ephraim Dunaway again. Every aspect of her freedom on this side of the Genesis Gate strikes her anew, now that she has the time to consider it. *There are so many people I want to talk to. So many places I want to go.*

But Genesis has to come first.

Within minutes, a return message chimes. Noemi wants to cheer. "Remedy?"

"Sort of," Abel says, putting the signal through to the main screen. There, larger than life, are Ephraim, Harriet, and Zayan, all together on the bridge of what looks to be a small ship, each one of them smiling.

"You found her!" Harriet cries, waving. "Hullo, Noemi!"

"Hi." Noemi barely gets the word out; her throat tightens from the sheer joy of seeing these lost friends once more. Traveling to the rest of the galaxy as a free person rather than as a prisoner—it's the greatest exhilaration she knows. It's no wonder she had so much trouble forgetting and moving on. Who would ever want to forget a universe so much bigger, bolder, and richer with possibility?

Ephraim says, "Glad you're all right, Genesis girl. I'm afraid I wasn't able to get any relay codes—"

"We obtained them ourselves." Abel sounds pleased with himself, but the glance he gives Noemi makes it clear he's proud of her, too. "We've sent them out. Hopefully, Remedy ships will soon respond."

The three people on the screen look at one another with mingled amazement and amusement. "That's all well and good," Zayan says, "but we dug up a few ships of our own."

Noemi frowns. "What do you mean?"

"We called for the Vagabonds, and they came. They've brought medical personnel and drugs and—well, and themselves." Harriet holds out her hand as she steps away, allowing the *Persephone* to see what's on their ship's screen. An entire flotilla of vessels hovers in space around them— no, an entire fleet. Are those dozens of ships, or more than a hundred?

Slowly, Noemi rises to her feet. "They came," she murmurs. "You told them what Earth did to Genesis, and the Vagabonds rose up."

Ephraim nods with satisfaction. "The chain reaction has just begun."

30

THE VAGABOND FLEET HAS ASSEMBLED NEAR THE planetoid Pluto, a location of which Abel approves. It has several advantages: isolation, relative inattention from Earth, and at this point in Pluto's orbit, not too great a distance from the Genesis Gate. It is an ideal place to hide, an even better place from which to strike.

Although he'd been able to extrapolate the size of the fleet from the image shown before, the impact of the assembled ships is far greater in person. More than a hundred Vagabond craft cruise in loose formations, all of them brilliantly, individually decorated by the people who work and live within. A quick scan reveals an ore hauler with Celtic knots in vivid green; another, smaller one with Sioux patterns in black, beige, red, and turquoise; and one tiny cruiser painted to look like a turtle. While many of the ships are small, not even as large as the *Persephone*, others reach impressive sizes; Abel even spots a few freighters, modified with extensive armaments.

Noemi notices the weapons, too. "That's some pretty heavy firepower," she says from her place beside him on the bridge. "Those modifications show some wear. They didn't do this just to help Genesis."

"Hardly." Abel is aware his voice has taken on the tone humans call *dry*. "While most Vagabonds perform honest work, there are bands of self-described privateers. They get vague licenses from marginal authorities on colony worlds that purportedly allow them to search other ships and 'reclaim' any unauthorized cargo."

Her eyes get big. "Wait—you mean they're *pirates*?"

"Some would call them that. Others would call them heroic for their defiance of Earth's supremacy."

"What would you call them?" Noemi asks.

"That depends on the ship in question. These vessels appear to be from the Krall Consortium, the largest of the organized 'free trading' groups—known for rampant thievery, but also for avoiding loss of life."

"Thieves but not murderers." She looks toward the ceiling, maybe to God. "I guess right now we have to take what allies we can get."

Abel considers her philosophical acceptance useful, as Remedy ships have also begun to arrive. They're not as

393

disparate as the motley Vagabond crews; these are mostly older Earth troopships or medical scows, one is even a retrofitted Damocles. Remedy prefers ships that were built to fight, though from the sight of them, the ships haven't seen combat in many years. Probably the Remedy fighters haven't seen large-scale combat ever. But they're here because they're hungry for battle—for the kind of conflict that will end their status as terrorists and turn them into a true army.

Virginia has remained at her console almost the entire time, searching for the info packet the Razers had promised her—if they were able to get it, which at this point Abel surmises they haven't. Humans are slow to give up hope. He thinks she hasn't even been listening until she interjects, "You're asking who your allies are? You've got a bigger problem."

Abel doesn't immediately grasp her point, but Noemi must already have been considering the issue. "Nobody's in charge."

At that, Virginia finally looks up, a strange smile on her face. "You'd better figure that out, quick. Or else the ship with the biggest guns is going to figure it out for you." A light on her console flickers, and she claps her hands together. "Oh, Ludwig, you flashiest of flashes, you!"

Noemi hurries to Virginia's side. "The new form of Cobweb—you've got it?" They marvel at the screen as though they can devise a cure just from looking at the viral structure, which even Abel himself couldn't do, but sometimes humans simply like to look at evidence of their accomplishments.

He, however, remains focused on the problem Virginia has highlighted. "We should call a meeting of all the captains, of both the Remedy ships and the Vagabond fleet." He may not understand the nuances and illogicality of human political thought, but he was programmed with basic tactics. "With Ephraim, Harriet, and Zayan to back us up, we should be able to assert that much authority. Afterward—"

Noemi finishes the thought for him. "I guess we'll see."

* * *

The next hour brings a few happy reunions—Harriet and Zayan running back onto the *Persephone* bridge, declaring themselves home; Ephraim scooping Noemi, then Virginia, up in his arms until their feet don't touch the ground—but the impending meeting, and potential battle, occupies the largest part of Abel's thoughts. To judge by his friends' jittery, uneven energy, they, too, are worried. More Remedy ships appear every few minutes, which on some levels is encouraging. This is truly a potential war fleet, one that would give even Earth pause.

If they can avoid internal power struggles, he thinks, the next few days could change the course of galactic history.

Both Abel and Noemi would've preferred to hold the meeting aboard the *Persephone*, but it's not large enough to house a gathering of more than one hundred Remedy leaders and Vagabond pilots. The biggest vessel of the fleet is the Krall Consortium's flagship, the *Katara*, and so that's where everyone is headed. (The *Persephone* is at least given the prestige of docking rights on the *Katara*; most captains have to take single-pilot craft over instead.)

"Couldn't we just, you know, interface via comms?" Virginia seems uncomfortable not relying on technology. "Everybody has to be in the same room?"

Harriet nods firmly. "Comms can be hacked. Voice messages can be faked. Back in the early days, Vagabonds sometimes had it rough telling the true from the false. Person-to-person talk, though—that you can prove. No Vagabond would negotiate something this important any other way."

With a shrug, Virginia says, "I guess if we run into trouble, we've got the galaxy's most badass mech here to help us out."

Abel freezes, but his friends don't catch it right away. "What trouble?" Harriet folds her arms. "You think all Vagabonds are criminals, don't you? Just like you pampered prats on Cray—"

"Hey," Noemi interjects. "Could we not have all the planets fighting among themselves here on our own bridge? Earth sets us all up not to trust one another. We have to do better than that."

The others nod, but Zayan's expression has become confused. "Wait a second. We have a mech to help us out? Where?"

Virginia claps one hand over her mouth. Ephraim, who doesn't understand as much of the context, simply points at Abel. Both Harriet's and Zayan's eyes go wide. The secret Abel's kept so long is out.

"I ought to have told you long ago," he says. "I'm a special prototype of the late Burton Mansfield, with capabilities and intelligence beyond that of any other mech currently in production." Once he would've said *in existence*, but Gillian's further experiments make him wonder.

Zayan stares. "You're a mech? You?"

After a long moment, Harriet laughs. "You're putting us on, right?"

"He's telling the truth." Noemi, at Abel's side, puts one hand on his arm. "It doesn't make him any less a person than you or me."

"But that doesn't make any sense," Zayan says, then shakes his head. "You can't be a mech. You don't act like one—except for the thing where you're really good at equations in your head, and being really strong, and oh my God you're a mech."

"Mechs with full personhood remain rare," Abel explains.

"I'm almost certainly unique at this time, though I expect others to follow. If it takes you some time to adjust to this, I fully understand—but I hope you'll both remain crew members and friends."

Zayan and Harriet share a bewildered look, one that lasts long enough for Abel to wonder whether they'll abandon ship at their next opportunity. Slowly, however, Harriet begins to nod. "You're a good captain. That's the main thing. We'll figure out the rest."

"We're still on board," Zayan promises. He doesn't hold out his hand to shake; instead, he gets back to work, the best proof he could offer that the two of them intend to stay with the *Persephone*—and to learn to understand just what and who Abel really is.

Docking keeps most of them occupied during the next 4.9 minutes. As Zayan brings the ship toward the *Katara*'s massive bay, Abel's sharp ears cannot help picking up the quiet conversation between Ephraim and Noemi, when she tells him what became of Riko Watanabe.

"It didn't have to end like that," he whispers, more to himself than to Noemi. "I tried to tell her there were other ways to fight. Other ways to live. She wouldn't listen. No— that's not right. Riko listened, but she couldn't hear me, not really."

This would be a natural segue for Noemi to mention Riko's doubts at the very end of her life. But she doesn't.

She says only, "She wasn't in pain for long, and she died bravely."

From what Abel can see via his peripheral vision, this information comforts Ephraim. Learning of Riko's doubts would probably have had the opposite effect. Is Noemi's omission kindness or dishonesty? The two are not as different as Abel has often assumed.

The *Katara* is shaped much like its namesake, an ancient push-dagger of South Asia: a long, pointed prow in front of a squared-off stern. Its decoration is modest for a Vagabond ship, with only a few black and brown stripes painted along the sides of its dark gold hull. Its grandeur is in its scale, which becomes even more apparent when they enter its docking bay. This space alone is larger than the average spacedock on a planet, much less anything Abel would have anticipated within another ship.

The meeting room isn't much smaller. It appears to be a cargo hold, one with a catwalk high above the floor. While the majority of the attendees crowd in down below, a handful of individuals have taken their place above. These will be the ones most interested in asserting power. Abel, Noemi, and Ephraim exchange glances before climbing the ladder, claiming their own positions of authority.

Body language alone tells Abel who the captain is, but they walk up to her for introductions anyway: female-presenting, of Northern European ancestry, with a weak chin, shoulder-length blond hair, and exceptionally wide-set green eyes. She seems to recognize them as well, or at least their right to present themselves to her.

"Dagmar Krall," she says. "Captain of the *Katara*, leader of the Krall Consortium. And . . . your host."

"Any Vagabond knows of Dagmar Krall," Abel replies, an answer crafted to sound more complimentary than it actually is. He respects this woman's intelligence, but remains aware of her potential viciousness. "I am Abel, captain of the *Persephone*, and this is Noemi Vidal, a soldier of Genesis and the person most responsible for calling us together."

Krall nods, gesturing for a sound module. Noemi leans closer to Abel. "What do you mean, 'most responsible'? You called Ephraim and Remedy. Harriet and Zayan called the Vagabonds—I was either trapped in a force field or in a shipwreck the whole time."

"During your captivity, you used your few moments of communication to summon help for Genesis," Abel points out. "You thought you were sacrificing your life by doing so. Everything else that has happened flows from your action in that moment. The rest of us have done our parts, but you're the one who set this in motion."

His gesture takes in the crowds beneath them, the armada around them.

"Hear and obey!" Dagmar Krall calls through the

module. This is a standard Consortium greeting from a captain, not quite as severe as it first sounds. An expectant hush falls. "We have gathered in response to biological warfare against planet Genesis. We've accepted Earth's injustice and tyranny for decades—near on a century, now—but a crime like this cannot go unpunished. If it does, we can never again expect safety, or freedom."

The speech is stirring. Krall's rhetorical skills are strong. But Abel doesn't lose sight of the fact that Krall has never shown herself to be a protector of the innocent. Her hatred of Earth is honest, but she wouldn't be here if she didn't also have something to gain.

"What proof do we have that any of this is really happening?" calls someone from below.

Krall swivels the sound module over to Noemi, who doesn't hesitate. "I'm a soldier of Genesis, sent through the Gate to help my world. That this is Earth's work was verified by Burton Mansfield himself, shortly before his death."

Someone on the catwalk mutters, almost below Abel's range of hearing, "When did he die? Thought it was a long time ago—"

"If you're asking for solid evidence," Noemi continues, "no, I can't show you that right now. Genesis sent me to negotiate with people on Earth who knew exactly what they'd done; I didn't know I'd have to offer evidence. But if you'll come through the Genesis Gate—either with a few scouts or as an entire fleet—you'll have all the proof you need."

Somebody else shouts, "Why should we believe you?"

To Abel's surprise, Krall takes the module back. "Why shouldn't you? There's nothing to lose by checking for ourselves, and everything to gain. Since when do Vagabonds sit on their hands and refuse to act unless everything's sure and safe? That's no way to own the skies." A few people raise fists; apparently "Own the skies" is a Vagabond saying, a way of claiming their homeless status with pride. Krall adds—in a more ordinary tone of voice, "Besides, some of my captains have been hearing rumors for a couple of months now. Whispers that Earth was going to make a move that would end the Genesis War, and to me, infecting Genesis with Cobweb sounds a whole lot like that kind of move. I believe her. So does Remedy." With that, she nods toward Ephraim Dunaway.

Ephraim gets a strange look on his face as he realizes he's become the spokesperson for his entire, leaderless group. Yet he doesn't hesitate either. "If we travel to Genesis, we could get the proof that will turn the other colony worlds against Earth forever. That's worth a trip through a Gate, don't you think?"

Murmurs of assent fill the room. Concern is turning to enthusiasm. At first Abel finds it odd that they're so easily convinced, but then he realizes, *Only those inclined to believe the report made the rendezvous to begin with. The doubters will of course remain far away from any potential uprising.*

Noemi gestures for the module, which Ephraim hands over with what looks like relief. "We don't have much time. Genesis was already suffering terribly when I left—what, five days ago? Six days? I've been on too many planets to tell." A few people laugh knowingly; this is a problem Vagabonds are used to. "My planet is weak, and Earth knows it. They must be planning to invade within a week or two. We can't afford to wait."

Krall claims the module again. "The longer we stay here, the better chance we have of Earth finding us. My Consortium declares itself for Genesis. Who's with us?"

Cheers fill the room. Noemi smiles at Abel, elated. He understands her emotion, but is also very aware of the greater authority Dagmar Krall has just claimed. As long as Krall intends to help Genesis, however, he will not object.

Another voice from below rises over the last of the applause. "A fleet this big, Earth's bound to see us headed for the Gate. What's going to stop them from coming after us right away, before we can even get through?"

Noemi steps forward. "We're going to give them their own problem to deal with. We're about to spill the biggest secret Earth's ever had."

•　•　•

Crews assemble. Weapons are double-checked. Engines are put into overdrive. The signal goes out from the *Katara*, and within 2.1 seconds, every ship in the new fleet zooms straight toward the Genesis Gate.

Not long after the Gate comes within visual range, Virginia sounds the alarm: "Earth defense systems near Mars are starting to look mighty awake."

"Let's give them something to wake up to." Abel nods toward Noemi, who settles herself at the comm station. He enters the codes that will patch them into pan-galactic communications arrays, then nods to Noemi.

It's time to change the galaxy.

"Citizens of Earth and its allied colony worlds," Noemi begins. "This is Noemi Vidal of the planet Genesis. The truth about the Cobweb plague—both on Genesis and throughout the galaxy at large—has been kept from you. Attached to this audio message are data files that will explain the disease's origin, and the method Earth used to distribute the plague to Genesis, an act of biological warfare forbidden by all Earth laws and every pan-galactic accord."

The Razers provided all of that information. One of those data files is a copy of the new, "improved" Cobweb virus unleashed on Genesis. Another is the assembled research Remedy's moderate wing has on Cobweb, which goes back to within a year of its emergence.

Noemi continues, "Your leaders will try to tell you these files are forgeries—which is why you should also look at the files that provide the location of another Gate in Earth's solar system—a secret Gate, one that leads to the planet Haven, a habitable world that's been kept secret, too. It's a dangerous planet, for a number of reasons; most human beings can't land there and survive. But there *are* ways to make it safe for billions of people someday, ways Earth has hidden from us all. Find that Gate, and you'll know Earth's been lying to you. Find Haven, and you'll know why Earth created Cobweb in the first place. Once you've done that, you'll know this is the truth—about Haven, about Cobweb, and about Genesis. Earth is responsible for all of this. Earth did it all knowingly, and cruelly. But we can undo that damage. We can take back the worlds that belong to us. We have to do it together."

Abel snaps off the comms. "Full message packet—distributed."

"That's it." Noemi leans back in her chair, almost in a state of shock. "Do you think any of them will believe me?"

"Lots of them won't," Virginia says blithely. "But some people are going to investigate. Curious people, people already suspicious of Earth, even bored people. You don't need many of them to follow the trail before word gets out. Trust me, the leaders of Earth are currently peeing their collective pants."

Abel understands the colloquialism, but the visual image this presents is... peculiar.

Over the comms comes the voice of Dagmar Krall. *"Prepare for Gate transit on our mark."* The specific split-second window for the *Persephone* appears in green lettering on the vast domed viewscreen; in deference to Noemi's status as a soldier of Genesis, they've been given one of the first berths. Abel inputs it into navigation himself.

"Here we go," he says, hands on the controls. "Ready?"

Ephraim nods. Virginia gives him a thumbs-up. But they all look to Noemi for the final word. She lifts her chin and says, "Ready."

The *Katara*'s signal comes through. Abel pushes the *Persephone* forward. The shimmering pool at the center of the Gate reflects his ship's teardrop shape as they move closer and closer, until light shatters. Lines disintegrate. Reality itself fractures around them, then suddenly snaps back into place. Other Vagabond ships appear nearby, a few of them streaking on ahead. In the far distance shines the small dot that represents their destination; Abel zooms in to reveal a soft green planet wrapped in wispy white clouds.

"Genesis," Ephraim whispers. "I never thought I'd see this."

Nor did Abel. He realizes that Noemi is the first person to have set foot on every single inhabited world in the galaxy: Genesis, Kismet, Cray, Stronghold, Earth, and Haven. Within a few hours, he'll become the second. The Loop will be closed; they will have come full circle at last.

When he looks over at Noemi, her expression is grave. "I had to make that transmission, but—we've shown our hand. Earth has to act now. Sooner or later, they're going to strike."

"They were going to strike anyway," he says.

"But sooner now." Noemi closes her eyes as if in prayer.

31

HOME.

Genesis grows larger on the viewscreen, like a flower blooming. The vast green continents take shape—the Eastern Peninsula, the Far Southern Islands, all the places she learned as a little child in school. It seems to shimmer before her eyes, but maybe that's only because she's blinking back tears. *I never thought I'd see my home again.*

All the unhappiness she's faced here can never change her love for her world.

"We have Genesis ships incoming," Zayan announces. Then he frowns. "Only about ten or eleven, though."

That's probably as much of a patrol as they can muster in their weakened state. Noemi aches for her broken planet's lost pride as she goes to comms. "Genesis patrol! This is Noemi Vidal, seeking landing clearance."

Of all people, it's Deirdre O'Farrell who says, in amazement, *"Vidal?"*

"Yeah, glad to see you, too." The patrol breaks off—
probably more in confusion than through any trust in her—
or maybe because of the sheer scale of the enormous fleet
beginning to appear. She memorized the codes for Darius
Akide's offices at the Hall of Elders months ago, so it's easy
to input them now. But the last time she saw Akide, he was
in a hospital bed. Could he be comatose now? Even dead?
"Noemi Vidal for Darius Akide. Urgent. Top priority."

Within less than a minute, Akide's voice comes through.
*"Vidal. Thank God. We thought they might've killed you. It
took them this long to accept our surrender?"*

"Oh." She'd almost forgotten that was her original mission. "Okay, here's what happened. I actually never got a
chance to surrender, *but* I'm coming back with antiviral
drugs, tons of doctors, and an entire war fleet to defend
Genesis while we rebuild."

The pause that follows goes on so long she wonders if
he's fainted. Finally Akide says, sounding nothing like an
august elder, *"Hold on, what?"*

As scared and wound up as she is, Noemi can't resist a
smile. "You're welcome."

·   ·   ·

Within the hour, the entire fleet has achieved Genesis
orbit, save for a strong patrol that remains on guard near
the Gate itself. Noemi brings the *Persephone* in for landing.

The silvery teardrop of the ship descends through the clouds, emerging above the rounded buildings of marble and stone. Two of the Remedy medical ships follow them in; this planet needs immediate help, but having every ship land at once would only create a panic. The breeze from their wake whips the tall willows by the river until their branches flutter free of the surface of the water. To judge by the rosy paleness of the sky, it's early morning, but not so early that a few people aren't walking around. Noemi sees them clutching the hoods of their robes as they look up in both fear and wonder.

As the ships approach the Temple, Noemi feels a quiver inside when she imagines facing the Council again. She's gone beyond her authority—almost unfathomably far beyond it. But what else could she have done?

Besides, she *is* kind of saving the world. That's got to help.

The enormous oaken doors of the Hall of Elders swing open at Noemi's touch. She strides through without so much as a sideways glance at the people watching her, agog. Beside her march Abel, Ephraim, Virginia, Dagmar Krall, and a half dozen of Remedy's top medics; behind them walk about ten Genesis guards, although their weapons remain holstered.

Noemi doesn't slow her steps until they're almost to the

doors of the Council chamber. Two guards there in ceremonial saffron cloaks look from her to each other and back again before they open the doors to let them all in.

Only five of the elders sit there, including three she saw at the hospital before. Good care has seen them through; even on a world as egalitarian as Genesis, elders get attention the average citizens can't expect. Darius Akide is among those present, his expression almost neutral until he realizes who's walking beside her.

Abel smiles at him. "Hello, Dr. Akide. It's a pleasure to finally meet you."

"Model One A," Akide whispers. The resemblance to a younger Burton Mansfield no doubt tipped him off. "Dear God."

"That's my designation, but I prefer to go by Abel. Professor Mansfield told me a great deal about your work; I understand you even helped design me. We should make time for a long discussion later on."

Akide blinks, but returns to the usual serene calm of an elder within minutes. "And these are our doctors? These are our new warriors?"

"That we are," Dagmar Krall says. "Any enemy of Earth's is a friend of mine—assuming, of course, you're not too proud to accept our help."

The taunt darkens Akide's gaze. Noemi doesn't like it

either, but she's not about to turn the Vagabond fleet away for something as petty as that. Surely Akide wouldn't either—but it takes him a long few moments to answer.

Noemi holds her breath until Akide finally says, "So be it."

And with that, Genesis gets to live.

● ● ●

Or so Noemi thinks at the time. Within the next hours, as the medical teams roll out planetwide, she realizes how dire the situation is.

Noemi left Genesis in a state of plague and panic. She returns to it in a state of shock and grief. Some cities have even buried hundreds in mass graves. The breakdown of normal record-keeping and communications means the teams have to go town to town to find and treat the sick— in some places, almost house to house. Already it's clear the new drugs help considerably; Ephraim is optimistic that, with the information the Razers got about the new Cobweb virus, they can design even more effective treatments within days. But the death toll on Genesis remains horrific. Nothing Noemi's done can change that.

When she returns to the Gatsons, she finds Mr. Gatson weak but recuperating. He doesn't know where Mrs. Gatson is. Nobody does. There's no way to be sure whether that's because of chaos at overburdened hospitals or because Mrs. Gatson died in a huddle of unknown people and is now buried in an unmarked grave. Noemi promises to find out. Mr. Gatson only nods. His gaze is far away, and while he briefly takes her hand, he doesn't welcome her back home.

She continually checks and rechecks long-range sensor reports. Nothing else has come through the Gate—yet. The Vagabond fleet remains in place, unchallenged, an entire day after their arrival. When Noemi receives a summons to a military hearing, she assumes they'll want more information about how this strange alliance came together, and about how the discovery of Haven could affect the Liberty War.

But that's not what her superior officers want to discuss.

"Not even in uniform, Vidal?" says Kaminski, the exact same guy who prosecuted her after her return from journeying around the Loop. His neck is nearly as thick as his head, and his veins stand out as if engorged with anger every second of every day. Of course he's perfectly healthy; maybe being a total ass makes you immune. "You can't even show basic respect to your former commander?"

Noemi doesn't answer him. She speaks only to Yasmeen Baz, who is again here, apparently to defend her. "My uniform was lost on my mission. I'd never intentionally disrespect you, Captain Baz. Please believe that."

Kaminski can't endure being ignored. "You override the

highest decisions of the Elder Council itself, substituting your judgment for their own, and you call that respect?"

"*That's* what this is about?" Noemi's astonishment makes her gape. It's all she can do to keep talking. "You're *prosecuting* me? I thought this was just to ask me about how I got the fleet together!"

"Which, in my mind, is a very good question." Baz sounds neither defiant nor angry, only tired. Maybe she was sick, too, but if so, the lines of Cobweb are hidden by her uniform or her head scarf. "Whatever issues the Council has with Vidal should be taken up by the Council directly."

"Disobedience to our government is a military offense. A *court-martial offense*," hisses Kaminski.

"What disobedience?" Noemi protests.

Kaminski smirks; clearly he thinks he's got her. "You were ordered to present Genesis's surrender to Earth authorities. You patently failed to do so."

"Yes, because I *patently* got kidnapped." She catches herself. Sarcasm is conduct unbecoming an officer. "It was impossible for me to deliver my surrender while I was in Burton Mansfield's custody, or while I was stranded on Haven."

"And after that?" Kaminski says. "Upon your return to Earth's system, did you contact their government?"

"I—no, I didn't." Hanging on to her temper is getting

harder by the second. "I'd been able to summon help by then. An entire fleet. That changed things—"

"So you made up your own mind!" Kaminski retorts. "On your own, without any input from the Council or any other Genesis authority, you decided the situation had changed enough to merit ignoring your orders. And in so doing you not only continued a war that was meant to end, but escalated it."

This is more than Noemi can take. "I escalated it by making it possible for us to actually win! Did you notice the war fleet up in the sky? The lifesaving drugs we have for the sick?"

Baz finally cuts in. "She's got a damned good point, Kaminski. Once Vidal got back to the Earth system, conditions had radically changed. We allow military officers a certain degree of discretion on missions. She used hers. The result might be the difference between Genesis's certain defeat and a real chance at victory."

Silence hangs in the narrow stone chamber where the tribunal's being held. Genesis's green flag hangs as a banner on the high wall behind the dais where Kaminski, Baz, and a blank-faced official sit. That person must be the judge for this trial she didn't know she had to face. Noemi stands before them, at attention, unsure how this all will end.

"I petition the court on Lieutenant Vidal's behalf," Captain Baz continues, back in official mode. "A record of the events shows that she conducted her mission with due diligence, despite considerable difficulty and danger to herself and a comrade—"

"A comrade?" Kaminski's veins throb visibly. Noemi wonders whether his head could explode from fury, and if so, whether it would be more satisfying than gross. "Are you speaking of a *mech*, Captain?"

The steel in Baz's glare could pierce granite. "If you'd like to give back all the medicines that mech arrived with, then you can sneer at him, Kaminski. But if you've benefited from anything this mech has done, it might behoove you to start thinking of him as *Abel*. Wasn't your husband one of the first to get treated in the hospital?" Kaminski's mouth opens and closes like a fish stranded out of water, and Baz gives him a thin smile meant to muzzle him before turning back to the judge. "Looking at the totality of the circumstances, Lieutenant Vidal's conduct must be considered not only appropriate, but also heroic. I submit to you that the most just disposition of her case would be to dismiss the charges immediately."

The blank-faced judge speaks: "Vidal overrode a surrender issued by the governing body of this world. She did so without permission, an act of grave disobedience. This cannot go without punishment."

Captain Baz obviously expected this. "Then I suggest we simply allow her to resign her commission immediately.

She will no longer, and never again, be a part of the Genesis armed forces. If I understand Vidal as well as I think I do, that's punishment enough. And this way, she's free."

No longer, and never again, will Noemi be the only thing she's ever been.

The first time she flew her starfighter into space—the first time she broke atmosphere and looked out at the stars as her destination—she felt prouder than she ever had before in her life. Maybe prouder than she ever will again. She closes her eyes tightly, willing herself not to tear up. Baz wouldn't suggest this if she didn't think another, worse punishment were possible. This is as much mercy as Noemi can expect, and she's smart enough not to throw it away.

But oh, it burns.

When she can open her eyes again to look at the judge, she knows her fate is sealed.

Afterward, in Baz's office, as Noemi completes the necessary documentation, she says, "Thank you for defending me, Captain."

Baz is leaning back in her chair like it's the closest thing she has to a bed; exhaustion casts shadows beneath her eyes. "You're a good soldier, Noemi. The thing is—you're always fighting your own battles. Not necessarily ours."

"I only ever wanted to protect Genesis." Does she get to want something else now? Now that she's free to determine her own fate, what will she choose?

What are you fighting, Noemi Vidal? And what are you fighting for?

"You did the right thing, and I'm not the only one who knows it." Baz sighs as she sees the dataread screen light up as the last forms are processed. Noemi's been cut free for good. "Believe me, I'm glad we're on the same side. May Allah help anyone who gets in your way. What will you do now?"

For the first time in Noemi's life, she has choices—dozens of them. It ought to feel like liberation. Instead it's terrifying.

"I don't know," she murmurs. "I have no idea."

The freedom to choose is the freedom to fail.

32

"DO YOU BELIEVE YOUR CAPTAIN'S COMMENT WAS A compliment?" Abel says one hour after Noemi's hearing, as he walks with her by the river with their friends. Only a handful of citizens are in the nearby area; what must normally be a bustling marketplace is quiet. It's been such a brief time since Remedy and the Vagabond fleet came through the Genesis Gate. While there's now medicine to help the sickest, recovery will take more than a few days— it will be weeks, or even months.

Most of the onlookers appear more weary than sick. Although most of these individuals gape at the outworlder newcomers and the now-infamous mech, Abel thinks some of the stares are...not unfriendly.

"I hope it's a compliment," Noemi replies. Her face is downcast, her energy low. Losing her military commission must be profoundly affecting for her, in much the same way that Mansfield's death is for him. The authorities that once governed their lives have vanished; the sudden freedom is both beautiful and bewildering. "How would you take it?"

Perhaps humor would be effective. "If the comment were made about me? With my superior strength, intelligence, and reflexes, it would make sense for a religious person to pray for divine help against me. They'd stand very little chance without divine intervention."

"Mansfield never did install modesty, did he?" Her dark eyes sparkle with suppressed laughter. His distraction is proving successful.

So Abel continues the joke with an exaggerated shrug. "What would be the point?"

She looks up at the sky, shaking her head as if in dismay, but he feels the affection radiating from her.

He continues, "But if I look at the comment as one made about you . . . I believe my analysis would be the same."

"What?" she teases. "You mean I'm just as much of a badass as the ultimate mech in all creation?"

". . . You're close."

"Close?" Noemi raises a skeptical eyebrow. "I can see I'm going to have to prove my strength."

"I look forward to it," he says.

"You know, I kind of thought it would be dull here," Virginia says. She's cleaned her baggy orange jumpsuit and added a green Genesis flag at the collar; like the others, she strolls a few paces behind Noemi and Abel, taking in this new, unfamiliar world. "You know, all virtue and straight lines and taupe."

"Why taupe?" Ephraim, who described himself as "too tired to sleep" after his first hospital shift in Goshen, is by Virginia's side. Coming from the severity of Stronghold, he must find Genesis even more surprising. His gaze moves from object to object, taking it all in. "Is there something especially virtuous about taupe?"

Virginia shrugs. "Nah. Just boring, like virtue often is. In other words, nothing like *this*."

She stops in her tracks and spreads open her arms, taking in the whole vista before them: the winding river sparkling in the morning sun, the cobblestone paths, the brightly canopied booths. The view is both stately and pastoral, a scene of beauty and harmony almost unmatched in the galaxy.

"This is what I thought Kismet might be like, before I ever went," Harriet says. She's woven green ribbons through her braids as a sign of solidarity with the people of Genesis.

Zayan leans on the wooden railing of the small bridge they're crossing and sighs. "I never even thought Kismet could be like this. I thought this kind of life was—only in the past, or in fairy tales." Virginia, who might be expected to scoff at such fulsome praise, simply nods. Even in its battered state, Genesis has overcome her cynicism.

No wonder they fought for this, Abel thinks. *No wonder Earth was so determined to have it. But if Earth had claimed it, the beauty would've been destroyed—soon, and forever.*

"'Scuse me?" says a tiny voice. Abel looks over to see a child, male-presenting, approximately four years of age. He wears the loose pants and shirt that seem to be common for children on this planet. The little boy takes a step back, as if intimidated by the attention he sought, but he manages to say, "Are you the good mech?"

Is that how he's become known? Abel must be careful with his answer. The boy's parents are a few paces away, wide-eyed at their child's audacity. He drops to one knee so that he's at the little boy's level and puts things in terms he might understand. "I'm the mech who came here with the medicine, yes."

"What's your name?"

"Abel. What's yours?"

"I'm Tangaroa." The name is of Maori origin, unsurprising given the tattoos on the father's face. "You don't *look* like a machine."

"I don't feel like one either," Abel explains. The child-psychology information in his databanks tells him that explanations should be kept simple. It didn't work with Simon—but Simon wasn't truly a child, only the remnant of one. This simple curiosity, the chance to grow and learn day by day: That's what Simon Shearer was robbed of, and it was a large part of what destroyed him. Abel finds it comes naturally, speaking gently to this boy, and that somehow it helps soothe the guilt he still feels about being unable to save Simon. "That's because I'm not entirely mechanical. I'm part human, too."

"What parts are human?" With wide brown eyes, Tangaroa avidly studies Abel's face. "Is it the nose?"

Abel laughs. "Here, see for yourself." He leans forward slightly, ducking his head and trusting the little boy to know what to do next. As anticipated, Tangaroa puts his hand out to touch Abel's nose, then laughs out loud. Behind him, the parents smile. A few of the other passersby have stopped to watch this interaction as well, and Noemi is beaming. He has the definite sense that this is going well.

"That nose is kinda superhuman if you ask me," Virginia says. "I know you're too objective to take offense at this, Abel, but you've got a considerable schnoz there."

"Just like my creator's." Mansfield's features live on within Abel's.

Tangaroa looks up at Virginia, then at Noemi, then at Ephraim, with new interest. "Are you mechs, too?"

"Nope," Ephraim says. "One hundred percent human. But I'm from another planet. Have you ever heard of Stronghold?" Tangaroa nods eagerly. His class must be studying the other worlds of the Loop in school.

"We're from Earth," Harriet chimes in, taking Zayan's

hand. "But we live as Vagabonds and travel all over the galaxy."

"Me, I'm from Cray." Then Virginia frowns. "I mean, I'm from Earth originally, but I've lived on Cray most of my life."

A woman a few years older than Noemi hesitantly asks, "Is Cray really just one big supercomputer?"

"Mostly!" Virginia agrees with cheer.

Then the few people by the river are all congregating in this one spot, wanting to hear more about Cray and Stronghold and everywhere else in the greater galaxy. Ephraim gets caught up in describing his world's deep mines, while Virginia clearly enjoys talking about the Razers' secret lab. It's Abel himself who explains the newly discovered world, Haven, with its blue pine trees and clouds of bats, and what may be happening there even now. Surely not all the listeners gathered near have fully accepted Abel as a person like themselves... but he sees signs that such acceptance could be possible. A few Remedy members have also begun to mingle with the group, and he's aware that Vagabonds have put in at ports across the planet. Genesis is still too battered to look far into the future, and the threat posed by Earth is very real—but already he can determine that the planet will never be as closed off again. Other humans will find their way here; they'll shape Genesis and be shaped by it.

Could that be true for someone who isn't human?

Abel looks over at Noemi, who's forgotten her sadness. He's been summoned to a meeting that night to answer questions, but now he can ask one of his own.

Maybe his future isn't out among the stars. Maybe it could be right here.

● ● ●

Darius Akide's offices are ventilated with natural breezes and illuminated primarily by sunlight. The economy of it is something Abel expected; the beauty of it surprises him.

When he says as much, Akide shakes his head. "That's one of the differences between mechs and humans. Where you see efficiency, we're capable of seeing something more."

Abel takes no offense. As he knows from his initial journey with Noemi, humans require time to fully accept him. "Upon consideration, it makes sense. Even in pure mathematics, the equations that appear 'beautiful' are most likely to be true. Beauty is not only a perception; it's also an indication of simplicity and strength."

That makes Akide blink, but he says nothing. His eyes narrow as he studies Abel from behind his desk. This allows Abel to study Akide in return. The images of this man in his memory banks are of him in his early twenties, when he was Burton Mansfield's protégé and friend. One holo showed Akide holding Gillian when she was only four months old. Some of Darius Akide's theories are woven into Abel's deepest programming and structures. Perhaps he should feel reverence, meeting someone who is in effect his co-creator.

He does not. Mansfield reserved that reverence—the devotion dictated by Directive One—for himself.

So Abel sees an ordinary human male in late middle age, of African descent and average height (impossible to gauge precisely while the man is sitting). Akide shows signs of recent illness: bloodshot eyes, ashy skin, and slowed reaction time. Yet he has resumed his post, helping to lead a planet in great peril. This is a sign of either great fortitude or great egocentricity.

"According to Vidal's report, Gilly managed to store her son's consciousness and transplant it into another mech." Akide steeples his hands. "One with even more organic components than you have yourself."

"The transfer wasn't entirely successful, but it's impossible to say whether the process is fundamentally flawed, or whether failure was due to premature execution." He then deliberately uses the same nickname Akide did. This is a connection they share. "Gilly certainly believes herself to have copies of both her son's consciousness and her father's. Had she been able to capture me, she would have attempted to transfer Mansfield's into my body. Given that I am both intact and functioning excellently, complete transfer might well have succeeded."

Akide shakes his head. "Thank God the *Osiris* crashed. Their work could've proved monstrous. At least it's been destroyed."

"I wouldn't be so certain. They had extensive plans to expand their work on Haven. The so-called Winter Castle may very well have mech labs she'll be able to use to further her research." Abel finds the idea of organic mechs highly interesting—something he'd like to investigate himself, for his own purposes—but senses this is unlikely to be a feeling Akide shares.

"Any data you can provide on these plans will be welcome," Akide says, as if inputting a command into a basic computer. "Visual images, if you can re-create them. I'll want to research this in much more depth once we've made it through this crisis."

The Vagabond fleet remains assembled above. It has been less than three days since Earth learned of that fleet's existence and its journey to the Genesis system—and since the galaxy learned of Earth's deception. Given the amount of time necessary for bureaucratic decision-making and military mobilization, Abel puts the likelihood of a major military operation within the next two days at 81.8 percent.

However, unlike humans, he can be aware of impending danger yet continue to focus on other subjects. "I wished to ask—will any of those who have come to defend Genesis be allowed to remain here?"

Akide nods absently. "The Council has had a preliminary talk. Some form of citizenship for the Vagabonds fighting for us...that may be appropriate. Of course they would have to follow our core philosophies, and we'll come up with forms for citizenship, but I imagine most of them will consider that a fair trade for a true home."

Harriet and Zayan might be able to have a place to call their own. Ephraim might choose to open a clinic here. Virginia— no, Virginia is happy on Cray and will certainly return. But even Abel's selflessness functions can't outweigh one core thought: He can stay with Noemi. "I would wish to apply."

"You?" Akide sits upright, startled back into the present. The surprise on his face slowly shifts into disdain. "You are...a piece of machinery. One built to serve humans, and a kind of machine we have no use for here on Genesis. Mechs are forbidden here, for good reason. Vidal may be caught up in her fanciful notions about your 'soul,' but no one else is likely to make the same mistake. I'm sure when you process this through your programming, it will make sense to you."

Abel is still not accepted. He is still *less than*. Genesis cannot be his home.

• • •

Later that night, when Noemi joins him aboard the *Persephone*, her outrage eclipses his hurt. "Akide said that to you? After what you've done for this entire planet? It's so—ungrateful, so mean—"

"It is a logical extension of his worldview," Abel says. "It's not a tragedy, Noemi. I will resume the existence I had before, as a Vagabond. It's a way of life I enjoy. Granted, if Harriet and Zayan stay here, I'll have to hire a new crew, but I'm confident other good people can be found." So many Vagabonds need homes, and as his friends have told him many times, he pays well.

Noemi stands on the other side of the bridge, suddenly awkward. She shifts her weight from foot to foot, then says, "So—you're hiring?"

Fresh hope floods Abel's mental processes as powerfully as excess voltage. It's a state of mind he's rarely experienced to such a degree. Not since the first time he saw Noemi in her starfighter, flying closer to his ship, about to set him free from three decades' confinement—

Maybe they're about to set each other free. "You would leave Genesis?"

She hugs herself; obviously she's thinking this through at the same moment she says it. "I can't protect my world in the military anymore. I've brought them medicines and allies—I don't know that there's anything more I could ever do. And nobody here's going to miss me that much." Her smile is crooked. "Maybe we both need a new Directive One, huh?"

Abel nods as he takes a step closer to her. "We can explore the galaxy together."

"Figure out what we want. Where we want to go. What to fight for."

She takes one more step—then bounds into Abel's arms, which are already open and waiting. He swings her around, a human gesture he wouldn't have thought he was programmed with, and hugs her tightly. Noemi laughs out loud with joy, and everything seems possible—

And that's when the ship's communications begin to shriek, an automated siren he's never heard before.

Noemi's face goes white as she slides from Abel's embrace. "That's the call to arms."

Earth's attack has finally come.

33

NOEMI RUNS TO THE NEAREST COMM PANEL AND SWITCHES to full audio reception in time to hear: "—*near the Gate suggests imminent intrusion. All military personnel are ordered to combat positions.*" But the true horror comes with the next words: "*All civilians should proceed immediately to designated shelters.*"

Stricken, she turns to Abel. "They don't do that. Ordering people to shelters, I mean—we've fought only in space for years and years now. It's been decades since they attacked us here, at home." Earth never wanted to mess up Genesis too much; they wanted to claim a prosperous planet, not a demolished one.

"As you predicted, the revelation of Haven has forced Earth's hand. Instead of admitting guilt and dealing openly with its citizens, they're trying to win a victory that could eclipse their own wrongdoing."

She thumps her fist against the wall, overcome with fury

at Earth but most of all at herself. "I shouldn't have said a thing about Haven until after we'd distributed the cure and Genesis was back to normal. While Earth thought we were helpless, they weren't in any rush to—oh, God, what were we thinking?"

"We made the best decision we could based on the information we had. We couldn't have predicted Earth would be petty enough to attack while vulnerable to unrest at home, out of what appears to be spite."

Is that really all this is? Earth's pettiness? Doesn't matter. "I've got to get to one of the exosuits."

Abel puts one hand on her shoulder. "Noemi—you're not a military officer any longer."

"Do you think I'd ever forget that? But if Genesis is in danger, I have to fight. If they want to reprimand me, they can do it later." She thinks fast. "How much work have you and Virginia done on the corsair? Enough?"

"It can fly," Abel says slowly, "but it's not a starfighter."

"It has the ability to disrupt enemy ship signals. That's enough."

She runs from the bridge down the long spiral corridor of the *Persephone*. Abel's footsteps thump behind her, but she wouldn't look back for him even if she could. It's like he said before: This is still her Directive One. Protect her world.

Time to come up with a new Directive One later.

432

When she reaches the launching bay, the exosuits are waiting. She steps in, puts her arms through the sleeves, and starts pulling it tighter around the shoulders. Abel stops in front of her. The fear in his eyes reminds her of the moment he saw her as Mansfield's captive. "Don't be scared," she says.

"Your life will be in danger. Fear is a natural response."

"Haven't you been paying attention? My life is always in danger."

Her joke doesn't break the tension. Maybe Abel's emotions don't work that way. "We could take the *Persephone* into battle together, instead."

"It's even more useless in combat than the corsair."

"But I had a thought that—"

He falls silent when Noemi takes his face in her hands. "Abel, I have to do this. You know why. You know better than anyone else. Please don't try to hold me back. Help me."

Abel remains still and silent for what feels like a long time but can only be a second. Then he zips up her exosuit for her. As the seams automatically seal, he leans his forehead against Noemi's. He says only, "Come back to me."

"I will. If I can I will." That's the best promise she can make on the verge of combat, and they both know it.

Together they turn their attention to the battered corsair. As Virginia-ordered penance, Abel's been repairing some of the damage during the hours the rest of them spend sleeping. A human might've done the cosmetic work first, repainting the blackened hull scarlet or polishing the sheen on the fins. Abel's more rational process has led him to restore primary functions. Noemi slides into the seat and activates the engine to check operations. She's low on fuel, but she can get to the Gate and back with a margin to spare. The cockpit is again airtight. There's no reason not to take this ship back into space.

Aside from the fact that Virginia will *for sure* kill her... but Noemi can deal with that later.

Abel reaches into one panel, performing some last-minute tweak that sharpens her navigational sensors to almost-normal levels. "If you can wait another ten minutes, I could—"

"No. I have to get up there." That's not her usual impatience talking; it's her military training. The soldier she so recently was still lives inside her skin, and knows this battle has to take place as far from Genesis as possible. Every minute she waits is another five thousand kilometers Earth's forces can travel.

He doesn't protest any longer. Instead he pulls her close and kisses her for a long, sweet time. She winds her fingers through his hair, her entire body responding. Her mouth is learning how he kisses; her breaths fall into tempo with his. She knows him in her very skin.

The kiss breaks. Abel repeats, "Come back to me." All Noemi can do is nod.

She punches the controls, and the cockpit slides shut. Abel walks backward a few steps as the landing bay door slides open. The cool meadow breezes from outside ruffle his dark gold hair. She stares at him, memorizing every last detail, until the go light flashes on her control panel.

After that, there's no time for anything but the fight.

34

ABEL SUSPECTS NOEMI WOULD'VE PREFERRED TO HAVE
been told that he intends to fly into battle, too. If she objects
later, he'll point out that he did mention the possibility of
the *Persephone* going into combat....

That won't be the full truth, so he rejects that option.
Noemi is more than his friend now; he wishes for her to be
the other half of his life. Dishonesty between them is inadvisable on every level. She'll rage at him, but ultimately
she'll understand. He could no more leave Noemi to go
into battle unprotected than she could fail to defend her
world.

He takes off immediately, setting course for the Gate.
The scene that unfolds on the vast domed viewscreen
reveals a battle of such staggering size as Abel has never
seen. Earth has sent through twelve Damocles ships,
which he reckons to be more than half the Damocles ships
in their entire fleet. The rebellious planets of Kismet and

Stronghold will soon realize they're unguarded. This can only be Earth's final invasion assault.

But Genesis is ready for them.

The Vagabond fleet is assembling itself—haphazardly, in the way of a group of ships never asked to work together before. Still, they're flying into action, every burst of blaster fire proof of the colony worlds' pent-up fury at Earth. He sees the *Katara* in the heart of the action, all weapons firing, Dagmar Krall proving herself again as a leader. A few medical vessels, courtesy of Remedy, hover nearby to treat the wounded—of which there will be many.

Genesis has sent its ships up, too, though they are less impressive. The age of the vessels is dispiriting, as is their relative state of disrepair. But then one of the older ships fires, hitting a Damocles and rupturing a solid fourth of its hull. Abel reminds himself, *Old is not the same as weak.*

Amid green streaks of blaster bolts and the large lumbering ships, he sees his fellow mechs in their star-shaped exosuits emerging from the Damocles ships to attack everyone fighting for Genesis. Queens and Charlies one and all, the mechs fling themselves into the best tactical positions, even if it means they'll be blown to shards within seconds. They risk themselves without fear. They can kill without guilt and be killed without guilt.

But Abel thinks there might be another way to use them.

There was no time for him to teach Simon Shearer what

he needed to know; however, Simon may have been able to teach Abel something.

He brings the *Persephone* in closer to the battle, until the starfighters and mechs are crisscrossing the space around him in every direction. No Queen or Charlie will pay much attention to an unarmed civilian vessel unless it makes overly hostile moves. Remaining motionless is dangerous mostly because stray weapons fire could hit him. The shields are at full power, which will have to be sufficient protection. Abel's going to need all his concentration for what he does next.

Simon told Abel that he controlled other mechs by being more machine than human. This is strange to Abel, who's worked so hard to explore his human side. Letting himself be wholly a machine—it would be the equivalent of telling humans to jump off a cliff, trusting that a force field would catch them. All their faith in the force field wouldn't make that jump easy. He doesn't want to surrender his human self, even for an hour.

His memories of Haven crystallize, and he sees the broken, battered mechs attacking him in concert, as if they were the limbs of a single organism. Simon learned how to control them as if they were an extension of his mind. The opportunity before Abel is immense.

So is the danger, but he considers it irrelevant. Compared to the risk to Noemi, what he's attempting is nothing.

He sits at ops and opens one of the interfaces. Then he withdraws an emergency repair edger and slashes across his wrist, reopening the wound he gave himself on Haven. The injury doesn't bleed as much as it would for a human, but red drops spatter onto the console. As long as it doesn't ooze into the wiring, this represents no significant problem.

The metal within Abel has been exposed. Simon hadn't found such hardwiring necessary; that was one of the few advantages he had. While next generations of Inheritors may have the advantages of greater organic content, Abel thinks with satisfaction, they'll lack the ability to interface directly with older computer systems, like the one that governs his ship.

He withdraws one long, slender rod and pushes the end into a small port. The effect is instantaneous and overwhelming; the full flood of *Persephone*'s data rushes around and into him, too much for even his brain to process. But he retains enough self-control to block out one core function area, then another, until he's eliminated enough to think clearly. That lets him focus on communications.

The signals the ship would normally send aren't on the same frequencies that tether mechs to their Damocles controls. They are, however, extremely close, and now that Abel's connected with his ship, he thinks he can push that frequency to exactly the right level. Shutting his eyes, he concentrates. The effort feels like static electricity crackling around his brain—

WE ARE HERE.

Abel's eyes open wide as he connects to every mech fighting for Earth. At first it's the same overload as when he initially connected to the *Persephone*, plus nearly five thousand. (4862, to be exact—the combined Vagabond and Genesis forces have already destroyed 138 of the invasion force mechs. He can feel their absence from the whole the way a human might feel the gap of a lost tooth.)

He bears down. Bit by bit, he streamlines the connection until far more information flows out to them than in to him.

Your grandson was able to do this with a human mind, he says to the Mansfield that dwells within his heart, the shadow-father he'll never stop defending himself against. *If he could, that means I can. I'll wield a kind of control you never even dreamed of.*

—*I am **more than you***—

Energy pulses from him, through the circuits of the *Persephone*, out into space. Every one of his muscles is tensed to the point of spasm, but his physical body has never felt farther away. Abel's mind is a part of these signals, the ones surging into every single fighter mech and redefining their new targets: one another.

4717. 4321. 3800. The mech signals wink out like snuffed

candles. He feels every single death—physically feels it, a dim reflection of the momentary pain he's discovered even mechs experience at the end. But as their numbers decrease, the level of control he has to exert lowers. He can bear this. He must. Every mech destroyed is another one that can't hurt Noemi.

2020. 1686. 1037. 548. 215. 99. 47. 10.

Zero.

Abel severs the connection. The concepts in his mind soften, deepen, becoming thoughts instead of data. As he leans back, his muscles quiver as they try to relax from the tension. The immense heaviness he feels at first seems like a malfunction, before he realizes it's exhaustion, even greater than that he experienced on Haven. He hadn't given himself sufficient regeneration time, perhaps. A faint sheen of moisture along his facial skin must be sweat. He has never perspired before.

Then he realizes the moisture on his upper lip is in fact blood. Abel puts his hand to his face, pulls it away to see red stains on his fingers. He gave himself a nosebleed, a new experience he swiftly decides he doesn't like.

He resolves not to try multi-mech control again until he has conducted extensive further study. Even his strength has limits.

While he carefully reassembles his arm and reseals the skin, he watches the domed viewscreen. The few human-commanded ships that accompanied the mechs to this side of the Genesis Gate are already trying to return, with a few ships of the Vagabond fleet in pursuit. Those Earth ships could put up a good fight on their own, but he suspects the people have forgotten how to undertake their own battles. Without the mechs, they're lost.

Meanwhile, the other Vagabond and Genesis ships swoop and swirl in crazy victory spirals. He wonders which one of the tiny darting lights on that screen is the corsair. Normally he'd focus in tighter to locate it, but he finds he doesn't yet want to.

He's...hurting. Not physically, except for the bright line of pain where he cut his arm open. What he feels is more like the absence of something so essential he takes it for granted, maybe similar to what humans experience when they get dizzy or are temporarily deafened by trauma. When he tries to take stock of his condition, he realizes there's a sort of numb place in his brain—an area he can't currently probe.

He decides to ignore this for the time being. His organic repair systems may heal it, and if not, he can have Virginia Redbird mend any damage. Currently Abel has higher priorities, such as finding Noemi amid the post-battle chaos, and dealing with the small ship that's now approaching the *Persephone*.

A transit pod, he realizes. These aren't fighters; they're

hardly even ships at all, with very little steering and propulsion. They exist purely to allow humans to move between ships in space when neither vessel can dock with the other. The green-and-white marks on its side reveal that this one was launched from one of the larger, older troop ships of the Genesis fleet.

Abel rises from his chair, surprised to feel his legs shaky beneath him. But he can walk through the corridor without stumbling. Weary as he is, he's still able to function.

By the time he gets to the launching bay, the air lock is already cycling. Maybe he should've demanded communication from the pod before allowing it to dock; maybe he should've set the door not to automatically open. Normally he would have done these things, but in his current daze, they're occurring to him too late. Everything is too fuzzy, too slow. This must be what having a human brain feels like.

The air lock cycle ends. Abel immediately steps inside the bay. He can't keep this individual from coming on board, but if there's going to be a confrontation, he intends to get it over with quickly. When the transit pod slides open, however, the visitor appears to be... if not a friend, at least an ally.

"Darius Akide," he says. "I thought you were a non-combatant."

Akide nods. "I went into battle to bear witness, and to

chronicle this stage of the war for the survivors, if there were any."

"As you see, survivors are numerous." Abel waits for praise or gratitude that doesn't come. The humans may not yet have realized what he did for them. However, other questions are far more important. "Did you see Noemi's ship? She was flying a red corsair."

Surprise flickers on Akide's face as he steps from the pod, his long white robes striking an oddly formal note. "She went into battle? I thought she was required to resign."

"Nothing could keep her from defending Genesis." Abel will need to send out a signal to her directly. What if she was one of the few Genesis pilots lost in the early, bloody stage of the fight?

Have faith, he reminds himself. Even if he can't believe in a deity, he can believe in her.

"What is the purpose of your visit, Dr. Akide?" Abel asks. "You could have simply reached out to me via comms, which suggests you have a message that is delicate and requires extra security. Or you may wish to conduct a confidential conversation." Could Akide have realized what Abel did to the other mechs? It would be a considerable mental leap, but his cybernetics background with Mansfield makes the connection possible. This would naturally be something Akide would have wished to investigate immediately.

"Yes, I have a message." Akide has a strange expression on his face. "Do what you were made for."

He straightens to his full height and withdraws a small device from his robe, larger than a comm link but smaller than a spanner. Before Abel can ask what it is, Akide hits a switch and—

The floor tilts and sways. Visual input shuts down entirely; touch and smell go to minimum. Abel staggers sideways and would fall except that Professor Akide catches him in his arms. Only sound remains to him, that and the panic of his own thoughts.

Akide helped design me, Abel thinks in a daze. *He knows how to shut me down.*

Whatever signal was sent doesn't render Abel completely unconscious, the way Mansfield's old fail-safe did; he retains some mental function and full auditory input. "Why?" he manages to say. If he's judging the sounds correctly, Akide is dragging him along the *Persephone* corridor. "What are you—"

"I'm sorry, Abel. I'm genuinely sorry about this. But I have to secure you." Professor Akide's footsteps stagger in irregular thumps; Abel's considerable weight is no doubt difficult for the older man to manage. "Make sure your consciousness is bound good and tight. Then I can take you back to the one cybernetics lab we have on Genesis. There, I can get some work done."

"What—do you—"

"This battle doesn't change anything." Akide sounds resigned, as fatalistic as Noemi described him. "Our victory today will only make Earth more desperate. They'll send human troops next, and they'll land on Genesis. They'll kill our children, burn our homes. We can't let that happen."

"But—Haven—"

"There's no guarantee Earth's people will accept Haven as a new home for humanity. They have to survive a life-threatening disease to even think about it! Even if they do, every person on every single colony world is going to feel betrayed by Earth. Haven can't be their home for a long time to come, if ever. So to avoid a mass uprising, Earth must conquer Genesis, immediately. The battle today proved that. That means this is our last chance to stop them." Akide takes a deep breath. "Long ago I learned to question the work I did with Burton Mansfield. I thought I'd left it behind me. Now I see God's true purpose in it. He led me to Mansfield, because Mansfield would lead me to you."

They want to destroy the Genesis Gate. The only way to do that is to send Abel through in a ship with a thermo-magnetic device—Noemi's original plan, all those months ago. In the resulting detonation, Abel would be utterly destroyed, possibly vaporized.

And Akide has the programming knowledge to force Abel to do it.

Noemi wouldn't allow Abel to choose the path of destroying himself to destroy the Gate. Instead it seems that destruction has chosen him.

35

THERE'S NOTHING WORSE THAN BEING AT THE HEART OF A *battle you're unable to fight.*

Noemi decides this about the fourth time a mech flies straight into what would've been her crosshairs. Her thumbs tighten on the controls, instinctively seeking triggers for weapons that aren't there. In the corsair, it accomplishes exactly zero, except for accidentally turning on Virginia's music.

Once she's shut that off, she tries to take stock. Without the combat map provided by command, or any communications with her fellow fighters, making sense of the battle is almost impossible. Genesis starfighters dart among Vagabond ships of every size and stripe. Mechs fly around her, random as gnats, sometimes so thick they blind her to the rest of the starfield. She's still registering as a civilian vessel to them, so she's safe, but Noemi didn't come here to stay safe. She came here to help.

Even without weapons, she can defend her world.

Months ago, she was on the verge of being captured by Stronghold authorities when Virginia flew by in this exact ship. Virginia had defended the *Persephone* not with blasters or lasers, but by scrambling the signals all around her.

Why didn't I ask her exactly how she did that? Noemi thinks as she goes through the various controls, familiarizing herself more with the corsair's less-critical functions. *That would've been an extremely useful conversation to have. Mega-useful.* Finally she hits upon a subroutine in communications that ought to work. *Here goes nothing....*

The corsair broadcasts on wavelengths that rise and fall in sine curves across the control panel. At first she wonders whether she's now playing Virginia's music to the mechs, which would be hostile but not effective. Then she sees a handful of mechs fold their strange metallic wings, almost like bats preparing to sleep. A smile spreads across her face as she realizes they've lost their command signals from the Damocles.

That's exactly what they're doing, Noemi thinks. *They're falling asleep!*

Laughing out loud, she pushes farther into the thick of the night and does it again. Once more, a dozen mechs fold up into uselessness, and the Genesis and Vagabond ships pick them off one by one. This isn't as satisfying as destroying them herself, Noemi decides, but it's effective.

The more Queens and Charlies she incapacitates, the better chance Genesis's forces have of winning this fight.

When she swoops into another cloud of mechs, they adjust formation. Noemi's heart sinks as she realizes the Damocles ship has detected what she's doing. So has the *Katara*; the massive vessel changes course, trying to put itself between the corsair and the Damocles, but it's too late. Any second now, those mechs are going to attack her—

—yet in one instant that formation breaks, and the mechs turn on one another.

"What the hell?" she says out loud, her voice echoing inside her helmet. Queens and Charlies firing on one another? Ignoring the Genesis fighters? A Damocles ship must be malfunctioning.

But there's something very methodical about the way the warrior mechs are fighting. Their movements are synchronized. Almost like they're separate parts of the same thing…

Just like Simon's mechs were on Haven.

Only one other person could do this. Only one other person in the whole galaxy, one person most people wouldn't admit is a person at all.

Abel! She looks around wildly for the *Persephone*, though of course it's impossible to glimpse it in the chaos. The mech-on-mech battle has escalated into an animalistic frenzy, one pouncing upon another in the same eerie rhythms. Shards of metal spin out in every direction; some of them rain against her cockpit.

Noemi presses a hand to her mouth in both horror and wonder. The wonder is for Abel—he's expanded his capabilities even further, done something so unprecedented and heroic that it fills her with awe.

The horror is for what Abel might've done to himself. Was Simon's mind doomed from the beginning, or did he break himself down by trying to control machines, trying to be only a machine instead of a person?

But the mechs have almost completed their violent self-destruction. Most of the ones remaining are the ones she put to sleep, and the combined Genesis/Vagabond fleet ships have resumed blowing those to smithereens. The lone Damocles ship in her field of vision turns away, clearly heading for the Gate. Earth's forces are in full retreat.

They'll be back. They'll dig deep. Earth has warships capable of being operated by humans. They may have forgotten how to fight their own battles, but war has a way of reminding people.

"This isn't over," she murmurs, watching the *Katara* take its place at the center of the fleet, a silent testimony to Dagmar Krall's contribution and potential new power.

The war hasn't ended. It's just entered a new phase, one

Noemi can't guess at. But she senses the danger will be even greater.

•   •   •

Flying toward Abel's ship feels like swimming against the current. Almost all the other ships in the fleet have begun their journey home, zipping past her, leaving wake trails in the debris of the battle. One of the larger Genesis vessels, the *Dove*, lingers near the Gate—for more readings, or another message, she figures. Other than that, she and Abel are going to have this corner of space all to themselves.

Don't worry about what's to come, she tells herself. *Go back to Abel. Live in the moment. Kiss him every chance you get.* As soon as she gets within range, she signals the *Persephone*.

No response.

Noemi straightens in her seat and tries again. Nothing. A chill sweeps through her as she accelerates. *He pushed too hard. Controlling the mechs did something terrible to him. Or maybe one of the mechs got inside the* Persephone *to stop him?* Abel can defend himself, of course, but then he ought to be answering her, and he's not.

She doesn't become truly afraid until the corsair slides into the *Persephone*'s launching bay and she sees the Genesis transport pod.

Someone came up here to see Abel, and that someone must be responsible for his silence.

The second the air lock's done cycling, she springs the cockpit, yanks off her helmet, and goes for the weapons locker. Blaster in hand, Noemi walks slowly into the corridor. Every nerve is on edge. Her ears prick at every small noise, but it's just the usual sounds of a spaceship—air filtration, the faint buzz of the mag engines, and—

Wait.

She listens closer and hears it again: The faint clink of metal on metal ahead, somewhere around the sick bay.

Noemi gets her back to the wall and keeps her weapon at the ready as she inches closer. The fear inside her as she ducks behind each strut, straining to hear what lies ahead—it reminds her of her first day on this ship. She was headed to the sick bay then, too. The doors on board close automatically, so there's no way she can get in there without giving away her presence. But she can at least listen and figure out as much as possible about what she'll face when she goes inside.

Even before she can make out words with any clarity, she recognizes Abel's voice, and she recognizes that something's badly wrong. Even his tone sounds...groggy, not quite right. Leaning her head against the nearest panel, the best conduit for sound, she finally understands a bit of what he's saying. "—impossible for you to be sure."

"We only learn through experimentation."

Wait, is that—*Professor Akide*?

Astonishment boils into fury. Noemi doesn't know how he overpowered Abel or exactly what kind of experiment he plans to run, but she's putting a stop to this, now.

She goes through the door, weapon raised, to see Abel lying flat on one of the biobeds and Akide above him, frowning at a scanner. "Back off!" she shouts. "Get away from Abel this second, or I swear to God I'll fire."

"No, you won't," Akide answers. He doesn't budge.

"Do you think I don't believe in God? So the promise doesn't count?" Noemi feels like her stare alone could kill him where he stands. "Trust me, I do, and it does."

"I believe in God, too." With that—quick as a flash— Akide pulls a weapon of his own.

No mech would ever have gotten away with that. She would've blown it to bits before it could even get its hand on its blaster. But she's so used to thinking of this man as a member of the Elder Council—as her protector, even her friend. Her fighting instincts didn't kick in fast enough.

"Noemi?" Abel turns his head toward her. He's visibly weak and dazed, even more than he was in his exhaustion on Haven. Whatever Akide did has turned him into a shadow of himself.

With his free hand, Akide activates some small device. Instantly Abel goes unconscious. Noemi remembers the fail-safe used to capture him months ago; Akide must have his own methods of shutting Abel down.

"You're not going to shoot me," she says.

"And you're not going to shoot me." Akide looks disappointed, the same way adults look at little children who have let them down. "We're only going through these motions because you've never accepted what Abel really is. What he's for."

She wishes she could shake him. "Did you happen to notice that we just won the biggest battle of the Liberty War? That we have a brand-new war fleet, one Abel helped bring here?"

"We're grateful for that. But gratitude isn't worth much, compared with the safety of our world."

Noemi doesn't agree, but that's beside the point. "*We don't have to destroy the Gate.* Don't you see? We can *use* that Gate now. Make contact with the other worlds of the Loop, force Earth to be the one on the defense for a while. Everything's changed. We can turn this uprising into victory."

"You don't understand war." Akide sounds sorrowful, but his expression is hard. "They'll send humans after us this time, and the fighters of Genesis will have to take the sin of murder on their souls. And in the end, if Earth doesn't succeed in taking our planet, the other colony worlds will decide to claim it themselves. They've seen our prosperity now; they won't be content to merely help us. No, they'll come after us next—unless we destroy the Gate now."

"We don't know that." She thinks Darius Akide has a lot of nerve telling her—someone who's trained to fight for almost a third of her young life, who's gone into countless battles—that she doesn't understand war. He's the one who's forgotten. "Are you really going to strand all the Vagabonds here, and all the Remedy members who came to help us?"

If he cares about their volunteer fleet, he gives no sign. "I'm willing to sacrifice one mech to ensure that Genesis remains safe. You're willing to endanger millions in the hopes the war has changed. That's not enough, Noemi. We have one more chance at ensuring the security of Genesis forever, and we're not going to waste it."

Hasn't he heard anything she's said? Noemi wants to scream. *The Elders don't want to win this war,* she thinks. *They only see two ways to end this war—through death or isolation.*

"I can't make you believe in victory," she says. "And I can't make you believe in Abel's soul. But I'm not going to let you hurt him, ever, so you can just—"

Noemi doesn't hear the energy bolt. She only feels it. Heat beyond imagining erupts in her chest, sears outward along every nerve. Her muscles lock up, and her weapon falls uselessly to the floor. For one instant she sees the horror on Akide's face, the way he looks from her to the blaster he just fired and back again in disbelief.

He meant to do it, she thinks in a daze. *He just didn't know what it would feel like to kill someone.*

Then she falls.

36

HEARING RETURNS TO ABEL FIRST. HE PROCESSES THE input automatically, then consciously: It is the sound of a man crying.

Next he regains proprioception, the awareness of his own limbs and physical body. Then touch, which reveals that he's lying on a flat, hard surface. Smell he finds with his next inhalation—

—and his receptors identify the scent of blood.

Abel opens his eyes and snaps back to full consciousness. He sits up quickly to take stock of his new situation and then realizes, no, he can't be conscious yet. What he sees can only be a nightmare; therefore he is still asleep. But most dreams dissolve upon recognition, nightmares especially, and Abel's still here, on a table, looking down at Noemi lying on the floor, unconscious or . . .

He looks toward the sound of weeping and sees Darius Akide on his knees, hands pressed together in the traditional shape of prayer. "Forgive me, Lord. Forgive your unworthy servant."

On the floor next to Akide lies a blaster. The scent of ozone tangles with that of blood in the air.

Abel stares again at Noemi and sees the scorch marks on her exosuit. The faint spattering of blood around her on the floor from the few capillaries not instantly cauterized by a blaster wound. And the very slight rise and fall of her breath, which tells him that as seriously hurt as she is, she's still alive.

This is no dream. This is reality, and he still has a chance to shape it.

He leaps from the table, landing between Akide and Noemi. Akide stares up in astonishment; apparently he didn't know how long the stunner's effects would last. Abel says nothing, just seizes Akide's head in one hand and his throat in the other, then snaps them in opposite directions. His sharp hearing picks up the faint pop of the spine before the corpse drops to the ground.

There is deep inner programming meant to keep non-warrior mechs from hurting human beings, and that programming now throbs within Abel, one brief pulse of pain, and then it's forgotten. Maybe it will trouble him later. Nothing matters at this moment except for Noemi.

He kneels beside her and brushes his fingers along her cheek. "Can you hear me?" Being stunned is a poor analogue of death, but he knows that in both cases, hearing is the last sense to go.

Noemi's eyes flutter open. Abel rolls her into his arms, cradling her shoulders in the crook of one elbow. Her pupils are slightly dilated and both her pulse and respiration are dangerously low. She opens her mouth, closes it again, then manages to whisper, "Abel?"

"Yes. I'm here. I'm going to take care of you."

With that he pulls her into his arms and dashes to the nearest biobed. He's able to keep her steady in his embrace, without a single jolt to hurt her more, and once he's reached his destination he lays her gently on one of the biobeds. Immediately readings light up on the monitors, each one of them more dire than the last.

Abel knows how a biobed functions. These readings are consistent with the injury Noemi has received. Yet he cannot believe them. Never before has he understood the human emotional response called "denial."

"Where's Akide?" she murmurs.

Hopefully in hell, Abel thinks, but he says only, "He's not a danger anymore."

"...Did he hurt you...?"

How can she worry about him while she lies on the biobed with a burned-out crater in her chest? "No. I'm all right, Noemi, I'm fine, and I'm going to make you well."

"Liar," she says softly, and somehow it sounds like the kindest name she's ever called him.

The heart remains intact, he thinks, looking up at the readings. The lungs are badly compromised, significantly past recommended regeneration limits but not absolutely beyond the range of possibility. Liver, spleen, and gallbladder destroyed, but only the liver is critical and could in time be regenerated.

Time. He needs time to save her, and all his intelligence and ability can't give it to him.

"It's starting," she murmurs. "You can feel it a little... like your body isn't yours really...."

"Try to remain conscious." Why does he feel such a strong need to say this to her when he knows it's beyond her power to obey? He wants to believe it's up to her. He hates even the idea of heaven, because if she has faith in some better place she'll want to go there. "Stay with me."

"Wish I could." Noemi's eyes close for a moment; when she opens them again, it's obvious she's fighting for even that. "...I'm going to find Esther's star."

"Noemi—"

"Come to me there someday," she whispers. "A long time from now."

Then her head leans to one side as her eyes fall shut again.

Abel stares up at the biobed monitor. Her heart's still

beating; her shallow lungs are processing what oxygen they can. But she's no longer conscious, and if this were any other human patient, he would judge it unlikely that she'd ever wake again.

This isn't any other patient. This is Noemi, and he *will not* endure this.

She deserves her life. He's going to give it to her.

Swiftly he gathers her back into his arms and crosses the sick bay in three long strides, which take him to the cryosleep pods. He hits the activator with his elbow. One of the pods slides from its place on the wall onto the floor; its translucent panels fold open like the petals of a flower. Abel settles Noemi onto the pale green interior, and the soft, elastic substance gives slightly under her weight.

Maximum skin contact is recommended for optimal results. The words from the cryosleep training manual are right there in his memory bank; they've waited there all these years for the moment when he'd need this knowledge. He gets to the surgical tools, pulls a scalpel from its robotic arm, and uses it to slash away as much of the exosuit as possible.

But her life signals are now in the red zone. Further delay means failure. Abel steps back and hits the activator again. The panels fold around Noemi, and he stares down at her face as the pod fills first with vapor, then with liquid.

Her features blur; her black hair floats around her in an uncertain halo.

A light on the control panel blinks green as an automated voice says, "*Cryosleep activated.*"

Abel feels as though he can breathe again. While the cryosleep pod rotates back into standing position, he watches the readouts to monitor her life signals. Already they're slowing as the chill settles into marrow, blood, and brain. That's entirely normal. But he also knows that she was so weak when he put her in that, even preserved this way, she might not survive any attempts to replace or regenerate her damaged organs. All this has bought her is a chance.

Abel will take what he can.

He waits until the process is complete, watching her the entire time. She seems to be floating in mist like some ethereal spirit in a fairy tale. His imagination is normally not so given to metaphor and simile; he has to gentle the truth of Noemi's condition to come to terms with it. She is suspended between life and death.

In a fairy tale, the hero would have to face great trials to bring the heroine back to life: slaying dragons, undoing spells. Abel only has to remember where he came from, and what the future generations of his people will become.

The Inheritors won't be equal parts man and machine; they'll be far more organic. More powerful than even Abel himself. And they'll live even longer. Gillian Shearer can't transfer a human consciousness yet. But what if Noemi's consciousness remains in her body, and then that body can be changed?

There must be ways to add organic mech components to a human body. The new transhumanism Gillian Shearer dabbles in—those technologies would be linked, too. It would be possible to synthesize both real and artificial DNA to make Noemi... not an Inheritor. Something else. A mech and yet not a mech. Something entirely new, but not *someone* new. It will still be *her*.

Abel's cheeks feel oddly stiff—salt from the tears he must have shed without realizing it. He can tell that now because he's begun to smile. The pain he feels is even greater than what he felt in the moment when he parted from Noemi before, greater than what he felt in the instant when he realized Mansfield had abandoned him alone in space, in an imprisonment that would last for thirty years. But he now possesses what he didn't have back then: hope. This pain is endurable because it points him in the direction he needs to go.

The pain will lead him back to Haven. To Gillian Shearer. And possibly to his own doom.

He can't do this without Gillian's help. The price of that

help can only be one thing: Abel's surrender. She'll want to replace his soul with the stored consciousness of Burton Mansfield. If it comes to that, Abel will agree. His life for Noemi's—it's a simple exchange, one he doesn't have to question.

Maybe it won't come to that. There are always possibilities. Always variables. Abel will do whatever it takes to save Noemi, but he refuses to admit defeat.

His entire body feels weak, and his chest aches as though he were the one who had been wounded. Still he presses on, transferring auxiliary control to a nearby console, so he can steer them away from the battlefield and toward the Genesis Gate.

Beyond that lies Noemi's last hope.

He walks back to her cryosleep pod again to double-check the readings; it helps to be absolutely sure she's in complete stasis. As he gets closer, he sees that one of her hands has drifted close to the outer shell. He presses his against it, feeling the burn of the cold against his skin. As he looks up at her face, Abel whispers the word that nearly destroyed him, Mansfield's old fail-safe code. It's the same word that will bring Noemi back to him again.

"Resurrection."

ACKNOWLEDGMENTS

As always, I owe a tremendous debt of gratitude toward my agent, Diana Fox; my valiant assistant, Sarah Simpson Weiss; and above all to the guidance and patience of my editor, Pam Gruber. Thanks also go to Stephanie Stoecker and Marti Dumas for sitting through brainstorming sessions; to Paul Christian, aka the "Word Cop," for making sure I got things done; to Tom and Judith at Octavia Books for all their help; and to the Peauxdunque Writers' Alliance for camaraderie and support.

CLAUDIA GRAY

is the *New York Times* bestselling author of many science fiction and paranormal fantasy books for young adults, including *Defy the Stars*, *Defy the Worlds*, the Firebird series, the Evernight series, the Spellcaster series, and *Fateful*. She's also had a chance to work in a galaxy far, far away as the author of the Star Wars novels *Lost Stars*, *Bloodline*, and *Leia, Princess of Alderaan*. Born a fangirl, she loves obsessing over geeky movies and TV shows, as well as reading and occasionally writing fanfiction; however, she periodically leaves the house to go kayaking, do a little hiking, or travel the world. She will take your Jane Austen trivia challenge any day, anytime. Currently she lives in New Orleans.